SURVIVAL
Part 1

Ellen May Hynes

Published by New Generation Publishing in 2022

First Edition

ISBN

      Paperback   978-1-80369-174-9
      Hardback   978-1-80369-175-6

The characters in this book are purely fictitious and not based on any person/persons.

Original Cover Paintings by Martin McCormack
www.martinmccormackart.com

www.newgeneration-publishing.com

I would like to dedicate this book to my three amazing sons, James, Jon and Will.

I also want to thank my husband for his unfailing support and encouragement throughout the writing of this book.

Thank you also to good friends who have offered many a wise and helpful word.

1. CONNEMARA

Along the rugged coastline of Connemara, the oystercatchers were wading through the ripples on the seashore, seeking a meal of shellfish on the incoming tide. The curlews were flying overhead, periodically swooping into the waves and screeching as they dipped and turned. The endless white sandy beach stretched as far as the eye could see, only broken by the sand dunes in the distance. Aoifa loved it there with all her heart, this beautiful wilderness that was her home. As she walked the sand, it came to her that she couldn't possibly live anywhere else. Echoes like spirits on the wind whispered across the huge expanse of grey ocean, bringing their messages of freedom and enlightenment to her.

As she turned to look inland toward the rugged rock formation and across to the distant hills which bordered the bay, Aoifa's mind was full of those whisperings. Suddenly, the horses came into view, galloping toward her, and she smiled with her arms outstretched, desperate to touch them. Rafa was in the lead, a stunning and powerful Connemara pony, then Roma, his mother, darker-eyed and slower but more reliable. Last was Brown Mane, who was no relation, a youngster and their constant companion. It gave Aoifa such joy to watch them kicking out their hind legs in play as they cut through the rippling waves on the shoreline. Rafa came across to nuzzle her and she stroked his nose, whispering words of endearment to him. She stayed with them some while enjoying their silent communion until she realised the sky was becoming dark. Threatening clouds hung along the horizon and the sea had become rough and unforgiving. A storm was on the way. Looking skyward, Aoifa searched out a plane that could be heard in the distance, but not seen. *Better be quick*, she thought as she wrapped her thick grey cardigan around herself and pushed her unruly red hair out of her eyes. *Storm's gonna get you if you're not!* She smiled to herself. What a wonderful life she had along these shores, yet she knew her girls would all leave one day and then it would be just her and Padraig. She would never leave to follow them. Her heart would always be here.

Aoifa had been out a long time and she felt the need to return home, her senses on the alert. There were changes in the air. The wind suddenly took her long skirt, blowing it around and whipping her tangled hair across her face. Yet she wanted to stay a while longer to prolong her contact with nature, which was necessary to her very existence. She sat down on a rock, stretching her long legs and pushing her feet into the sand. The smell of seaweed was coming in on the tide as she watched the rush of the waves picking up height and momentum and crashing down in front of her. Rafa nuzzled her once more, but Roma belonged to Padraig and stood back. Then all of a sudden, they took off and galloped the full length of the bay as if sensing something. The clouds soon closed in, so she brushed the sand from her feet, put her shoes on and turned to follow them home. As she reached the track to Muir Farm, a few drops of rain hit her forehead and she heard distant thunder. Aoifa turned around for one last look at the beautiful vista before hurrying toward the house. The girls would all be home soon in their usual carefree way, frolicking and giggling around her. Aoifa felt a wisp of sadness as she contemplated their future being elsewhere one day, especially since Lois was in her final year at school.

Life had been hard for them all living on these shores, but Aoifa always dwelt on the beauty and carried the rest lightly. She spent little time worrying over her fate. She and Padraig worked hard and took everything on the chin because she had an inner sense just like her ma. She had been born with it, a second sight. It paved the road for all of them, giving them a security beyond the reach of most human beings. She considered herself lucky that there was nothing to worry about that day or any day, as she had learned to rely on her sense of foreboding. It had served the family well, always preparing them for what lay ahead.

Friday evenings were special in the O'Brien household. It was tradition that they spent time together in front of the fire, often with Lois telling one of her unlikely stories and Clara, her youngest daughter, believing every word. Aoifa pictured the other three, always captivated but rarely saying a word. Maybe that evening they would tackle a crossword together with Padraig chipping in now and again, she thought with a chuckle. Niamh could bring her fiddle down and they could play a duet, with her on the piano. They'd not done that for a while.

Aoifa opened the front door in elated mood at the prospect of an enjoyable evening. Stopping abruptly, she caught sight of herself in the mirror and examined her reflection. It reminded her of nineteen years before when she had met her husband on the beach. Her long red hair had been dishevelled then too with her skirts all askew. Her husband had come along on his Connemara pony that day, picked her up and off they went. He told her she had wisps of real gold in her hair, and she believed him! Brushing the sand from her skirt, Aoifa made her way upstairs to tidy herself before everyone returned. She soon came back down to earth as Lois was calling her.

"Ma, the school bus has broken down and you have to fetch the girls!"

"Ah, OK. Be down in a min." Aoifa sensed a touch of irritation in her daughter's voice. "Are they waiting now, Lo, because I wanted to start dinner?"

"They are, Ma, and I need to get to the beach."

Aoifa shook her head disbelievingly, murmuring to herself.

"Surely not in this weather! Oh, Lo, couldn't you begin dinner, then?"

Lois threw her mother a petulant look as if she knew that was coming.

"Oh, Ma, must I? I've a lot to do down there."

Aoifa shrugged, figuring she could manage, and let it pass, not having the desire to argue. She observed her daughter looking quite the serious student in her heavy shoes with her hair up in a tidy ponytail and carrying a load of books.

"I'm off to change, then. See you later."

Aoifa sighed at the sudden change of plan, although it was no surprise in the O'Brien household. Now there would be no quiet evening but all a mad rush instead. As she left in the family car, the storm came over, the rain lashing against the windscreen, and Aoifa hoped her girls were able to wait inside the school. As she travelled the coast road, she could see Padraig coming toward her with his cart full of seaweed. He was sopping wet, and her heart went out to him as she stopped and pulled the window down.

"Hello, chara, where are you off to?" he asked.

"The bus has broken down, so the girls are waiting for a lift just now."

"Ah. I have to put the horses away in this rain. See yers later. Don't wait, you all start your meal."

Aoifa didn't like dinner without him on a Friday, but she shrugged and carried on her journey, determined to make it back in good time. With the heavy clouds overhead, it was a total contrast to earlier that morning when the sun had been warm on her hair. Yet Aoifa knew such was the way in Connemara with its changeable weather systems. It was a big part of the allure for her, the fluctuating climate and the wild flora and fauna which made up her homeland. Aoifa's heart told her that she was on this utopian journey through her life, although her head probably knew otherwise. She nodded to herself. She must hurry; all of this pontificating would not bring her family home for dinner.

As she reached the school, Aoifa could see her girls out on the pavement, Mairead waving madly. She had a scowl on her face as she jumped in the car, her long dark hair dripping wet.

"Oh, Ma, where've you been?! We've been waitin' hours."

"No, you haven't, Mairead, maybe twenty minutes at most."

Aoifa smiled at her middle daughter's familiar sense of drama as Siobhan and Clara jumped in after her.

"Ma, I'm so hungry. Can I have some of that apple cake when we get home, please?" pleaded Clara.

"Of course," said Aoifa, relieved that she and Padraig had not finished it at lunchtime.

Aoifa considered how different these girls were. The youngest, Clara, was always polite and considerate. Siobhan, the middle of the three, wanting nothing and saying little, and Mairead, well, had plenty to say for herself, to be sure!

"Where's Niamh, Mairy?" Aoifa asked as she drove off.

"Oh, she gotta lift with her friend. They were going to do some studyin' for the GCEs or something."

At sixteen, Niamh usually managed to make her own way home, always resourceful and sensible with it.

The clouds parted as they reached the farmhouse and the sun shone through as if to welcome them home. The autumn leaves on the trees glistened from the rain and a shaft of sunlight spread right across the sea in front of them.

"Will you look at that, girls! The colours of autumn. They don't last long."

"I must paint it soon," said Siobhan quietly. "Ma, look over there, two beady eyes – it must be the hares coming out! They make my arms prickle!"

"It is too, Sheve. You draw them well – they must know you by now."

The girls jumped out of the car and ran indoors as Aoifa spotted Lois coming up the footpath from the beach.

"What on earth are you up to down there in this weather, Lo?"

"Oh, just checked on the animals, makin' sure nothing got washed up or injured. All OK."

Aoifa knew Lois' priority was always the animals and nothing came before them.

"Now can you help me, Lo? Dinner's running late."

"Why me, Ma? Always me!"

Aoifa took the girls' coats to the scullery to dry out as she looked patiently at her daughter and sighed. "The others will help, but as you're the oldest, you're quicker, Lo." It seemed like an uphill struggle with Lois at the moment and she watched as Lois reluctantly made her way into the kitchen, tossing her mop of red hair as she went.

"Girls, can you all fetch some veg and herbs from the garden?" she asked her sisters crisply.

"Come on," said Clara to Mairead and Siobhan.

Just then, Niamh walked in.

"Hi, Ma, guess what? I learned a new piece of music today. Can I sing it to you later?" She did some dance steps around the kitchen, humming a little song and making Aoifa laugh.

"You already have, chara," said Aoifa, looking at her daughter's colourful clothes, her shiny straight red hair bobbing up and down around her smiling face as she danced her steps. "I don't know how you get away with those colours in school."

"Well, at sixteen, you get some privileges, you know!"

"Oh, is that right, my girl!" Aoifa replied, tickled by her daughter's boldness. "Well, go dance your steps an' fetch the cutlery, then!"

Aoifa lit the wood-burning stove and went to help Lois with the meal whilst Niamh laid the table. Before too long, Mairead came running in with baskets full of greenness, kale, herbs, various edible fronds from the seashore and potatoes from the garden. She dumped them on the table, shouting, "I'm off to play some music now, Ma!" and she ran upstairs, quick as a flash, not waiting for a reply.

"Where's Siobhan and Clara?"

"Clara's just comin', Ma. She has crabs – don't give me those for tea!"

Aoifa shook her head. Clara always found crabs, and no one wanted them, but she hadn't the heart to tell her as she soon came running in.

"Look, Ma!"

Aoifa could see the live crabs in her basket as Clara handed them to her.

"Thank you, my love."

"I did well, didn't I? I know where to find them now!"

Aoifa grimaced but didn't say anything, as she knew Clara was always keen to please. At ten years old, her youngest daughter was already as tall as the others with clear milky-white skin dotted with freckles. Her fair hair was thinner and straighter than her sisters with wisps of gold running through it, just like Aoifa's. Clara herself was like a little butterfly, always flitting around as if sprinkling fairy dust as she went.

As Clara closed the door, a blast of cold air came in with a suggestion of something more, making Aoifa shiver. Something was happening, she could sense it, but she was looking forward to a lovely family evening and nothing was going to spoil it. Maybe it was just the storm outside, Aoifa surmised as she dished up the meal and Padraig came rushing through the door.

"Here's your knight without the armour," he whispered to her.

"Flattery gets you… nowhere! Come on, meal's ready."

Aoifa laughed. Padraig was a picture of solidarity to them all with his calm easy ways and gypsy looks too. He gave her a playful kiss and ruffled her hair.

"And you, always looking dangerously gorgeous with your tousled hair," he murmured.

Aoifa smiled back at him as Flynn, the family Collie, helped himself to the fire.

"Caught the storm, then, Flynn? Go on, the fire's yours!" she added, giving him a stroke and putting his dinner down on the flagstones.

"Ma, the phone's flashing," said Lois.

"Oh, Pad, pass me the phone. I think there's a message."

As Aoifa listened, she could feel the blood draining from her face.

"It… it's Ma. She's… very sick. I have to go there immediately. Pa's been trying to reach us, but I had to go to the school, and he called again, but that was over an hour ago. Shall I call him back or…" Aoifa knew she was babbling, but her brain was working overtime. Confusion and shock set in as she dropped her knife and fork and ran around the room, trying vainly to find the car keys.

"I have to go now. Pa said 'quickly'."

"Why? What's happened to Grandma?" Lois asked. "Is she… dying… Ma?"

"No, Lo, she is not. We saw her last week. She's fine. Don't say that!" There was a sharpness to her voice as she felt the alarm rising inside.

"Ma, take her my new scarf to wear!" Niamh cried. "The weather's cold. She would love the colours too."

Aoifa took it with tears in her eyes as the girls asked her endless questions, but she was miles away. Her thoughts without any direction and without any idea of what lay ahead. What was happening to her dear ma? And why didn't she know about it?

Clara started to cry and Aoifa gave her a hug, gently brushing her tears away.

"Clara, don't upset yourself, my darling. It will be OK. Grandpa just needs my help, try not to worry. I'll get off now and call you all tomorrow."

Aoifa was trying hard to maintain her composure for the family's sake, but inside her stomach was churning. She ran upstairs quickly to fetch an overnight bag, her movements jerky, agitated, as Padraig helped her out to the car.

"I wish I'd got to the phone, Pad." Aoifa was in tears.

"My love, you cannot be everywhere. Go now and drive carefully. Your pa is just worried. She'll be OK, especially when she sees you. Don't fret too much."

He embraced her, holding her tight, then she suddenly broke free and jumped into the car.

"I'll call you later," Aoifa called as she drove off, her eyes filling up again with unspent tears.

"Take care, my love," he replied and waved as she pulled away into the darkness.

Aoifa sped along as fast as her old car would permit, taking no heed to the stones on the lane as it rocked from side to side. The rain had returned, and she could hear the wind whistling around the car. She could also hear the wind inside her head. It felt like thick fog. Aoifa could make no sense of it all and her hands were shaking as she made her way to Home Farm. Yet she had received no messages about her ma! Where was her second sight? In her confusion and haste to arrive, her driving was erratic, and she couldn't seem to change gear. "Drat this old car!" she shouted loudly as a mixture of worry and frustration ran through her.

Her pa's cattle were baying along the shore in protest to the storm. It distracted her for a moment then she saw the farmhouse with its dim lights in the distance. The last mile was the longest she had ever travelled. It seemed that she was driving through mud and would never get there.

She pulled up at the bottom of the lane, jumped out and ran up the track toward the house. Her pa opened the door, his face taut, his eyes red, and as the wind preceded her, he took Aoifa into his arms.

"I tried to reach you, chara, for you to come… before…"

She remained motionless as it slowly dawned on her what had happened. She couldn't speak but stood in her pa's embrace, her arms by her side feeling as heavy as lead. He started sobbing and her younger brother Sean was sitting on a chair near the range, looking into space. They were like two lost souls, and she had not been there for them. She had not been there for her ma. Aoifa spoke in a whisper, tears rolling freely down her face now as the emotion began to rise.

"Where is she, Pa?"

Aaron didn't speak but pointed up to the bedroom.

Aoifa pulled herself gently away and made her way upstairs, her body shaking with longing to be with her ma. When she walked into the bedroom, the cold hit her. The curtains and window were partially open and there were soft shafts of dusky moonlight coming into the room. She could hear her own footsteps walking on the wooden floor and felt like an interloper, an unwelcome guest in her ma's bedroom. She was afraid in some unearthly way that she may disturb her, but it was too late for that. She should have been there. Aoifa stole a cursory glance at her mother then looked away. She could still feel her presence – there was an aura in the room. As she approached the bed, she could see a serenity and peace in her face. She wanted to touch her but couldn't, not yet. She moved forward slowly and sat on the bed then stroked her hair, which was barely there, grey and thin, spread out on the pillow. Aoifa recalled how it had once been, rich auburn with dense curls. Cara O'Connell was a shadow of her former self. She tentatively took her hand and it felt cool like the air coming through the window. Her face was like polished porcelain with no suggestion of pain whatsoever and she hoped that was how it had been.

Putting her hands over her face to shut out the tragic scene, Aoifa sobbed uncontrollably, taking great convulsive breaths, the grief pouring out of her. She didn't hear her pa come in. He put his arm protectively around her and she turned, wrapping her arms around him. They stayed like that until her tears subsided when he helped her into the old armchair and left so that she could spend time with her ma for as long as she needed.

When Aoifa came downstairs, Aaron O'Connell was sitting in his familiar chair next to the wood-burner. He looked totally distraught, his gaze fixed on the floor and pain etched in his face.

"I can still feel Ma's spirit and soul in here. She hasn't left yet, Pa," she said in an effort to comfort him.

He turned to look at her, his eyes betraying the intense grief he was feeling. She sat on the floor and leaned back against him, next to Casey and Brody, the Collies at his feet.

"My heart is broken, chara. We were together more than fifty years. How do I carry on?"

"You have us, Pa, and Sean. We will help you," Aoifa said vaguely as she got up and put the kettle on. Her legs felt heavy as she rubbed her eyes, all her energy of the afternoon gone. "You're trembling, Pa," as she put a shawl around his shoulders, her ma's shawl.

"It's just the shock, chara."

"I am so sorry I wasn't here for Ma, or for you. I would have been had I known, you know that. I always knew what was coming, Pa, but I did not. For the first time and most important time in my life, I didn't receive any forewarnings."

"Your ma will understand, chara. Dunna chide yourself."

Aoifa put her head in her hands and sobbed inexorably once more. She took some deep breaths, trying to gain some measure of control, when Sean came through the door. His arms were limp by his side, and he was looking at her, not knowing what to do, his eyes full of tears. When Aoifa saw him, she composed herself and held out her arms as he walked straight into them. She could hear his almost imperceptible tears, his usual reserve momentarily forgotten. Aoifa had always been close to her youngest brother, for which she felt truly grateful.

"She was ill a long time, Aoif," Sean spoke in his usual quiet, unhampered and pragmatic way. Aoifa squeezed his arm in response and they both sat down on the sofa by the fire. A peacefulness soon entered the room, calm amidst the storm of emotion which had just taken place. Aoifa made some tea and they all sat in silence as the night drew in, watching the flames from the fire flicker around the room.

Sometime later, Aoifa walked around the kitchen, trying to make some food for them all, unable to form her thoughts nor regulate her actions. Her pa broke the spell of silence.

"Chara, your ma left a message for you. She said, 'Tell my Aoifa to watch her girls, especially...' but she didn't finish the sentence, Aoif. She tried to, but it was too late."

Those words were of little consolation to Aoifa, as she knew her second sight had gone. Her sense of what will be had left her. She had been born with it and now it had gone with her ma to the next life. But how would she manage without it? Mixed in with all the sadness, Aoifa suddenly felt another – unfamiliar – emotion: panic.

2. HOME FARM

That night, Aoifa sat in the chair alongside the range in the kitchen but hardly slept a wink. As dawn approached, she looked out at a glimpse of blue sky peeking through the clouds, the storm of the night before having passed. Her pa and Sean were out on the farm and Aoifa was all alone. A feeling of abject loneliness crept over her, and life felt unreal. It was as if she were floating above reality, looking down on a scene which did not include her. Yet, it did include her, and Aoifa was acutely aware that her life would continue very differently from before because not only had she lost her mother but also a part of herself, her guiding light.

Throughout her life, Aoifa had been used to hearing a voice from within – messages which told her what lay ahead. She had inherited the gift from her mother. Now it had gone, and her ma had gone, and she felt totally lost, rudderless and disconnected as if there were a huge void between her and everyone else. Why did she not know of her ma's passing? Aoifa shook her head in utter disbelief. How could she possibly know what lay ahead for her and her family now?

Aoifa's biggest challenge that day would be speaking to her elder brother, and it filled her with dread. They were not close and had chosen very different paths. Liam was an ambitious man, his mind always on worldly things, and he showed no care for Aoifa's gift. In fact, it had come between them. Slowly making her way upstairs, she walked directly passed her mother's room, closing the door quietly as if afraid of disturbing her. Although Cara still lay in her bed, Aoifa knew her spirit and soul had left them, and she was no longer present in any form.

She undressed and stepped into the shower, allowing the hot water to soothe and embrace her. As she washed her long red hair slowly, mechanically, she knew she would somehow find a way through. It was what her ma would want. Aoifa just wished she could speak to her one last time, but that was never to be. Her best friend had gone, and her mind now had to work on its own. It was a hugely daunting prospect for Aoifa as she envisaged the conversation with her brother.

"Aoifa, are you there?" her pa called up the stairs, breaking into her thoughts.

"Coming now, Pa."

She went downstairs and gave her father a hug.

"You didn't sleep much, chara?"

"No, Pa. I suppose I kept waiting for Ma to walk downstairs, but she never did."

Aoifa turned away to hide her unbidden tears.

"No, my chara, not anymore."

Aaron O'Connell sighed and went up to have a wash, his step heavy and his shoulders bent.

"Where is Sean, Pa?" Aoifa called after him.

"Coming. Just feedin' the dogs."

"I'll make us all a nice breakfast," she said shakily.

Aoifa glanced at Sean as he came in and turned toward her.

"How are you, Sis?" he asked quietly.

"Lonely, Sean."

"Yeah," he replied, the dogs at his heel.

Aoifa prepared bacon, eggs and fried bread. A while later, they all sat down together, a sombre trio, the sadness between them palpable as Aoifa stole herself to speak.

"We need to contact Liam this morning," she told them, looking around as if searching for courage from within the room.

"Sure. Will you call him, Aoif?" Aaron asked carefully, aware of the difficulties between the two siblings.

"I will, Pa." Aoifa turned to Sean, changing the subject, "What's it doing outside this morning?"

"Oh, not too bad, not like last night. The shore's had a batterin'."

They all sat around the table, but no one ate the hearty breakfast Aoifa had made. As she cleared the plates away, her pa shook his head. "Give the bacon to the dogs, Aoif, shame to waste it."

"I'll make some tea," she said. Tea was more welcome, and they all sat holding their mugs, united in their melancholy as Aoifa said a little more brightly, "Ma liked autumn, with all its colours," as she looked out of the window at the rising sun and the changing leaves on the trees.

"She did too." Her pa managed a slight smile. "I felt her outside on the breeze this morning, gentle just like she was."

"I've no doubt, Pa."

Aoifa could think of nothing more to say. Her heart was bleeding and she felt like there was a gaping hole, a rawness inside of her. She watched, deep in thought, as Aaron and Sean left to return to work. After two cups of tea, she felt slightly better and knew she couldn't delay making the phone call any longer.

"Liam?"

"Hey, Aoifa. What's up?"

A call to her brother was so rare that she couldn't blame him for presuming something was wrong. What would she say? Everything was wrong.

"Liam, I…" But Aoifa's resolve weakened and her voice broke. "Oh, Liam, I… I don't know what to say."

"What is it?" he asked directly.

"It… it's Ma…"

"What about Ma? I saw her last weekend. She did look weak, to be sure."

"She has passed, Liam. Last night." The line went silent for a few moments. "Li? Did you hear me?"

Aoifa could hear him clearing his throat.

"I did. Well, she'd been ill so long, I suppose it was to be expected. How's Pa?" Her brother's perfunctory tone asking the next thing already didn't surprise her.

"He's bearing up, carrying on as best he can. Sean too."

"Well, he'll be OK, a practical lad. We need to make arrangements for the funeral. We'll have it here; more room and I can get caterers in."

This took Aoifa by surprise as she felt her heart beat faster.

"Oh, Li! It's too soon to think…"

"We must think," Liam broke in. "We can't leave her where she is."

These words felt brutal to Aoifa, but she mustered some strength and spoke her truth.

"Pa would want it here, Li. The girls and I can prepare food and maybe Danny and Scorcha too." She spoke quickly then held her breath.

"Danny and Scorcha will not do it, nor Emma. I suppose I will have to pay anyway!"

Aoifa felt her legs weaken, but she had to be strong for her pa.

"It's better here, Li. It's what Ma and Pa would both want. We'll split the cost right down the middle, and Dolly, the housekeeper, will help." Aoifa felt her bravado slipping away as grief and anxiety churned in her stomach. "That's it, Li, for now. Please."

"Tell Pa I'll call him tonight."

"I must go now." Aoifa sensed there was more conversation to be had. "Look, I'll visit later. They… they're taking Ma away – now."

Aoifa couldn't continue. She put down the phone and collapsed into a nearby chair, her hands shaking and sweat pouring off her brow. She wrapped her arms around herself, and tears rolled down her face as Cara was carried out of the front door. She caught her breath as the last sight of her ma passed before her eyes. Aoifa would never understand the coldness of her older brother. He always lacked warmth or indeed any emotion at all. It simply increased her sadness, and she knew she would need to find courage to cope with it all. Then the phone rang.

"Hello, my love. How are you this morning?" asked Padraig gently.

"Oh, Pad, lovely to hear from you. M... Ma... they've just taken her." A sob caught in her throat. "And I've just spoken to Liam, upset me all over again. He was so cold, Pad – wants the funeral at his. We can't–"

"Deep breaths, chara. Calm yourself, don't be worrying about that yet. He can be a funny one, you know that," said Padraig reassuringly.

"I'm going to see him later, talk it over. I wish you could come, Pad. I feel so alone." The tears fell once more.

"The girls want to see you, chara. They're all so upset, especially Clara."

"I know, give her a big hug from me. But I must sort this out. I will find the strength, some inner... Oh, my love, I can't seem to think straight. Please bring them tomorrow, then. You know I have never understood my brother, his frostiness. It's as if he has some residing resentment against me."

"Try not to fret, Aoif. Liam will be fine, kind. He's an intelligent man and knows this is a time for family unity, and Emma is always the sensitive one," Padraig replied positively.

Aoifa's face was contorted with anxiety. "Well, I just hope she is the sensible one too because he will not be kind. He never is toward me!"

"It will be OK. Believe me. He will want peace to prevail, you watch."

"Please tell the girls I'm looking forward to seeing them. We need their love and laughter here, and you too, Pad."

"I'll bring them after lunch tomorrow, chara. They'll help to raise everyone's spirits. Take care, my love."

She rang off, feeling a little better as if Padraig was at her side.

Aoifa wanted to look the part to visit the O'Connells. Sober, but not sombre. She put her jeans and white shirt back on instead of the colours she had brought. They were for when colour returned to her world once more. She put on the Aran cardigan her ma had made to feel enveloped in her spirit and pulled her hair back in a gold braid, then she was ready to leave and called out to her pa in the yard,

"Pa, I'm off to Liam's. Shall I make you a bite to eat first?"

Aaron called back wearily. "Not too hungry, chara, maybe a bit of ham for later?"

"Sure, Pa, I'll leave some with a cake in the dairy."

Aoifa called Casey and Brody up to the house. She loved the dogs and needed something to hug. When she bent down to stroke their silky coats, she could smell the sea and Brody licked her cheek as she whispered, "It'll be OK, guys." As they all made their way along the path to the beach, Aoifa took in great gulps of air to bring renewed energy for the task ahead. The dogs ran on ahead, barking excitedly, and it made her smile. When would she feel joy again? She felt shaky as she walked down the lane but ignored it and allowed the wind to take her forward on her first walk from Home Farm without her ma. She could see Sean in the distance repairing the cattle shed.

"Sean, I'm going to Liam's, but I'll be back for dinner."

"You sure, Sis?" Sean was aware of the relationship difficulties.

"I need to… to sort things out. Fresh air and a walk will help."

He nodded as she passed on by.

Aoifa tried not to think but instead concentrated on her breathing, taking in the fresh scent of wild lavender after the rain of the night before. She could see her pa's cattle below on the mudflats and the sheep high up on the moorland. There was a thick mist over on the horizon, above the azure blue of the sea, and the gulls were flying overhead in the hope of something to eat. The dogs led the way along the well-trodden path, snaking through some late-flowering heather and faded bracken in all its hues. Dew was glistening all around, reflecting the autumn colours, as Aoifa chose her footing carefully across the moorland.

Aoifa contemplated her loss as she walked steadily on, feeling her ma's presence along the way. It was as if she were walking alongside her, and absent-mindedly, she almost reached out for her hand. Death was so finite, so unfathomable, so painful to accept, the eternal absence of one so dear, but she kept walking, taking in the beauty all around to help lighten her load and keep her in the present. Then her mind turned toward her relationship with her brother. The gulf between them created by their differing personalities, checkered past, the five-year age gap and disparate lifestyles. Deep in thought, Aoifa was acutely aware that she would normally feel protected by a spiritual cloak, a prior knowledge of imminent encounters, but she felt nothing, no warning, no messages on the wind. Where had they gone when she needed them most? She stopped and stamped her foot in despair and frustration, her face contorted, when suddenly the sun appeared from behind the clouds and she turned toward it, basking in the fleeting comfort it gave.

Aoifa stopped and sat on a favourite rock looking out to sea, now a sheet of calm tranquillity in front of her as the dogs ran in and out of the gentle waves and snuffled around in the heathers and reeds along the shore. She threw off her shoes and buried her feet into the cool sand, which brought a feeling of familiarity and solace, the white foam of the waves making their way toward her. She listened to the sounds around her to take her mind off the angst she was feeling inside. The dogs knew something was amiss too, as they stayed close, periodically looking up into Aoifa's face.

As she closed her eyes, Aoifa whispered, "Ma, if you are there, please come with me, hold my hand," as she lingered for just a moment longer. Then she put on her shoes and resumed her journey, hoping the long walk and calm reflection would serve to blow her fears away for what lay ahead.

They turned off the moorland and soon reached the O'Connell Estate. She could see Liam's daughter, Scorcha, in the garden with a young man and Aoifa smiled warmly as she approached them. A beauty, Scorcha had her mother's looks, rich brown curly hair, shapely long legs, a ready smile and a confidence about her as she came running up to greet her.

"Hi, Scorch." Aoifa gave her a warm hug and smiled at them both. She was very fond of her effervescent young niece, just two years older than Lois.

"Poor Grandma. I'll never see her again now!" Scorcha exclaimed with tears in her eyes.

Aoifa looked at her kindly. "Keep talking to her, chara, and keep your memories strong. Lovely you have Mikey for company. Is your mother here?"

"Yes, in the kitchen." They both walked off hand in hand to sit in the garden.

As she reached the door, Emma opened it, greeting her with open arms.

"Lovely to see you, Aoif, come in. I'll put those dirty creatures in the scullery," Emma smiled at her, "then make some tea. It's a sad day, to be sure. Your brother's in his office – I'll fetch him."

Aoifa watched her sister-in-law as she left the room, admiring her tall, elegant stance, neatly cut clothes and graceful ways, her warmth palpable. She always felt very welcome in their home and valued Emma's strong presence.

"He'll join us for tea shortly," Emma said on her return.

Aoifa sat by the range wishing she didn't feel quite so apprehensive of seeing her brother, but then she always did.

"How is Pa, Aoif?" Emma asked.

"Oh, not too bad," she lied, not wishing to speak in too much detail. "He keeps on. You know Pa."

Emma nodded.

"How have the twins taken it, Em?"

"Well, Dan was brief on the phone, but Scorcha talks about her grandma all the time. She wears her heart on her sleeve that one, but at least she has Mikey here with her." She turned to Aoifa. "Cara is out of pain now. She was ill for so long and sadly wouldn't accept any medical help. We would have paid, you know?"

"I know, Em. It wasn't what she wanted, but thank you. Never mind now."

The door opened and Liam walked in, his bulky frame filling the room. He was not a handsome man and had a formidable presence but an engaging smile. Aoifa got up to embrace him. She knew it would feel wooden, but she was used to that.

"Ah, Aoifa. Good of you to come over."

"No trouble. The walk did me good and the weather's eased a bit. It's nice to see you both." Aoifa felt warmth in his embrace, which took her by surprise and eased her anxiety somewhat. She searched Liam's face for traces of emotion, but he gave nothing away.

Emma had prepared tea on a tray with cake and scones. "Let's go and sit in the drawing room – it's much more comfortable," she said as they all crossed the hall, the sun streaming in through the sash windows.

The pretty blues and chintzes of the drawing room and its high, decorative ceiling were a soft contrast to the clipped hedges and rather austere, formal garden, which could be seen through the window. Aoifa felt out of place in the sumptuousness of her surroundings with her tousled hair and jeans against her sister-in-law's formal style. Yet, she had always loved this room, so she settled into a pretty sofa, gaining comfort from its opulence.

"How are you feeling now, Aoif?" her brother enquired.

"Empty, Li. Totally bereft." She told him the truth.

"Really?" Liam looked at her strangely. "You with your second sight and all?"

"Well, um," she started, avoiding his eyes, feeling guilty – but for what? She looked up and met his gaze, shivering slightly.

"Is something wrong?" he asked.

"It's the shock, Li," Aoifa replied apprehensively, feeling not just grief and confusion, but trepidation too. She felt completely devoid of any thoughts and her inner voice, suspecting it showed on her face.

"You have always claimed to have second sight, like Ma, all your life – why didn't you see this coming, Aoif?" Liam was direct.

Aoifa's heart missed a beat. There was condemnation in his tone. He had always questioned her gift and now she was questioning it too.

"I don't know," she replied quietly, averting her gaze and blinking furiously as she felt close to tears. "I saw nothing, Li, and I have no idea why."

"If you had seen it, Aoif, we may have been able to help her before it was too late." Liam looked stern and Aoifa sat up with a jolt, composing herself. What was Liam saying? Did he blame her for Cara's passing?

"When Pa called, I was out. The school bus had broken down and I had to fetch the girls. I didn't get the message until much later, so I couldn't get there in time. It's something I shall regret for the rest of my life, but now she's gone, and…"

Aoifa broke down in tears as Emma came over, handed her a tissue and spoke gently,

"Don't upset yourself, Aoif." She handed her a cup of tea. "Nothing will bring Ma back. We must just get on now."

Liam's words had cut through her like a knife, and she noticed the sharp look which took place between the two of them. She sat still, frozen, as if she had an open wound, bare to the elements.

"I wish I had known, Li, but I didn't. I'm sorry. Anyways, Ma was a spiritualist and believed her time had come." Guilt and regret were rising inside as she tried to remain composed. She so wanted to make contact with Liam to alleviate the pain and any dissent between them, but she made no move. If he knew what she was feeling, he didn't show it.

Liam sighed. "Don't be sorry, Aoif. It was nobody's fault Ma died. Anyway, we've been talking. We think Home Farm is the best place for the funeral," Liam conceded, his tone softer.

"Small mercies, thank God," Aoifa murmured to herself, looking out of the window. "Yes, it'll be for the best, Li."

The conversation was nearly at a close and Aoifa had myriad emotions travelling through her, but one prevailing: anger. She pushed it away determinedly, replacing it with a touch of acceptance. As Aoifa stood up, her hands were clenched, but she managed to fix a grin on her face as she said goodbye to her brother, then left the room.

"I'll take you back, Aoif, too far to walk at this time."

Emma touched her arm and Aoifa smiled her gratitude.

They gathered the dogs, jumped into their Range Rover and set off, shouting their goodbyes to Liam and Scorcha. As they travelled in companionable silence, Aoifa began to relax alongside Emma, who was a natural at returning karma to a situation.

"Don't take any notice of our Liam. He has an uncanny knack of saying the wrong thing sometimes. He meant nothing by it. He knows Ma's cancer sadly got the better of her. He'd wanted to pay for treatment, but she wouldn't allow it, so it's rattled him slightly."

"No, Ma didn't want intervention, Em. She knew it would get her in the end and she preferred to see her time out naturally," making no mention of her brother's accusatory comments. "I'm glad and relieved she will make her last journey from her own home."

"Yes, it will be a sad day, but everyone will come and bring their support."

Aoifa was thankful for Emma's company at the end of a painful day. She began to wonder if her inner voice would come back one day, that maybe it was just a temporary blip because of the shock. Aoifa fought to put it all out of her mind and brightened as she saw the farmhouse up ahead and Sean in the yard, locking the barns for the night.

The two women got out of the car and hugged one another. There was a fine delicate connection between them for a moment then they went their separate ways.

Aoifa was trembling by the time she went inside, and she felt cold, needing the warm company of her pa and younger brother to put her thoughts back on an even keel. She made a nice meal for the three of them that evening, and they all sat in quiet reflection by the fire with the dogs.

"Padraig is bringing the girls over tomorrow to raise our spirits, Pa. They will need comforting too."

"Aye, they will, lass. Bring a ray of sunshine into this house for sure," he said, looking vacantly out of the window at the sunset.

Aoifa nodded in agreement. She didn't speak to her pa of the painful conversation that day and what Liam had alluded to, not wishing to upset him. She wanted to believe Liam had meant nothing by what he had said about her inner voice, but the comment had taken Aoifa back to a time when they had all lived at home. All she could remember was the shouting about the second sight. What had happened between Liam and their parents at that time? Something had sent the whole family reeling, but she had no recollection of it whatsoever.

3. A TIME TO REFLECT

When Aoifa opened the curtains the next morning, the sky was a mixture of oranges, pinks, yellows and mauves, her ma's favourite colours, with the sea shimmering below. It was mesmerising. She went downstairs, grabbed a coffee then returned to watch. As the minutes passed, it changed to an enchanting array of golds and pinks. She could hear the gulls calling and the trees outside the window were swaying, the leaves dropping one by one, and it went through Aoifa's mind that here was the most beautiful place to be laid to rest.

She dressed carefully, wanting to look her best for the family's arrival later. As she walked past her ma's room, she detected a suggestion of Cara's familiar perfume and sighed. There were memories of her dear ma everywhere.

After breakfast, Aoifa pulled on her cardigan then went out into the cool autumn sunshine and sat on a rock in the garden with a clear view out to sea. Little white horses were gently undulating on the shore and there was a ship in the distance also making its journey to another place.

"Hello."

Aoifa turned around.

"Pad!"

She ran into his arms. "You're early, my love!"

He held her for a long moment as she sobbed into his warm coat, relieved to see her family as she turned to them.

"Girls!" There was an outpouring of emotion between them as they all hugged one another. "Let me see you." Aoifa held them back. "Are you all OK?" She took a deep breath. "We will all miss Grandma very much. Just remember her stories and they will always make you smile."

Niamh, Siobhan and Clara gathered around her in floods of tears.

"But where is Grandma now?" wailed Clara.

Mairead let out a loud sigh, "Oh, Clara, she's died, don't you know?"

"She's gone to heaven now, Lara," said Niamh gently, and turning to her mother, "Ma, you OK?"

"I am, Nevey," said Aoifa warmly, "but you know, girls, I was just sitting here talking to Grandma, hoping she could hear me." She noticed Lois made a face and turned away and it occurred to her maybe she didn't like her second sight either, although Aoifa couldn't imagine why. She watched as Siobhan collected up a selection of fallen leaves.

"I think I'll draw these for Grandma. She loved autumn colours."

"A lovely idea," said Aoifa, stroking the leaves, then Siobhan's dark silky hair, which was gleaming like ravens' wings.

"Come, girls. Let's go and give Grandpa a hug," said Niamh and they went across the yard to find him whilst Aoifa and Padraig sat down on the rock together.

"Ma's spirit is out there, Pad."

"I know, my love. She'll always be there for you to talk to and check out any messages you receive…"

"But that's just it, Pad. I don't receive messages. Not anymore. Nothing!"

Padraig turned to look at her. "What do you mean, chara?"

"I mean my… gift. It's gone. Otherwise I would have known about Ma!"

"It's just the sadness and shock, Aoif. Give it time."

Aoifa remained deep in thought as they went inside and she made some coffee.

"How've the girls been?" she asked.

"I spoke to them, as you said. Clara has taken it quite badly. The others are more accepting, but it'll help them to be here today."

"Pad – you know Liam and I have never seen eye to eye?"

"I know. Was it OK?"

"Yes, but he was so matter of fact about Ma's passing, showed no emotion whatsoever. In fact, it was as if he wanted it to happen. I can't believe I said that," she added with a pained expression.

"Folk are very different in their ways of coping with death, Aoif. I'm sure he was feeling as sad as you, just couldn't show it."

Aoifa's mind was in a whirl. "Also... he..."

"What?"

"Oh, nothing." Aoifa avoided his eyes. "He just seemed relieved, that's all, but he did agree to having the funeral here. He put up no fight for that at least."

"Well, he possibly was relieved, Aoif. Your ma had been ill for some time."

Aoifa shook her head and let the matter drop with an air of resignation.

The girls always loved being around the farm with their grandpa and Aoifa was pleased they were spending time with him. It would ease his pain too. Before too long, Siobhan came in, followed by the others.

"Ma, we found a hare's den. Lois says it's called a form."

"It was quite old, I'd say," Lois added.

"And we didn't disturb it," added Siobhan. "I'll come back some time to draw them. Do you think it'll be White Fur, Ma, from our beach?"

"It may be the same family, Sheve. You'll have to see."

Aoifa smiled at them, warmed by their interest in nature rather than weighed down by events. Mairead sidled up to her and whispered,

"Ma, could I have something of Grandma's, you know, to remember her by?"

Aoifa looked at her unsurprisingly. "I'll see what there is, Mairy. You may have to wait."

Clara reached up to her mother's ear. "I felt closer to Grandma, as you said, out on the beach. I thought I saw her, Ma."

Aoifa smiled knowingly. "Yes, I understand that. I feel her presence out there too, as if she is watching, Lara." Aoifa took her hand as they shared the same thoughts.

The girls' mood was subdued over lunch without the usual hilarity of days gone by at their grandparents' house. Yet their presence brought a semblance of sanity and normality into Aoifa's otherwise tarnished world.

"This is nice, Aoif, like old times." Aaron looked around at his family and smiled.

"Yes, Pa, having the girls around the table has brought some lovely memories back – only not like old times, because Ma is not here," Aoifa added with a heavy heart.

Aaron tapped his glass loudly, quickly expelling the gloomy mood around the table.

"Can I raise a toast to happy memories – my dear Cara." They all chinked glasses, making the younger girls smile.

"Can I have some wine, Ma?" asked Mairead.

Aoifa threw her a disdainful look and topped up her glass with lemonade.

"I'll stay for a few days now, Pa. Do you mind?"

Sean was always the quiet one, but he spoke up. "We'd love that, Aoif. You remind us of Ma, with your gentle ways about the place," he said shyly.

"Yes, to be sure," her father added, "Anyways, you're a grand cook!" her father added jokingly, when quite out of character, he got up and embraced Aoifa warmly. It was a poignant moment for everyone.

After lunch, Lois took the younger girls around the farm and Padraig helped Aaron outside. Aoifa cleared up in the house quietly with Niamh, a serenity replacing her angst of previous days.

As the sun came out a bit later, she and Padraig took a walk down to the beach. There was a chill in the air with autumn colour underfoot creating a warm glow around them as they stopped and sat down on an old tree stump.

"We will all need Ma's strength for the funeral, Pad."

"I know she will help you through on her last journey, chara. You may get her messages then?" he told her encouragingly, but Aoifa doubted it and changed the subject.

"I must visit Pa over the coming weeks, support them both."

She bent down to pick up some leaves with bronze, red and golden hues, feeling their smoothness as she brought them together on her lap. She took in their salty scent and softness, noting their imminent departure from the world too. Nothing stayed the same forever, she thought to herself.

"I guess so. You could come across once a week for a while?"

"Definitely."

Aoifa felt pale and wan despite the bright sunshine, her movements jerky as the grief took its toll. They sat with their bare feet on the cold sand, looking out across the sea at some fishing boats making their way to shore. She snuggled up to Padraig, wrapping her arms around him.

"You know, your relationship with Liam may change going forward, Aoif. He never did get along with your ma too well."

"Maybes," she whispered. "He always showed distain for Ma's predictions. Mine too."

"Well, every cloud an' all that."

Aoifa shrugged and took his hand.

"I don't feel so fragmented with you here, Pad. It's like I've been partially put back together, but my soul and spirit still feel fragile."

"It will ease, chara. Just give it time."

As Aoifa looked into her husband's deep blue eyes, a rush of love came over her and she emitted a loud sob. She took a few deep breaths and they languished in a moment of togetherness, holding each other close, then Padraig roused her.

"Come on, let's go back and have a cup of tea with your da and Sean afore we have to leave." They put their shoes on and walked back up the path just as the sun popped behind a cloud.

Clara came running up behind them and gave her ma a hug.

"Ma, so where is Grandma now?"

"She has gone to heaven, my sweet, to rest."

Aoifa felt touched by Clara's questions, always wanting to know everything and crying at the drop of a hat. Aoifa stroked her fair hair, which was in tangles around her freckled tear-stained face.

"So will I never see her again?" Her mouth was twisted in pain.

"Who knows, my sweet, maybe one day, but probably not for a long time," as they walked into the house, hand in hand.

Niamh had made some scones and tea for everyone, and they all gathered in the large kitchen. Shafts of sunshine touched the golden streaks in Clara's hair as she sat on her mother's lap. There was some scratching as the front door opened and the dogs walked in, Brody sidling up to Clara, his tail wagging.

"Come here, Brody." She reached out to stroke him.

"Ma, will Grandpa be OK?" Niamh asked quietly.

"I hope so. He will have Sean by his side, Nevey."

After tea had finished, Aoifa read to them from one of their grandma's favourite children's books and Clara exclaimed,

"Oh, Ma, I love that story about mermaids and golden fish in the sea. I want to read it every time we come to see Grandpa."

"A perfect idea, Lara. We will so." It was getting late as Aoifa embraced them all and Padraig collected Roma and the cart to take them all home.

When they had left, Aoifa made a decision to visit her ma's bedroom, but a flutter of anxiety came over her at the very idea. She continued to sit on the window seat in the hallway and, in the stillness, listened for any familiar messages to come into her head to show her the way. Aoifa breathed deeply to calm herself and waited. Several minutes passed, but nothing, just silence from within and without.

All she could hear was the distant lapping of the waves and an intermittent cry of a seagull as it came in to roost. Aoifa realised when her ma had been with them, she had never felt alone. They even used to share the same thoughts, but now Aoifa felt entirely alone, her emotions stripped naked. She pulled her cardigan tight around her, but it was not enough; she began to shiver. The evenings were getting chilly. No, it was just her blood running cold.

Aoifa gave no thought to other human beings who stood alone in the face of illness or calamity and managed to negotiate their lives with courage and faith, without any foresight of misfortune coming their way. For now, she could only think of how she could possibly do that for the rest of her life. She got up but was suddenly immobilised by fear. Gritting her teeth and with all the effort she could muster, Aoifa made her way upstairs one step at a time and pushed open the bedroom door.

Her pa had left the room as a shrine to Cara, her final outfit laid out neatly on the bed. Aoifa suddenly realised that Aaron had always been self-sufficient and not dependent on spiritual support from Cara, like she had. She wondered what that actually felt like, to have the ability to navigate your own actions and emotions every day. How did he do it? Aoifa had a notion that she was about to find out. It was a fact and she had to face up to it. Common sense told her she would have to allow herself to feel the grief and then, maybe, a slow healing would take place.

She forced her thoughts back to the present. Photographs were what she needed to remind her of happy times. Aoifa sat down at her mother's dressing table and caught sight of herself in the mirror, her sickly pallor and the dark circles under her eyes. Where had the brightness gone? Pad had always told her he loved her beautiful hazel eyes. Now they looked grey, dull and lifeless and her red hair was pulled back harshly. Aoifa yanked at her hairband, and it fell freely around her shoulders. She imagined it was how her ma had looked once in that same mirror, but now she felt not a fraction of what her ma had been. Cara had been a guiding light for everyone, Aoifa had wanted for nothing, yet any feelings of gratitude eluded her. She became aware of a rising anger at her change of circumstances. She didn't like it one bit as feelings of terror crept over her.

Aoifa gathered herself and opened the draw where the photographs were kept. She bypassed some envelopes containing locks of hair and continued her search. They were all labelled, and she soon found them. There she was – full of fun, laughter, her brothers alongside, Liam standing tall and proud, Sean, nervous, sullen. There were others, of parties long ago with her friends. She tried to work them out. There was Rachel, Mary, Chloe, Declan, Eamon and Laurel too. Poor Laurel. Aoifa recalled the last time they had spoken, some months back. Her parents and brother had all passed, and she was feeling desperate. How did she come to terms with that, with no foresight? One day she would meet up with her and find out. She looked at early photos of her mother – they looked identical. Cara's hair was curlier, thicker, but also long and spread around her shoulders, as Aoifa wore it now, and it comforted her to see the likeness. She took several photos out to keep, also selecting some small items for the girls to have as keepsakes.

Aoifa looked out of the window at the sun going down and suddenly had an urge to break away from her mourning, needing some wind in her hair and sea spray on her face. She rushed downstairs, threw on her coat and wellies and set off down the lane toward the beach, waving to Sean as she passed him by.

"Back later," she called out. "Supper at 6pm. Just need a walk."

"Sure, Sis."

Aoifa made her way to a place where she and her ma used to sit together. She looked out to sea and could see the pod of dolphins in the distance – her ma had loved them. She tried to recall the last time they had sat there together, maybe six months before. It had been a hot day, midsummer, and the sea had been a deep sapphire blue. But what did they talk about? Maybe something about the girls and where they were heading. Cara had actually made reference to the gift, but how? Ahh… Aoifa did remember. She said that Clara was of the element Water – that she was emotional, intuitive, creative, spiritual. So maybe her ma had meant that Clara would have the gift! Her message was to watch out for her girls, wasn't it? And 'especially' – who? She must watch out for Clara, then. After all, she, her ma and Clara – they were of the same element. As she looked back, Aoifa wondered if Cara had been trying to prepare her for her passing and times ahead. Suddenly feeling more confused than ever, Aoifa made her way back to the farmhouse for dinner.

Aaron was stoking up the fire and closing the curtains for the evening when she arrived.

"Hi, Pa – had a nice walk in the fresh air. Cold now. I've got your favourite lamb stew cooking too."

"I can smell it, chara. Smells like your ma is here – stew, cosy evening and a blazing fire." Aaron sat down with a sigh. "Wish I had an appetite, Aoif."

"Me too, Pa, but Sean will, so we must try. Cup of tea be nice now."

After they had finished their meal and cleared everything away, Aaron and Aoifa sat alongside the fire whilst Sean went back out to work in his shed.

"Pa, I hope you don't mind, but I would like to give some small trinkets of Ma's to the girls and also take a few photos?"

"Take what you want. She'd like that, chara."

"Can I talk to you about something that's been bothering me?"

"Go on – what is it?"

"You know I had no messages of Ma's passing?"

"I did see that, Aoif."

"I've lost my gift, Pa. I have no messages anymore. Not since just before Ma passed."

Her father remained silent, looking intently into the fire. Aoifa thought he had fallen asleep.

"Pa?"

"Yes, chara, I hear you. You see, this happened to your ma after she lost her own mother, so it is no surprise to me. But then, when the grief passed and she was healin', it came back."

"Oh, Pa! That is a relief. So it will come back to me too?"

"I don't see why not, chara. Just be patient and all will be well."

"And in the meantime, Pa, I feel... so lost, without direction, unable to make decisions at all."

"Ah, that's just the sadness. Don't expect much for now. I feel that too and I miss her second sight as well. She always told me what was comin', now I'll never know."

"Sure, Pa, I hadn't thought of that. We can support each other, then."

Aaron nodded and looked away, staring into space. Aoifa touched his shoulder to bid him goodnight, then turned to face him once more.

"Pa – the message Ma left for me – did she mean to look out for one of the girls in particular, d'you think?"

Aaron looked at her and his eyes glazed over, "Her face showed nothing, chara. It was all so brief..." and he returned to the warmth of the fire. Aoifa left him to his thoughts and made her way upstairs to bed, feeling a lightness and hope she had not felt for a while.

Two days later, Aoifa knew it was time to go home to her own family and stop this self-pitying. She was determined to be sensible. Taking the stairs two at a time, she strode forward into her day and called out of the front door,

"Pa! Sean! Breakfast is ready!"

Aaron threw off his boots, a sad smile on his face. "You off today, then, chara?"

"For a bit, Pa. I'll come back in a few days to prepare for the funeral." Aoifa felt a lump in her throat, so changed the subject, wanting to remain upbeat. "You two got a busy few days, then?"

Sean looked at her suggestively. "Don't you know, then, Aoif?"

"I don't, Sean. I don't quite know everything you know – and I didn't even know about…" But she didn't finish, and Sean looked taken aback, clearly embarrassed.

"Ach, Sis… I thought you did, with your sight an' all. I thought you could see all the important things. I'm buildin' sommat special."

Aoifa took a deep breath. "Like what, then? You're a dark one!"

"Well, if you dunna know, I ain't gonna tell yer! For once, I have a secret from you, Sis!" he told her furtively.

Somehow Sean's tone irked Aoifa. Everyone expected so much of her all the time, but she had nothing to give anymore.

"Guess so," she replied despondently.

Aoifa could think of no further response, so cleared the dishes away, then made her way upstairs to pack her bag. This time, instead of grief, Aoifa felt anger and she wasn't sure why. Then she realised – toward her ma! Why had she taken her precious gift? Her resolve to be strong vanished and she contemplated, once again, a life of her own making. It seemed that her pa, Sean and definitely Liam had walked straight back into their lives, without Ma. Why couldn't she go forward with the same courage? Aoifa considered whether she should reveal to the whole family about her loss. They surely would sympathise. But what if they didn't – or worse, didn't believe her? Perhaps her ma wanted her to cope without it, was that was why she took it away? Or was it because she hadn't been there for her passing?

Oh dear. Too many questions, too much agonising and heartache. Aoifa sat on the bed amongst her packing, conscious of the dark clouds and gusts of wind rattling the window. What next? Would she become a shadow of her former self? Who was she without a part of her ma inside? Her ma had gone, her gift had gone, Lois was making plans for her future too. Where would Aoifa end up, who would she become? Or would she too disappear along with everything and everyone else as they departed slowly from her life? What if the void inside got bigger instead of smaller and she became a nothing and couldn't think at all? As far as Aoifa could make out, her future looked bleak. But wait a minute. Her ma's sight came back, so hers would too – surely?

4. THE FUNERAL

As Aoifa drove along the coast road toward Muir Farm, the ponies were galloping toward her along the beach, and she pulled over. It brought Aoifa such joy to be around these horses, born and bred on Connemara. They were so genuine it brought out her own truth and gave her a feeling of belonging. They stopped close to the car and looked into her eyes, shaking their heads, excited to see her. Rafa put his head near the open window, and she fondled his nose, then as she set off, they followed alongside, racing along the sandy shore.

As Aoifa approached home and her family, she felt apprehensive. She would need to be strong for them over the coming days, but she didn't feel it just now. As she pulled up the drive, the girls ran out of the front door, thrilled to see her. Even Flynn was at the garden gate, his tail wagging exuberantly.

"I've missed you all so much," said Aoifa. "How've you been? Everyone been helping you, Lo?"

Lois gave her disgruntled reply, "Just a bit, but mostly Clara," and Aoifa gave an understanding nod as the girls flocked around her.

"Ma, I've made a flower wreath."

"Oh, Nevey, in twisted willow and autumn colours, very pretty, my love.

"Can we hang it on the front door – I read somewhere – to keep the good spirits in and the bad ones out – for Grandma?"

"We sure can," said Aoifa as she put down her bag and took off her Aran cardigan. There was a roaring fire in the hearth and a smell of something cooking. "OK, who's the chef tonight?" she said brightly, attempting to pave the way for the coming days.

Clara smiled coyly and put up her hand. "Me!"

"Now, let me see, is it… fish and chips? No? Um, shepherd's pie – but you'd need help with that. Bacon, eggs…? Hmm. Sausages? Yes! With chips and peas and your special seaweed dish, then? Ah, lovely, Lara."

At ten years old, Clara had quite the culinary flair and Aoifa knew she preferred to cook the same meal but wanted to humour her, smiling good-naturedly as they all sat down together.

"Where's your da?"

"He's still at market, Ma, had a lot to do today, but I helped him," said Mairead.

Aoifa glanced at Lois, who was shaking her head.

"What did you do?"

"I took some baskets down to him for his seaweed haul," she said proudly.

"He will have appreciated that, Mairy." Aoifa sensed that everyone had pulled together in her absence. Siobhan was her usual quiet self as Aoifa looked across at her, a couple of years older than Clara, but so very different.

"We missed you, Ma," said Niamh, giving her a hug. "How are Grandpa and Sean?"

"Grandpa's doing OK, as independent as ever. Sean has a new project on the go or something."

"What's that, then?"

"That's just it, he was quite secretive about it!"

"But you know, Ma – right?"

"Not sure yet, Nevey." Aoifa gave a quick response as the door opened and Padraig came rushing in.

"Hello, my love." Aoifa got up to greet him. "Drink?"

"Hey – let's break open one of our elderflower wines as a welcome home!" Padraig exclaimed, turning to give her a kiss. "I think at sixteen and eighteen, the older girls can have a taster too?" he added with a cheeky grin. Padraig went down to the cellar for the wine, and Aoifa fetched the glasses as Mairead sidled up to her.

"And what about me, Ma? Fifteen is nearly sixteen too!"

"Hardly, Mairy." Aoifa scowled at her wayward daughter.

"Well, I've had plenty a'ready," Mairead muttered defiantly, but her parents ignored the remark.

"This tastes good, Pad, your best yet. Don't you think, girls?" Aoifa smiled at Niamh as the wine was making her eyes water.

Later that evening, Aoifa and Padraig sat together in the cosy sitting room with his arm protectively around her.

"How are you feeling tonight, my love?" he asked gently.

"Oh, Pad. So-so. I wish I had some foresight of what was coming instead of butterflies in my tummy," she replied dismally.

"It'll be OK, and the girls will help. I'll be there too, Aoif. Lean on me whenever you want," he added good-naturedly.

A few days later, on Saturday morning, everyone was up early, as Aoifa and the girls were making their way to Home Farm to prepare for the funeral. When they arrived, Lois, Niamh and Siobhan washed the plates, cutlery and glasses, ready for laying the table. Mairead was never anywhere to be seen when there was work to be done, but Clara had a way of roping her in to help.

"Mairy and I will go and collect some flowers from Grandma's garden," she said, pushing her older sister out of the door.

"Lo?" Aoifa called out. "Can you come with me to do the food shopping? We can leave the others to carry on here."

As they got into the car, Lois turned to her mother with a solemn expression. "Ma, are you OK?"

"I am Lo, thank you. Although I feel I've lost a part of myself, to be sure."

They chatted as they went along in the car. Lois had been close to her grandma, although there were no similarities between them. She felt her way in the world by working it all out, never going with the mood or leaving things to fate – Lois was far too pragmatic for that.

"I will miss her so, Ma, her stories and the way she took such an interest in us girls. Yet…"

"What, Lo?" asked Aoifa tentatively.

"She used to talk so much about her mysterious beliefs in the unknown, her predictions and all that, like you get too."

"Mmm. That was just how it was."

Although Lois was her daughter and she loved her dearly, their differences were often quite apparent, yet it rarely came between them. She considered sharing the loss of her second sight, but the moment passed, and the conversation turned to their shopping list.

"I am so relieved Dolly and her friend will be coming to help us tomorrow, Lo. I prefer not to bother Danny and Scorcha."

"We can do it, Ma, all of us together."

"Yes, I know we can, and we will."

Aoifa found the prospect of the food preparation rather daunting and suddenly felt grateful for her daughter's practical approach.

When they got back, Aoifa opened the front door and gasped. The table was laid, there were flowers everywhere and the place was as spotless as a new pin.

"It all looks brilliant, girls – just like Grandma would want it!" she exclaimed.

"And look at all the flowers too, Ma," cried Clara and Mairead.

"All reds, yellows and autumn leaves. Perfect!"

Aoifa was moved by all their efforts and felt emotion rising up inside, but she turned away from it quickly, gathered the girls and they all left to make their way home.

That evening, the family sat harmoniously together, each feeling their own sadness, yet it was no longer palpable, more a quiet, settled ambience.

"I think Grandma's spirit is here with us, Ma," said Niamh. "I can feel it, but it no longer hurts in the way it did."

"That is death, Nevey," Aoifa whispered gently. "The more you get in touch with it, the more you understand and accept it for what it is. I must say it hurts me terribly at the moment, but it will be easier after we've laid Grandma to rest tomorrow."

Aoifa had always been the strong one, an inner strength spurring her on, but at that moment, she found everything quite overwhelming, her thoughts still without clarity or direction.

It was late when Padraig came through the door that evening.

"I had such a journey to market today, Aoif. The cart broke. I had to make my way back on Rafa to fetch another wheel. He and Roma did me proud in the end."

"Treasures, those two!" said Aoifa with a smile.

"We got ourselves there but missed a lot of market. Never mind, there'll be another."

"Maybes we can get you a new cart one o' these days?"

"Rubbish. Nothin' wrong with the old one!"

"Now you sound like Pa."

He punched her playfully and took his dinner to the table, his cheerful ways lightening her mood.

The next morning, Aoifa sat on the side of the bed and looked out of the window across at the vivid blue of the sea and the fluffy clouds on the horizon. It was a lovely fine day.

Padraig came into the bedroom. "How are you feeling, my love? A silly question – big day ahead."

"I'm ready in my head but not my heart. A bit of me will go out on the tide with Ma today, Pad." She took a deep breath, her voice breaking.

"Not too much of you, though, I hope," Padraig replied, taking her into his arms and pointing out of the window. "You'll be able to connect with her spirit out there. Just look at the natural elements all around you and imagine…"

Aoifa shivered and suddenly felt cold.

"I feel she's gone already, Pad. The wind has taken her."

"Come on, Aoif, you can do this. We'll support each other."

Aoifa suddenly snapped out of her mourning and maudlin. She selected her most colourful outfit with a pretty necklace her ma had given her and matching braids for her hair, although when Aoifa looked down at her wellies, she frowned. They looked more than a little incongruous, but it brought a small smile to her face, easing her tension a little. Her ma would have loved the contrast.

After they had loaded up the car, the family left for Home Farm. It was a quiet journey, with each of them deep in their own thoughts.

"Ma?" Clara called from the back seat, her voice muffled as she stifled a sob.

"Yes, Lara?"

"Can I hold your hand when we take Grandma to the beach, please?"

"You can hold my hand for as long as you want."

After they had laid out the food amidst the girls' elaborate decorations, the O'Connell family and some close friends arrived and gathered outside the farmhouse.

Aaron O'Connell greeted everyone warmly, his smile belying the pain and distress beneath. When everyone had arrived, Aaron led the procession down to the bay, carrying his wife's ashes in a wicker casket for her to be laid to rest on the shores of her beloved Connemara. A lay minister said some poignant parting words as Aaron carefully opened the casket and scattered her ashes on the departing waves. Everyone stood in silence and watched as the tide went out and all that remained of their beloved Cara drifted out to sea, then Clara whispered to her mother,

"Ma, where will Grandma go now?"

"She is on her way to foreverland, my love, where she will remain, peaceful and content. She will have no pain and we can think of her out there any time we want."

Clara accepted this and watched, still holding her mother's hand as tears flowed freely down Aoifa's cheeks, Padraig alongside, his arm around her.

The girls had each brought a flower from the garden, which they dropped onto the waves, "to brighten Grandma's journey," said Niamh. As they did so, almost uncannily, a ray of sunshine appeared across the water.

"As if by magic," Aoifa muttered.

Everyone watched as the ashes floated away into the shimmering light then Aaron turned and led the way slowly back up the hill. It had been a serene moment, Aoifa thought as she followed her pa, as if the whole ceremony had been cathartic, bringing comfort to them all. When they reached the top, Clara turned around. The flowers were still floating on the surface of the calm waters, and she waved goodbye to her grandma as they all went indoors.

There was a lovely spread in the dining room and Aoifa greeted everyone warmly as they came in, telling them to help themselves. Padraig and Sean served the drinks, his blackberry wine and locally brewed beer, with home-made elderberry or chamomile cordial for the children. As Aoifa took a glass from him, she caught sight of a couple coming in just as Liam and Emma walked by.

"Liam, who are the elderly couple at the door?"

"Aoif, surely you remember? It's Aunt Beth and Uncle David."

Aoifa looked puzzled, then it dawned on her. "Oh. Ma's sister! I'd quite forgotten she had one. Goodness, how did you track them down?"

Liam looked surprised, taken aback. "I never really lost touch with them, Aoif."

"Was Ma in touch with them, then? She never mentioned her."

"I'm not sure," said Liam dismissively as he turned to his family, handing them all drinks, then turned back. "I wonder what made you bring a minister after all, Aoif?" he asked her, a touch of irony in his tone.

"It was Pa's idea. He's a friend and adored Ma. Not a true minister of the cloth, Li, just a layman preacher. It was nice, though. Don't you think?"

Liam shrugged, a disapproving look in his eye, but Aoifa pretended not to notice and turned to Padraig.

"I'd better go and talk to my aunt," she said reluctantly and took a deep breath as she approached them.

"Hi, Aunt Beth, how are you?"

"Ah… you must be Aoifa? You look like your mother. This is an unfortunate event, to be sure. Was she ill for long, then, my sister?"

Aoifa was surprised at her aunt's question. "But you knew – didn't you, Aunt?"

"I'm afraid not. Cara and I hadn't been in touch for many years."

"It must have come as a shock, then," said Aoifa. "Please, come and eat something."

She took her aunt over to the dining table. "The girls prepared it all, mainly Clara, our youngest." Aoifa pointed to her nearby. "She loves cooking."

"How nice," said her aunt vacantly, looking over Clara's head.

"She did well," Aoifa added, smiling kindly at Clara and giving her arm a little squeeze. "Well, good to see you again. Please would you and Uncle David help yourselves."

Aoifa was pleased to move away from her aunt's obvious frostiness. She decided it must be the shock and grief as she watched the pair walk away to sit apart from the other guests.

"Pad… my aunt… so unlike Ma, a bit of a cold fish, I must say. Says she had no idea Ma was ill."

Padraig glanced over at them.

"Well, I've never seen them afore," he replied thoughtfully.

Aoifa went up to Aaron as he sat in his armchair next to the range.

"Pa, you OK?"

"I am, chara. The flames are warming me inside and out."

Aoifa put her arm around his shoulders. "Do you remember Aunt Beth, over there?"

Aaron glanced across to where Aoifa was nodding.

"Not seen her for many a long time. Surprised she came. Any tea going, Aoif?"

Aoifa frowned, none the wiser.

"I'll fetch you some, with a plate of food."

Emma came across to them and touched Aaron's hand.

"Very moving ceremony, Pa. Cara is at peace now."

"Aye, she be," he replied sadly as Emma and Aoifa nodded in agreement.

"Lovely spread, Aoif. You and the girls have done well."

Aoifa looked at her warmly, grateful for her generous comments.

"Thanks, Em. I just hope there's enough." Aoifa made a quick decision. "Emma, would you all like to come over this Christmas? It's only a month away. Would you like that too, Pa?"

He smiled in agreement.

"I think that would be lovely," Emma replied. "I'll ask Liam and let you know."

So far so good, went through Aoifa's head.

There was a gentle aura around the house that afternoon, Cara's calm spirit omnipresent, permeating the atmosphere. There was a gaggle of youngsters in the study, snippets of laughter erupting now and then, and the adults collected in small groups throughout the rest of the house. Aoifa noticed her aunt and uncle remained alone. She watched them carefully, thinking how unalike the two sisters were as she delved into her past, but nothing came to mind. Approaching them once more, she said, "Aunt Beth, where do you live now?"

"Oh, not too far away," was the vague reply and Aoifa thought quickly,

"As Pa will be missing Mother this year, would you like to join us with Liam's family on Christmas Day?"

There was a moment of silence.

"Thank you, but I think not. We prefer to spend Christmas at home."

Aoifa smiled her understanding, offered them another drink, and as she moved away, Lois came up to her and whispered,

"Ma, why didn't you tell us that lady, Great-aunt Beth, was coming?"

"Because I didn't know, Lo," Aoifa replied nervously, turning away from her daughter, not ready for the conversation.

"Ma?" Mairead whispered, "Can I take a look in Grandma's bedroom, please? You found the keepsake, maybe there's something…"

Aoifa looked at her reprovingly. "Not now, Mairy."

"But, Ma, as we're here…"

Aoifa spoke more sternly than intended. "Not now! We can look another time."

Mairead stomped off with a long face and Aoifa sighed. She had a lot on her mind and needed some fresh air, so she slipped outside for a moment. It had become cold. She could feel winter approaching. The leaves were no longer evident in their multitude of colours, just a semi-barren grey landscape all around, echoing her mood.

"Please, Ma, things are happening around me of which I know nothing. Don't leave me yet. Can you linger a while and help me to cope as they unfold?"

As Aoifa continued to sit in the porch with the dogs for company, watching the night close in, it occurred to her that when someone passes, life still continues for those left behind as they all take faltering steps toward their mutated future.

The front door opened, interrupting her thoughts.

"Aoif, what on earth are you doing? It's freezing out here!"

"I just needed air, Pad. It's a bit claustrophobic in there and…"

"What?"

"I don't know. I just feel out of sorts, what with my aunt appearing from nowhere, me not knowing, and she and Ma hadn't spoken for years. It's hit me a bit."

"Old skeletons, my love, leave well alone."

"Yes, to be sure, but rests uneasy with me, that's all. Ma and I were so close – why didn't I know?"

"Ah, dunna worry now, chara. 'Twas a peaceful day, too."

Just then, Clara came running out. "Ma, can we start the cake I made? I put real marigold flowers on it just for Grandma – she loved bright orange!"

Aoifa smiled at her daughter, her natural exuberance bringing them back to the present. "Of course, Lara, and tell Siobhan to bring hers out too, the chocolate one. I'll get the plates."

Aoifa looked at her husband. "Trust Clara to diffuse a situation with her sweetness in more ways than one!"

As they went to rejoin the party, Aoifa mentioned to Padraig about having a big family Christmas.

"Good idea, Aoif, if your pa would like it. Be grand."

"Do you think it may give me a chance to spend some time with Liam, ease our differences, Pad?"

"Well, I think Christmas is a good time for healing old wounds."

Aoifa considered this as she stood up and gazed out to the inky blue sea and approaching clouds.

"Come, my darling," he whispered, "this is not a time for morbid reflection. Let's rejoin the group and think positive!"

"Yes, you're right. I only hope I can," Aoifa replied with her fingers crossed. As they turned to go inside, Padraig stroked her hair, which was cascading in rich red folds down her back, highlighted by the setting sun.

Although her sadness had lifted somewhat, Aoifa couldn't help but reminisce and remained deep in thought as the day drew to a close. Since her ma had passed, changes were occurring which she had no knowledge of nor any control over. Skeletons, for sure, were on her mind.

After they had cleared up, the family were exhausted; it had been an emotional day. They all piled into the family car and made their way back to Muir Farm. When she was getting ready for bed, Aoifa did get a premonition – but, she sadly realised, it was more of an idea. One day, she would write her memoirs in a journal, her own truth, for everyone to read. But, she admitted with a rueful smile, she clearly had some research to do first.

5. THE O'CONNELLS

After the funeral, Liam took himself off for a walk along the beach. He wanted to make sense of things, breathe in some sea air. When he had learned about his ma's passing, it had immobilised him. He felt numb, especially toward his sister, with whom he had endured a difficult relationship most of his life. Aoifa had always been the favoured one, which was why he spent so much time with his gran. He remembered the relief he felt on leaving the farm to go to university. When he returned to live at home again, that was when things got really bad.

When he had heard the news, Liam was reminded of when his own gran had passed. He was at uni at the time and remembered how devastated he had been. She had shown him the ways of the world, instilled in him ambition, a confidence and a belief that anything was possible. He hadn't got that from his own parents; all they thought about was the farm. Yet this time, it had been his own ma's funeral and he didn't feel the same.

Down on the shores earlier, he had been transported right back to his gran's funeral when he had been eighteen, Aoifa thirteen, and Sean only eleven. Her passing had affected him deeply, making him more determined than ever to continue with further education. He recalled keeping this resolve from his family at the time, as it had seemed like disloyalty. Feelings of guilt had returned in recent weeks because of the lack of emotion he had felt, acutely aware of lingering resentments. Would they ever go? Should he deal with them – get them out? Liam shook his head.

As he looked across at his pa's cattle on the shores, Liam's mind wondered as to how Aaron managed these animals every day, taking them across the bay to fresh pastures and back. He had a reasonable relationship with his pa these days, although he could never figure out why he was so resistant to change. His ma had been vehemently against it, but now she had passed, he would choose a good time to discuss with Aaron and Sean about updating their farming methods. He could even offer to make an investment, to help them out.

As he turned around to return to the farmhouse, Emma was coming toward him, a tall slim figure with her hair up in a fashionable topknot walking elegantly along the beach. She had such a chic style, which he so admired, her looks belying her advancing years. As he walked slowly toward her, his thoughts drifted back to when they had met, when Liam had been a fun-loving but hard-working student. It crossed his mind that he hadn't been endowed with the looks of his sister, nor Sean. They were both tall, with thick red hair, whilst he was stockier with brown hair, now receding, but he knew he had been blessed with the old Irish charm. There was no doubt he had been a success with the ladies, he admitted to himself with a furtive smile.

"What are you smiling about, then?" his wife asked as she approached him.

"Oh, nothing, trying to bring a little humour into a sad situation, that's all, my dear, and something funny came to mind." They continued walking hand in hand as the sun went down and a gentle breeze whistled around them.

When they got back to the farm, everyone was sitting around in small groups. He noticed the easy camaraderie between the cousins; they all got along remarkably well considering their differences. He and Aoifa had managed an acceptable rapport that day, which had to be a good omen, but he could see with some relief that the party was starting to break up. He shook his pa and Sean's hands, gathered his family and they all set off in the Range Rover.

"Shall we go to the Traveller's Rest for a meal, Li? Be an uplifting finish to the day?" asked Emma.

"Why not?" he replied, looking forward to a large pint. Their local pub was a homely place; it would indeed lift their spirits. He looked in his mirror at Dan and Scorcha in easy conversation, their mood light given the circumstances.

As they arrived at the pub, they were greeted by a warm atmosphere, familiar old sofas and a roaring fire in the hearth. After Emma had placed their orders, Scorcha took her father's arm.

"Come on, Dad, let's find that nice table near the fire."

"Liam, you look lost in thought, penny for them?" asked Emma as they all sat down.

"I was just thinking how much Ma would be missed."

"Will you miss your mother, Li? I know you were not that close," asked Emma carefully.

"I couldn't cope with her funny ways, Em. If she'd left them alone, it would have been better between us, but yes, I will miss her."

Dan looked up. "Do you mean her beliefs in the supernatural, Dad?"

"Yes, Dan, she was always predicting the way for all of us."

"But was she right?" added Scorcha.

"Usually," Emma answered quietly. "She had a sixth sense, but sometimes it was just uncanny and rather spooky how she knew things."

Their meal arrived and they all tucked in ravenously.

"I wish we'd been closer to Grandma, like our cousins were," Scorcha declared, a sadness wafting over her pale freckled face. "They spent much more time over at the farm than we did when we were all little."

"That's because your dad and his parents didn't always see eye to eye, Scorch. Sometimes these things happen," Emma explained.

"And he didn't get along with Aunt Aoifa much either," added Danny. "Why, Dad?"

"Argh, all water under the bridge now, son. Times were hard on the farm in those days, and they wouldn't accept that I had ambitions beyond it."

Scorcha's face crumpled. "So didn't you spend time on the farm helping Grandpa, then?"

"Not much, Scorch, if I'm honest. I was always over at my gran's, my head in her books and ideas."

"Poor Grandpa – so who helped him?" Scorcha replied scornfully.

"Your uncle Sean was the practical one then and still is. Hey, if I'd stuck around there and not got an education, you wouldn't have the luxuries you enjoy today, now would you?" Liam said with an ironic smile. Danny looked slightly disapproving too but nodded reluctantly.

"I left home so young. University life took me away from all that."

"And then you met me!" said Emma.

He nodded with a wide smile. "And you were far too aspirational for the ways of the farm. You're a product of your fancy upbringing in London! It just so happened you came across to Dublin Uni or we would never have met." He looked warmly at his wife as she added,

"Hey, easy, I can be practical too!"

"I know. But we moved away and chose a different road. The only regret for me is that it fragmented my relationships with those left at home."

"It's never too late to make amends, Dad," his son said sagely.

"I suppose you're right, Dan," Liam replied, a doubtful look on his face.

As they moved into the lounge area for coffee, Scorcha spoke up.

"I wanted to talk to you both about something."

"Go ahead," said Liam curiously.

"Mikey and I want to move in together."

Emma looked worried, although not surprised. "But what about your studies, wouldn't they suffer, Scorch, you know, if you're together all the time?"

"I believe it's not been three months yet?" added Liam. He too looked concerned. It had been such a whirlwind romance.

"We're both very committed to our studies, but we love each other and want to spend more time together. We've less than a year to go, so it will be heads-down for sure."

"Well, you've obviously thought this through, what can we say to deter you?" said Liam, galled at the news. "I'll probably have to foot the bill too?" he added irritably.

"Not at all, Dad. We'll pay the rent, half each. Anyway, when we're done, we'll probably both get jobs in London. It's the place to be for our respective fields at the moment."

At this information, Danny scowled. "I thought we were going to work together over here at the end of uni, Scorch? We think along the same lines… want the same things."

"I don't know yet. It's a long way off. What if we can't find a suitable place together in the research fields we want? It's unlikely, Dan."

Danny got up and left the table, disappointment and rejection written all over his face.

"Come on, you two, let's not have a fall-out on the eve of Grandma's funeral," Liam chided. "Anyway, neither of you can plan that far ahead. If your heart is with Michael, then I suppose you must give it a go, my girl," he acquiesced.

Scorcha jumped up and hugged her parents then whispered,

"I think we have to spread our wings sometime."

Her mother took her hand and smiled in agreement as Scorcha went off to find her brother. They always made up one way or another and Dan soon returned with a smile on his face.

"She said there are no plans for looking ahead yet… a way to go! So all good."

Liam knew that his twins were quite inseparable, although one day it would be inevitable.

"What are you studying at the moment, Dan? You had to prepare a paper some months back?"

"Oh, that one, Dad, gone long since. You mean the one about global warming? Yeah, got a First for that."

"Wow, brilliant. Would love to hear about it."

Although, Liam knew the level of his twins' studies were mostly over his head these days.

"OK, Dad, I'll go through it with you some time," Danny replied vaguely as he rejoined Scorcha at the bar.

"Em, I'm worried about Pa. I'd really like him to mechanise the farm, to help him and Sean take it forward. Neither of them is getting any younger and it would bring more value to it."

"I know how you feel, Li, but they nor Aoifa want any interference, not just now anyway. I think your da needs to find his way on his own for a bit."

"I wouldn't interfere exactly, you know that. I just want to help." He looked at Emma imploringly. She had such a way with his sister; they seemed to understand one another. "Could you speak to Aoifa, Em, then we could join forces and approach Pa?"

"Maybe. In time, but not before Christmas. I think we'll leave things alone until after. I forgot to say – Aoifa mentioned Christmas, but we can talk about it tomorrow now."

It had been a tiring day and they soon left for home, but the evening with his family had definitely helped to restore his equilibrium. Everyone took an early night, except Liam, who needed time to unwind. He fetched a nightcap and made himself comfortable with his feet up in the semi-darkness of his study. His mind drifted back to his sister again; he was so conscious of the differences between the two families. Padraig had his bohemian ways, coming from a deeply traditional Irish gypsy family, going back decades. Yet he had to admit, he had been loyalty itself toward Aoifa and they seemed very happy. Their girls had lovely temperaments, good looking lot, some lucky enough to have their grandma's rich red hair. They had a pretty decent outlook on life too, myriad talents between them, although slightly naive in some ways, Liam admitted to himself. Two out of five stood out to him. Mairead was heading for trouble in his book, lacking both direction and discipline. Maybe one day a strong partner would have some influence over her headstrong and self-seeking ways, and Siobhan – a deep one that, quite serious with a rather intense nature for one so young.

Liam's main concern about his sister's family was that they had their heads entirely in the clouds. Literally. Padraig made quite a reasonable living and Aoifa was very resourceful in making ends meet, although he wished she hadn't given up the teaching. He knew she followed her sixth sense, living day to day, and Padraig never seemed to worry about a thing as he managed his kelp farm. They believed their future was pre-destined. Well, there was no denying that the future was mapped out one way or other, but they were both romantics and he was a pragmatist. Just maybe it was OK to live with those romantic mystical notions, especially as they lived in the back of beyond where the pressures of urban life never seemed to touch them. They may get away with it. Although, he felt they'd do better to catch up with modern technology and how the world was changing. Liam yawned and took himself wearily up to bed to stop his mind from whirring around, giving him a headache.

After breakfast the next morning, Dan and Scorcha headed out of the door.

"Come on, Dan, a bit of vigorous exercise on the tennis court will help ease the tensions of yesterday, release the old endorphins!" Scorcha gave him a playful punch.

Everyone had an emotional hangover, the mood of the day before lingering in the air as Liam and Emma enjoyed a quiet coffee together.

"Aoifa has invited us all over for Christmas, what do you think, Li?"

"Hmm," said Liam.

"Well, the kids do get along surprisingly well. I'm all for it. Be nice for your pa, too."

Liam nodded. "I think you're right," he said thoughtfully. "Maybe it'll be an opportunity for some good ole family cohesion," he said, encouraged. "Say yes, then. I may even get a chance to catch Aoifa on her own for some make-up time – you never know."

Liam knew that he and Aoifa sat easily with one another when they were surrounded by their respective families, so it shouldn't be a problem. He figured everyone will have come to terms with their grief somewhat by then and he hoped that he and Aoifa would have a clearer view of the way forward for their pa. He certainly didn't wish to have a fall-out with her, not now, not ever.

As he travelled to work, Liam pondered over Scorcha's news about moving in with Mikey. It took him back to when a similar thing had happened to him. Unfortunately, it had not ended well, but he preferred to not revisit it and certainly not that morning. He would put it all out of his mind; after all, it happened a long time ago. His residing memory of the situation was when his mother had said, "Be sure your sins will find you out." That saying would haunt him forever.

As he drove along toward the city, a thought came to him about the day before. When he had told his aunt Beth that his ma had passed, she was adamant that she wouldn't attend the funeral. Now, he was concerned that her turning up out of the blue would create a further disparity between him and his sister. Aoifa was sure to bring it up again, and he definitely preferred not to have that conversation.

6. AOIFA'S GIFT

It was the day after the funeral and Aoifa was curled up on the sofa covered with one of her ma's rugs in all the colours of the sea – blues, greens, silver, with a hint of mauve. It reminded her of Cara, and Aoifa was suddenly overcome with emotion. She allowed it to pour out of her until exhaustion halted her tears and she could barely get her breath.

The girls had gone to school and she and Padraig were taking time out that day, so as she slowly recovered, Aoifa made her way upstairs to get ready, her tension relieved a little. By the time Padraig returned from feeding the animals, Aoifa had put on a pair of thick jeans, long wool cardigan and prepared a picnic to take with them. It was cold outside but dry and crisp, a perfect day for a walk to ease away her churning emotions.

"You've been crying, chara."

Padraig grabbed the rucksack, took her hand and they walked slowly down the lane toward the beach. The sun was peeking through the clouds and the horses beckoned. When they reached them, Rafa gently pushed Aoifa from behind, amusing her. They all made their way along the muddy shoreline, the tide just turning as Aoifa walked in tandem with Rafa, who nudged her periodically, and she responded by fondling his long white mane affectionately. As she watched Flynn racing ahead, she felt a surge of energy and her mood began to lift.

"It never fails to amaze me, the power of the sea, Pad. I feel better already. Come on, let's find our favourite spot, near the old bothy."

They soon reached the creek at the end of the bay then headed up onto the moorland, leaving the horses behind and turning inland past the lighthouse. It was still early, and the gulls were in the air squawking ahead of them until Flynn barked them away. Although the sea was calm, it had a grey murky hue and there was a chilly wind coming in.

"Winter's on its way, Pad, when everything goes to sleep, like Ma. The difference is that everything else will waken again, but not her."

Padraig put his arm around Aoifa's shoulders.

"But when spring arrives, you'll know Cara is there watching the new life, sharing it with you."

"Yes, for sure." Aoifa sighed then brightened as they walked on in close companionship. "Liam and I were good yesterday, Pad. Although, he did have a quietness about him."

"Yes, that's his way sometimes, but in all, the day went well. The food was grand – the girls did their grandma proud."

"What are we going to do about Pa, my love? I think he'll need some help with winter approaching." Aoifa looked worriedly at him. "He seemed quite frail yesterday."

"We can visit often, offer support then have a chat with him early in the New Year?"

"But what sort of help would he accept? You know how stubborn he can be."

"We need to tread sensitively. Maybes talk to Sean and Liam, too."

Aoifa felt a cloud descend over her at the mention of her older brother.

"I wish Liam and I could talk more easily to each other."

"Did something happen when you were young, chara?" Padraig asked carefully. "To come between you?"

"Where do I start, Pad?" Aoifa gave a sardonic laugh, looking straight ahead and freezing slightly. "You know we never got on."

"But I don't know why," Padraig said gently. "Do you know why, Aoif?"

"Not any. I really can't recall," she said dejectedly.

"Can't you both just move on, forget the past for your pa's sake?"

"If only it were that simple," Aoifa said. "There was a big fall-out, I know, but the details escape me."

Aoifa sat down on a rock, running her hand over its smooth surface and looking out to sea. If only life could be as simple as a rock: solid, stable, reliable, unchanging, but Aoifa knew humans were just not like that with their fickle, fanciful and unpredictable ways.

"D'you want to talk about it?"

"I can't, Pad. It hurts too much with everything. Anyway, I've buried it so deep. He never got along with Ma or Pa either, which made everything worse. I think it was to do with my second sight, but I don't have that anymore or it could help me. Just a huge void inside. It feels strange and very scary that there'll be no forewarnings, no visions and no more messages."

"Don't worry about it, Aoif. You've been so lucky up until now that you had such a gift. It doesn't matter, does it? Our lives are solid and happy here."

Aoifa stood up abruptly, her face contorted.

"Padraig O'Brien – don't you mess with me!" Her eyes flashed in anger as she shook her head indignantly and poked her finger at him. "I feel like I've lost everything and you make out it's nothing!"

"Everything, Aoif? You've lost everything?" Padraig looked at her wretchedly.

Suddenly, Aoifa was crest-fallen, arms hung by her side, her eyes downcast. "It feels like everything, that I have nothing left, nothing to give."

She fell to the floor, sobbing as if she were breaking into tiny fragments and would float away on the tide like her ma.

Padraig sat down next to her.

"You have me. You have our wonderful girls. You have a good life and a future ahead and you will be OK without your ma's help."

Aoifa remained silent and looked out over the vista of her homeland. Eventually, she spoke more calmly.

"I know. I just can't feel any gratitude right now. I... I'm sorry."

"Well, it just might be excitin' not to know what's comin' anyways?" Padraig told her with an encouraging smile, but Aoifa wasn't so sure. Could she learn to enjoy the unknown after a lifetime of no surprises? She shivered involuntarily then rallied quickly, aware she was sounding irrational.

"Let's go, Pad, walk it off and forget it for now," said Aoifa resolutely, but she was still shaking.

Padraig helped her up and they set off, walking close together but separate. They moved into dense forest, underneath a gold and amber canopy from the trees overhead, and meandered along the familiar path, picking their way carefully through the prickly gorse bushes on either side.

Aoifa felt her anxiety ease as she put one foot in front of the other.

"Look, Pad, there's still wild lavender here; it's shielded from the wind."

Padraig picked some, handing it to her, and Aoifa rubbed it gently over her skin as they walked on.

"Mmm… still a strong smell too…"

Padraig leaned close to her, and she laughed as he went in for a kiss.

"It's not that lovely!"

They embraced and the discord between them passed.

As they reached the bothy, Padraig pushed open the door and noticed something inside.

"Look, Aoif, over there – a rough den – in the corner."

Aoifa checked, not wishing to disturb it. "What is it, d'you think?"

"From a pine marten – there's some fur." She bent down to look.

"So it is. What luck is that! I've not had glimpse of one around here for years – good luck for us, Pad. We were meant to come here today and see this."

"We'd better vacate, though. Let's sit outside." So they left, pulling the old wooden door slightly behind them.

They moved on to a clearing in the forest where the sun streamed down from above, warming an area around some rocks as they sat down. Padraig laid out their lunch and they listened to all the familiar noises of the forest, squeaks and rustlings coming from the moorland, birdsong overhead in the dense trees and the rush of the sea in the distance with gulls and terns calling to one another. Padraig opened a bottle of wine and Aoifa took a glass from him.

"Hey, what's this?" she asked, raising an eyebrow.

"I thought it'd be nice to make a toast to your ma. She loved this walk too."

Aoifa closed her eyes and offered her glass to the elements all around her, whispering,

"To you, Ma, wherever you are." She held her glass out, her mood softening. "You know, Pad, we are so lucky to have found one another. Not all folk get the chance to find a life like we have here. How can I not feel grateful for that?"

A warmth came over her as she sipped her wine, replacing her angst of earlier.

"In some ways, I thank my old ma for that, the honesty and integrity she taught me just to be me. So when you came along… I fell for you and never questioned it! My parents showed me so much love and a belief in myself, but I was bestowed with… my inner voice too, this sense of what will be. I hope it comes back, Pad, because Ma left me a message. She said to look out for our girls, and especially *one*, so I need to keep my wits about me. Just maybe Clara could be the next chosen one…" Aoifa told him hesitantly. "She and I are at least from the same element, same as Ma too."

"Ach, well, time will tell, chara," Padraig reassured her. "Just be patient, Aoif, a day at a time, eh? Believe if your ma speaks to you again, it's meant to be."

"What made you so wise, Pad?"

Aoifa could feel her sadness lifting, a calmness taking its place as she smiled.

"You!" Padraig replied. "Come on, we can do some exploring. Let's take something home for the kids – you know they love that."

This notion took Aoifa out of herself. Wandering amongst nature always made her feel good, like music to the soul.

"Oh, I left my bag in the bothy. Wait a minute."

When Aoifa went to find it, the clasp had opened, spreading her coins all over the old stone floor. As she bent to gather them, she saw tiny glints amongst them, close to the den. She moved her hands over the area and saw minute green stones under her fingers, shining in the darkness.

"Padraig, come here…"

As he entered the bothy, she told him to tread carefully.

"Look, what do you think?"

Padraig examined them. He seemed to be holding his breath.

"Aoif, I think these are precious pieces of Connemara marble. They would be centuries old." His eyes were wide in disbelief.

"I think the pine martens must have disturbed them – or found them, attracted to their brightness and smooth surface. Dare we take any?" She looked at her husband excitedly.

"Well, I don't see why not. They are residing inside our bothy! It would be our best gift yet to take back to the girls."

"If they are *the* green gemstones, Pad, they would have a great deal of value?"

"More value to us, I think, Aoif, from our history here. We can keep them safe in the family all the same."

They made a selection, amounting to at least half a dozen, leaving some behind, and Padraig put them safely into the rucksack.

"I may sneak back quietly sometime," she said, "to get a picture of the pine martens, wouldn't that be great!"

"Definitely a good omen, Aoif, to see a pine marten in these parts."

Aoifa figured it may be wise to seek out all the good luck she could find just in case she needed it in the future, when a recollection of the day before came to mind.

"Pad, what did you make of my aunt Beth? She was fairly impenetrable."

"Well, I can say nothing really, since I never knew of her."

"That's true. I just wonder why she and Ma never saw one another."

"Ah well, we'll probably not see her again either!"

They gathered everything up and made their way back, soon reaching the beach, Flynn refreshed after his sleep over lunch, bounding on ahead. The tide was out, and they could see the horses frolicking in the distance. As they left the wood, Aoifa caught a movement out of the corner of her eye and stopped.

"Shh… look, Pad, over there, watching us."

The doe eyes were unmistakable. It was a large female roe deer watching them as they walked quietly past. Such a beautiful sight with the late sun shrouding her from behind, but she didn't come any closer, not with Flynn around, and then bounded off, quick as lightning.

"Do you remember, Pad, about a year ago I came here and drew a white hare as it sat close to me? We both watched the world together. I brought the picture home, and ever since, Siobhan has been out searching but hasn't found her again. I do hope one day she will."

"When she's older and knows where to look," he replied wisely. "There is much to find along these shores, to be sure. Her life has barely begun, but she's such a quiet one, Aoif. Do you worry about her?"

"Sometimes. I try to bring her out, but the only time she is loquacious is when she has a story to tell – then there is no stopping her! Lois is my main concern just now; she's so distant from me, Pad. She hated my second sight anyway." Aoifa smiled ruefully to herself. "Small blessings, eh?"

"She is just growing up, chara, let her be. She'll come round. I worry about Mairead the most! We hardly ever see her these days. She's always with that friend from the village, but quite what they get up to beats me."

They walked along the top of the bay, the horses following slowly behind, ready for their evening meal.

"To be out here today has been sheer bliss, Pad. I think it's been good for us both. To think, we were only coming for the morning!"

Aoifa sat down for a moment on the sand dunes and watched the sun go down, the purple rays filling the bay with a warm glow as the light faded.

"Sheer beauty, Aoif," Padraig whispered, "like you."

"Aw, give over the flattery, O'Brien. Won't win yer favours, you know!"

She laughed and took off across the sand, but he caught her up, grabbing her in a bear hug as they both fell to the ground, giggling.

Then Aoifa sat up. "I get such insight from being close to nature, Pad, although no visions, but I still love my poetry – that hasn't left me! Can we stay a moment, and I can write my thoughts of the day down?"

Padraig lay back, closing his eyes whilst Aoifa took out her pen and notepad and wrote down her musings alongside him, but it soon started to get cold.

"I'm done, my love. Let's go back to our not-so-little ones. They'll be waiting, wondering. These stones will cheer Clara up and Mairead loves anything precious!"

"Shall we say where we found them?" Padraig asked.

"No, I don't think so, not just now," Aoifa said decisively.

When they arrived at the farm, the girls were home from school.

"Hey!" Niamh greeted them cheerily.

"Dinner's in the range. Do you feel better, Ma?" asked Lois.

Aoifa smiled her gratitude. "I most certainly do, thanks, Lo. Your pa and I have walked off the sadness of yesterday. Look – we've brought you something!"

She reached into the shoulder bag. As she took out the gemstones and laid them on the table, they twinkled a bright green, catching the girls' attention.

"Ma!" Lois exclaimed. "Are they the green stones, the marble of Connemara, the ones which have been on these shores forever?"

"Well, maybe, Lo. Or they are just pretty stones anyway! Here – have one each. Remember your grandma by them."

"Maybe she helped us to come upon them!" Padraig suggested. They each took one and Aoifa had two left, which she put safely into a little trinket pot, placing it above the fireplace.

"Pa – can we go out on the horses?" Lois asked, always wanting a small piece of him.

"Yeah, if you want, Lo, after dinner. They'd love a quick ride before bed."

Aoifa knew he couldn't resist pleasing his girls. After they had eaten, she and the younger girls sat down together.

"Do you want a good story from today?"

They were all waiting, knowing their ma would create something interesting, partly real and partly her imaginings. There was a great deal of laughter as they listened to her tales about goblins, pine martens, pirates and gem-seekers.

"I wish I could tell stories like that, Ma."

"Well, you write music instead, Nevey."

"I write poetry sometimes," added Clara, quietly, "but I hide it away."

"Do you, Lara?" asked Aoifa. "It will be lovely, because it's yours."

And Siobhan added, "I write stories too, Ma, and it always makes me hot!" but Aoifa was unsure if she'd heard correctly, as she smiled at her benevolently.

As the evening drew to a close, Aoifa felt the familiar consternation setting in as she became apprehensive of the following day. When she awoke each morning, it was if she had lost a phantom limb. What Aoifa had actually lost was a phantom friend who had talked to her all of her life. She felt physical pain some mornings, running her hands all over her body searching for its location, but it came deep from within. She would take heed to her husband's advice, she said to herself determinedly. Leave well alone and surely her inner voice would come back one day.

They both retired early, the fresh air and walking exhausting them. As they were settling down in bed, Aoifa whispered,

"Pad… are you asleep?"

"Well, I'm not now, my love, what is it?" He turned toward her.

"Why didn't I know we were going to find the stones? It was a big deal. I always knew about the bigger things coming… and Aunt Beth too, ghosts from my past, but I didn't, Pad."

"Hmm…" Padraig said, "I can think of times you didn't know when there were big things comin'… just think of the babies. Did you always know?" he asked, smiling in the darkness.

"Yes," she said definitively.

A walk into the unknown, Aoifa mused. *That's my future now.* Vicissitudes of life were on their way. Aoifa had no doubt of that whatsoever as she curled into Padraig's arms and they both fell fast asleep.

7. CLARE ISLAND

Winter was fast approaching and with it would come the harsh weather off the Atlantic; Aoifa was sure of that. As a storm was forecast, she and Padraig had been out in the yard all day securing the animal housing and their final task was to enlarge the pig pen, ready for the piglets' imminent arrival.

The family had finally returned to relative normality after Cara's passing. Aoifa still had her moments of sadness, but the girls were mindful of this, helping out wherever they could, and were coming home early that day to help with some chores to prepare for winter. As Aoifa worked, her mind wandered. The family always went on an annual outing just before Christmas and the girls were looking forward to it, a light at the end of a period of darkness for them all. The click of the garden gate interrupted her thoughts.

"Hi, Ma, back early as you asked," said Lois.

Her mother noted an edge to her voice.

"What is it, Lo?" she said, frowning.

"Ma, why do you want us? I need to go down to the beach."

Now Aoifa understood.

"We have the vegetable garden to prepare, all the fodder to unload off the cart, a big Christmas ahead with guests, piglets coming, and we also have to plan our outing."

"Can I do supper instead, later?"

"I would prefer you were a part of the plans, Lo. What do you do down there anyways, or is it a secret?"

Lois didn't look at her mother but carried on upstairs to change.

"It's not a secret, Ma," she called back. "You know I need to make sure the sea mammals are safe with a storm on the way."

"Well, please be quick, Lo. Niamh's already made a start with the fodder."

Siobhan and Mairead rushed in with Clara running up behind, shouting,

"Ma, can I put the manure out?"

"Yes, please, Lara, then I'll cover it," when Aoifa caught sight of her middle daughter disappearing behind her. "Oh no, you don't!"

She reached around, grabbing her hand good-humouredly. "Back here, young lady – you're needed!"

It was all hands on deck outside before darkness fell.

Later on that evening, Aoifa smiled around at her girls.

"Thanks, everyone, for your help today – many hands an' all that! Now we can concentrate on Christmas properly, with most of the jobs done, and we have the outing to look forward to!"

"Where to this time, Ma?" asked Clara.

"Now, Lara, you know I never tell…"

Two days later, Aoifa heard the pitter-patter of raindrops on the kitchen window as she looked out at the threatening clouds coming in off the sea. Then all of a sudden, the sky came over as dark as slate, rain started lashing down in sheets and the wind had picked up. The expected storm had arrived. She quickly threw on her waterproofs and it took seconds, yet she was drenched through as she locked the chickens, geese and pigs into the big barn. She ran back to the porch and looked across the bay at the heavy clouds filling the sky when there was a sudden flash of lightning followed by a loud crack of thunder, then the heavens opened as the rain came across the sea in torrents. Aoifa watched as the trees blew horizontally across the garden. She was afraid of severe damage, and she looked frantically around for Padraig. At least the horses were safe in their stables, so where was he? The tide was in, and nothing could be heard above the roar of the waves as great mountains of water pounded the shore below.

Aoifa ran indoors and grabbed the phone, but the line was dead. As panic set in, she looked for the car keys to fetch the children. Where was Padraig – and Flynn? She needed to know everyone was safe! As she made for the front door, it flew open and Niamh ran in dripping wet, followed by Lois, a look of horror on their faces.

"Ma, we… we had to run from the bus. It couldn't get up the hill – there was a waterfall comin' down!"

"Where are the others?" Aoifa asked, white-faced.

"They're at school, with the housemistress. She wouldn't let them go to the bus and Clara was in tears."

"This is the worst storm ever! Put on some warm clothes. I must find your pa."

Bracing the gales once more, Aoifa went to search around the farm. Outside, she heard a barn door banging then noticed the light was on and ran across the yard.

"Padraig! What's going on? Are you alright?"

"Flynn was swept up into the waves, Aoif, and I had to go in to rescue him. It was treacherous, a'right. He's OK but in shock."

Aoifa could see he was shaking on the straw and so was Padraig.

"I'll prepare some food and warm milk for him."

She felt such relief that everyone was safe, albeit shocked and shaken about as Padraig soon came indoors carrying Flynn and placed him in front of the fire.

"It's torrential out there, but I must away to fetch the girls!"

He ran upstairs to change then returned quick as a flash and set off.

"Take care!" Aoifa shouted after him as she stoked up the fire. She would be happier when everyone was safe indoors. Before too long, Padraig returned with a tearful Clara, the other two running behind, drenched through.

"Can't stop shivering, Ma. Flynn, gimme some fire!" shouted Mairead, pushing him to one side.

"Mairy, he nearly drowned!" Aoifa told her indignantly. "Away upstairs to warm up in a hot bath, all of you! Use ours too."

"Everyone safe now, Pad, although how much longer that gale can rage out there heaven only knows. Too many hurricanes these days."

The next day, as if by magic, the weather was calm once more. There was much debris around the farm, although luckily little real damage. As she took the girls to school, Aoifa was mindful that for the first time in her life, she'd had no forewarning of such a horrendous storm and it had left her truly shaken. It had been a miracle that no one got hurt.

The day of their annual outing arrived and Aoifa knew a day with the family would raise everyone's spirits. Having some family fun, she surmised, was long overdue. In total contrast to a few days before, the sun was shining brightly onto a calm translucent sea and the wind had dropped. There was just a nip in the air to remind them that winter was coming.

"Ma, tell us – where are we going?"

"You'll see soon enough, Nevey!"

"On foot?" asked Lois. "Ahhh… to the boat, I see!"

Aoifa smiled as they all tried to guess. Padraig was already down on the beach with the horses at the ready.

"Oh, Ma – it's Clare Island, surely!" cried Niamh.

"It may be, then."

Aoifa took off and raced them to the shore, all shrieking with laughter for the first time since the loss of their grandma. It filled Aoifa with joy to see and feel their happiness once more. They all loved the island and they'd not been across there in six months or more.

Clare Island was a little way out to sea. To get there, they had to walk the huge expanse of sand when the tide was out and stay until they could return, some six to eight hours later. The horses carried all the provisions and enjoyed it too, as they took their fill of the lush grass over there. As they made their way across the bay, Siobhan walked alongside her mother.

"The storm and the waves, Ma, what makes them? So different today – look – the gales gone – a lovely colour of pink too."

Aoifa considered her answer as she looked for the colour pink.

"Well, it is indeed mysterious, Sheve, how the weather and behaviour of the sea can suddenly change. You'll learn about it all at school, but I believe it's a mix of the unknown and science, my love." And she was sure there was no pink anywhere to be seen.

Clare Island was a special place for the family, as it held such poignant memories. Ten years before, Padraig had taken them by boat to the island for the first time and Clara had been born that day. It had taken them all unawares, yet all was well, and they had since given the island her name. It was a very rugged, wild place with high peaks and jutting rocks. Then, last year, Padraig had built a treehouse high up in the biggest oak tree on the rocky landscape. Rafa and Brown Mane brought the wood from the mainland and did him proud. It took several months to complete and now the family came across for the day from time to time.

"Ma, d'you remember the last time I found some trinkets? I still have them," as Lois caught up with her.

"Where do you keep all these little beauties, Lo?" Aoifa asked, but Lois turned away and Aoifa frowned as she made no reply; she was always doing that these days. "So, what will we find today–"

"Oh, Ma, none of your messages now, surely!" Lois interrupted.

Aoifa caught her breath but said nothing and the girls ran on ahead.

"She can have a sharp tongue, that oldest daughter of ours, Pad."

"Well, maybe, but she won't know she touched a nerve just now."

"No, that's true."

Aoifa walked alongside him, his reply posing yet more questions in her head. "How much longer will we get the girls to come over here?"

"Oooh… about thirty years!" he said with a chuckle.

"D'you mean that?" Aoifa asked.

"For sure. I expect they'll always come back here, even with their own families," he said.

"We'd better make sure the treehouse holds up, then!" she said, wondering how many people it would hold.

The horses were galloping ahead, swishing their tails and shaking their heads in anticipation. They knew what was coming. Flynn too had his own rucksack; he didn't get a free ride. The walk across took thirty minutes, and when the horses stepped onto the island, Padraig took off their haul and they wandered off to find the grass near the lake. The girls took off at speed, keen to reach the bay on the far side of the island. They were in high spirits, laughing and chasing one another around the rock face, disappearing out of sight.

The island was approximately three miles by two, dominated by two great peaks and a steep rugged rock face on one side and over the other side was the most beautiful sandy bay. Aoifa and Padraig climbed onto the rough grass and worked their way up between the craggy rocks to a favourite sheltered area of rock pools which lay between the peaks. The area was covered in trees of varying heights and species as they weaved amongst them, soon reaching the summit where they could see the children below, running into the sea, barefoot, their shoes, bags and coats discarded as they went. The water would be icy cold, but they gave no thought to that.

"Relax today, chara. Let the magic of this place wash over you. We've a busy time over the next few weeks."

He pulled her to him and Aoifa could feel her worries diffusing.

"My mind's clearer now and the anxiety is easing a bit, Pad," she sighed. "I guess I've been worrying that Lo will be off soon, too."

"Don't worry about her, chara. She'll be OK wherever she goes – she's like me. I was a born traveller at that age, and she'll always come back."

"You were like that, so... then you met me. I tied your feet down, Pad. Any regrets?"

"None whatsoever. You were the best thing. I got a sixth sense that day – from you, no doubt!"

"Tell the girls about your past. Your life story will fascinate them."

"I know," he told her wistfully. "I shall have to dig deep."

"Lois especially will want to know."

Padraig nodded in agreement as Aoifa continued,

"I think the air speaks to the girls in whispers here because they're always full of stories when we get home! Uncanny, I know, but it's Clara who loves it here the most. Have you seen how being here changes her? She seems wilder somehow... like she's in her own little bit of heaven."

"I have. I think she feels more at home here than anywhere."

Aoifa shivered as if someone had walked over her grave and she had butterflies in her tummy, a familiar feeling, as she considered what Padraig had said.

They watched as the girls left the water and made their way up the precipitous rock face toward them, treading carefully between the crags.

"Look!" shouted Mairead as she reached them. "There it is!"

The huge oak looked surreal, stretching up toward the sky, leafless, with the branches pointing outward and the sun gleaming down, shrouding the treehouse like a halo.

"Let's do some crabbing," said Siobhan as she and Lois went across to the pools. Siobhan wanted to take them home, but she was never allowed.

"How would you like it, Sheve, if someone suddenly plucked you up and took you away from your family?" Lois asked.

Siobhan considered this. "I think I'd see it as a bit of an adventure, Lo, but it'd be a bit noisy with too many crabs an'… I'd want to sleep in my own bed at night."

"Exactly!" said Lo as Aoifa noticed a slight look of alarm crossing Lois' face.

Padraig and Niamh started a fire while Clara and Mairead went to catch some fish. Those two, like chalk and cheese, rubbed along well together. Clara always considered Mairead's needs before her own, which in turn pleased Mairead but not their ma.

Niamh started singing an old Irish ballad to herself while she searched for bits of wood and dried seaweed for kindling.

"Love those old songs, Nevey. You should play some, you know, on your fiddle."

"I wish," said Niamh shyly to her mother.

Padraig joined in and soon they were all singing at the tops of their voices and Niamh started a dance around the fire.

"Hey, you're not a squaw, you know, indigenous to the island!" laughed Padraig. "But you sure look like one, with yer wild hair an' all!"

Niamh pushed him playfully then fell back herself, just missing the fire. "I'm having it all cut off soon anyway, Pa!"

"Mind out!" he laughed. "Or that hair'll make good kindlin' – save money at the hairdresser too!" he joked.

The girls returned and they all sat around the fire.

"Let's cook these small fish, Pa," said Siobhan. "Look – herring. They smell like the island, too."

Lois was the last to arrive. She sat down and took something out of her pocket.

"Look, Pa, I found this in a rock pool."

Padraig took the object, a tiny replica of a fish, and it shone like gold. It had an almost imperceptible clasp on the top as if once there had been a thin chain passing through.

"It looks like a lucky charm," said Aoifa.

"It seems to be very old," added Padraig. "Aoif – do we have a plate with us, an old pottery one?"

"We do. I only brought the old ones." She handed him one.

"I should be able to tell if it's gold. You run the piece across the plate, applying light pressure. If it leaves a gold mark, then it is gold, but if the mark is black, then it's not."

The girls watched him in earnest. The fish was gold, he told them!

Mairead jumped for joy. "Come on, Clara… let's go find some more!"

They searched the pools, but there were no more, nothing precious of any kind. Padraig told Lois that as she had found it, it was hers, as the island was unoccupied, and no one ever came here.

"Could I have a gold chain for Christmas so that I can wear it for good luck, like someone did before?"

Her mother nodded and smiled. Maybe her older daughter was a romantic after all, she mused as they all set off toward the old oak tree.

"The rope ladder is still here!" Mairead shouted, running on ahead. She grabbed the ladder but in her haste missed the rung and fell, gashing her foot on a rock. "Oh, Ma! It hurts so!"

Her mother rushed over to examine the wound.

"What are we to do with you, Mairy?" Aoifa chastised her gently. "Now I don't know how you'll make it up to the treehouse."

Mairead's face crumpled.

"If I can't go up, Ma, I wanna to go home now!" she cried. "I think it's broken!" But the wound was not deep, and it had stopped bleeding.

"You go on, everyone. I'll stay with Mairead. Maybe she'll be OK in a while." She washed the wound with some salt water from a rock pool.

Niamh hesitated.

"Really, Niamh, go. We'll try and join you later."

Aoifa took another look at the wound. "I know, Mairy, I'll give it support it with my scarf and I'm sure your pa and I will manage to hoist you up."

"Oh, Ma, what a pain! I really wanted to do more exploring to find more trinkets."

Aoifa tutted as she wrapped the wound up carefully, then they helped Mairead up and she managed to weight-bear a little.

Lois looked down from the tree. "Ma! I don't think Mairy should come up, what if she breaks her ankle?"

"Don't worry, Lo. Pa and I will support her."

"But… she's making such a fuss!" Lois went to add something when she got a stern look from her pa as he lifted Mairead onto his shoulders then hoisted her up the ladder.

"See!" shouted Aoifa. "All's come good in the end. Now… take care!"

Mairead joined her sisters at the top, scowling at them.

"It was all your fault, pushing ahead of me. I lost my footing."

"Well, you should have taken more care, then," said Lois. "Anyways, thank Ma for making that support and Pa for lifting you. Be grateful, Mairead!"

Aoifa and Padraig exchanged a knowing look as the girls squabbled up above.

"After you, chara, or you'll be left behind," Padraig laughed.

"More's the pity," muttered Aoifa.

Padraig held the ladder for her, offering his hand with a lop-sided grin.

"Oh no, you don't, Paddy O'Brien, make out you're fitter than me. Just you watch…"

Aoifa took the ladder two rungs at a time, making it up in just a second, then she taunted Padraig by pulling it up and laughing out loud as he bellowed,

"You seem to have forgotten… I was the one to climb the tree in the first place. You wait until I get up there… youse all in trouble!" and the girls screamed at him to stop teasing and join them.

"Look, Ma… in the resting place – some flattened straw. Someone's been here," said Niamh.

"Just someone passing, Nevey. Nothing sinister!" said her pa with a reassuring smile.

"Look," Lois told them, "the horses are watching us, Ma. They love it here; they get more grass than back at home."

Mairead was the only one with a long face, as she was unable to move around and had to rest with her foot up.

"Ma, can I have a snack? I'm suffering here!"

Aoifa gave her a cupcake, hoping it would go some way to mellowing her mood.

On their last visit, Padraig had created a small recess in the corner with a tiny door and Aoifa remembered the girls had placed some shells in there and went to check. When she opened the tiny latch, she was amazed. Inside, there were some sharp objects like tiny spears, short and stumpy, beautifully made from stone and others long and thin, carved out of wood. It smelt of rotten fish. She looked more carefully and, using her fingers, scratched around the objects and found some tiny hooks attached to miniature vines. Aoifa didn't say anything but turned away to conceal her surprise – and irritation – as she handed two tiny shells to Clara and sighed. Why didn't she know of someone else's presence? But no messages had come, and she regrettably had to accept it. She brought her mind back to the job in hand with feigned enthusiasm.

"Right, girls! Put your skills to good use. We need to make this table then we can finish our lunch on it before Mairead eats it all!"

So the girls set to shaping the willow for the legs and pieces of leather for the joints. Aoifa used some twine to attach it all together whilst Padraig stripped the wood and carved out the top. After it was all done, they spread out the remaining food. Clara gave up her tiny shells to Mairead, who took them without a word, and Aoifa shook her head perceptively.

"D'you think the treehouse will withstand another winter, Pad?"

"Aye, for sure, and more to come."

They were all lost in their own thoughts for a while, sharing the remains of their picnic and looking out at the beauty of the surrounding landscape.

"You know, Pad, maybe put an upper floor on top one day too?"

"Oh yeah – me and who's army, chara?!"

"Maybe one of the girls could…"

Padraig gave her a withering look. "Yeah, on a good day, eh?" he laughed. "Hey, look, time to go, girls, or miss the tide!"

"We'll go down, Pad, and leave you to secure the winter cover."

They went down the ladder one by one, helping Mairead when she reached the bottom. As Aoifa went to follow, she whispered to Padraig.

"Will you put the contents from the recess safely into your rucksack, Pad?"

He looked puzzled but nodded in agreement.

When they reached the bottom, Flynn ran around wagging his tail furiously and they set off, supporting Mairead between them and making their way slowly back to the horses, who were waiting patiently.

"Come, girls, just time to load the horses then Pa'll be here. Mairead, we need to get you onto Roma."

They hoisted her up just as Padraig arrived.

"We better get a move on. Tide is rising," he told them.

They were back on shore within half an hour and Roma took Mairead dutifully up to their front door. The horses had certainly earned their keep that day and were more than ready for bed. That evening, it was Niamh's turn to tell the story with Clara's help, as their outing had fired imagination as usual, and she had them all in stitches.

"What a great time we had, girls. Off to bed now, more work to do tomorrow," said Aoifa as Niamh touched her arm and asked,

"Ma, did you foresee that we would find that little fish?"

"No, Nevey, I didn't. I had no idea," Aoifa told her then whispered to herself, "and I didn't know about the other things either."

Aoifa made a decision that she would speak to Niamh one day about the loss of her second sight. She had always shown an interest in it and was sure to understand. It would be good to have an ally.

Later that evening when they were alone, Padraig laid the miniature tools out on the table.

"I think these were made a long time ago, just two more recently, Aoif."

"So, maybe Niamh was right. Someone has been living on the island?"

"Very likely. I wouldn't mind if they had, give them a roof for a few nights. No harm done," Padraig concluded.

"I think the little trinket Lois found probably came from the same source."

There was an expression of wonderment on Aoifa's face. She couldn't deny the idea was enchanting but disconcerting at the same time. So where was their mysterious guest now, she wondered, and one so skilful at that?

8. CHRISTMAS

It was three days before Christmas and the family were rushing around to get everything ready. During the summer, Padraig and Sean had renovated a bothy on the edge of their land, with two bedrooms above and a sofa bed, a galley kitchen and shower room downstairs. The girls used it as their space too, where they could make as much noise as they liked and nobody minded. Right now, Aoifa needed to prepare the sleeping quarters.

"Grandpa and Sean can sleep in the bothy, give them some peace and quiet, Lo. Would you help me get it ready?"

Lois gave a disgruntled look but reluctantly agreed.

"Won't it be fun having your cousins too?"

Lois nodded. "But what about Uncle Liam, Ma?"

Aoifa hadn't told the girls of their difficult relationship, but everyone knew.

"It'll be fine. We can all help create the mood, you know, plenty to eat and drink, a walk, some games and maybe a sing-song too. Liam and I can get along when needs be, Lo. We'll be fine."

They worked harmoniously together, Aoifa grateful for the time with her eldest daughter.

After lunch, Siobhan and Mairead were putting decorations up, Niamh and Lois brought in the vegetables and Clara was laying the table when Padraig came in with a pile of wood.

"Aoif, I think those piglets will arrive on Christmas Day – or before!"

"Now that would be interesting! We'll get those twins' hands dirty yet!" said Aoifa with a chuckle. "You know, Pad, this Christmas, our girls may learn a thing or two."

"Like what, my love?"

"Well, Danny and Scorcha have aspirations that ours haven't even thought of yet. It'll certainly open up their minds when they get talking," Aoifa mused with a twinge of regret that her brother's kids were on an ambitious path like their father, and they would be an inspiration. "It'll be a lesson to me too, Pad – I know our nest will empty eventually and I need to go with the flow more." She pushed back her red hair with a sweep of her hand, her face suddenly downcast.

"Which you never usually have a problem with!" Padraig smiled at her and Aoifa nodded, acknowledging that was because she always knew what lay ahead. But no more. She would simply have to work things out for herself and accept everything more readily. She carried on the cleaning with renewed vigour to help overcome her inner doubts.

Christmas Eve arrived. The tree looked spectacular in the hall with its snowy white lights and the girls had made some colourful decorations radiating an iridescence of colour throughout the house. Aoifa had created a display of family photos in the front hall too, carefully assembled for everyone to see.

"These look lovely," said Niamh, picking up a picture of her grandma.

"She will be in our thoughts, Nevey. A nice reminder, I thought," said Aoifa sadly.

"Will Grandma visit us tomorrow, Ma?" asked Clara.

"I don't think so, Lara. You can talk to her all the same. Maybe write her one of your poems?"

Clara's face brightened. "I will too, Ma."

Aoifa went into the scullery for some time alone to get a perspective on the days ahead as her energy at the start of the day together with her assumed confidence started to wane.

Padraig called through the door, "I'll just put the horses away and come back and help, chara."

When he returned, they prepared the Christmas pudding together.

"It will be a mix of emotions tomorrow, Pad. Liam's lot will bring some new energy into the house, for sure."

"It'll be swell. There'll be laughter and presents all round! A typical Christmas, you'll see."

"But not typical, without Ma." Tears ran down Aoifa's face.

Padraig passed her a tissue and took her hand.

"She will be missed, Aoif, but we'll all pull together to make it good."

"I just hope my brother doesn't pull the other way, Pad."

"He won't, not Christmas Day, chara. We'll ply him with the good stuff, put him in good spirits. Hey, how many presents for these girls – too many I see!" He checked underneath the Christmas tree.

"Just two each but never enough for Mairead," said Aoifa with a smirk, wiping her eyes.

"I'll give her not enough – get her to do the washing up, more like!"

"Her smile wins her through that one. She has your gypsy ways!"

Padraig grabbed Aoifa in a close embrace. "I'll show you the gypsy ways!"

"Not now, you won't." Aoifa turned away with a flicker of a smile. "We must share the load between them more, Pad. I put too much on Lois and it's not fair."

"I agree. We will lose her soon too. She said…" Just then, Siobhan came in.

"Pa, can you fix the DVD player, please? It won't work."

"OK, Sheve, just coming."

As Padraig left the kitchen, Aoifa called after him, "What did Lois say about leaving…?"

"Oh, nothing much, chara." Niamh put her head around the door.

"Ma, how about we play some of those Celtic ballads together?"

"Be great. Gimme ten. I'll just finish off the pudding."

Aoifa soon opened up her piano and Niamh brought down her fiddle. Before too long, their playing filled the house. The girls sang along merrily, Padraig tapped out the beat, and at the end, Aoifa was in floods of tears as they played her mother's favourite.

"Well, that'll wake your ma up for sure!" Padraig said to diffuse the melancholy.

"Then she can join us tomorrow after all," added Clara solemnly.

They all smiled but shook their heads sadly and Aoifa got up.

"Come on, girls, mince pies all round, then bedtime."

"Ma, you read the story, please – Pa's are never real," said Siobhan.

"Well, he'd better make up a real one, hadn't he? Tell him to dig deep into his past – that'll do it!" Aoifa told her as Padraig took the younger ones up to bed, chuckling to himself.

Aoifa and Padraig always had a special time of their own on Christmas Eve. They had just finished wrapping the presents when there was a creak on the stairs.

"Lara?" whispered Aoifa.

"Ma, I can't sleep. I'm too excited."

Padraig turned to his young daughter. "Lie on the edge of the bed, chara, you'll soon drop off!" making Clara giggle as she went back upstairs.

Padraig waited a while then went to put one present quietly on each of the girls' beds. When he came down, he poured out two glasses of his fiery home-made seaweed wine, infused with lavender.

"Plenty more where this came from, Aoif, to warm everyone up tomorrow!" he said as they raised a glass to each other and then retired early to bed. "Chin up, chara." He held Aoifa tight. "It'll all be grand. A family Christmas – it's what your ma would want."

Clara awoke early the next morning in particularly high spirits.

"When is everyone coming, Ma?" she shouted.

"In a couple of hours, Lara. Now can you stand still for a minute and help me!"

"Did Father Christmas drink your special wine, Pa?" she asked.

"Of course," said her father. "Look, some has gone from the bottle."

The family soon started to arrive. First were Liam, Emma and the twins. They burst in, bearing myriad gifts, baskets of food and lots of bottles.

Aoifa exclaimed as she gave them all a hug. "Goodness me, Li, you are spoiling us!"

"Merry Christmas, Sis," he replied warmly.

Danny and Scorcha gave the girls a high-five and Padraig offered drinks all round as Emma walked into the kitchen with a broad smile.

"Come on, show us what Father Christmas brought!" she exclaimed, and the girls fetched their presents while Aoifa looked on proudly.

"Aoif, these are beautiful. Clara's cardigan, Lois' painting from Siobhan, the shell necklace for Mairead, all hand-made. So clever. I'm afraid we bought ours. Hope they're OK," she added.

"Emma, they're not expecting presents. It's very kind."

Clara beckoned to her cousins. "The piglets arrived yesterday – come and see!"

As they all went out to the yard, Aaron and Sean were just pulling up and Aoifa ran out to give her pa a hug. She could see a sadness in his eyes but a big smile on his face.

"Happy Christmas, Pa."

"I hope you've not gone to much trouble 'ere?" he said, stretching as he got out of the truck.

Aoifa laughed. "Not at all, Pa, just a bit of toast each – oh and a glass of wine!"

As Sean came up the path, Clara noticed a shadow behind him.

"Hello," she said to a young boy.

He smiled but said nothing.

"Come on, lad, don't be shy. All family here," said Aaron, pushing him gently forward. "Aoifa, meet Conor. One more OK?"

Aoifa tried to conceal her surprise as she greeted him warmly. She could see he was about thirteen but with a maturity about him.

"Come and join us, Conor, most welcome."

As they went indoors, the others looked on curiously as Clara announced,

"This is Conor. He's come with Grandpa."

Dan went over and shook his hand. "Good to see you, Conor, meet the O'Connells!" he said amicably.

"And the O'Briens!" added Mairead more loudly while everyone laughed.

Conor was slightly taller than Siobhan with a mop of dark hair and a cheeky expression on his face. Aoifa was surprised her pa hadn't mentioned him – and why didn't she see it coming? Pah! She was going to have to get used to surprises, as they seemed to be coming thick and fast.

Shortly afterwards, they all sat around the large farmhouse table with Padraig's special wine in abundance as Aaron stood up, clearing his throat.

"Can I make a toast – a very Merry Christmas to those present – and absent – to your dear grandma." He raised his glass. They all sent their wishes to Cara, and Clara blew her a kiss. "Also, I have an introduction to make. This 'ere is young Conor. He is now living with us and assisting Sean on the farm. We're very pleased to have an extra pair of hands."

"So, Conor – where did you spring from?" asked Liam with a blatant look of interest.

Conor looked down, too embarrassed to reply.

"Liam, easy. He's only just met us," said Aoifa gently.

"One day, I came across him in the barn," Aaron explained. "He'd been sleeping in the loft and was very sorry, said he'd move on. So we had a chat, and it seems he had nowhere to go. He's a good lad." He affectionately ruffled Conor's hair. "And I had a spare room in the house, so everyone's happy!"

Conor looked abashed and no more was said as they tucked into a wonderful spread, all home-made from the farm.

When Padraig served the pudding, Clara shouted,

"I've found the five pence piece!" eyeing Conor, who's eyes were sparkling, clearly mesmerised by the warmth of the family gathering.

"I don't know about the sixpence, but this pudding is making me drunk, Pa!" exclaimed Mairead.

Padraig chuckled. "Ah well, I put the fiery wine to good use!"

After they had cleared the dishes, most of them set off on a walk to the beach and Aoifa went to look at her brother's new car.

"Wow, Liam. This is special!"

"Very special, Sis. It's electric."

"You mean those new ones?"

"Well, 'tis one of the first. An experiment, you might say!" Liam told Aoifa about electric cars and why they were devised.

"But they're surely more trouble to fill than to pull up at a gas station?"

Liam sighed. "You've heard of global warming?"

"Of course I have," said Aoifa sharply.

"The world is heating up, Sis. Because of all the fuels we burn, they're making our planet hotter, causing extreme weather conditions, melting the ice in the northern hemisphere and making the sea rise too. More floods, storms, wetter summers – and warmer winters are coming.

"Well now, that would be nice!" Aoifa said, drifting off to join the others, keen to get away from Liam's know-all ramblings, but he followed her.

"Aoif, this young boy… what if he stays long-term?"

"So what, if he helps them, Li?"

"Hmm. He may get his feet under the table, though."

"You are such a cynic, Liam O'Connell!" Aoifa chided.

"Well, one of us needs to be. Anyway, you didn't have any foresight of this, did you?"

"Nothing, Li."

"Well, I think your inner sight is letting you down. We can't rely on you anymore, Aoif." Liam's tone was acerbic as he spoke with some satisfaction and Aoifa felt herself bristling.

"Maybe you can't, Liam. We can't all know everything, yet it seems you know enough for all of us!" She walked off irritably.

Aoifa was shaking after this exchange. She returned to the house and walked right into Emma.

"Aoifa – you're as white as a sheet!"

Aoifa got flustered. "It's turned so cold out there!" she told her as she made her way to the fireside to sit down. Emma followed, seemingly unconvinced.

"I'll make a cup of tea," she told Aoifa. "Can you find Padraig?"

Aoifa was pleased to, and she found him in the snug with her pa.

"Pad, Emma's making tea."

"Sure. The others will be back from the beach in a minute. Tide's coming in," he told her.

The children soon returned, conversation in full flow.

"That was pretty impressive, Lo," Dan said as they came through the door. "The animals really trust you."

"An' I had no idea about your collections down there," said Mairead.

"What collections?" asked Scorcha. "I must have wandered off."

Lois explained, "Oh, all the sea mammals, Scorch. I help the injured ones and take all the rubbish away."

"Lois collects treasure too!" Mairead told her and Scorcha laughed.

"Unlikely, Mairy!"

"No, really, she hides it down there!" Mairead whispered.

"Lois knows the sea life get caught in old fishing nets and swallow sharp objects, Mairy, so she puts all that stuff away," explained Aoifa.

"I plan to save them all!" said Lois with a determined smile.

Danny told the girls about his recent project at uni, about global warming and climate change and how they all need to do their bit by recycling and using less plastic, which ends up in the ocean. Clara and Siobhan listened, a look of awe on their faces.

"But Lois doesn't want to go to uni like us," he continued. "You'd rather go over to America, isn't that right, Lo?"

Aoifa came into the room. "What's this about America?"

"Oh, nothing, Ma," Lois added quickly, avoiding her mother's eye.

Emma had made the tea and was calling them all – it was present time!

"Ooh, Aunt Emma, have you really brought us presents?" asked Mairead.

"Only for good girls, Mairy!" said Aoifa playfully.

"Oh, you better stay in 'ere, then!" Padraig told her as Mairead scowled at him.

Clara opened hers first, trainers with wheels and flashing lights and a small cookbook. "Cor, Aunt Emma, my best presents ever! Thank you."

Niamh received a personal music recorder. "Thank you so much!" as she ran off to the barn try it out.

Mairead was beside herself with excitement and could wait no longer. "Me, me!" she cried. It was a pair of studded jeans, a designer sweatshirt and some hair slides. "Wow! Thank you. I can wear these to the school disco!"

Siobhan guessed hers – a book by her favourite author and a new set of paints. "Thank you, Aunt Emma. I love painting, you know – and I love to smell the colours too," she said quietly.

Emma smiled at her curiously. "You must show me some time."

Lois took hers gratefully; it was a new mobile phone.

"If you're off to America, you'll need that to keep in touch," Emma told her.

Lois looked uncomfortable but thanked her politely.

"You've been spoilt, girls," said Padraig.

"Even me, Pa!" exclaimed Mairead jubilantly.

"You've been too generous. Thank you," Aoifa told them.

Then Clara handed something quietly to Conor, and his face lit up too.

As Aoifa walked into the kitchen, Aaron and Scorcha were deep in conversation.

"But Grandpa," Scorcha said. "If we ignore climate change, the rubbish will kill all the sea life – and the seas will keep rising because of all the carbon dioxide gases going into the atmosphere. Danny and I are specialising in this at uni and plan to work in the field of global warming."

"But, lass, we've been OK till now," Aaron said. "You say we live in a changing world, that it makes the seas stronger and the sea life weaker, well, I don't see that. We raise our cattle and sheep the same, on the same pastures – doesn't affect them. We'll be OK, for sure. Anyway, your uncle Sean has ideas, don't you, lad?" he said, looking across at Sean. "And he has a partner in crime in Conor, so watch out!"

A curious look came over Scorcha's face.

"Tell us, please! Dad – listen to Grandpa!"

Liam came into the room, but Aaron had picked up the newspaper and the subject was closed – for the time being at least.

While most of them settled in the family room to play some games, Aoifa sat down next to her pa in the kitchen.

"'Ere, Aoif, what d'you make o' those ideas of young Danny and Scorcha's, then? It's the modern way, but maybes they're just gettin' carried away or it's all a long way off?"

Aoifa nodded. "They're ahead of their years, those two. No doubt it will all become clearer as time goes by, Pa, the rising seas and changing seasons. If it comes, we can't stop it, that's for sure," she said vaguely and turned to Padraig as he walked in. "My love, has Lois talked to you about going to America?"

"She did mention it briefly, but I didn't know she was serious."

"Well, why am I, her mother, the last to know, I ask?"

Padraig looked at her kindly. "You are not the last to know; it's just that I was the first – she must have told her cousins on the beach. Well, Aoif, it's possible she thought you already knew, of course! Let it go. We can chat to her after Christmas."

Aoifa's mind was reeling. First a stranger in their midst then an attack from her brother and now her own daughter making plans behind her back. What next? If only she knew. Aoifa sighed and turned away from Padraig, exasperated and lost for words.

"Who's for a piece of Clara's cake?" she announced vehemently. "I've made up the fire in the sitting room now."

They all followed her in, and Liam walked up to her.

"So, Lois is off to America, Aoif. What a surprise. The first to flee the nest. Do you know her plans?" Liam asked his sister directly, obviously still smarting from earlier.

"Not yet, Li. I… I don't think she has any."

Liam tutted and Aoifa changed the subject.

"Hey, we had a Christmas card from Aunt Beth and Uncle David. Be nice to ask them over. What do you think, Li?" Aoifa asked him brightly. "I'd love to get to know her, you know, for Ma's sake."

"But she and Ma didn't get along, Aoif, so why bother?"

"But why not?"

"Best left alone, don't you think, Pad?" Liam frowned.

Padraig nodded. "I think Liam's right, chara. You never know what happened. Leave it be."

"Hmm. I think I may like to know."

Aoifa's face was set, and silence filled the room until Mairead came running in.

"Ma, can you play some music? Niamh has written some too."

Aoifa welcomed the light relief. "What a wonderful idea, Mairy! Come on, everyone, over to the barn. Padraig, bring some of your fiery wine for us all."

As they left the room, Aoifa approached Liam.

"I'd like to know what happened between the two sisters, Li. If you know, maybe you'll tell me some time?"

"It's such a long time ago, Aoif," Liam answered more gently. "No more talk of it today, eh?"

Aoifa shrugged then linked arms with Emma as they set off for the barn. "Ma loved a sing-song, Em. This is for her," as she pushed open the old door.

She and Emma prepared the wood-burning stove and had soon built a roaring fire. "OK, go on, Pad, open the wine!"

As he did so, he whispered to Aoifa.

"Family feuds at Christmas – tradition, isn't it?"

Aoifa gave him a knowing look and sat at the piano with Niamh alongside.

"I love this tipple of yours, Pad," said Emma.

"Wild and fiery, like my sister!" Liam retorted with a cheeky grin.

Aoifa took it on the chin, poured out some more then started her playing, and Niamh accompanied her on the fiddle.

Just then, Clara came running through the door.

"Pa, Conor and I've been feeding the piglets. They nearly escaped too!" Padraig looked at them in mock horror.

"Well, Conor can come here anytime to help with them little critters!"

"Yes," said Clara happily.

The family all joined in with a Christmas sing-song, and at the end, everyone was in tears. Even Aaron had taken his handkerchief out.

Afterwards, the children remained in the barn to play some games whilst the adults returned to the house and Aoifa and Emma laid out a buffet for supper.

As the evening drew in, the O'Connells prepared to leave. As they all got into the Range Rover, Aoifa called out boldly,

"Next time, we'll get Aunt Beth over too!"

"We'll see you then!" replied Liam, shouting out of the window. "Happy Christmas and thanks, one and all!" He speedily pulled away.

Aoifa knew she'd had the last word – for the time being.

Back in the kitchen, Aaron got up from his chair, not without effort.

"I need my bed too, chara, but thanks to you both for a grand day. Cara would have loved it."

He reached out and gave Aoifa a hug.

"I think at times she was watching over us, Pa."

He and Sean bid them all goodnight and made their way across to the bothy.

"Ah, here come the young'uns now. Send Conor over, would you, Aoif."

Conor walked across the yard, and to Aoifa's surprise, he came right up to her and held out his hand, saying nothing but with a big smile to express his gratitude. She took it and bid him goodnight as he went across to the bothy.

Later that evening, Aoifa and Padraig sat alone, curled up together watching the flames from the fire as they threw a warm orange glow into the darkness. The Christmas tree lights sparkled as the decorations swayed gently in the warm air, and the candles emitted scents of amber and spice around the room.

"All's well that ends well, my love. What a day!" Padraig exclaimed. "Wonderful but exhausting, eh? I think your ma would have been proud."

"I think she was with us, Pad, helping us to enjoy a lovely family day, despite our differences. I felt she wrapped me in a warm gossamer cloak to help us all get along."

"I know there are some conversations to be had, Aoif, but we must trust and look for the right time." Aoifa nodded in agreement.

"Talking of conversations, I promised to say goodnight to Clara."

As Aoifa got up and made her way upstairs, it passed through her mind, at the end of the day how important is family, one way or the other.

When she got to Clara's room and sat on her bed, she was busy writing. "Can I read this to you, Ma? It's for Grandma.

'On Christmas Day,
after Grandma passed away,
there was a knock at the door,
in came Grandpa, Sean and Conor.

Conor loves to swim in the sea,
Just like me,
A nice lad, all good, not bad,
so I gave him a green stone
to remember me.'"

"Grandma will love that, Lara. Nice to give Conor that little stone too. I'm sure we'll see a lot more of him."

Clara smiled then opened her hand to show the tiny goldfish which Lois had given her and the chain too. "She said because I was born on Clare island, Ma."

Aoifa smiled at her. "It was kind of her, Lara."

"I haven't told anyone, Ma," she said proudly, putting it in a small box with the tiny shells.

Aoifa was warmed by Lois' gesture, her willingness to part with something so precious. It helped to soften her previous convictions.

"I'll look after this little fish forever, Ma, but I will always wonder where it came from."

"Well, my darling, maybe one day you might find out. Happy Christmas." They hugged one another and Aoifa wished her goodnight.

9. LOIS' BIRTHDAY

It was Saturday morning and Lois awoke feeling out of sorts. She lay for a time, trying to figure out why she felt so guilty. Suddenly, she sat up: she knew why. "But I'm only trying to plan for my future," she said aloud, not without a touch of frustration. "I suppose I should talk to Ma about it, but o' course, she'll already know. She always knows everything, and I just don't like it anymore!"

It was a dull January day, and the sun was hiding behind the clouds. As Lois got out of bed, her room felt very cold; there was even frost around the window. Deciding on an early walk down to the beach, she threw on a warm sweater and thick waterproof trousers then went downstairs, quietly made herself some toast and popped it into her pocket. Flynn was running around, excited at the prospect of an early walk too. The coldness hit as she opened the door, put on her padded jacket and pulled her beanie down over her mass of red hair. Lois knew she would feel better as soon as she was outside, breathing in the salty air.

"Come on, Flynn, let's get to the cave and see how Sally seal is doing. Race you!"

When they arrived, Lois could see the tide was turning and they didn't have long. As she fed the two seals their ration of fish, she read the trust and gratitude in their eyes and loved them for that. Their comical expressions amused her as they romped around in the rock pools, but soon a trickle of water came into the cave.

"Flynn, we must go!"

Lois had an intuition about the sea, an awareness instilled into her since she was young. They left the cave and made their way up onto the rocks where they sat looking out over the bay, enjoying the ebb and flow of the water. Lois was in love with the sea, the beach, and all it offered. She always found a use for herself there. She knew she wasn't a romantic like her ma, nor as carefree as her pa. Her inclinations were more of a practical nature – a doer rather than a thinker, as one of her teachers had told her. As she sat nibbling away at her cold toast, she watched the seagulls and terns coming in on the tide and threw some crumbs onto the sand for them. There was no wind and slowly the clouds made their way out to sea, a touch of cobalt blue appearing from behind them with the promise of a fine day ahead. She spotted her pa making his way towards her, Roma pulling his cart full of seaweed and the other horses trotting behind. Every day, Padraig had to make his catch on the incoming tide and Lois knew the earlier in the day, the better his haul.

"Lo!" he called, waving. "You're up early for a Saturday?"

"Couldn't sleep, Pa, so came to feed the seals."

"You're good to these wild animals. Bet they're grateful too."

"They're more grateful for the fish!" She smiled at him.

"I'll just bring this catch in and be back with you."

Lois nodded and watched Padraig working quickly and efficiently, sorting the seaweed ready for market, his speed and skill fascinating her. He would soon be done then maybe they could go for a ride. The horses watched him too, as if they understood it would be their turn soon, but Roma held back – she knew a full load meant work. Rafa came up to Lois and she stroked his thick, pure white mane as he tossed his head, loving the attention as she tugged on his forelock which fell down over his eyes. Impulsively, she jumped as light as a feather onto his back, which was covered with his dense winter coat, and they walked across to where Padraig was working.

"Pa, he's asking for a trip out, look!"

Rafa had started to bob his head up and down and paw the sand in anticipation as if to hurry them along.

"I'll be done in an hour then we can take them across the bay and over to the moors if you like, as the tide's coming in?"

"Be great with the sun coming out too."

Lois' mood brightened as she walked along the bay through the shallows on Rafa's back. She took deep salty breaths and felt her head clearing, bringing an air of positivity. When she reached the point where the waves hit the pebbles, she jumped down, abandoning Rafa for the seashore. She decided to make good use of the hour her pa was working and collect what debris she could find. This was Lois' favourite occupation: to be on the seashore surrounded by her beloved animals. She checked carefully what had come in on the tide with Flynn running alongside her, picking up detritus and throwing it about, amusing Lois with his antics. She soon had quite a collection to add to her booty, safe from harm's way. Then, turning to watch the birds up on the cliff face tending to their winter nests, to her delight, she could see a pod of dolphins coming in on the swell of the waves.

"Pa, look!" she called out, running over to him. "I've seen them here before. I think they're hoping for a meal on the tide. One day, I will train the dolphins. I'm sure they try and communicate with me. I've read about something called clicker training. It's some form of kind training technique – positive reinforcement, I believe it's called. They use it for domestic pets now too. I will learn about it, Pa."

Padraig didn't look up but added, "I know you will, Lo. You have a way with these animals."

As she worked along the shoreline, Lois' troubled thoughts of earlier returned, unsettling her mood. She made her way uphill to take her booty to the barn. As she entered the yard, she spotted her ma through the kitchen window talking to Niamh, which increased her unease, and she hoped they hadn't seen her. She grabbed the bridles and reins and crept out of the back door. She didn't want to use a saddle, as she loved to feel Rafa underneath her, feeling closer to him that way. Lois knew a ride would help her to unwind and hopefully release her pent-up emotions. Her pa always knew how to alleviate her fears and she was looking forward to sharing with him what was on her mind. The horses saw Lois return with the reins and they galloped over, splashing in the waves and giving her a soaking.

"Hey, guys," she said with a laugh, not minding a bit. "Comin' for a ride, then?"

She could see her pa had finished, so she put the reins on Rafa and Roma, Brown Mane frolicking around them.

Padraig took the cart up to the store, ready for market on Monday. When he returned, the sea was rough, so they sat high up on the rocks and shared his flask of coffee before their ride.

"Pa, you know Ma was a bit cross with me the other day?"

"I do," he answered carefully.

"I feel so guilty."

"Why, chara? Because of the conversation?"

"Not exactly. I guess I just haven't been ready to talk to Ma about my future yet. Maybe I feel guilty about wanting to leave home."

"It's just part of growing up, Lo, as you look for what to do next. Listen to your heart. Just because your choices may be different from ours, you don't need to feel guilty, chara."

"I guess I worry that Ma won't like my plans. She seems quite anxious these days. Is it to do with losing Grandma?"

"She is grieving at the moment, for sure. We all need to give her some slack."

"I know she is grieving, Pa, but I just can't get this inner voice of hers, the promise of what lies ahead. I don't want her to tell me what to do anymore!"

"Ach, no, chara. She won't do that."

Lois noticed a strange expression cross his face but said nothing.

"But she does, Da! She goes on about Grandma always being out there, but I believe when you're gone, you're gone, and she knows everything about us! A funny thing, but she didn't know about Grandma's passing, did she?"

"It seems not, chara," Padraig answered vaguely. "Well, your ma has her own ways, and you have yours. She never had this wanderlust, though. That's something you get from your da! Just be honest with her, Lo, that's all she'll ask. If travelling is in your blood as it was mine, so be it. Come on, let's go for a ride – blow your worries away!"

They jumped up onto the horses and took off along the narrow stretch of sand, catching the ripples as they crawled up the sand. Lois always rode Rafa, who was the faster of the two, and she overtook her pa, laughing and racing ahead.

Padraig called after her. "You see what good the horses do – take you out of yoursel' for a while!"

They carried on at the speed of light, the horses' manes blowing in the wind and the spray soaking their faces. As they reached the moorland, they slowed to a trot, the horses and Flynn all out of breath as they eventually came to a standstill on the soft sand.

"Look, Pa, fishing boats. They're out late today." They waved across at them.

"Mackie and his mates often get lucky a second time. They can tell by the marine mammals around, bringing the message that there are fish to be had on the turn of tide."

They walked along in close harmony, watching as the fishermen pulled their boats in to shore.

"Talk to your ma about your plans, Lo. It will bring you closer. Anyway, you can't go foraging along these shores forever, you know!"

"Why not? I love it. You do!"

"I know, but it's my life, my livelihood. You've had an education. You can go further, chara."

Lois suddenly felt bewildered at the thought of growing up. She knew her mother was almost married at her age, but times had changed. She also felt the pressure of being the oldest, to achieve and set an example for her sisters.

"I do want to work with animals, Pa, to learn about how they think, how they behave."

"Go on then," her pa said. "You know my parents were travellers, Lo?"

Lois nodded.

"They lived off the land, but never the same piece of land, so I became used to moving about all the time. It was a good life but nomadic, and I was pleased to finally put down some roots when I met your ma. So I do understand your desire to travel. It reminds me of the constant expectation of pastures new when I was your age and the curiosity about what lay ahead. I can totally understand your desire to go out and explore the world."

"Oh, Pa! I knew you would. It's a pity Ma doesn't."

"She will, Lo, give her a chance. It's just she never got the opportunity. It's OK to be different from your ma – and more like me!"

"I get that, Pa, I really do."

Lois nodded with hope in her heart, although she could feel the tears pricking the back of her eyes.

"Be happy, chara. It all sounds grand – look to your future!"

Lois took some deep breaths as she felt a wave of relief come over her. They made their way out across the moorland past the lighthouse as the sun came out and turned the sea into a sheet of deep silky blue. The scene lifted Lois' mood as she contemplated leaving this enchanting homeland of hers and hoped deep down that one day she would find a new paradise elsewhere. They slowed the walk right down, the horses breathing heavily after their gallop along the bay as their hooves fell heavy onto the bracken underfoot.

"Hey, Lo, another subject – you've a big birthday next week!"

"I don't want a party, Pa."

"No? Not a celebration, then?"

"Yes, maybe. But not a load of my school mates around playing loud music and carryin' on."

"What did you have in mind?"

"I don't think Ma will allow it." Lois looked dubious.

"Why? Is it illegal, Lo?"

She grinned. "O' course not! I would like us all to go out for dinner," Lois spoke tentatively, "with Liam and the family."

"Ah, that's an easy one, then. Good idea."

"I hope Ma thinks so too."

"She'll go along with it, Lo, if it's what you want. Talk to her."

Lois finally agreed to do just that. She would be honest with her mother and just hope she agreed.

They turned off the moors through the woodland, the trees dark and bare ahead of them. As they walked the path single file, Lois felt angst once again at the prospect of talking to her mother, but she would stick to her decision.

Later that afternoon, Lois found Aoifa all alone in the kitchen and seized her opportunity.

"Ma, it's my eighteenth soon."

"It is too. Have you given thought to your party yet?"

"Well, I don't really want a party."

"No party! For your coming of age, Lo?"

"I know that's what you've predicted for me, Ma, but it's not what I want!" Lois spoke sharply and immediately regretted her tone as her mother turned away and silence ensued, making Lois feel guilty all over again.

"Sorry, Ma, to be rude," said Lois, and Aoifa nodded an acknowledgement.

"Don't you want a celebration, then?"

Lois tempered her tone. "I do, but I'd like all the family to go out to dinner, would that be OK?"

Aoifa smiled her approval.

"Of course, Lo, just us, then, a cosy celebration. Wouldn't that be lovely?"

"Well, I had in mind to invite Grandpa, Uncle Sean and Liam's family too?"

Lois could see her ma's misgivings at the suggestion. "Unless you don't think…"

"If that's what you want. It's your birthday, Lo."

Aoifa's response was cool yet agreeable. "I'll talk to your pa, and we can look at where to go." The conversation petered out as Aoifa carried on with her chores.

Lois sighed. Her ma had been reasonable, but Lois knew she'd been unnecessarily blunt once again. She had been unkind in the face of her ma's willingness to take the family out for her birthday. Chiding herself, she knew she needed to talk to her mother at length some time to explain what she wanted to do with her life but without guidance and without her predictions. Get it all out in the open. Things would be easier between them then, as her pa had said.

Later that evening, her parents expressed their approval for a family meal celebration, and they soon settled on a hotel not too far away. Lois was so relieved that equilibrium had once more been restored and she retired that night in excited anticipation.

On the morning of her birthday, Lois was awoken by whoops, loud cheers and a jolly arrangement of 'Happy Birthday' by her sisters, with Niamh playing her fiddle. They all flocked into her room, showering her with balloons and streamers and throwing presents onto her bed.

"Awww, girls, it's too early!" she exclaimed, sitting up and rubbing her eyes.

"Hey, Lo, you're only eighteen once! Wish I was that old!" cried Mairead. "Come on, we have to choose your outfit, something trendy and glamorous!"

"No, you're OK, Mairy. I'm not getting married, you know!"

"And why not?!" Mairead asked saucily. "Ma was married at your age!"

"Not quite," said Lois as she jumped out of bed.

"And I'll be married by eighteen too!"

"Good luck with that, then." Lois smirked.

"Out, you lot!" she added good-naturedly. "Leave me to dress in peace – and thanks!" she called after them.

The girls all chose their best outfits, Mairead wearing her designer t-shirt and denim mini skirt. Siobhan wore a pretty blouse and jeans, her dark hair back in a neat ponytail, and Clara chose some pink leggings and a pretty matching top. When Lois came downstairs, they all gasped. She'd donned some new diamond-studded jeans, a bright yellow shirt and denim jacket with some new yellow sparkly trainers. It was her hair which received the most acclaim – curled with several shiny gold slides to create a messy swept-up style.

"You look so grown up, Lo," cried Niamh.

"That's a shame, Nevey, as I don't feel any different. Maybe I will tomorrow." Lois smiled at her sister.

The two of them were so unalike, Lois in a smart but simple outfit and Niamh looking very gypsy-like with her colourful layered skirt, orange and yellow cardigan her ma had made and her hair a bit shorter than Lois', adorned with coloured braids.

"Look at you all!" cried Padraig. "A picture for the album."

"Aww, give over, Pa!" Lois added coyly, noticing a tear in his eye.

"No, Lo," said her mother in serious tone. "A coming-of-age birthday is special, with you nearly all grown up, too."

Lois shuffled awkwardly as Mairead saved the day.

"You can have your first drink now, Lo, although I ain't gonna wait until I'm eighteen!" she added defiantly.

"I don't doubt it," said Lois with a smirk.

They all left to make their way to the luxury hotel, which was ten miles along the coast road, the girls chatting excitedly as they went, and Lois was full of anticipation as she laughed along with her family.

As they walked into the magnificent foyer, Niamh gasped.

"Ma, it's very grand!"

"It is too. Enjoy it, Nevey – won't be something we do every birthday!"

They made their way into the lounge where everyone was waiting, and Lois ran to hug her grandpa.

"Happy Birthday, Lo," he said warmly.

There were congratulations all round as the family in turn gave her their best wishes.

"Here, Lo." Liam passed her an envelope. "Something for your future."

Everyone looked mystified, but Lois tucked it away.

"Thank you, Uncle Liam – and thanks for coming, everyone!"

They soon found their table, lavishly prepared with a centrepiece of wild lavender sprigs and white heather, Lois' favourite flowers.

"Ma, which knives and forks do we use?" whispered Clara as they sat down.

"Just watch, you'll see!" Aoifa told her.

It was with fresh eyes that Lois observed her cousins during the meal, their worldly ways unmistakable. She sat next to Scorcha, who filled her head with adventures about their recent field trip to Alaska. She became wide-eyed as her own aspirations were taken to a whole new level when she heard her ma addressing her uncle Liam.

"Liam – I hope you haven't spoiled Lois too much there, although it's very generous of you, to be sure."

"Not at all, Sis. Just helping to pave the way to a bright future for the kid."

"How so, Li?"

"Well, you know she has some great plans ahead?"

Lois choked on her drink as she couldn't help hearing.

"I don't know much about it, Li."

"Ach, course you do, Aoif."

He turned to Lois. "Isn't that right, Lo? Ready to spread those wings, eh?"

Just then, Padraig intervened. "Drink up, everyone – we've a lot of celebrating to do! Let's raise our glasses to the birthday girl!"

As they did so, Liam shouted, "Speech, speech!"

Lois turned bright red and wished for the floor to swallow her up, deciding being the centre of attention wasn't her thing after all. Her grandpa, sitting next to her, spoke quietly.

"Don't you take any notice. They's just winding you up, chara. Enjoy today and this lovely spread, eh?"

Lois smiled at him, grateful for his understanding.

"So, Lo, eighteen – nearly the end of school for you. What comes next, then?" asked Scorcha.

"She be getting married next, Scorch!" exclaimed Mairead.

Lois snorted. "Not likely. Prefer animals to humans any day!"

"You can't mean that, Lo. Don't you want a boyfriend?" Mairead asked cheekily.

"I'm not boy-mad like you, Mairy. There's more to life."

She turned to her cousin. "I'm not sure, Scorch. Can't quite believe I'll be leaving school – maybe a nice holiday first!"

"You mentioned at Christmas you wanted to work with animals across in America?" Dan chipped in.

"I've not decided yet," replied Lois as she shot an uneasy glance toward her mother, who was talking to Emma.

"I do want to work with the sea mammals but don't fancy uni. I think I prefer some hands-on stuff."

"But Lo, I've heard uni's a lot of fun!" shouted Mairead, her voice a little shriller, courtesy of the glass of wine she'd had.

"Well, it is that, but it's a whole lotta work too!" replied Scorcha, looking at Mairead scornfully, but Lois ignored the exchange and added,

"I would really love to train the dolphins!"

"Sounds exciting," said Liam with an encouraging smile. "I can help you to find an opening, if you like? I have my contacts."

Lois was flummoxed, not knowing what to say as she leaned across to her ma and whispered,

"If you know what lies ahead, Ma, don't tell me!"

"I don't have those answers just now anyway, Lo. Too far away."

"Ah, don't pay any attention to your ma. She just wants to keep you in suspense!" said Liam, giving his sister a sidelong glance, but Aoifa remained quiet, and the conversation moved on.

"What a grand spread, won't you look at this!" said Emma as they all tucked in. "Li – why don't you get a couple more bottles of that white wine? It's delish."

"More for me, please!" added Mairead.

"You've had enough, my girl." Aoifa frowned across at her and a short while later added, "Now, girls – don't you need to do something?"

Niamh got up, pulling Mairead to join her. "Oh yes. Come on." As they ran off giggling, Siobhan turned to Lois.

"I can hear water and lots of splashing. Can you smell it, Lo?"

Lois looked outside and could hear nothing, especially as they were inland, but Siobhan's words were soon forgotten as the girls returned carrying an elaborate birthday cake adorned with a dolphin and surrounded by eighteen candles. Lois gasped in amazement as the whole family gave a rendition of 'Happy Birthday' accompanied by the guests on the surrounding tables. There were tears in Lois' eyes as she blew out the candles, looking across at her ma's emotional expression and smiling her gratitude. Much laughter ensued as everyone in the restaurant clapped and cheered.

The party soon drew to a close, everyone going their separate ways. On the way home, Lois felt a rush of gratitude as she contemplated her future, especially since she'd taken a look inside the envelope Liam had given her. It meant the opening of all sorts of exciting doors. Lois knew now, without a shadow of a doubt, and with her heart full of hope, that there was a world of opportunities out there waiting for her.

10. CONOR

It was late January and Padraig had come up with an idea.

"You know, Aoif, I was talking to Liam at Christmas about our kelp farm, telling him demand's picked up these past months and he said it was because of climate change. Seaweed is a valuable resource against global warming apparently and is now used widely for all manner of products."

"I had noticed it was flying out at market, Pad. All good, eh?"

"For sure. It's just taking up more and more of my time, fitting in the sortin' with the animals an' no help from the older girls, as they're busy with exams."

"They can't be spared, Pad, you know that."

"No, sure. I was just wondering about somethin' else."

"Hmm?" Aoifa was looking at him with interest.

"Well – what does young Conor do with your pa?"

"I'm not really sure. I got the impression that he just helps out to pay for his keep."

"Guess so. I think I'll take a trip over and find out."

When Padraig pulled up at Home Farm, Sean and Conor were clearing up the yard and Sean came across to greet him.

"Hiya, Pad, what brings you here?"

"Oh, need a reason to call on family now, do I?" he asked good-naturedly.

"Nah, course not. Come and get a coffee with us. Would'ya give us a hand with the wood a minute?"

They all made quick work of bringing in the pile of chopped wood, then Padraig spoke up.

"It may be this young fella I've come to see!" He looked over at Conor with a smile.

"Come on in, then," replied Sean curiously as they went indoors, and Aaron greeted him warmly.

"Good to see you, lad, in time for coffee and some of Niamh's home-made biscuits!"

"Be grand. Colder out there now," said Padraig, rubbing his hands. "So, I'll come straight to the point, Aaron, you know me! Thing is, I need an extra pair of hands on the farm. The girls are busy with their studies and there seems to be more demand for the seaweed now... so... I wondered..."

Aaron gave him a canny look and cut in, "About this young'un, then, eh?" as he gestured toward Conor.

"Well, he's a good lad, isn't he?" said Padraig, smiling at him encouragingly. "You settling in OK?"

Conor nodded happily then disappeared discreetly outside.

"Could you spare him a bit?" he asked Aaron.

"Maybes we could, eh, Sean?"

Sean smiled agreeably. "He's a nice lad and a good worker an' all."

"We all get on swell, and I think he's happy enough," Aaron added. "Would a couple o' days a week do yer?"

"Be great, Aaron. Truth is I barely have time to harvest and get to market these days. I'll pay him, o' course. He may even get to know the trade a bit too, be good for him."

When he heard of the proposition, Conor agreed willingly.

"See you tomorrow, then, lad?"

"Yes, Sir!" Conor replied shyly.

"No need for formalities – call me Pad!"

They shook hands and Padraig set off to tell Aoifa the good news. He'd never employed anyone before, so new ground for him too.

Aoifa was enthusiastic when he told her. "Sounds grand, Pad, and we can get to know him a bit better too."

"He seems a good sort – quiet, shy, but I reckon he'll soon get over that. Now you mentioned earlier some plans of your own, Aoif?"

"Yes. I think I'll paint the girls' rooms – and ours too, Pad. What do you think? It's too cold to do much outside at the moment."

"Why not? Keep you out of mischief with all your wonderings and wanderings!"

Aoifa looked crest-fallen, and Padraig realised what he'd said and caught his breath.

"I'm sorry, chara, I forget."

"Well, don't, Padraig O'Brien! I get enough jibes from the girls without you too!" said Aoifa bitterly.

She sat down and put her head in her hands. "You see," she wailed, "my mind is empty, and I worry about absolutely everything these days."

Padraig knew Aoifa was still reeling from the loss of her gift and how her life had changed, and he knew how it would ultimately make a difference to all of them.

"It must be hard, chara, but there's nothing you can do to change it. Things will work out, you'll see," he told her, hoping his tone didn't reveal his own misgivings.

They sat together listening to the waves and the wind in the trees as Padraig stroked her hair and kissed her brow, which he knew soothed her. "We'll go forward together, my love."

Aoifa nodded, with her head still bowed.

"It's getting colder now," he said with his arm around her shoulders. "The horses have their winter coats and look, here comes Flynn. He knows when you need him."

Aoifa gave her beloved dog a hug, and when her tears had subsided, she spoke quietly,

"I thought if I could just be… kind, not even thinking bad things, a truly good person… it would all come back."

"But Aoif, you are the kindest person I know."

"I can't be, Pad, or Ma wouldn't have taken my second sight away!"

She started to cry again, tremors going through her body as she tried to recover herself. "But why has it gone? And if I don't have it, who does? Someone always has it."

"Your ma loved you and you are not to worry about it. Just keep on being you and don't be so hard on yourself. Listen, are you afraid I won't love you the same, that none of us will, if you can't tell us what lies ahead?" he asked gently.

"No. I just feel I've let Ma down in some way."

"Your ma knows every minute of every day, you do your best by everyone. Come, now. You've managed so far, eh?" he said encouragingly.

Aoifa composed herself as she leaned closely against him.

"Now – what colour do you want to paint our bedroom?"

She thought for a moment. "Yellow, like the sun. To bring hope, light and joy as we awaken on these cold mornings."

"Yellow it shall be. Why not get the girls to do a mural on one of the walls? Bring in their bit of happiness too."

Aoifa rallied slightly. "They would love that," she murmured as she got up. "I'll fetch the paint, then, no time like the present."

She put on her coat, gave a half smile and left without another word.

Padraig got up slowly and sighed. He knew a period of mourning was normal when a loved one died, and he would need to be patient and trust that it would all come good when it was meant to. Aoifa had more than most to cope with, to suffer two big losses at once was a lot for anyone.

The next day, Conor arrived down at the beach right on time and Padraig was waiting for him.

"Hi, Conor. How are you today?"

He held out his hand and Conor took it shyly.

"Well, lad, it's good to have you here, to learn a bit of my trade. Nice to have your company, too. First, let's see if you can handle the boat!"

It was a small wooden barge with a throttle engine and some sails at the ready should needs be.

"Have you managed one before, lad?"

"Oh, yes, lots of times."

Padraig was surprised but didn't show it.

"Ah, that's great, then."

"I was brought up around boats. My da built them."

"He did?" Padraig answered, his eyes wide. "I'd love to hear about it sometime. Come on, let's get this haul out and onto the cart. It's market day today and we need to be away."

They attached Roma's harness to the cart, and as he observed Conor out of the corner of his eye, Padraig got the distinct feeling that he had a way with horses too.

"Hey, lad, give me a bit of history, then. How did you come by Home Farm?" asked Padraig as they set off on the cart together.

"Well, I lived down south, and I found mesel' alone one day – hard to believe, I know – so I just took off."

"What – on your own – at home, d'you mean?"

Padraig looked across at Conor disbelievingly.

"Yeah, that was it. My parents died from the flu. We couldn't afford the doctor, and, well, they passed away at home. I have an older brother and we sort of managed for a bit, but then he got very down with it all and so he left."

"He left you alone, lad?" Padraig was shocked.

"Yeah. He wanted me to go too, but I wouldn't leave. I don't know where he is now. I wish I did."

"So, what did you do?"

"I was eleven at the time and there was no food, so after a while, I packed a bag and set off mesel'. I didn't know where I was headed." He let out a small laugh.

Padraig could see it was distressing him. "You OK talking about it?"

"Yeah, is good to talk. Never done before. I made my way along the shores finding bits of metal and trash, became a pedlar really, sellin' it in villages I passed through. It worked for a while. My folks had lived rough in the old days, so I suppose I had their ways. I used to think of them, how they used to hunt and live wild like wolves. My family had always told me they were like a pack of wolves." Conor laughed again. This time, it was more genuine. "When I was very young, we all lived in the open, more like animals than humans, catching and eating wild birds, berries, small animals and fishing like bears. No fixed abode, I think they call it. We'd build a den in the woods until it fell down, then we'd move on. We made boats from the pickings of shipwrecks and travelled to nearby islands to look for treasure from pirate landings.

"I felt the wolf was in me that day, so I travelled miles just like them. In fact, I imagined I was a wolf – it helped me to get on. I did that for a while."

"How long?" Padraig asked.

"Probably two years. I saw seasons come around twice, so it must've been."

"Two years! Good God, lad. You had such courage."

"My great-great-grandparents had lived in the mountains and forests – with the wolves, my grandpa used to tell me, until the wolfhounds hunted them all down. I think I was born with some of those ways! My grandad taught me everything I know, reckoned I didn't need school." Conor chuckled. "Then it got cold, last winter, really cold. I had no money for clothes, so it was a stroke of luck I came upon the barn. I remember being so tired. I didn't care in the end, just wanted to get warm and sleep... then Aaron found me. It was like sommat sent him from above."

"I'm from a travelling background too, lad, so I do understand. You just get this canniness to cope with anything life throws at you, don't you?" Padraig confided. "You did well, but such hardship. I'm sorry about your parents."

Conor shrugged.

"My parents went when I was a bit older than you are too. I have a sister, but she lives a long way away. So you've no idea where your brother might have gone?"

"No. I miss 'im if I'm honest."

"You may come across him, I guess."

"I reckon I'm meant to be 'ere now. I enjoy working the land and am quite happy considerin'."

"Well, you know how much we appreciate you, especially Aaron and Sean. You have a home with us all for as long as you want."

"I'll never let you down," he replied sincerely, averting his eyes.

"I know, lad," said Padraig warmly. "Your skills will take you far. You're good with your hands and that's very much valued in these parts."

They sat peaceably alongside each other on the cart as they travelled along the coast road. The only sound was the splash of the waves as the tide came in and the monotonous clicking of the cart and Roma's hooves. Padraig pondered over what Conor had told him, concluding he seemed unfazed by his earlier life, some of which Padraig could identify with, but he hoped leaving so abruptly would not come back to haunt him.

"This is a much-travelled route for Roma. She needs little guidance," said Padraig. "I could send her to market on her own, I reckon, and she'd still get there!" He laughed out loud at the thought.

Conor let out a small grunt as he had drifted off into his own little world, so Padraig left him alone for the rest of the journey.

When they arrived at the harbour, they worked together sorting the seaweed swiftly and efficiently and Padraig observed him in awe. He knew without any shadow of a doubt that Conor was a good soul and deserved to be with them now.

He got them both a crab sandwich and they enjoyed their lunch sitting side by side on the harbour, watching the hustle and bustle of the fishermen at work. They were soon chatting like old friends, or more like father and son, and when lunch was finished, they carried their haul into market.

"Swimming is what I do best," he told Padraig. "Learned it long afore I could walk! Used to make a catch for dinner with my bare hands faster than any of my family.

Loved it. Still do, no matter how cold it feels. It… what's the word… exhilarates me!"

"Our Clara loves to swim too, like a mermaid out of water that one. She's ten – just a bit younger than you, eh?"

"I'm fourteen now," Conor said proudly. "At least, I think I am."

"Nearly a man, to be sure!" Padraig smiled.

He could see how Conor's experiences had matured him, his skills and demeanour belying his years more so than their little Clara, just a few years younger.

On the way home, Conor chatted openly to Padraig, with none of his old reserve.

"I can remember my first night under the stars – it was so beautiful, so quiet. I wasn't a bit afraid. The next day and the days after that, I caught my own supper. I felt close to nature, and it was enough. I were always on the alert, though, and could smell a human half a mile away. I liked the idea of livin' outdoors in many ways, movin' through the forest like one of the wild animals. I lived under cover of woodland or caves in bad weather."

"Primal instinct, lad," muttered Padraig.

"S'pose so," Conor nodded and continued, "I must admit, when I saw the farm ahead, I felt at odds with mesel', whether to join other humans or be alone. But I figured then, I might be alone for the rest of me life. So by the time I reached the barn and found the straw, it felt very warm and comfy. There was no goin' back after that," he smiled gratefully.

"Well, I'm glad you did, son," said Padraig.

"You know what I felt when Aaron came in and found me? I felt I had come home."

Padraig patted him on the back as if to reinforce his welcome into the fold.

They had a successful morning at market. Padraig had got much more for his haul because it was bigger, and he was delighted it had all gone so well.

"D'you think you could do this a couple o' days each week, Conor? Would it suit you?"

"No doubt about that. Be grand, thank you," he said with a jubilant look on his face and surprise too when he received his wages for the day, mumbling his thanks.

They made their way straight to Home Farm after market, and on arrival, Conor jumped down quickly, obviously keen to tell Aaron and Sean about his day.

"Come in a minute?" he asked Padraig.

"OK, see the boys a while." He pulled Roma to a halt and fetched her a bucket of water.

Sean opened the door. "Pad, glad you've come. I've somethin' to show you."

He led the way across to one of the larger barns, and when Padraig went inside, he couldn't believe his eyes. In front of him stood the makings of a huge machine resembling a catamaran and he gasped.

"So, what's this, then?" His eyes were wide with speculation.

"It's something to help us on the farm. Is what Liam calls mechanisation. Not sure how it'll work yet, though!"

"Impressive or what? I'll ask no more. Can't wait for a demo when it's all done, lad! So, Liam, put that in your pipe and smoke it!" Padraig added with a satisfied grin.

"Exactly!" added Sean proudly.

Padraig went home that night, his head bursting with the day's events.

"You'll never guess what, Aoif? Sean – he's making some sort of invention or other to do with mechanising the farm."

"What's it all about, then?"

"Don't know yet. It's a way off completion – huge contraption, it is."

"Well, Liam – eat your heart out!"

"That's what I said! He's a clever lad that brother of yours an' a bit of a dark horse too! Also, I've a new employee…"

"Conor!" Aoifa said with a smile.

Padraig told her about Conor and his past life. "His history, Aoif, it's fascinating. He's had a hard time of it." There was a look of incredulity on her face as he explained. "Lived rough in the woods and caves, hunted his own food. Amazing…"

At that moment, Padraig saw something flicker across Aoifa's face.

"What are you thinking, Aoif? Incredible young lad, uh?"

Aoifa looked across at her husband then out of the window toward the deep blue of the sea and the white clouds of winter hovering in the distance.

"You say he's a swimmer?" she murmured.

"Yes, he told me he could swim long before he could walk!"

"Just like our Clara, then."

"We'll have to watch those two," Padraig chuckled, "or they be swimmin' across the Atlantic together!"

Aoifa suddenly seemed miles away, so Padraig went outside to bring in some more wood for the evening and to say goodnight to the girls. He was looking forward to putting his feet up with a glass of wine – the day had been something of a success, one way and another.

11. OLD FRIENDS

One month later, Aoifa stood back smiling proudly as she looked at their bedroom, bright yellow throughout, and letting the brilliance wash over her. Just one wall left bare for her girls to work their magic on a mural. She then went to check Clara's room, and whilst standing in the blaze of yellows, oranges and golds, a feeling of déjà vu came over her. She remembered helping her ma decorate her own bedroom in the same colours! Wait, something else happened. Her friend Laurel had come to stay – and had knocked over a full can of paint! Aoifa could see it in her mind's eye, a sheet of orange all over the floor. It was the only time she had ever seen her ma in a rage, but somehow her pa managed to remove it and save the day. Aoifa's thoughts wandered to Laurel, as she too had endured great losses some years back. Several times since, they had resolved to get together, but somehow it hadn't happened.

Aoifa sat in the glory of her new bedroom, looking out of the window at the flurries of snow falling onto the garden when she shuddered and was suddenly overcome by a profound feeling of loneliness.

"Lotta good that did," she said to herself, looking around miserably. The silence was ubiquitous. Outside there was no wind, only the snow falling tacitly. Even the animals were quiet and inside all she could hear was her empty heart beating and the sound of the clock ticking in the hall. Aoifa's thoughts drifted to her ma – she so missed their chats, outings and her companionship. Now those days had gone, but how could she fill this eternal void of nothingness with no thoughts of the future to console her? As she recollected times of long ago with her ma, Laurel and her school friends came to mind, and it occurred to her – they must come to stay! They didn't know about her ma's passing, yet they had all adored her. Aoifa was excited about the very idea and hummed an old Celtic ballad to herself as she washed the brushes and cleared away the paint.

When the girls came home that day, she greeted them jubilantly.

"You're in fine mood, Ma! Did you finish the rooms, then?" asked Niamh.

"I did indeed. Yours in purple, pinks and silver, right?"

"Sounds fab! Is that why you're so jolly, though?"

"Not entirely. I've decided to invite my school friends over if your da doesn't mind."

"What – a party?" said Mairead eagerly.

"Well, a houseful, Mairy, for sure!"

When Padraig walked in, Aoifa flung her arms around his neck.

"Wow – what's going on?" as he extricated himself.

"Chara, can I invite my school friends over to stay? We can go to the pub and walk and… talk and…"

"Hey – what – a celebration?"

"Indeed it is. I've finished the bedrooms!"

"Ah, but for the magic mural, girls, it's over to you."

"So, what d'you think?"

"You deserve a bit of fun, Aoif. Why not!"

Aoifa set about contacting them and arrangements were made for their visit in a few weeks' time.

"Who's coming, Ma?" asked Lois. "And have we met them before?"

"Yes. You came to Dec and Meg's wedding last year. Then there's my best friend, Rachel, recently back from working abroad. Clodagh can't make this one, but Laurel can. She's been unwell but seems better now."

"I remember Laurel, Ma. She's a hoot!" added Mairead.

"Well, yes, she has her moments," Aoifa replied.

It was Saturday morning a few weeks later and Aoifa was feeling elated, as her friends were due.

"We're walking over to the pub when they arrive then we'll come back and spend the evening with you all," she told the girls.

Clara ran downstairs. "We'll do dinner, Ma!" she declared, clapping her hands.

"Well, that'd be a great help!" Aoifa smiled gratefully.

Lois walked in, taking a step back. "Wow! So on trend! An up-hairdo – makes you look younger too, Ma."

"Well, that's lucky, then, as I'm one of the oldest!" A compliment from her eldest daughter, things were looking up. Then a car could be heard coming up the drive, Aoifa checked herself in the mirror and they all ran outside.

Two cars pulled up in the yard and everyone jumped out.

"Hi!" Aoifa shouted, running toward them. "Oh!" Aoifa let out a sob. "I told the girls I wouldn't blubber!"

Before long, everyone was crying.

"It reminds me of when you came years ago," she said tearfully, but they were soon laughing and there were hugs all around.

Aoifa walked over to Laurel, her arms outstretched, taking in her jaded appearance. "So good to see you, Lors. This is well overdue."

Laurel nodded, overcome with emotion as the tears ran down her cheeks.

Declan stretched his legs. "Lookin' good, Aoif, d'you wash your hair in Padraig's seaweed or what?!" Aoifa laughed again, reminded of his raffish ways. "Have you all met Megan?" he asked.

Megan stepped forward like a pretty wisp of lightness in a pink fluffy sweater, tight denim jeans and a long blonde ponytail as she smiled a greeting.

"Lovely to see you again, Meg. Right – we're to walk all this emotion off – to meet Rachel in the pub."

Megan turned toward the girls, who were beaming from ear to ear. "Are these stunning beauties all yours, Aoif?"

Mairead giggled and gave a curtsey.

"Don't be cheeky, Mairy!" Aoifa chided, laughing, as they set off toward the bay with Flynn leading the way.

Laurel and Aoifa linked arms and walked on ahead.

"It's lovely to see you again, Aoif. I am so sorry about your ma; she was very kind to me."

"They were great times, eh, Lors?" She squeezed her hand.

"Well, after my parents died in the accident, your family always made me welcome. And then my brother passed too…"

Aoifa looked at her sadly. "I can't imagine losing both parents together, Lors," she said as they walked onto the soft sand.

It was a crisp, fine day. There was frost along the shoreline and some mist still hung in the trees. The tranquil sea lay out before them like a sheet of deep sapphire blue.

"Will you look at that?" said Laurel, riveted to the spot. "Sheer beauty, Aoif. I'd forgotten."

The seagulls were following them, screeching from above, then the horses appeared up ahead.

"The two bigger ones are our workers, mother and son, Roma and Rafa. The youngster, Brown Mane, well, he's just a hanger-on!" Rafa came up to them and nuzzled her as Aoifa gently stroked his mane.

"Where does Padraig work, Aoif?" asked Declan, looking out to sea.

"His kelp farm is round the far side of the bay. He could do with some help if you ever get a minute, Dec!"

"Ha! Like, as if. Our farm keeps me going non-stop! Our condolences about your dear ma, though," he said and Aoifa gave a wan smile.

"So, how was Christmas?" Laurel asked.

"Liam and his family joined us actually. It was pretty full-on, a houseful, but took our minds off things."

"Your bro, I remember. You didn't use to get along?"

"Not much change there, but it was OK. We kept our heads!"

"I remember – he didn't like your predictions, Aoif," said Declan.

"What's that?" Meg interjected. "Some sort of telepathy?"

"Well, yes and no, Meg, but no, he didn't, Dec."

Aoifa moved the subject on.

"We reach the woodland in a while then you'll recognise the route."

They followed the shoreline around the peninsular, then climbed up over the low rock face and headed inland.

"This is real wilderness," said Megan. "South Wales is quite mountainous, but here the landscape is open moorland, more rambling."

"It's our land all along this coastline, but not many folk come here anyway, as we're quite isolated."

"How's your pa and Sean?" Laurel asked and Aoifa thought she spotted a flicker of interest cross her face.

"They're managing OK, thanks. Sean has some idea or other. Don't know what it'll come to, though."

"What idea?" asked Laurel.

"For the farm. We'll have to see."

They soon left the rocks and entered the woodland, walking in single file through a plethora of pathways flanked on either side by dense gorse bushes.

"Ah, there's the old bothy we used to play in!" shouted Declan.

"Sshh, look…"

Aoifa pointed to a clearing and there was a white hare up ahead, eyeing them suspiciously.

"Wonderful eyes!" Aoifa whispered, then Laurel started to giggle, and she was gone, quick as a flash!

"Lors!" said Meg, slightly irritated. "I wanted to get a picture."

"Siobhan draws them all the time. She'll show you later," said Aoifa, then she turned back to Laurel.

"We've not spoken since the summer, Lors. How've you been?"

"You don't want to hear my troubles, Aoif," she whispered.

"Of course I do. That's what old friends are for."

Laurel pulled her to one side. "I had a miscarriage, then my boyfriend and I broke up, but he was a rotten apple anyway." A sob caught in her throat, and she pulled her hand across her face.

"Oh my, Lors. I am so sorry."

Aoifa touched her friend's arm, shocked by her news and feeling a twinge of guilt that she hadn't been in touch, then the others caught up. The group continued in companionable silence whilst negotiating overgrown scrubland, when Laurel exclaimed,

"Ah, I remember once we met some boys at the pub here – The Fisherman's something? I got home late and was in trouble with your ma!"

Aoifa smiled at the memory. "Sounds familiar! The Fishing Net."

The sun was streaming through a canopy above of stark branches, which formed eerie shadows ahead of them, but soon they reached daylight and left the wood.

"Come on, Flynn, we're nearly there, show us the way!" Laurel shouted.

Rachel was in the pub garden as they approached.

"Hi, everyone!" she called.

Aoifa observed her friend, a tall Irish beauty, with dark hair gleaming like ravens' wings flowing down her back.

"Hi, Rach, so good to see you. It's been a long time." They embraced warmly. "Have you been waiting long?"

"Actually, I came yesterday, but Brendan here's been looking after me."

"Hey!" said Brendan, looking around. "So, a group o' locals, eh?" he said, grinning at everyone and giving Aoifa a kiss.

"What bliss," said Aoifa. "Great food, home-made wine, good old company and a roaring fire!"

"Old? Who's old?" asked Rachel.

"Well, definitely not you, Rach. Still lookin' good!"

Aoifa looked at the contrast between her friends. Declan and Meg in the throes of marital bliss. Rachel looking radiant and glowing from her worldly experiences. Laurel's depression, however, was acutely evident, etched into her face. Her hair was thin, streaked with grey, her features pale and the pain in her eyes unmistakable. Aoifa drew her in as they went into the pub.

"Come on, Lors, let's sit close to the fire."

Soon they all settled around a large table and fell into their usual banter.

"I remember us meeting here before you were married."

Aoifa frowned at Declan in embarrassed anticipation.

"Aoifa used to lead us all astray in those days," he told Brendan. "Always the one with the ideas – what to do, where to go."

Everyone laughed at the memory when Rachel added,

"You know, recently, I got thinking about old times and wondered if you still live by the elements?"

Aoifa was startled but held her beliefs. "Actually, I do, Rach. I believe the raw elements around us have a bearing on our lives."

Laurel looked up. "In what way, Aoif? I didn't know about this."

"Well, Ma used to say if you're born near the sea, that the elements of nature enter you and live in you forever."

"So – is that true, then?" asked Megan. "Sounds a bit mystical, like reading the stars."

"This is the land of myths and legends, me darlin', don't you know?" Declan's eyes were gleaming.

"Some," said Aoifa. "The belief originated in Ancient Greece. They say we all come from four main elements depending on when you are born."

"Ah, I see," said Declan, "so which one are you?" he asked mischievously.

"Water, like Clara, our youngest. We have empathy, intuition, but can have a jealous streak too! Clara's a sweet, sensitive girl, helps me more than the rest put together!"

"And the others?" asked Rachel.

"Lois, just eighteen, is of the Earth, practical, reliable and logical. Aims to save all the sea mammals!"

"Wow – impressive – wanting to change the world already!"

"Padraig is Earth too – stable, solid, fertile…"

"Hey, steady on, Aoif, too much information now!" said Declan as laughter ensued.

"No! Tell us more. What about naughty Mairead, then?" quipped Laurel.

"Ah, Mairead. Fifteen going on twenty-five. She's Fire. Passionate and unruly. We have to watch her!"

"I can teach her a thing or two, then, Aoif!" joked Laurel as Aoifa tutted amiably and continued,

"But there are two sides to Fire. Niamh, sixteen, is on the other side – lots of positive energy, plays the fiddle and loves to dance."

"Lastly, your quiet one, Siobhan…" asked Meg. "She hung back earlier."

"Creative, always writing or drawing. Twelve years old, an enigmatic soul for her years, floats around on her own and is Air. You can see them all for yourselves later!"

Brendan brought in a delicious meal, and they all tucked in, ravenous after their long walk. Feeling warmed by the company of her friends, Aoifa turned her attention toward them as they went over old times, and after the meal, they went outside to catch the last of the sun.

"Won't you look out there?" Declan reflected. "Across the moorland, shades of winter and endless nothingness for miles. Just sky, sea and fresh Atlantic air. Glad I brought you, Meg. I'd forgotten this beautiful landscape with the mist swirling in the distance. Truly evocative."

Brendan arrived with the coffee. "We have rooms here, Dec, plenty of peace and quiet for you two lovebirds!"

Meg looked embarrassed as Brendan disappeared back inside.

"Ach… he just wants some himself!" Declan added jovially. "Nice guy, Aoif, not married?"

"He was, but she died, baby too. It was five years ago now, but it was all so very tragic." The group went quiet. "He certainly gets lonely," she added.

"He'll meet someone soon," said Laurel dejectedly. "Just wish I had his charm."

"Someone be around the next corner – you watch, Lors," suggested Declan cheerfully, but Laurel had already turned away.

By the time they went back inside, Rachel and Brendan were deep in conversation.

"…Global warming? A problem, for sure. It's all our rubbish doin' it," said Declan, chipping in.

"The trouble here isn't global warming… We need a new school," Brendan said. "Incomes are down because parents have to home-tutor."

Brendan's community spirit was plain to see, and Rachel was listening intently. Aoifa looked across at her friend, as stunning as ever, and wondered why she was still single.

"Rach, you've done so much good, setting up schools abroad. How about bringing your skill set closer to home? Then we get to see each other!" suggested Aoifa with a twinkle in her eye as Rachel gave her a perceptive smile.

"It would be nice to spend time back home, Aoif, as my parents live in Belfast now."

Aoifa and Laurel took their coffee and went back indoors to sit near the fire.

"It must have been so hard, Lors, what you've been through. I wish I'd known; we could have got together."

"I took myself to rehab, only just come out. Took to drink an' all. I have to take meds, balance my moods. It helps a bit. I just hope the depression is passing, but I wonder at times. My life is slipping away, Aoif."

Aoifa didn't know what to say. She felt so helpless.

"Life can seem very unfair," Aoifa agreed.

She tried to imagine Laurel's pain at the loss of her baby, but it was impossible. Her expression was so sad and severe with her hair pulled back in a thin ponytail it made Aoifa sigh. "Your work is going well, though?" she asked dismally.

"Yes, I'm shop manager now, which I do enjoy. Maybe I'm better off without a partner – at least no one has come along since."

"There will be someone out there, Lors. They say when you stop looking!"

Aoifa spoke lightly, but suddenly Laurel's face darkened.

"I am not looking!" she growled, her eyes flashing, taking Aoifa unawares. "And I am not desperate! It's alright for you. You've got everything!"

Laurel looked away, seemingly upset, then turned back to Aoifa.

"I am so sorry. How could I? You've just lost your ma. I just, well, get agitated sometimes."

Aoifa started at her friend's reaction but spoke calmly.

"It's fine, Lors. I know you're not desperate, just in pain at the moment."

Laurel's sudden outburst triggered a flashback as she recalled her bad moods when they were teenagers. Once when they had fallen out, her ma had to bring them back together, but Aoifa couldn't recall details and it occurred to her that Laurel just needed a good friend right now.

"Come and stay with us a while, Lors. You always loved the sea and it's so soothing to be out there with nature. The girls will keep you amused, too!" Aoifa smiled at her good-naturedly. "Be nice for you to see Pa and Sean, wouldn't it?"

"I remember Sean," said Laurel pensively. "Quiet chap. Didn't like school, though. He was always in the bike shed repairing the bikes instead of at lessons!"

Aoifa laughed, explaining that he was still happiest when fixing things.

"Sean is a good man, but loneliness is his enemy. Maybe one day he'll find his passion – and a partner too."

Laurel said nothing then added, "I would love to come and stay."

They went across to the others at the bar, who were laughing over something, and Aoifa broke in reluctantly.

"We need to make our way back before dark, but it's been great, Bren. Did you find cover – you coming back with us?"

"I can actually," he replied with a grin. "Wouldn't miss this party for the world!"

A while later, they all squeezed into Brendan's large pick-up and headed back to Muir Farm.

"Can't wait to see the girls again, Aoif. They must be so grown up now?" said Rachel.

"Sometimes!" Aoifa smirked.

"How do you cope with them all?"

"Go with the flow – easier than battling them, Rach!"

"Well, you have the sight of what's to come. Must help," added Laurel. "Can you see what lies ahead for me, Aoif?" she asked boldly, but alarm showed on Aoifa's face and Rachel intervened, clearly sensing something.

"Ah… save for another day, Lors. We're nearly there and the girls'll be waiting!" Aoifa responded with a hint of a smile.

"Bet they're all beauties too. Who looks like you?" said Declan, his eyes twinkling,

"I guess Lo and Niamh, red-haired with hazel eyes. Clara too, but with fair hair. Mairead and Siobhan have dark hair and blue eyes, like the gypsy in their da!"

When they got back, Megan got to the door first.

"Ah… dark hair, smaller – you must be Siobhan? Would you show me your drawings, please?"

Siobhan nodded. "I do hares…"

"I know. I paint too," smiled Megan.

"I smell food," said Aoifa. "Wonders may never cease! Where is everyone?"

Mairead came flying down the stairs. "I'm here, Ma. Look, Niamh made me some braids."

"Lovely. They match your hair, Mairead," said Laurel, "but I should give it a good brush before you put them in!" she quipped.

Mairead chuckled, shaking her mop of unruly black curls. Then Padraig came in with Lois, and Aoifa made the introductions. It took her by surprise, but Aoifa thought she noticed a frisson between Padraig and Megan and her heart missed a beat, but she shook her head, pushing out the twinge of anxiety.

"Pad, where's Clara?"

"Feeding the piglets, chara, be back now."

"Ah, OK. We'll have dinner in a couple of hours. Bit of time-out, guys? Nevey, can you help with their bags and show our guests to their 'quarters', please, and Lo, could you help me with the table?"

"Ma, I've been clearing up, can't you ask the others?" Lois snapped.

Her refusal added to Aoifa's growing tension, so she asked Siobhan, later remembering her vow not to overload Lois as she made her way wearily upstairs to have a wash.

Later on, Brendan and Padraig were preparing the drinks in the scullery when everyone slowly joined them.

"So, beer, Dec? Or some home-made wine?"

"Surprise me – and Megan too." Megan walked in with her naturally blonde hair spread about her shoulders; she had a look of pure beauty about her and Aoifa noticed, to her consternation, that Laurel was glaring at her, and she waited until Meg was out of earshot.

"Lors – you OK?"

"Fine. What's up?"

"It's just the way you were looking at Meg – stunning, isn't she – and a lovely girl with it, eh?"

"If you say so," replied Laurel sourly.

Aoifa wanted to believe her own words, but with such a beauty in their midst, she couldn't help comparing herself too.

"You look gorgeous tonight in that green dress, my love," said Padraig, sidling up to her. "A bit tight, but that's how I like it …"

He went in for a kiss, but Aoifa wasn't in the mood and shrugged him off. Suddenly, the responsibility for everything without the benefit of foresight overwhelmed her and she took a big gulp of wine to settle her nerves.

"Can I raise a glass to the O'Brien girls for a fantastic spread!" shouted Declan, and Padraig turned to Aoifa.

"Had no idea there were budding chefs in our midst, did we, chara?" But she was looking out of the window and didn't respond.

"Aoif?" Padraig called her back to them.

"Yes, brilliant…" Aoifa hadn't eaten much, and the wine was making her light-headed, but she had something on her mind.

"Rach, you have a good memory. Do you remember Aunt Beth, my mother's sister, ever coming to the house when we were young?"

Rachel considered her question. "Wait a minute. Did she have fair hair?"

"Yes, not red like Ma's."

"I do indeed. On your twenty-first. I was staying over. She wasn't there long, just spoke to your mother as I recall."

"She was a bit of a sourpuss at Ma's funeral. She told me she and Ma hadn't been in touch for many years but didn't say why."

Rachel frowned. "I do remember now. They were in the kitchen talking for ages. Maybe raised voices? And then I think she left."

Aoifa had no recollection of any of it, which galled her, and she turned back to her guests, suddenly acutely aware of Megan's svelte figure next to her and the way she sat so elegantly, her conversation flowing naturally.

"More drinks, everyone? Nevey, shall we have some music later?"

Aoifa decided a distraction would help.

"Um, OK, Ma." Niamh was reluctant.

"And singing and dancing in the barn?!" asked Mairead hopefully.

"You like dancing, Mairy? We'll have to go together some time!" Laurel exclaimed, helping herself to more wine.

"You're a few years ahead with that, Lors!" said Aoifa.

"Why, Aoif? I wouldn't lead her astray, now would I?!" Laurel teased.

During dessert, Aoifa suddenly felt nauseous, the wine and her thoughts going around in circles. She excused herself and went upstairs, overcome with confusion and torment.

A few minutes later, Padraig followed her.

"Chara – what is it?"

Aoifa was crying silently into her pillow.

"Oh God! I… I just can't seem to cope with all the dynamics down there. Ma has taken my sense of what will be – as well as my common sense and confidence – and brought Megan here to catch your eye!"

Padraig sat down close to her. "Your imagination is playing tricks on you, chara. You're just worn out with all that decoratin' too."

Aoifa seemed unable to move, her guilt and distress overwhelming, but she was powerless to overcome any of it.

"Look, stay and rest, my love. I'll explain downstairs."

Padraig returned to his guests and told them,

"Aoifa has come over so tired just now with all the excitement and the decorating too. She's sorry but will stay upstairs a bit."

"Can I go to her, Pa?" asked Niamh.

"Not just now, Nevey. Clara, fetch that delicious trifle you made! I'll get more wine, and Siobhan, can you put cheese and biscuits out? Come on, more drinks all round!"

Niamh fetched her fiddle and played some Celtic songs and an aura of conviviality soon returned to the party.

The next morning when Aoifa woke, she found herself wrapped in Padraig's arms.

"I love you," he whispered.

Sometime later, they showered and made their way downstairs.

"It's so quiet here," said Aoifa. "Where is everyone? Pad, they've gone! I've chased my friends away."

As she opened the kitchen door, there was a huge uproar. They were still there! A grand breakfast had been made and Aoifa could even smell fresh coffee. Meg came over and handed her a cup as tears ran down her face.

"Hey, you'll have to come more often!" she laughed through her tears.

Clara came rushing in carrying a bunch of Christmas roses in one hand and Percy the piglet in the other, offering him to her ma.

"What's this for, Lara?" Aoifa asked.

"Percy wanted to give you a cuddle!"

"Well, I'd rather the bacon on the plate mesel'… so out he goes! I am so very sorry to you all for last night. I felt emotionally exhausted. But I'm so glad you're here. Truly."

The happy atmosphere of the previous day was gradually restored, and Declan entertained everyone over breakfast with tales from their school days, making the girls roar with laughter.

"I've to take some medicines across to Home Farm. Would any of you like to come and see Pa and Sean?" asked Aoifa.

"I'd planned to show Declan the farm, chara," said Padraig.

"I'd love to see them, but Brendan and I have something to discuss," Rachel announced mysteriously.

"And I'll stay with the girls," Megan said, smiling at Siobhan.

"That leaves you, then, Lors – you coming?"

"Yeah, why not. Be good to see Sean again."

"I'll come too, Ma!" said Mairead.

"Hello… anyone home?" Aoifa opened the front door as her pa stood up from his chair.

"What do we have here – a troupe of lovely ladies visitin' me?"

"Pa, you remember Laurel, my friend from school?"

Aaron looked puzzled.

"Hi, Mr. O'Connell. I was really sorry to hear about your wife."

A shadow came across his face, but his hand rubbed it away.

"She is sorely missed, lass," he sighed, "but we're managing," he added more brightly.

"Is Sean about, Pa?"

"He's bringing the cattle in. Take your friend down. She'll like that."

"Um, is it really mucky? Shall we wait?" said Laurel dubiously.

Mairead soon found an old coat and wellies. "Come on, Lors, I'll take you." So off they went whilst Aoifa stayed with her pa.

"I've brought the linctus for your chest."

"Oh, grand, chara."

"Bitter cold out now. Wouldn't be surprised to see some proper snow soon," as she made some tea.

"Aye, they say it's comin'."

"I've finished the bedrooms at home, so thought I'd come and do some decorating for you?"

The door opened and Laurel rushed in, followed by Mairead and Sean.

"Oh, it's so freezin' out there. Who's decorating?" asked Laurel.

"I'm going to do some for Pa, freshen it up a bit here."

"I can help – come for that break you promised me!"

"A woman's touch wouldn't go amiss around here, young Laurel!" said Aaron encouragingly.

"But right now you have to come down to the beach with me," cried Mairead, "so, Ma, we have to go!"

They had finished their tea and Aoifa noticed that Laurel seemed to be making eyes at Sean, who was clearly embarrassed.

"OK. We'll leave you now, Pa."

"But we'll come back before too long with our paint brushes, eh!" called out Laurel.

Back at Muir Farm, Rachel and Brendan came out to greet them.

"Guys – Brendan and I have some news." Aoifa turned toward her, raising an eyebrow as they all went indoors. "We're going to build a new school!" Rachel cried, her eyes sparkling with excitement.

"What?! Oh, Rach!" Aoifa grinned happily at her. "So you'll be staying here, then?" she asked.

"For a while – eh, Bren?"

He put his arm around her shoulders, nodding and smiling as Aoifa took Rachel to one side.

"You're a fast worker, my girl!" she said playfully.

"We just formed an instant bond, Aoif. I can't believe it myself."

"He's a good man – and a very lucky one." Then Rachel whispered, "Serendipity."

Aoifa turned to Laurel. "Oh, Lors. Fantastic news, eh?" She spotted her downcast face and asked, "What?"

"I'm always the one left behind, Aoif. When will it be my turn?" Then Laurel's expression lifted. "Ah well, one down, one to go!" and Aoifa knew what she meant.

Lunchtime was a very jolly affair. Padraig brought out his elderflower and bramble wine amid the laughter and celebrations. The table looked very colourful with birds, bees and butterflies hanging from above, which Siobhan, Meg and Clara had made earlier.

"You know – for climate change, Ma?"

"Oh no, Lara, not you too."

Aoifa groaned, but she was laughing with them. She looked across at Rachel. "Your new project will bring so much to the area, Rach. Come on, Nevey, let's celebrate – fetch your fiddle, give us all a dance."

Very soon they were all singing traditional Celtic songs whilst Niamh gave a demo of her Irish step dance around the spacious kitchen.

"Wow, give me another drink and I'll have a go," Laurel added.

"I'll teach you one day!" cried Mairead, clapping to the beat.

As they finished dessert, Siobhan asked her ma to play some ballads on the piano, which, it turned out, evoked many memories and reduced them all to tears.

"The sound of milk and honey, Da," Siobhan muttered to her father.

"Mmm," he replied, giving Aoifa a bemused smile.

It was soon time for everyone to leave as they all gathered their bags.

"I'm going to miss you," sighed Aoifa, giving them all a hug.

"Sorry we didn't get down to the beach, Mairy. Pity the tide was in. Next time, eh? What's there to see anyway?"

Mairead just smiled excitedly. "When are you coming back, Lors?"

"Well, ask your ma. I think they need some help at your grandpa's."

"In a few weeks' time, maybe?" said Aoifa distractedly.

"Definitely!" Laurel replied with some satisfaction as Aoifa turned to her.

"Taken a shine to my brother after all these years, Lors?"

"And what if I have?" she chuckled.

"Just friends then or…?"

"A place to start," Laurel replied with a smile.

Padraig put his arm around his wife as they waved their goodbyes.

"Wasn't it grand in the end, Pad?"

"You see – you did well with no prior knowledge of any of it!"

Apart from a tiny blip, Aoifa too felt she had coped pretty well. So that was what going with the flow was, occasional brain overload, a few surprises, a bit of fun, with no harm done. Easy-peasy and she had even managed to let go of her misgivings too.

"See you before too long, then, Aoif," yelled Rachel as she left with Brendan. "Thanks again."

"We've all had a great time – thanks, both!" Declan and Meg shouted from their car while Laurel jumped in the back and leaned out of the window.

"Can't wait to come back! Next time, Aoif, can you look deep inside and tell me what my future holds…?"

12. NIAMH – COLOUR, MUSIC AND DANCE

It was a sunny Saturday morning in March and Niamh had been trying to put a new song together for some time, so she decided a walk along the beach would help to inspire her. As she set off, Niamh considered the changing seasons, how colour in nature, or a lack of it where she could add colour in her own mind, all helped to ignite her imagination. Spring was the best, though, new beginnings and a budding vibrancy evident as she skipped along, practising her steps as she went. She based her sequences on a step dance, drawing from her love of the acclaimed show, *Riverdance*, which was founded on traditional Irish dance movements. When she went to see the stage show a year before, it had filled Niamh with inspiration upon which to build her own dreams.

As she reached the sea, Niamh watched the frothy waves turning into ripples and creeping toward her. She kicked at the water, and it splashed over her wellies, shiny droplets landing on her short skirt and colourful leggings. Images of spring and thoughts of new life came into her head followed by a flowery tune with a light rhythm, like the ripples on the shore. Niamh took out her music recorder, sat on a rock and hummed the tune into the microphone.

Turning away from the seashore, she headed up onto the moor, the ground cover coming to life all around her with signs of marsh marigolds appearing above the dearth of winter. The tune in her head changed to a moving melody, a love lost, a bleeding heart, greyness for a moment. She looked up as the sun reappeared from behind the clouds, giving a brightness to the trees as they came into leaf. Her music took a turn, the timbre more upbeat, faster, with poignant pauses. Niamh hesitated to record once more. When she looked up, there were two bright eyes watching her, peeking out from behind the gorse bush. She couldn't wait to tell Siobhan; it was one of the white hares! Suddenly, it hopped, skipped and jumped away, disappearing out of sight. There was a further frisson of movement up ahead as a red deer lifted its head and it too pranced across her path. The music adjusted itself to a sharper melody of vibrant action, young life and love entering the scene. She replayed the piece and was pleased with the results. As she made her way through the woodland and back down to the seashore, there was a brisk wind behind her, pushing her forward. She put her earphones on and began to dance, bringing her movements and her new song together, her actions perfectly synchronised with the music. She pointed her toes and tapped out the beat as she reached the hard sand, laughing to herself, elated by the fusion. Nature had played its part as it always did – guiding her and bringing colourful thoughts and motion into her head, merging as if one. As the song finished, in her euphoria, Niamh threw herself onto the wet sand, laughing out loud as another thought occurred to her. This time, it was especially exciting, as it would take her musical ability to quite another level, moving it forward as if on a natural course, and she stored the idea away in a corner of her mind.

She soon settled in a sunny spot to enjoy her picnic. The tide was out, and the horses were coming over to see her. As they cantered across the sand, she watched and listened. She heard something surreal in the beating of their hooves, a tune which resembled a sombre tap dance. It was autumn, winter, going into spring then they stopped in front of her, so the beat came to an abrupt end. This scene sent Niamh's mind reeling as she began to record the cadence of their hooves. Old Roma ambled up to her, putting her nose into the rucksack.

"Hey! Ah well, I guess you've helped me, so I'll keep you some!"

Her grandma had always told Niamh that "Colour made her smile, music made her laugh, her fiddle-playing gave her pleasure and she always wanted to dance." As these thoughts came back to her, they brought a waft of sadness as a gentle breeze came across the sea toward her.

"Thank you, Grandma, for your inspiration today. You always encouraged my music," she whispered.

Her mother and the loss of her gift came into her mind, and she spoke aloud, "Gran, can you tell me – where has Ma's sight gone? I just want to make her happy again. She doesn't do so well without it. At least can you show her what the rest of us do, how we cope?" Although Niamh was unperturbed about having no foresight of her own future, she did worry about her ma.

Enough! She jumped up, turning away from her worries and throwing off her wellies and socks as she ran across the sand and jumped into the icy cold water. As she breathed in the sea air, smelling her da's seaweed, it brought renewed vigour, warming the blood in her veins. Niamh was aware of nature's influence on her spirit and soul as she looked around at the buds on the trees, the birds calling and the suggestion of fresh nests in the rock face. Even the horses had a spring in their step, trotting alongside her as she made her way back home.

Although she was almost in her penultimate year, Niamh's heart was not in her studies. She enjoyed art and languages, but there it ended. Niamh knew she was not artistic in the style of drawing or painting; she would leave that to Siobhan. Her inclination was to create music and dance in the physical sense, yet she loved colour and it shone through everything she did. Niamh brought an alternative meaning to art entirely.

Her mother came through the front door and broke into her thoughts.

"Did you have a good time on the beach, Nevey? Clara and I have seen the snowdrops waking this morning. Fetch your fiddle – I feel a song coming on to welcome spring!"

Niamh brought it and played a gentle lullaby. She was in pensive mood because she knew her grandma would never hear her play again, but her ma had other ideas.

"Play something lively, Nevey – make us all laugh!"

So she chose a favourite – one from the Transatlantic Session musicians. Their music filled her with an unspeakable sense of fun. The colours Niamh was feeling shone through her hazel eyes as she stepped out some dance moves at the same time. Her ma soon picked up the tempo as they danced a traditional Irish jig around the table and they both laughed and laughed, and Niamh couldn't stop, as it epitomised what life was all about for her. Suddenly, she felt intoxicated, and her head was spinning. They each fell into a chair, overcome with emotion. Aoifa followed with a quiet ballad on the piano as Clara and Siobhan went and sat alongside her.

"I smell hot chocolate, Ma," said Siobhan. "I can taste it too. It's in the song," she added as her mother looked across at her curiously.

When the other two had left the room, Niamh spoke up,

"I don't know what Siobhan was on about, but that was lovely, Ma. I've been thinking, you know you were worried about losing your gift? Well, maybe we girls can take over, you know – predict everyone's future, and *tell each other what we can see – all the bad stuff for my sisters and the good stuff for me…*" She read it like a rhyme and looked at her mother, her eyes twinkling.

"Oh, you rascal!" Aoifa said and told her the dancing had made her daft, but she had seen the funny side and it was Niamh's way of making her mother smile with her quick humour.

"Next Saturday, me and my friends – we're going to start a dance group. What d'you think, Ma?"

Her mother looked uncertain but smiled.

"Ah… I know your love of dance, Nevey. Do you have any plans for this group?"

Niamh was thoughtful. "Not yet. We want to try out some different styles, then maybe we can do a little show in the village hall for the old folk, the children too, you know, spread the music around a bit. It may inspire the little ones."

"Absolutely – share your passion!"

That evening, Niamh told her pa about her idea.

"You having boys in this dance group?" he asked with interest.

"Nah, be a distraction for the other girls, Pa," she said. "I know what Chloe's like!"

"Not for you, though, eh?" he asked with a cheeky grin.

"I prefer to keep my eye on the steps for now, Pa!"

"Well, you watch out, cos the boys will have their eye on somethin' else with those short skirts!" He looked across at her, with her mop of shiny red hair and pretty pale freckled face.

"Leave her be, Pad," scolded Aoifa. "Let her have a bit of fun with her music! So what if she does like short skirts?"

"Ah well, no different to you at that age, I suppose!" Padraig retorted and they all laughed as he went out the door.

Saturday came and Niamh was off to meet her friends. It was a long walk to the village over the mountain, but it would only take half an hour. She was carrying her fiddle, her music recorder and there was a piano at the hall for her friend Aisling to play. When she arrived, her three friends were waiting for her excitedly. They soon agreed on a selection of musical pieces and started to practise some dance routines when a few of their classmates walked in.

"Hey, Niamh, can we join you?"

"Well, we have a music session going on here, Aidan. Can we meet you at the cafe later?" They left reluctantly, closing the door behind them.

Niamh felt bad about sending them away, but she knew they weren't ready for an audience yet. At the end of the session, the girls were all satisfied with what they had achieved and set off to the cafe.

"Be great to hold a performance on stage, wouldn't it?" suggested Aisling, her eyes shining with excitement.

"Maybe we could perform in the Easter concert at school?" said Niamh. "Mrs. Butler always encourages my love of music; I could ask her?" But the very idea filled Niamh with trepidation, and she suddenly wondered where that idea had come from.

There was quite a crowd at the cafe, but she soon spotted Aidan, who smiled and came over.

"I wish we could have watched you in action," he told her.

"It was our first time, so we wanted to get it right – without you lot jeerin'!"

"We wouldn'a done that, too!" he said indignantly.

Niamh looked thoughtfully at him, surprised at how much she enjoyed his attention.

"Another time, then. I have to get off home now – it's getting late."

Aidan offered to walk her, but she declined, saying she was used to walking over the mountain alone.

"Maybe next time," she told him.

Aidan returned her smile, and they went their separate ways.

When she arrived home, her mother was putting the tea out.

"Ma, is it next weekend Laurel's coming to Grandpa's?"

"I believe so, Nevey. Why?"

"Well, I thought we could do a show for the family in the barn, and they can all come too?"

"Great idea. Yes, let's do it!" agreed her mother.

"Ma – Laurel fancies Uncle Sean, doesn't she?"

"Nevey! Anyway, I don't know."

"Well, I do. She'll eat him alive – and come back for more!"

Her mother smiled as they both giggled and Niamh knew it was true.

Saturday soon came around and Padraig and Conor had built a stage in the barn for the occasion. As her friends arrived, Niamh felt the excitement, but was admittedly slightly nervous too, especially when the rest of the family pulled up in their old Land Rover and her grandpa got out. Niamh was a bit in awe of her grandfather.

"So, my girl, your grandma always said you could dance, eh?"

"This is just a bit of fun, though, Grandpa, nothin'
serious. Way to go for that!"

"You'll get there, gal, keep at it. Be on the telly in no
time!"

They all made their way across to the barn, where they
were greeted by a roaring fire. Aoifa and the girls brought
some snacks and Padraig followed with the drinks.

"So, where did you get this talent from, Nevey?" Laurel
asked.

Niamh noticed she was wearing a tight mini skirt but
thought she'd gone a bit overboard with the make-up.

"I don't know, Lors, I just love it. But you're not going
to be able to join us on stage in those heels, you know!"

"Aw, that's a shame!" she laughed. "You ain't seen my
step dancin' yet!"

They all took their seats, the adults on chairs at the back
and the girls and Conor on straw bales in front.

"Phew, Pad, what's in this wine? Don't give it to the
troupe or they'll fall into our laps!" shouted Aoifa.

"No way, they're on the soft drinks – this brew is for
serious grown-ups!"

"Serious grown-ups or those who are silly and fall
over?" asked Laurel.

Before too long, Niamh appeared, taking centre stage
with her neat bob swinging stylishly around her face, a body
top, frothy skirt and sparkly dancing shoes. She began with
a lively intro on her fiddle, followed by a solo step dance
routine. Looking out at her family's rapt expressions,
Niamh soon began to warm up and really enjoy herself.
Next came a group dance, carefully synchronised with
Niamh bringing in fancy acro-moves at the end. The dancers
gave a lavish bow, and everyone stood up, applauding and
whooping loudly.

"Wow! Brilliant!" Aoifa called out.

Niamh beamed at them as the group came down off stage
for some refreshments.

"Very clever, Niamh, a great routine!" Padraig exclaimed and Aoifa gave her the biggest hug and told them all how impressed she was at their combined talents.

"Can we have a taste of Pa's wine, then, Ma?" Niamh asked.

"Well, just a taste, to give you energy for the second half!"

Aoifa reached across to the table, but there was none left in the bottle as Laurel confessed to emptying it.

"So sorry, guys. Can we get some more, Pad?" He politely fetched another bottle, offering them all a glass each.

The performance soon resumed with even more complicated and challenging routines, but they did themselves proud with no mistakes. At the end, all four girls were exhausted but laughing with relief that all had gone well.

Laurel shouted, "Encore!" and eventually, Aisling and Niamh played a duet together. She told them it was written in memory of their grandma.

Padraig stood up at the end to begin the clapping.

"Excellent, girls! Please raise your glasses to… what are you called… 'The Ceilidhs'…"

Tears were rolling down Aoifa's face and Laurel stood on her chair, whooping and shouting, "More, more… show us a bit more leg!"

Aoifa looked across at her warily and tried to help her down, but Laurel resisted.

"Could I get another glass, Aoif?" As Aoifa shook her head, Laurel yelled, "Mairy'll get me one…"

Mairead grabbed what was left in the bottle and filled Laurel's glass, which she drank in one, but as she leaned back, she promptly fell off her chair, her skirt up around her waist. Padraig helped her up off the floor, laughing to detract from her inebriated state, and suggested Sean chaperone her out to the car. Niamh came over and gave her grandpa a hug as he was smiling from ear to ear, clearly impressed by her performance, then Sean soon took them all home.

In spite of the drama at the end, everyone was in high spirits afterwards, which made Niamh glow with pride. The group expressed their thanks to the O'Briens, and Padraig delivered them all home safely. Niamh basked in her bit of glory that night as she dreamt happily of a bright and colourful future filled with music and dance.

On Monday afternoon, Niamh came rushing through the door.

"Ma, you'll never guess what?"

"I won't," replied Aoifa, "so tell me, quick!"

"Mrs. Butler has said we can do it!"

"Do what?"

"A performance at the school's spring concert!"

"Wow, that's brilliant. Do we get to see it?"

"Of course, anyone can come!" she said, beaming ecstatically and pirouetting out of the door to find her pa. Her mind was full of colour and sparkle, and she hummed her favourite song to herself as she saw her outfit in her mind's eye. Her mother made it from their remnant box and the only problem was Niamh wanted short skirts, but her pa thought otherwise.

"But Pa, they need to see my legs!"

"Yes, that's what we're worried about!" he said, concealing a chuckle.

Niamh spent a great deal of time practising over the following weeks. Mrs. Butler watched their rehearsals and told Niamh she was stunned by their combined skill set. Aidan too had become a regular at the practice sessions and gave her lots of encouragement, as he too was a music student, but piano was his instrument. Niamh knew he wanted to play a duo with her one day and just maybe they would.

The final dress rehearsal came around and her mother dropped her off at the school, wishing her well, and went for a coffee. Afterwards, Niamh rushed along to the coffee bar to join her.

"Seemed to go OK, but, Ma, it was hilarious! We *nearly* all fell about laughing... but we couldn't really!" chortled Niamh.

"What was so funny?"

"Mrs. Butler was watching from the wings, and when she passed us a microphone... it caught... on her hair..." Niamh broke into fits of giggles. "It... was, I mean, her wig was dangling from the top of the microphone, but the show went on...!"

Niamh tried to, but she couldn't stop laughing.

"Oh, poor Mrs. Butler. Did she laugh too?" said Aoifa, suppressing a smile.

"Yes, she definitely saw the funny side!"

"Oh dear, but it ended well. Come on, we must get everyone ready to come back later."

After they had finished their tea, the family made their way to the school. Mrs. Butler met them on arrival and told her parents how proud she was of them having the confidence to go ahead with this as Niamh looked on shyly. The family took their seats in the main hall along with the other parents when a hush came over the room. The curtain went up and Niamh stood centre stage, ready with her violin – a debut performance and it was a very technical piece. She felt her hands shaking but took a deep breath and began with gusto. It went well with no mistakes and afterwards she gave a deep bow to a big round of applause.

The dance routines came next based on a modern step dance. The main sequence went on for at least ten minutes and was a version of what Niamh had created out on the beach that day. Niamh lost herself in the performance, and at the end, she could see her sisters on the edge of their seats. Then everyone stood up and stamped their feet, calling for an encore, so Niamh played a quick coquettish finale on her fiddle followed by a short piece from Aisling on the piano, slowing the pace at the end. Afterwards, the troupe stood together and gave an elegant bow. The applause seemed to be never-ending, and Niamh couldn't stop smiling, her face radiant, then she stepped down to join her family.

Her ma came over and gave her a huge hug. "Brilliant, Nevey – your solo was such a complicated piece and you played it with such delicacy and skill."

"Yes," said her pa, "and note-perfect too. We are really proud of you, chara."

Siobhan made her way over to Niamh and nudged her arm.

"Your music sounded like rippling waves, and I saw snow flurries coming in then thunder and a smell of custard at the end," at which Padraig laughed.

"A very good interpretation, Sheve. Couldn't have put it better meself!"

Other pupils flocked over to give their congratulations to the group as a feeling of pleasure and satisfaction glowed on their faces.

During the journey home that evening, Niamh was aware of a palpable feeling of family pride in the car. She couldn't believe it had gone so well. She had thoroughly enjoyed performing and the praise from her family was what mattered the most.

The next day, Aidan appeared after school and gave Niamh a quick kiss, telling her how much he had enjoyed the concert.

"You are such a natural performer, Niamh. I would have been petrified. It was brilliant."

"Well, thanks, Aid. It was rather nerve-wracking for a first time, I must admit. At one point, I nearly fell off the stage!"

They left school together, and this time, Niamh accepted Aidan's offer to take the long walk home with her. She was thrilled with his compliments, which warmed her inside almost as much as the performance.

They both shared a passion for music and chattered incessantly. Soon Aidan suggested they sit on a bench, as the bags were heavy. They sat close together, and Niamh wondered if he would kiss her again, but he didn't, and they soon headed off once more. Nonetheless, Niamh felt elated because she had made a decision that night that would change the course of her life forever and it had begun with her walk on the beach several weeks before.

13. SOULMATES

Mairead was pondering over something whilst having her breakfast in front of the TV. She wanted to talk to her ma but would have to choose her moment. Her parents were none too happy after the Laurel incident in the barn, but what she didn't get was why they blamed her.

Her mother came in from the garden with a smile on her face and Mairead took her chance.

"Ma, when's Laurel coming back to Grandpa's again?"

"I'm not sure. Not for a bit, I think."

She carried her breakfast dish out to the kitchen and went over to give her mother a hug.

"What's that for?"

"Do I need a reason to hug my ma, then?"

"No. I just wondered what you wanted, that's all? Simply a guess on my part, Mairy!"

"OK," said Mairead, conceding, as her mother always knew stuff.

She took a deep breath. "Could you call Laurel and see if she can come over at the weekend, please?"

Mairead noticed the fleeting displeasure on her mother's face.

"She only just came, chara. Leave it, don't be a bother now."

Aoifa turned to resume her cooking as if the subject were closed, so Mairead stomped off upstairs. She could feel a dark mood coming on. Why were her parents always against her? Anyway, her ma didn't seem to like Laurel anymore and she couldn't think why. She threw on some old jeans and a t-shirt, wondering what to do next. As she went downstairs, she overheard her parents talking in the kitchen.

"Pad – just had Mairy asking when Laurel's coming again. It was a bit of a scene last weekend, nearly spoilt Niamh's performance, didn't it?"

"Ach, high spirits that's all, chara. Laurel's not too bad. Mairead's got quite a thing about her. Soulmates, I'd say!"

"Don't say that! There are so many years between them, too. I can't keep tabs on our middle child, and with Laurel's influence, there'll be no chance! She's always up with the Kellys too. What does she do over there anyways?"

"Beats me, Aoif. What do teenage girls do these days? No… don't answer that. One thing's for sure – she's gone a bit moody. Hormones probably, but you'd know about that, eh?"

"Oooh… you…" Aoifa chuckled.

As Mairead listened, a cheeky smile came over her face. She knew she'd win her pa over now!

At fifteen, Mairead was quite the teenager. She had no time for staying around the house. It filled her with boredom and made her available for all the tasks which she tried hard to avoid. She spent most of her time over at her friend Catrina's, who, to her delight, would be having a birthday party soon. Mairead had a secret desire – she wanted to borrow Laurel's silver dress for the event and decided if her ma wouldn't call her, she would. As she stomped around her room, it came to her that Laurel's number would be on her mother's mobile phone, so she went to look for it in her bedroom. As she tiptoed around, she heard footsteps on the stairs and froze.

Siobhan put her head around the door and Mairead breathed a sigh of relief.

"Mairy, what are you doing in here?"

Mairead had little time for Siobhan; she had some funny ideas and boring ones too. All she thought about was drawing hares and making up stupid stories.

"Don't you dare tell!"

"I won't, but what are you looking for?"

"I need Laurel's phone number, if you must know."

"Well, it'll be in Ma's phone book in the hall."

Mairead mumbled her thanks and ran downstairs. She found the number, waited for her mother to go shopping, then picked up the phone.

"Lors? It's me, Mairy. I just wondered when you were coming over next and if I can borrow your silver dress for a party, please? It won't be too small, Lors, we're nearly the same size! I won't spoil it, I promise. Ooh… thanks! See you at Grandpa's, then."

When Mairead rang off, she wanted to jump for joy! She would look the biz in that dress but knew she had to keep it quiet. Laurel was so kind; just maybe she would lend her something else too.

It was one week later when Mairead opened the front door and told her ma that she was cycling over to meet Laurel at Home Farm.

Aoifa gave her a quizzical look. "She's back so soon, after all, Mairy?"

Mairead was surprised her ma didn't know with her foresight and all.

"I think she wanted to see Sean, Ma!" giving a sly smile. "Can you pick me up from Catrina's party later, please?"

"Not too late, then, and will her parents be there for this party?"

Mairead knew her parents didn't like her out late and something else which infuriated her – they always felt she needed to be supervised.

"They will be, Ma. Is 10.30 OK?"

"No later, then. Pa'll be there on the dot."

Mairead rode off in a huff at her mother's idea of a late night out, shaking her head in exasperation. When she arrived at Home Farm, Laurel was pulling up in her car.

"Hi, Lors. You made good time. Must have been driving fast!"

"I never drive fast, Mairy."

Laurel smirked as they both went into the house.

Aaron looked up as they came in. "Ach, my girl, there you are! Sean asked can you go and give him a hand with sommat?"

Laurel raised her eyes to Mairead and sighed,

"I have to give something to Mairy first. I'll go in a minute," and they both made their way upstairs.

"I don't know, Mairy. As soon as I arrive, they have jobs for me to do. Who'd be a farmer's wife? Dirty work and heavy too, eh?"

"Not me!" Mairead made a face. "Lors – you wouldn't lend me some money for the party – please?"

"What d'you do with all your pocket money, then, Mairy?" Laurel took out a twenty-pound note and handed it to her.

"Well, these days I spend it all at the youth club," but she averted her eyes.

"You sure, Mairy?" Laurel asked her in disbelief. "In the pub more like!"

A huge grin came over Mairead's face. "How did you know?"

"I was your age once, remember? You can't fool the likes of me, yer know!"

Laurel unpacked her bag, took out the silver dress and handed it to Mairead, who beamed her thanks. She put it carefully into a carrier bag and spotted a tiny bottle of perfume on the bed.

"You don't think I could give this to Catrina, do you, please?" she asked, picking it up and trying some on. "Mmm, it's lovely. I haven't time to get her a present now."

Laurel shrugged. "Oh, go on then. It's not a good one. Take it."

Mairead was overcome with excitement. "Oh, Lors, this'll be a great party – thanks to you!" She popped the perfume into the bag, then jumped up and ran down the stairs.

"Well, have a good one!" Laurel called after her, laughing. "And behave yourself!"

Mairead was keen to get home, so she gave her grandpa a quick peck on the cheek, jumped on her bike and pedalled off at top speed, laughing loudly. She wondered if this was what ecstasy felt like – going to a real, grown-up party, wearing your very favourite dress – and with some money in your pocket! She would look so glamorous – and with maybe a little squirt of Laurel's perfume too.

When Mairead arrived home, she ran upstairs for a quick shower. She had to do something with her hair – it was so *black*. She just needed some glitzy slides and popped her head around Lois' door.

"Lo?"

"What d'you want, Mairy, just working…"

"Do you have any silver hair slides I can borrow, please?"

"Silver! What for?"

"Catrina's party… and your silver shoes? Are they size 5?"

"Size 6. Anything else, by the way?" Lois asked with a hint of sarcasm.

"Yes. Can you lift me in a while, please?"

Mairead knew Lois had just passed her driving test.

"Well, be quick, then. I have to get back."

Mairead couldn't believe her luck; everything was working out swell. After her shower, she felt hot with excitement, so gave herself a quick squirt all over with the perfume before putting her dress on. She stood back, looked in the mirror and did a little twirl, trying to balance on Lois' high-heeled shoes, and giggled as she fell back onto the bed. She popped her coat on over the dress and made her way carefully downstairs.

Aoifa took one look at her and gasped.

"Mairy! Far too grown up… those heels – and purple streaks. What will your da think?"

"It's all the rage now, Ma, especially purple. It washes out anyway," she said defiantly.

"Well, definitely too much make-up, my girl. Now go and see to it!"

Mairead groaned, knowing she wouldn't win that one, so rushed upstairs to remove some but slipped the make-up into her coat pocket for later and went back down.

"That's better," her mother smiled at her. "Have a lovely time, Mairy, and give my best to Mr. and Mrs. Kelly."

When they reached Catrina's house and Mairead got out of the car, exposing Laurel's dress, Lois gasped.

"Mairead! A silver mini dress. Where did you…?"

Lois looked shocked, but Mairead shouted her thanks and ran toward the house, laughing loudly, and entered quietly by the back door. She ran upstairs to Catrina's room to re-apply her make-up.

"Cat, shall we meet the others in the pub?" Mairead whispered.

"Mairy, we won't get served."

"We will if we go out of town – they don't know us there!"

Catrina reluctantly agreed, so they called their friends to arrange it. As they set off, Mairead suddenly remembered about the perfume but figured she'd used it now, so may as well keep it. However, a feeling of guilt crept over her as they walked along, arm in arm. It was Cat's birthday, after all.

"I'll buy the drinks this time, Cat." She waved the twenty-pound note in front of her, and Catrina's eyes opened wide. "Laurel lent it to me!" Mairead liked Catrina and she spent so much time at her house; she wanted to show her appreciation. "This is my treat – you're only fifteen once!"

Catrina smiled at her gratefully.

When they reached the pub, there was quite a crowd gathering.

"Come on, what shall we have to drink? Coke – with rum?!" Mairead sniggered. "Barney'll get them for us!"

"I'm not sure, Mairy. We can't be long. Ma's got food waiting for everyone."

An hour later, they were on their way back when Catrina suddenly felt sick, so they sat down on a bench for a minute.

"Here, Cat – have some of this, make you feel better…"

Mairead offered her a swig from a full bottle of rum.

"Mairy, where did you…?"

Cat took a sip and made a face. "Yuk!"

Mairead laughed. "Never mind that, come on." She pulled her friend up, keen to rejoin the party.

When they arrived at the house, several friends were there already, including Callum, who was smiling at her, and they all tucked into the lovely spread Catrina's parents had prepared. Soon the party was in full swing and Mairead turned the music up as she and Catrina started to dance, but the swaying made Catrina feel unwell again, so she went up to her room. The Kellys had taken themselves out to their summerhouse to give them some privacy and Mairead was having a grand time, but as the noise levels rose and hit an almighty high, it began to bother her.

"Hey, guys, keep the noise down or..." when suddenly Mrs. Kelly walked in through the back door to see what was going on.

"Where's Catrina, Mairy?" she asked, looking worried.

Mairead tried to tell her she'd been unwell but couldn't stop giggling.

"Mairead, have you been drinking?"

"Well, someone gave us one each, Mrs. Kelly, just a bit of fun! I think... hic... Cat's upstairs."

Mrs. Kelly went up to check on her.

Just then, somebody put some jazzy numbers on, so Mairead did a jig around the room and reached for her bag to take a swig of rum as she went, but she lost her balance and fell off her shoes. The bottle crashed to the floor just as Mrs. Kelly was coming back down the stairs.

"Mairy – you know Cat is very sick? What has she...? Oh no!" Her hands went to her face. "All over my new rug!"

Mairead was on the floor amidst the contents of the bottle. She tried to stand but failed, her drunken state more than obvious. She grabbed some cushions and attempted to mop up the red rum but only succeeded in rubbing it further into the carpet.

"Leave it, Mairead!" shouted Mrs. Kelly hysterically as she called out of the door for her husband.

Mr. Kelly rushed in immediately and roared at everyone.

"I want you all to leave – now!"

Two of the boys picked Mairead up and took her outside. She stuttered an apology to Mrs. Kelly as she passed her by, but once out in the garden, it was dark, and she fell over again. She managed to get up that time, but her heel caught in her dress, and it split right up the side.

"Oh no, Callum," she groaned. "Ah well, she won't want it back now, will she?!" Mairead started giggling all over again and couldn't stop.

"Who?" Callum asked.

"Laurel, my friend."

"Looks expensive, Mairy."

"Nah. Pass my bag, got another bottle in there…"

They both sat down heavily on a garden bench to wait for her pa and Callum put his arm around her. "Best keep you warm, Mairy."

"I know you like me, Cal," Mairead whispered as she leaned on him, swinging the bottle in front of her. "Come on, just one kiss, then." She turned toward him.

Mairead didn't hear the car pull up and her father walking up the garden path.

"Mairead!"

Padraig spoke sharply, marched over and tried to pull her upright.

"Sorry, Da," she slurred, unable to stand by herself and her dress gaping open at the side.

"You are coming straight home, my girl!" he said, glaring at them both, and they all left without another word.

The next morning, it was after midday when Mairead came downstairs and stopped by the kitchen door.

Her parents were sitting at the table having lunch.

"Come in, Mairead," said her father without turning around. "I have just been speaking to Maureen Kelly." He glared across at her as Mairead looked down at her bare feet. "Did you and Catrina take rum to the party last night? Because Mrs. Kelly found some and it appears it was trodden into her best rug."

"Well, someone gave it to us, Pa. They put it in our cola."

"Is that the truth, Mairead?"

"Yes, Pa. It made Cat and me very sick, so we didn't have much."

"I see. So what happened with Callum, then?"

"Callum?"

"Yes. The boy who was attempting to kiss you as I arrived?"

Mairead had absolutely no recollection of Callum doing any such thing. She had to think fast.

"He was smelling my breath, Pa, to see if I'd had my drink spiked."

Mairead looked across at her parents, guilt and upset written all over her face, suddenly worried that her ma would know the truth.

"Well, Mairy," said her mother solemnly. "A lesson learned, I think. Beware the company you keep in future. Also, an apology to Mrs. Kelly is in order."

Mairead nodded and took herself upstairs, wondering what was wrong with the company she kept. As she got dressed, it slowly dawned on her that her ma hadn't known any of what had happened at the party, had no foresight of it either, and she felt lucky to have got away with it. This puzzled Mairead, but it went out of her mind as she remembered falling over, so she went to check on Laurel's dress and discovered the long rip down the side. She was horrified. Laurel would be so mad! How could she fix it? She couldn't, not without telling her ma, so decided she would put it in a bag and hope Laurel wouldn't notice.

That afternoon, Mairead went into town to give her apologies to Catrina and her parents, which, thankfully, they took very well and put it down to someone sneaking in the drinks. As she left on her bike, Mairead breathed a sigh of relief. The sun had gone in, and it was getting cold, but Mairead didn't feel it. All she could feel was her pounding heart as she made her way to Home Farm. When she arrived, feeling pretty exhausted, Laurel was waiting for her eagerly.

"So… how was it?!" she asked excitedly, but Mairead couldn't bring herself to tell the truth in case she told her ma.

"It was OK, bit noisy, so my head hurts today, Lors."

Laurel laughed. "Won't the be last time you wake up with a headache after a party, my girl! Want some tea?"

"Yeah and some biscuits too." Mairead helped herself from her grandpa's cupboard.

"What you up to later, then, Lors?" she asked, hoping for an opportunity to pop the dress upstairs without Laurel seeing it.

"Sean wants me to help outside, but it's too cold, so I said no!"

"Won't he mind, then?"

"He doesn't have to. I'll make them some dinner instead. Doesn't pay me enough attention as it is, so I'll stay here and make meself up for him!"

"You fancy him, then, Lors?"

"Now, don't you be cheeky, and what if I do?" said Laurel with a devious grin.

"Is he… a bit young for you, though?" Mairead asked.

Laurel carried on making the tea and didn't reply, then turned and glared icily at her.

"How dare you be so rude! Who d'you think you are, talkin' to me like that, young lady? Take the dress upstairs and mind your own business."

Her sharp tone shocked Mairead as she stood frozen to the spot.

"You'd better make sure that dress is OK, and I want my money back too!"

Mairead flew upstairs without speaking, frightened by Laurel's sudden outburst. She thought they were friends. She sat on the bed shaking and felt the tears pricking her eyes. Why had Laurel screamed like that? What would she do when she found out about the dress and that she had no money? Mairead stayed there a few minutes but knew she had to go down and hoped her grandpa would be there. She entered the kitchen nervously, but Laurel was smiling brightly.

"Stay to dinner, Mairy! I want to show you my new make-up!"

"I… I told Ma I wouldn't be long. Thanks for the dress, though." She left before Laurel had a chance to say any more.

Mairead was very upset after she left the farm. Why had Laurel been so angry? She hadn't meant to be rude to her. Ah well, maybe she had a late night with Sean and had a headache too.

As she cycled along the coastal path, Mairead got to thinking about the party. She had really enjoyed it until she'd fallen off her shoes, and her parents had forgiven that she'd been drunk. Catrina had been OK about it too and she was looking forward to seeing her at school on Monday. School! How she hated it. She wouldn't be there long, just one more year, then she'd be off to London! Her friends told her they had great clubs and pubs over there, the best. She looked out to sea and Lois' cave came to mind. Lois would be gone soon; she'd said so. Surely Niamh would do something with her dancing too and then she would be the oldest – and her parents would treat her differently – and give her more pocket money!

As she replayed the previous evening, Mairead was surprised and pleased how easy it had been to get the rum and how relaxed and happy it made her feel. She'd been to the pub a few times now and couldn't wait to go again! Callum had been so nice to her. Maybe he really liked her, and he would buy the drinks next time, or she could borrow money from her sisters. Clara had some, she knew.

As Mairead opened the front door, she overheard Niamh talking to Lois and her ma.

"It's just a small music festival, Ma. I only want to see the local group play their Celtic jive music. Lo, would you come? I think Ma would be happier if we went together?"

"No, yer OK. A folk festival? Couldn't think of anything worse, Nevey."

"Aww, Lo. Please drive us. We won't stay long, just to see them. They're my friends, you see?"

Mairead was listening through the crack in the door.

"Alright, then. But not late back, agreed?"

"Definitely. Thanks, Lo!"

Mairead rushed in as Niamh went to give Lois a playful hug.

"Ooh, Nevey, can I come too?" she asked, her eyes gleaming.

Niamh groaned. "Ach, no, Mairy. I can't look on yer as well."

So Mairead asked Lois, "Can I, Lo?"

"You're too young, Mairy. In a couple of years, eh?" But Mairead had an idea.

"I know, Laurel can look after me!"

Aoifa looked anxiously from one to the other. "Och, Mairy, it's too much to ask. Anyway, I'm not sure she likes festivals."

"She does, Ma. She told me she always used to go."

Mairead looked across at her pa imploringly, who was quietly reading the paper and appeared disinterested. There was a moment's silence then her pa nodded his approval. "Be OK, Aoif. Laurel's a grown-up."

"We can ask her, then, just this once, if it's OK with the girls?"

They both seemed reluctant but nodded and Mairead shouted,

"Yes!" thinking to herself that she could get used to all this dressing up and going out.

The following evening, Aoifa was putting supper out when there was a knock at the door.

"I'll get it, Ma!" shouted Mairead, jumping up.

"Hello, Lors," said Mairead nervously.

"Can I come in, Mairy?"

Mairead stood back and Laurel stepped in, smiling around at everyone.

"Hi, Aoif. In time for dinner, I see! Just thought I'd call by on my way home."

"Erm, we can make room for one more, Lors. Come on in."

"Aw, thanks! I've come to see Mairy, really." She turned to face her. "Can you show me how you did your hair with that purple colour, then?"

They made their way upstairs, and as they reached the bedroom, Laurel touched Mairead's arm lightly.

"What?" Mairead asked her, holding her breath.

"I just wanted to say I'm sorry for raging at yer, Mairy, had a late night too. So, if you don't tell your ma about it, I'll say nothin' about the dress – an' no more about the money either!"

Mairead couldn't believe her ears.

"Course not!" she replied, grinning at Laurel, who offered her a high-five and Mairead happily reciprocated.

"Well, I have another favour, Lors. Will you chaperone me to a music festival with Niamh and Lo in a month's time, please?"

Laurel looked at her in delight.

"Wow, Mairy, I'm likin' that! It'd be a pleasure!"

Mairead ran downstairs, shouting,

"Ma, it's all settled, then. Laurel's coming to the festival!"

14. SIOBHAN is AIR

Niamh had told Siobhan about White Fur and she couldn't wait to get to the beach. It was a rare occasion when she took herself down there on her own; it was generally not allowed. However, on this occasion, her da had said he would be close by, and she could go, but she was to be careful and stay away from the sea. The sun was shining and her whole body tingled at the thought of it.

Siobhan put her notebook, drawing pad, pens, camera and binoculars into her bag together with a snack in case she had to stay a while and set off. She could hear the waves crashing onto the shore, although couldn't quite see them. Whenever Siobhan heard the rough seas, the colour purple came into her head and she had no idea why. She soon reached the beach and cut across the soft sand, eventually turning up onto the moor to the location Niamh had described. It was quite close to the old bothy where her ma had seen the pine marten den. She moved forward as quietly as she could, keeping vigilant in case she missed something. She waved to her pa; he was sorting his seaweed in the distance. Ahead of her, the spring flowers were open on the moor, speckles of purple, yellow and white all around. She could smell jasmine and violet and lavender oil, a floral mix, and colours of the rainbow wafted before her eyes.

Her grandma had told Siobhan about the elements around her, where she had come from and what was inside of her. Her element was Air. Her ma had said creativity was in her blood but was sometimes intangible, which to Siobhan meant you couldn't touch it. Sometimes you couldn't see it, but you just felt it. Apparently when Siobhan moved around, she was like a breath of fresh air, imagination in action with material or matter in varying forms entering her head. No one else could quite see, feel or hear these ideas, only Siobhan herself. No one else could quite catch her. She was a free spirit, or at least that was what her grandma had said. Siobhan likcd that; it meant that she didn't have to feel tied down, nor engage with anything or anyone if she didn't want to. She'd heard her ma say that she was 'expression in all its guises'. Hmm. She must look that one up.

As she reached the exact spot Niamh had mentioned, she sat down very quietly, not moving a whisker, and waited. If she kept very still, she would become air, not present in any form, so White Fur maybe wouldn't even see her! As time passed, Siobhan listened and could see time, numbers on the wind whistling around her. The number six was rumblings of moving cloud, or two when the wind reached a whistling high note. She was amused by how alive her senses felt. There were rustlings ahead. She saw colours – reds, browns, yellow. What was it? Then they disappeared. There was no white, the sound and sense of frozen rain and the colour of White Fur.

She got out her notebook and began to doodle, nothing with any shape or structure, just a practice. Then she sensed something up ahead. She raised her eyes carefully but kept her pencil on the paper. She could hear a light squeaking sound like the crack of a whip or a firework, and she saw the colour of snow out of the corner of her eye. There she was. White Fur! Ahead, about twenty yards. Siobhan just stared, mesmerised. She had waited many months for this moment, and it had come. Could she take a picture? No. Bright sunlit colours played all around with White Fur in the middle. She must draw quickly. She had very tall ears and long whiskers, huge dark eyes and mixed brown fur with a white chest. Her feet were very big, for prancing and a quick exit. White Fur turned slightly. Perfect. Siobhan could see her bushy white tail now and her eyes were captivating, like two pools of liquid chocolate, soft and deep. Just then, her whiskers moved, her nose twitching, smelling her. She lifted a front paw as if to wave then rubbed her nose a few times. Soon, there was movement alongside her – the leveret came out of the den behind her!

Tiny, the colour of cream, all aglow, her eyes two tiny black dots and a halo of sunshine surrounding her. There were shooting stars, streamers of different colours circling them both in her mind's eye as she sketched them quickly. What a sight; she would never forget. One photo. She had drawn them now, but she just needed one photo.

Her dream fulfilled, these words came into Siobhan's head. "Dream big," her pa had said. "Dream on," Mairead had laughed. "Just dream," her grandma had told her. It had come true.

She got a photo, not a good one, but she could enlarge it. Happiness filled her whole body, and she felt the warmth of amber running through her veins. Time to go and leave them in peace.

Siobhan carefully got up, but the hares did not move. They were in no hurry. They watched her a while until she moved... When Siobhan had gathered up her things and turned to leave, they took off with a flying leap over the bushes and were gone.

She made her way home, overjoyed with how it had all turned out. She would work on her drawings and put them up on her attic wall.

As she walked, Siobhan thought about what she would do the rest of the day. The hares were her new friends, but they were elusive and never stayed long. Siobhan had thought for some time that maybe she should find some real friends, but they would not be Air like her. They would be like Niamh or Mairead or of something else entirely and would not understand her. Her classmates were different from Siobhan; they didn't think of colours or sounds or numbers. Siobhan wondered why she did. Was it part of being Air? Maybe if she had been born another time, not October, and in some other place, she may have been Fire or Earth. The others in her class seemed much better at talking than she was. Did she have to talk anyway? If she wanted friends, she would have to talk. She could talk to her ma or Clara. Not her pa, though; he was always moving, didn't sit still and sometimes looked at her strangely. Lois was OK too; she loved animals and understood her. But she didn't think in colour or sound or smell. Oh dear. Who did? Niamh loved colour, but it was not the same. When Niamh played her music, Siobhan always tasted lollipops. Clara especially understood her, but she didn't care for drawing; she was always busy helping their ma, and she knew Clara was sunshine. Then she thought of Mairead. She knew Mairead didn't like her. She didn't look at her drawings, never spoke to her either. Maybe Mairead didn't even see her. When Mairead spoke, Siobhan felt the colour scarlet. What about Laurel? Siobhan didn't like Laurel; she always teased her and paid her too much attention, making the hair on her arms stand out. It stopped her feeling like Air and more like deep water or red hot, unsafe, dark and too mysterious. She heard strange things at those times, grinding noises, the roar of a lion, and she saw the colour of the devil through cracks in the floor or doorways.

Making her way across the rocks, Siobhan watched the swirling spray from the waves and thought of the number three and the colour of bright orange and purple together. The sun was low, throwing its beams along the sand. As she walked through the shadows cast in front of her, she had visions of wild animals. They showed her the way ahead and she could smell their scent, the colours of blues and greens in flashes before her eyes then the sun took them away.

Siobhan had always wanted to write stories. Now that she had a picture and a drawing of White Fur, she would write a story about her, using smells, touch and colour too. When she made up her stories for Clara and the others at bedtime, they always believed them because she made the characters real so that they could hear, feel and smell them, like she could. She mimicked the sounds they made, their colours and shapes and the way they breathed. Even her voice changed to create the avatars, the mystical beasts and beings in her head. They moved through her unconscious, figments of her imagination, becoming real as they entered her stories. Her ma had told her they were ethereal. Siobhan's head was full of them much of the time.

As she went indoors, her ma was sitting at the kitchen table.

"Ma… guess what? I found them. White Fur and her leveret!"

"Oh, Sheve, that is great news. What were they like? Did they hop off immediately?"

"Well, that's just it, Ma. They didn't. I got to draw them, and I got a photo too. Look!" She got out her drawings and her camera.

"Brilliant! I knew you'd find them in the end."

"Did you know, Ma? That I would see them? Why didn't you tell me?!" Siobhan was excited now. "I'm going to write a story about them. Did you know that too? Bet you won't have sight of the stories, though – they're not done in my head yet! There were colours around them and I smelt peppermint when I was with them, Ma!"

Her mother hesitated, then smiled wonderingly at her daughter as if she didn't quite understand. "Peppermint?"

"You see! You didn't know that. It was all mine!"

Her pa came in for some tea followed by Lois, and Siobhan showed them too. Lois had a look of fascination on her face.

"Could you take some photos for me too, Sheve? I need some for my CV, of the seals, terns, gulls, and try to capture the dolphins and whales too? You obviously have the knack… and good timing."

Siobhan looked doubtful, saying she'd think on it.

Aoifa explained further. "Sheve says they smelt of peppermint and there was a lot of rustling in the bushes, which threw out bright colours too."

Her pa added with slight alarm on his face, "Well done, Siobhan. All your patience paid off, then. Find the peppermint thing hard to get, though!"

Lois smiled proudly at her younger sister. "Wow! It must have been some sight out there. Can I come along with you next time, Sheve?"

"Maybe, Lo. If you don't talk to me."

Siobhan suddenly felt overwhelmed by all the attention, and in her mind's eye, she saw a big puff of smoke with colours swirling all around her family and there was a noise in her head like a spinning top. Then her ma spoke, and she smelt lemons and honey as she came out of her trance.

"There are deer too, Sheve. You might see them one day, but you may have to wait longer," her ma told her.

"I think you have a grand imagination too, Siobhan," said her pa.

"Yes," her mother agreed. "This daughter of ours puts an unusual spin on things, Pad." Her mother gave her an encouraging smile.

"You'll probably make a fortune one day with all your tales!" her father added.

Siobhan heard the word 'fortune' and knew that meant a lot of money, but these things were mostly just in her head and were not for sale.

Mairead came into the room. "Who's going to make a fortune?" she cried.

"Your young sister, here," said her mother, her eyes twinkling.

"What's she done now, then, Ma?"

Mairead looked curiously at Siobhan.

"She got some pictures of White fur and is going to write some stories, Mairy. Isn't that good news?"

"Huh, anyone can take pictures, Ma, but good luck, Sheve, with your stories! I suppose they are good'uns when she makes them up for us," Mairead admitted. "I could help too… and then I can get some of the money!"

Siobhan considered this and thought Mairead was being serious, as she was always looking for money. Then she figured if her stories ever were for sale, they would be her stories. Suddenly, she could taste vinegar, sharp and stinging, and she wanted it to go away.

"I don't know, Mairy. I don't really need any help. You'll need to make your own money, I think."

Their parents looked on, listening with interest to their conversation. Somehow, Siobhan had a knack of putting her finger right on the button, and just maybe Mairead would take the hint.

Later in the evening, the girls had just finished their supper and Padraig had built a roaring fire when Mairead turned to Siobhan excitedly.

"Come on, Sheve, tell us one of your new stories about the hares, then." She turned the lights down to create a mysterious atmosphere. Siobhan still felt exhilarated from her trip out that day, so she thought up her best story. The girls all sat on the floor with Siobhan in the middle and her pictures lay all around them. She could hear colours outside again as she began her story, magenta, pink, a rainbow and all shades of the sea as she painted a picture. In her mind, the hares got up to some frolicking and high jinks, getting themselves into mischief as there was magic and menace afoot. As the story unfolded, Siobhan could feel fur touching her skin and her feet began to tickle, making her giggle, as she let her imagination fly. When the story had ended, Mairead stood up, shouted her thanks and ran off upstairs, calling back,

"Got this one, Sheve!"

It took a second to register, but then Siobhan called out, "No, Mairy! It's mine!"

Siobhan ran after her, but Mairead had locked her bedroom door and Siobhan could hear her laughing inside. The colour of a thunderstorm, silvery purple and heavy grey, crossed before her eyes, accompanied by the sound of loud drums. She decided she would keep her stories to herself in future.

Siobhan sat quietly, feeling confused and disturbed for the rest of the evening, her senses on the alert, her skin itchy. She could hear the stars in the sky, feel the heat of the moon on her skin and smell the sound of anger rising, the colour of fire. It was late when Siobhan went up to her attic bedroom. She locked the door and was calmed by the familiar smells and noises inside. She stayed there for two days. Her mother couldn't entice her out, so put her food under the door for her.

"Siobhan, please come and join us for lunch today?" she asked her on the third day.

"No, Ma," Siobhan whispered to her through a crack in the door. "I feel safe in here. This is my own room. They're my own hares and my stories. They're all mine." *Sometimes a whisper is louder than a shout*, she thought to herself and didn't remember who told her that.

"I don't understand, Sheve. Of course they're yours. No one is going to take them from you."

Siobhan didn't reply to her mother, but she could see in the silence that followed, the colour lime green and she could hear something else, a strong wind, and before her eyes lay a field of nettles.

Later on the third evening, Siobhan could sense the sound of crying downstairs and she knew it was her ma. She could see jagged shapes in the dark of her room and the crying sounded like the howling of a wolf. Then she heard and smelt her pa, coming up the stairs and stopping outside her room. The silence was loaded; hot air seemed to be rising up the stairs, warming her, and with it came the smell of roses. Bright lights swirled underneath her door, but her bedroom door remained closed, and Siobhan knew she was… free, of air, of nothing. Uncatchable. She would stay in her room. This was her air, and no one could take it from her.

15. EXTRAORDINARY AND EXCITING EVENTS

It was a warm Friday afternoon in June, Mairead had just got home from school, and she was not happy. She always went to the pub on Fridays. Or to Catrina's. At least, that's what her parents thought. She'd told her friends she'd meet them, but the problem was, she didn't have any money.

Mairead had asked her parents if she could do some extra chores for more pocket money, but they always refused, as they wanted her to concentrate on her schoolwork. Yuk! Now the afternoon was passing her by and so far she'd found no solution. She could have asked her sisters, but they weren't home yet. Siobhan still wasn't talking to her after she pretended to steal her story. As if! Those stories never made any sense to her anyway. Then something came to her. She knew Clara had money. No, she couldn't just take it. Yes, she could, and she would tell her later. Clara wouldn't mind; she never spent it anyway. Mairead found her moneybox and quickly took a handful of coins, not too much, or she wouldn't be able to pay it back. But she needed a bit for the festival too, so she took a bit more. She soon got herself ready, left a note for her parents and set off for town.

She reached Catrina's house and knocked on the door.

"Hello, Mrs. Kelly. Is Catrina in, please?"

Mrs. Kelly frowned slightly, mumbling that she would fetch her. It seemed that Mrs. Kelly was still cross with her, but she had apologised for the party. What more could she do?

Catrina soon appeared. "Hi, Mairy. Can't come out tonight. I've to go out with my parents, sorry."

"Oh, Cat. You always let me down these days!"

Mairead turned and stormed off. She would just have to go it alone to the pub. As she continued on, it occurred to her that Cat hadn't come out with her since the party. Well, thought Mairead, it was her loss.

On arrival at the pub, she popped into the cloakroom to put her hair up in a topknot. She checked in the mirror, feeling quite the grown-up in her smart jeans, heels she had borrowed from Niamh, swept-up hairstyle and careful make-up as she opened the pub door. She looked around and recognised a few lads at the bar. They called her over, so Mairead joined them, grinning flirtatiously as they showered her with offers of drinks.

Before too long, one of the boys, Shane, invited Mairead outside and offered her a cigarette. Apparently, it wasn't a normal cigarette, but it would give her an amazing experience in her head, and she would feel like she was flying with no worries in the world. Mairead had heard of these, and it sounded like just what she needed. She certainly had a lot of money worries at the moment. She took one and soon got the hang of it, laughing along with Shane at the experience. The only trouble was when she'd finished it, she couldn't stand, which gave her a fit of the giggles. She seemed not to be able to think at all and her head started to spin. For sure, her worries had gone! A while later, Shane took her home and they laughed and laughed all the way. Her parents were still up when she got in and asked her what was so funny. Mairead told them Catrina and her friends had been playing some jokes on each other and that she'd better go to bed, as she couldn't stop laughing. They were pleased she'd had such a good time, but as Mairead left the room, she noticed her parents looking anxiously at one another.

The next morning, the girls were all sitting around the kitchen table having lunch and discussing the plans for the festival that evening when Mairead came down and joined them.

Clara had a particularly big smile on her face. "I know you like music an' dancin', Nevey, so did you know there's a circus coming to town? Conor told me. Someone on the boats told him."

Niamh's face lit up. "Circus? Ah… now, Lara… I love the circus! All those acrobatics! When?"

"Not sure. I'll ask Con for you."

"'Con' now, is it? What next, eh?" Niamh asked good-naturedly, but her dry humour was lost on the innocence of youth in little Clara.

Suddenly, Niamh turned to Mairead.

"Whatever's the matter, Mairy? You look like you've seen a ghost. You need to go back to bed – get some energy for later!"

"Leave me be," Mairead said sulkily. "I'll be OK in a while. Catrina and I walked miles last night."

The truth of the matter was that Mairead had no recollection of the night before whatsoever. The last thing she could recall was walking into the pub. Where did all her money go? *Clara's money*, she thought as she let out a moan. And why did she feel so ill?

Niamh whispered to her, "What is it, Mairy?"

"Nothing. I just need some breakfast," Mairead snapped as she grabbed some toast.

"Aww, cheer up…" Niamh tried to jolly her. "We've a special night out later and Laurel's coming too!"

"That's what I'm worried about," she muttered to herself. She didn't want to say the wrong thing to Laurel again but might if she didn't feel better soon.

Mairead needn't have worried. As the day passed, she began to feel her usual self and Laurel was in good spirits when she arrived. She'd won a bottle of champagne in a raffle the night before and had brought it along to show them.

"Look, girls! For me and Sean later."

"Lucky Sean, then," added Mairead. "Can't we take it to the festival?"

"Give over, Mairy, not likely. It's champagne, you know!"

A couple of hours later, they were all ready to set off. Mairead was so excited. She hoped Shane would be there, as she'd told him about the festival, but she didn't tell the girls that.

When they arrived, the field was water-logged due to so much recent rainfall, so they parked up and got out carefully, trying to avoid the muddy puddles.

"I hope it doesn't rain some more, Niamh," said Lois.

"Ah well, we've good coats and boots, so no matter. Come on!" said Niamh.

Mairead made a quick decision. She couldn't resist the temptation of the champagne, quickly popping it into her rucksack as she closed the car door. Carrying rugs, the picnic basket and bags, they all made their way up as close to the stage as possible. Lois laid out the rug and everyone sat down in excited anticipation.

"When are your friends on, Nevey?"

"In the second half. You never know, you may enjoy the other bands too, Lo!"

"Hmm. I'll try, although I'd rather be at home – working!"

Laurel looked at her aghast. "You can't mean that. You need to let your hair down sometimes, Lo! Life in the sea isn't everything."

"Ah well, that's where you're wrong, Lors. It is everything. Unless we save the marine life, one day there'll be no planet!"

"Aw, not tonight, Lo," Niamh groaned. "We're gonna have some fun, eh?"

Lois nodded and smiled good-naturedly.

Just then, Mairead stood up. "Anyone want a drink? I'll go get some, just over there," she said, pointing to the beer tent.

The girls all gave her some money as she took their orders and set off.

"I'll come with yer and be the eighteen-year-old, Mairy!" Laurel called after her, but Mairead had gone.

The field was now full to bursting and she had difficulty seeing through the crowd as she pushed her way forward when a sudden applause went up and the first band came on stage to warm up. As she crossed the field, trying to avoid the mud, Mairead decided to have a quick look for Shane; he would probably be around the bar. Then, out of the corner of her eye, she spotted Laurel heading her way. She had followed to help with the drinks! Mairead quickly darted behind the loos to give her the slip, then cautiously crept out and made for the bar. She recognised some lads from her hometown, spotting Shane amongst them, so she made her way over and nudged him,

"Hi – thought you'd come," she said, grinning around at them, but no one answered, so she looked at Shane. "I've got some dosh this time. Do you have any…"

Shane took out some rolled cigarettes from his pocket, saying, "Money first!" to her.

Mairead wondered why he wasn't being friendly but paid him then asked for a light. After he'd pocketed the cash, he grinned.

"Be a much better festival, Mairy, after a couple o' those!"

Mairead was relieved when he smiled at her, so she sat down next to him, lit up a cigarette and sighed with pleasure. She'd found her friends, got some drink in her bag, a smoke, and the music was about to begin. Her sisters and Laurel were but a distant memory and Mairead felt so grown up. It was to be a grand night! But suddenly, the heavens opened, and the rain started to come down in sheets, taking them all by surprise.

"Oh no, Shane, I've forgotten my coat!"

"No matter, look."

He put his umbrella up over them both and Mairead huddled in close. She took out the champagne, handing it to him, which he shook, then opened with a loud *pop*. It went over everyone as they all fell about laughing. Mairead whispered to herself, "This is better than I could have imagined!" The music blared out, everyone clapping to the beat when she heard someone calling her name. They sounded very far away, and she looked around vaguely but didn't care; she felt so relaxed and happy. Now someone was shaking her shoulder. Mairead roused, turned around and looked straight into Lois' face.

"Lo, you're all wet!" she giggled as if she hadn't noticed the rain.

"So are you, Mairy, sopping wet. Now, get up, you're to come and sit with us! And I don't know where Laurel's got to either."

Lois tried to pull her up, but Mairead objected.

"No, Lo, I'm not coming. Can't you see I'm with my friends? Shane'll bring me home anyways."

Lois pleaded with her. "Mairy... you'll catch your death and Pa'll never forgive us for leaving you! Please come."

"Na... Lo... I'm enjoying meself."

Mairead went to light up another cigarette, oblivious to Lois watching.

"Mairy! Who gave you this?"

"Go away, big sis, and leave me alone for once!"

Lois tried once more with tears of frustration running down her face.

"Shane... do you know how old she is?"

He suddenly got up and walked away, leaving Mairead sitting alone in the rain, but Lois called after him,

"She's not fifteen yet!"

Shane kept walking as Mairead pulled herself up, shouting,

"Shane, I'm comin'," and staggering after him, following him into the darkness as the crowd swallowed them up whilst Lois looked on helplessly.

It was in the early hours of the morning when Shane dropped Mairead off at Home Farm. She knew it was too late to go home. After he drove off, she looked for the bucket where her grandpa kept the key. She seemed to have lost connection with her hands and feet as she scrabbled around on the floor of the porch in the darkness, giggling to herself. Her movements were jerky, and as she became aware of scurryings and squeaks all around her, the giggling stopping abruptly. She felt herself come over very cold as a hint of confusion and panic set in, when suddenly she touched the key. Relief allowed her to breathe again, but she felt nauseous now and badly needed to lie down. As Mairead struggled to stand, she realised to her horror that her feet were bare. Where were her shoes? Niamh's shoes. As she put the key in the lock, the click of the door broke the silence, but luckily the dogs recognised her and wagged their tails. Mairead stumbled her way to her grandpa's study, where she fell onto the small sofa. Her head was burning now, and she wished she could close her eyes, but that would take longer, as she felt the room spinning around her. She lay there and waited for the whizzing to stop, but she was nowhere close to sleep. Mairead felt as if she were plugged into an electricity socket, and she had something hot running through her whole body. She had no idea when sleep eventually came, but it felt like hours later, just as the sun was rising.

The front door opened with a light click, but it woke Mairead. It felt like a thunder bolt piercing her head. When her ma walked in and shook her by the shoulders, Mairead could hear her but was unable to respond.

"Mairy, wake up! We've all been so worried about you. Where did you go last night?"

Mairead's tongue felt like cardboard and wouldn't work. Her head was glued to the cushion, and she simply couldn't open her eyes.

"Mairead!" her ma shouted, more loudly this time.

Sean popped his head in from the yard. "Hi, Aoifa, what's goin' on? I didn't know Mairead was here."

Mairead told herself to speak to them and finally managed to open her eyes.

"M... Ma?"

"What is it, Mairy? Are you ill?"

Her ma's voice sounded like an echo.

"Yes, M...a. My words won't... Have bad th... thr...o...at. Can't speak."

Her mother muttered something about Laurel as she ran upstairs. Mairead lay still and waited. Her heart seemed to be jumping out of her body and she couldn't stop shivering.

She heard her ma talking to Laurel, which only served to increase the thumping inside her head.

"Laurel? You up?"

Laurel let out a loud moan.

"I fell down the steps in the yard last night, Aoif, and gashed my leg badly. I can't move it!" Aoifa helped her to the bathroom but proceeded to question her about the night before.

"Did you know Mairead is very ill? She's downstairs and can hardly speak."

"I didn't see her much last night, Aoif. I looked out for her, but she… ran off."

"Where to?"

"I just don't know. Now I've got my gashed leg to worry about."

"Look, I think it best if you go home now, Lors. You can't help here anyway with your leg like this. I can drive you to the station if you like?"

Laurel jumped out of bed, screaming as she put her leg down,

"Ah, that's it, is it, you want rid of me? Well, I've got news for you – I'm not going anywhere. I'll stay here as long as I want and make myself at home – until my leg is better – and they can both look after me! Your brother ignored me when I got home; he won't do that too often either!"

Laurel hobbled past Aoifa aggressively, pushing her out of the way, her face blotched and red with anger as she limped back to bed and threw the covers over her head.

As Aoifa came back down to the study, Mairead looked up through bleary eyes to an expression of abject horror on her ma's face as Sean came in through the front door. They both helped Mairead out to the car and all she could hear were Laurel's angry words replaying inside her head, over and over again.

"Sean, Laurel's hurt her leg; you'd better see to her. I need to take Mairy home…"

Aoifa stopped, obviously unable to continue as she jumped in the car and drove off at speed, skidding in the mud as she went, leaving Sean to look on anxiously.

When they reached Muir Farm, Aoifa helped Mairead into the house.

"Girls, Mairy has a headache, a sore throat and she seems exhausted, probably taken unwell after a soaking last night as Laurel took her back to Home Farm."

Mairead said nothing as Niamh and Lois exchanged an uneasy look.

"Some breakfast will help, I think, Ma," she said with a small smile.

"Have a wash and brush up first, chara. I'll make you some."

Once Mairead had freshened up, she came down feeling a bit better and the family all sat together.

"Ma, my friend's band were brill last night." Niamh's eyes were gleaming. "I loved their numbers. We had a great jig around, until the rains came. Shame, but it didn't spoil it for us."

Aoifa was clearly warmed by Niamh's light mood. "That's nice, Nevey. I can remember going to a festival once but didn't care for the crowds much and I remember it rained then too."

"Ma, did Clara tell you – the circus is coming to town! My friends have been already and there's a troupe of very accomplished dancers, can we all go?"

Clara jumped up excitedly. "Ooh, yes, Ma, and can Conor come?"

Mairead was unable to finish her breakfast and looked around, wondering why everyone was so jolly when she felt so awful. She glanced at her mother, noticing how weary she looked, and a pang of guilt came over her for causing so much worry. They were still discussing the circus when Niamh added,

"You don't need to answer now, Ma."

"We can go to the circus, of course," Aoifa said brightly. "I'll ask your da to get the tickets." She smiled around at them all.

Mairead sat back in her chair and sighed. She was so relieved that the night before wasn't even mentioned, yet she knew no one had really forgotten about it.

Early Monday morning, the telephone rang just as Aoifa was taking the girls off to school.

Mairead picked it up as she walked past.

"Hi, Laurel," she said. "Yeah, here's Ma…"

She handed the phone to her mother and felt herself trembling.

"Glad your leg's better and they pampered you," Aoifa replied into the phone with more hostility in her voice than surely was intended, Mairead thought. "I'll get the girls to look in the car… so you'll be back again soon, then? OK. Bye."

Mairead looked at her mother as she put the phone down, her face etched with concern. Why did they have to look in the car? But Mairead knew why.

"I have things to do now, girls." Aoifa sighed, got up and made to go upstairs. "Lo, can you take everyone to school, please?"

Lois nodded and spoke quietly with a mounting tension in her voice. "We need to help out around here a bit, girls – I think Ma needs a break." They all piled into the car.

Mairead frowned at this. It was she who felt unwell – and she really didn't want to go to school. As they all set off, she was aware of Lois looking at her in the mirror and kept her head down.

"Mairy – whatever got into you at the festival, running off like that? And smoking too."

Mairead looked up at Lois' worried expression. Niamh shifted awkwardly.

"I came looking for you all at the end, Lo, but you'd all left without me." Mairead tried to recollect details, but they didn't come to her. "And one cigarette didn't hurt nobody anyways!" she added gruffly.

Lois grunted something impatiently and they all travelled the rest of the journey in silence.

Later that evening, the family were sitting quietly watching TV when the phone rang and Aoifa picked it up.

"Hi, Rach, lovely to hear from you! How are you both? Any news on the school? Other plans – what are they, then? Oh my goodness! That is fantastic. I'm speechless." She turned to the family. "Girls! Rachel is pregnant! I knew it wouldn't be long before we had some good news. No, no, Rach, I didn't mean that – I had no idea. No, no messages. A ray of sunshine in an otherwise rather grey day, that's all. Weather has turned. We'll come over and wet the baby's head before too long. Wonderful news – congratulations to you both. Take care of yourself. Bye for now!"

Mairead was sitting in front of the TV. She'd been pondering miserably over how much money she'd spent at the weekend and none of it had been hers. Laurel had obviously mentioned the champagne too and her head started to hurt all over again. She had also ruined her best jeans in the mud – and what had happened to Niamh's shoes? Everyone would be so mad at her again and she wouldn't have to wait long for that. As she listened to the call from Rachel, she felt so depressed. Why, oh why did the good stuff always seem to happen to everyone else?

16. CHANGING TIMES

It was a warm midsummer's day and Aoifa was sitting in the garden surrounded by a stunning spectacle of summer flowers, but despite the magnificence, she looked out with unseeing eyes. It had been over six months since her mother had passed, but sometimes Aoifa still struggled with life. Although she had found a touch of acceptance as she adapted to her change in circumstances, there were problems that she couldn't deny. Mairead was seemingly travelling a dark road and she spent too much time with Laurel, whose unpredictable behaviour was a worry in itself. Siobhan lived in her own often impenetrable world. It had been a real worry when she had stayed in her room, but neither she nor Padraig had figured that one out. With regard to Lois and her plans – Aoifa was none the wiser. With some relief, she told herself, there was Niamh, always vibrant and enthusiastic and Aoifa's driving force. And now there was Rachel's new baby! Miracles do still happen; she nodded and smiled reprovingly to herself.

Clara would be back in a minute to plant her vegetable seeds. Little Clara, spreading her sunshine wherever she went. Aoifa looked out beyond the garden to where sky met sea, the resplendence of the oceans lying before her and the heady summer fragrance as she felt her mood lifting. She watched the bees enjoying the nectar and the garden birds singing as she breathed in deeply, allowing nature to permeate her very soul.

Clara broke the spell as she rushed over.

"Ma – I've got all the seeds from the greenhouse, but when I found my small spade, the handle broke off, so I thought I'd buy myself another and went to my moneybox and… there was…"

"Wow, slow, Lara," said her mother and Clara burst into tears. "What is it?" Aoifa asked gently.

"My money, Ma. It's gone, just two notes left. You must tell me where it is, find a message!" she exclaimed through her tears.

Aoifa considered her reply carefully and waited for Clara to calm herself. She knew the time had to come to tell all the girls her truth. She went over and gave her a hug.

"Well, maybe you forgot how much was there, chara?"

"No. I know exactly! I was saving it."

There was a look of abject misery on Clara's face and Aoifa hoped the thoughts going around in her head were not real, just her imaginings.

"Well, we'll look into it, Clara. But for now, borrow mine, and if we can't find the money and there's some mistake, I shall buy you one, is that OK?"

Clara answered in a small voice, "Yes. Thanks, Ma. I'll pay you back."

They continued their work in the garden quietly as Clara became more composed, but Aoifa resolved to get to the bottom of the matter. Soon, Clara spoke up quietly,

"Ma, I know where my money went."

Aoifa held her breath.

"Where, Lara?"

"Mairead stole it. I hear her coming in late when she's been out with Catrina. No one else needs it, Ma, only her."

"I don't think she needs it, Lara," she said, avoiding her eyes.

"She does, Ma, I know it."

"Don't worry, we'll get to the bottom of it. If it was her, she'll have to pay you back."

Aoifa masked the angst she was feeling and changed the subject.

"Now, plans for our circus outing, yes?"

Although Aoifa had made light of the problem, if Mairead had indeed stolen the money, it was of grave concern. She told Padraig what had happened, and when all the girls came in from school, they were both waiting for them.

"Get yourselves a drink and snack and come sit with us, girls," Aoifa told them solemnly. You could hear a pin drop as they obeyed. Immediately, Lois and Niamh looked concerned, Siobhan thoughtful.

"I can smell burnt toast, Ma," she said, but no one had made any. Mairead had a nervous look about her and Clara was crying as she sat next to her mother. "What's up?" asked Mairead, looking around warily.

Padraig cleared his throat. "Clara has some money missing from her moneybox. Have any of you taken or borrowed it?" he asked.

Mairead's eyes darkened as the older girls looked knowingly at their parents and Lois spoke up.

"On the subject of money, Mairead, you still owe me five pounds from the festival."

Niamh looked sheepish and added, "Me, too, Mairy, and where are my shoes?"

"I just spend my own money on drawing stuff," added Siobhan.

"So, Mairead, did you take any of Clara's money from her moneybox?" Padraig asked.

Mairead looked around furiously. "So, why me, then?"

Her father looked at her steadily. "Because the others have money, and you don't. So, was it you?"

Mairead was defensive, but her face was bright red as she replied,

"Well, if you must know, yes, it was. I never have any money! I don't get as much as the others."

Padraig kept his tone neutral. "You know that was wrong, Mairead. You get the same as the others for your age. It's just you spend it."

"Why didn't you ask me, Mairy?" Clara wailed. "I would have lent you some!" She leaned in closer to her mother.

Padraig continued his line of questioning.

"What do you spend it on, Mairy? Alcohol, I think?"

"Sometimes, but not much."

"Only alcohol, would that be, Mairy?"

Mairead looked indignant. "Yes, Pa, only alcohol. Can I do more jobs, then, to get more pocket money?"

Lois interjected, "You'll need to. We all need our money back, Mairy!"

Padraig stepped in. "We've had this conversation, Mairy. Not until you are sixteen. If you go out too much, your schoolwork will suffer. You need to pay everyone back by doing their chores, starting now."

There was a finality to Padraig's tone.

"I can't, Pa, I'm seeing Catrina!"

"What about the circus, Mairy? We're all going together, later."

"I can't let Cat down, Pa. I'll do extra chores tomorrow, I promise."

Aoifa and Padraig looked at one another, shaking their heads in agreement that it was time to let the matter drop for the time being. As the girls left the table, Aoifa spoke up,

"Pad, I have an idea. Pa is bringing the two rams over to put on our pasture tomorrow. We could put Mairead in charge of them, to feed, clean out their shed and take them for walks at weekends. We could pay her a little to allow her to make good with the girls?"

Padraig concurred with this idea. "It would keep her around here more and I think it might make her feel more useful too."

"Exactly," agreed Aoifa as she took herself out to finish the chores in the garden. After a while, Flynn came over to see her and she fondled him affectionately when she saw Padraig coming up the path with Conor.

"Not much on the tide today, chara. Weather's too calm just now, but tomorrow be different. There's another storm comin'. Summer storms can be bad'uns. They're getting worse, too."

"Hmm. That's what Scorcha said. But they go as quick as they come?"

"Maybe. Maybe not," Padraig replied.

Aoifa looked at him questioningly, remembering the talk with the girls about climate change.

"Good we got all the seeds planted then, Pad. I'll cover them for a day or two." She took a deep breath. "Pity Mairead won't be with us tonight, eh?"

Padraig replied with a nod. "Yeah, but I like Catrina's family. Good influence, Aoif."

"You think? They can influence our Mairead?!"

"Ach, possibly not, but we can," he said decisively.

They stood a moment, both deep in thought as the sun changed from bright illuminating yellow to burnt orange. Evening was approaching and Aoifa checked the time.

"We need to be off soon, Pad. Prepare yourself for a night of entertainment! Colour, music and dance, just up Niamh's street, eh!"

"Yeah, I can see her feet twitching now!" he smiled and added, "Just pop the horses to bed." And he hurried off with Roma and the cart.

Aoifa watched him go as she felt the last of the sunshine on her face and looked forward to an enjoyable evening with her family. As she returned to the house, Aoifa heard music, a quiet, soft melody. Someone was playing the piano. She looked through the dining room window and could see Clara, playing a slow, simple song, using all of her fingers. Aoifa was amazed. She had no idea Clara could play; she had never shown an interest. Yet, why would it surprise her? Her ma had played by ear and so did she. She would say nothing to her for fear it may break the spell, so she made a clatter of opening the door.

"Hi, I'm back, girls… let's have a bite to eat. We need to be off soon!"

Clara came running out to greet her, followed by Conor.

"Conor's here! Oh, Ma, I can't wait! Do you think they'll have animals too?"

Niamh shouted from upstairs. "They do, Lara, elephants, horses, dogs, even a monkey!"

Lois muttered from the study, "I don't need to go to a circus to see how clever horses are – just wander to the beach and watch ours a while!"

"Ah… acrobatics too! I'd like to see you do that with the horses, Lo!" Niamh tested her cheekily.

"They'd soon learn, I know." Lois was adamant.

Mairead called over the bannister. "Ma, can you drop me at Catrina's on the way, please?"

"Sure," replied Aoifa. "Now, no dressing up too much, Mairy, not for an evening with the Kellys."

"No, Ma."

Clara sidled up to her mother and whispered, "Mairy said sorry for the money, and she would pay me back, Ma."

Aoifa wanted to believe it and smiled. "Lovely, Lara, so she will."

After they had all finished a snack and Padraig had hurriedly changed, they jumped into the car, Lois and Siobhan having walked on ahead to make more space. There was lots of hilarity on the journey and they soon arrived at Catrina's house as Mrs. Kelly opened the door.

"Well, how's ye, Aoifa?"

"Ach, well, Maureen, thanks. Off to the circus!"

"Yes, fun, to be sure. We'll take care of Mairead here, then. They be upstairs doin' I don't know what! Pick her up later, eh."

Aoifa shouted, "Have a nice time, Mairy!" but she'd gone already.

They soon reached the Big Top and Padraig found their seats. They didn't have long to wait before the band started up and the clowns came running in to rapturous applause, carrying a performing monkey which landed in Niamh's lap and stroked her face, making her laugh.

"Oh… how sweet is that…!" Then he pranced across to Clara as she squealed with delight, but Lois clicked her tongue and Niamh whispered to her,

"You like the animals under the sea, Lo, but I like them to have four legs!"

"Well, we got them covered, then, ain't we?" She smiled back at her sister.

In came the team of prancing ponies looking very glamorous with their grand headdresses. The acrobats ran in and leapt onto their backs as if they could fly.

"Wow!" whispered Niamh. "How do they do that?"

"Their learning goes back centuries and is passed from one to t'other," Aoifa told her.

The music was loud and engaging and the horses note-perfect in their rhythm as Niamh tapped her feet to the beat.

"Do you think Rafa could do this, Pa?!"

"Nah, too wild, to be sure!"

When the horses left, the troupe of dancers came on, their routines perfectly synchronised as they skipped, twirled and somersaulted, smiling broadly at the crowd.

"You can do that, too!" her ma told her as Niamh was on the edge of her seat with her mouth wide open and her eyes glazed over.

"I wish," whispered Niamh.

The finale to the first half was a team effort, with the children on the smaller ponies and joined by a baby elephant.

"Would you look at that!" cried Clara.

There was huge applause and some stamping of feet as they left the arena to signal the interval.

Niamh sighed. "Phew, that was incredible, Ma! The musicians next!" She was enthralled whilst Lois took it more in her stride.

"Everyone to their own, Nevey – rather be on the beach mysel'."

For the opening of the second half, the clowns came tumbling into the arena followed by the dancing dogs. Next came the troupe of dancers and accomplished musicians, a collaboration of movement and music. Niamh couldn't help herself as she hopped onto the floorboards, her feet tapping away as much whooping went up from the crowd. As the performance finished, the whole troupe came in for a final bow and everyone stood up clapping furiously. For the finale, the leading horse entered with a young acrobat standing astride her. As they circled the arena, she jumped into the air, landing elegantly, over and over again, with impeccable timing. It was an amazing feat, and at the end, the young girl and her horse gave a bow. The evening drew to a close and there were sighs of appreciation as everyone got up to leave.

The family made their way back to Catrina's, talking animatedly all at once when their pa told them,

"I remember some of my family got involved with the circus and it's hard work as well as skill, you know. Every day they have to practise, but it becomes a way of life, too."

Clara said thoughtfully, "I'd rather be swimming instead of all that jumping about, Ma."

Aoifa looked unsurprised, and Conor murmured, "Me, too."

Niamh seemed to be lost in her own little world. Siobhan was sitting quietly next to Lois and muttered that she'd seen shooting stars and wished she could have eaten some of the candy floss she'd smelt. Lois was always philosophical about Siobhan's vivid imagination and nodded agreeably.

They soon arrived at the Kellys' house and Aoifa knocked on the door. She had to wait a while, then it opened.

"Sorry, Aoifa, I was up with the girls. They've gone off to bed now. Mairy said can she stay, and I drop her back in the morning?"

"Yes, that's fine, Maureen, thanks."

They resumed their journey in silence, everyone exhausted. When they arrived home, Niamh stayed down a while with her mother.

"You enjoyed this evening the most I think, Nevey?" Aoifa asked with a twinkle in her eye.

"I did, Ma. The best. In fact, the ringmaster came over to me after my step dancin' at the end."

"Oh, why?"

"He told me I was as good as any of his dancers!"

Aoifa smiled. "Well, that's a compliment, alright!"

Aoifa locked the front door, put the lights out and joined Padraig in their bedroom.

"This evening touched a chord with our Niamh, Pad."

"Hmm. She did enjoy it so. Did you see the rapture on her face?"

"Well, I saw her element of Fire in her; that to be sure of!" said Aoifa as she replayed in her mind the elation on Niamh's face.

The girls were up and about early the next morning, all sharing the fun of the night before over breakfast, then going their separate ways, as there was a knock at the door.

"Good mornin' to you, Maureen," Aoifa looked around. "Where's Mairy?"

"Erm, may I sit down, please, Aoifa?"

"Of course," said Aoifa, her voice trembling as she stood back to let her in.

"I'm sorry to say, I've some bad news."

Mrs. Kelly looked distraught, and she was wringing her hands. "Mairead's in hospital. You see, she sneaked out when we were all asleep last night. She's had treatment for poisoning."

Padraig looked at her gravely. "Poisoning, Maureen, what sort of poisoning? Did she eat something?"

"Well, no. Apparently she'd taken something. She's OK now, although weak."

Aoifa stood up and held on to the table.

"Is… is she still there, then?"

"She's to come home this morning," said Mrs. Kelly. "I think maybe she and Catrina shouldn't go out for a while. Let some time pass."

After a brief silence, Padraig shook his head in disbelief and took a formal stance.

"Well, thank you kindly, Maureen, for letting us know. We'll be fetching her soon. I'm very sorry for your trouble."

Aoifa touched her friend's shoulder as Maureen Kelly got up to leave. "The only person responsible for this, Maureen, is Mairead. We'll be speaking to her presently."

Grim-faced, Padraig stood up. "I'll see you out, then, and make my way to fetch her. No one else comes – she doesn't need an audience." And he left without another word.

When Aoifa was all alone, it felt like her world had turned upside down yet again. There was no future because she couldn't see it, and the present was too painful to contemplate. Aoifa put her face in her hands and sobbed, deep convulsive sobs, because she felt so useless, so weak. She had no insight to help her with the parenting of an errant teenager. She needed her messages! With this thought, Aoifa felt her grief disappear to be replaced with a bubbling anger. She picked up her coffee mug and threw it across the room as hard as she could, emitting a shrill, deafening scream. Lois and Niamh came rushing downstairs to find their mother kneeling on the floor with her head in her hands. They helped her up onto a chair without a word.

There was the sound of a car coming up the hill and the girls cleared away the broken cup as Aoifa took some deep breaths to try to prepare herself for what was to come.

When Mairead walked in, she caught her breath. She looked exhausted, bleary-eyed, her face ashen, her hair and clothes were a mess.

"I'm taking her straight up to bed," Padraig announced. "They said she must rest."

As Mairead walked passed her ma, she didn't look at her.

When Padraig came back down, he too looked pale and upset.

Aoifa summoned some strength, made a pot of tea and asked him with some trepidation,

"Whatever had she taken, Pad?"

"She was the worse for wear with drink and…" He looked out of the window.

"What, Pad, what else?"

"She had taken drugs of some sort. They weren't sure."

Padraig had a sad, serious expression as he sat down at the table and it came to Aoifa that he couldn't, and shouldn't, carry this alone. She had to be strong too.

Lois spoke up, "To be honest, Pa, these things are easy to get hold of now."

"Is that so?" said Aoifa, in a voice that didn't belong to her. "Then we need to have a good talk with her, Pad. And soon."

"If she weren't so big, I'd tan her backside and more, that I would!" Padraig shouted, frightening the girls.

"That you wouldn't, Padraig O'Brien!"

Aoifa felt her anger returning, yet she knew that approach would help no one.

"We must turn her ideas around, Aoif. Before it's too late. She needs to know the dangers of these things. She's only fourteen!"

"Nearly fifteen, Pad. But she can't go on like…"

Aoifa's face crumpled and Padraig put his arm around her.

"Don't be frettin' now. We'll all pull together, Aoif. Anyhow, she's safe and asleep for the moment."

"It'll all be OK," Aoifa replied but without any conviction whatsoever and Padraig stood up with renewed vigour.

"Come on, Lo, you wanted a ride down at the beach, eh?"

"OK, Pa," Lois said reluctantly.

Aoifa immediately went upstairs, picked up her mother's photograph and looked out of the open window.

"Ma. Please help me. You've always been there for us. What can I do? Can you send me just one last message!"

She emitted a sob and waited, but nothing came to lighten her load. There were clouds lurking outside with no hint of sunshine, only the promise of a storm, as Padraig had said. She remembered her ma's parting words. She had to look out for her girls – was it Mairead now? She thought it was Clara or Siobhan.

Aoifa felt totally overwhelmed. "Stop the world, Ma, I want to get off," she muttered in her desperation. She didn't know how long she sat there, just that it was getting dark when there was a knock on her bedroom door.

"Ma? You in here?"

She sat up straight, attempting to conceal her torment as the question flashed through her mind: *Why do I always want to bury everything?*

"Yes, Nevey. Come in. Just relaxing a while."

"Ma, I've decided. I'm going to join the circus."

17. AOIFA'S TRUTH

Early one morning, Aoifa was sitting at her dressing table brushing her hair when there was a knock at the door.

"Ma?"

"Yes, Nevey?"

Aoifa looked at her daughter as she entered, a radiant smile on her face.

"Come here. Let me look at you," Aoifa said. "I am proud of you, you know."

"Are you, Ma? Are you happy for me, too?"

Padraig came out of the bathroom and replied, "We both are, Nevey. You must follow your dreams, as I did. Your ma will vouch for that!" They smiled happily at her.

"Thank you." Niamh breathed a sigh of relief. "I will miss you all but not too much, I hope."

"You won't have time for that, chara. Dancing, music and song will fill your life!" Aoifa exclaimed.

"Yes. Only five weeks to wait!" Niamh whispered and left the room in a state of euphoria, skipping and dancing as she went.

"That was only bravado, Pad," said Aoifa, tears spilling down her face as she put her arms around him and thought, *there I go again, burying my true feelings*.

"I know, chara," he replied.

A month had passed since the drugs incident with Mairead, and they were having a talk with her before school that morning.

"Come and sit with us, Mairy," said Padraig warmly and they all sat on the sofa in the snug with Mairead between them.

Her pa spoke first. "I must say, chara, it's been great having you around lately and you do well with those rams. They can be a handful, but you have them eating out of your hands!" he added with a wink.

Mairead had an expectant look about her but said nothing.

"I've enjoyed your company too, Mairy, and you've been a great help. Not been that bad being around your family, has it?" asked Aoifa with an impish grin.

Mairead considered her reply, her face downcast.

"No, Ma. It's been good, but I miss my friends."

"Not anything else, I hope?" her pa asked.

"No, not anything else, Pa," she replied indignantly.

"I've been speaking to your form teacher, Mairy."

"Oh no, not another lecture, Ma!"

"Hear your mother out, now," Padraig interjected.

"She tells us your maths is excellent and apparently you're a whizz on the computer too," she said brightly, but Mairead was disgruntled.

"So? You know I hate school!"

"Well, it's encouraging to hear her comments, surely, Mairy. I've been thinking, you love to read and so do I, so we could pop to the library each week, combine with a shopping trip?" Aoifa smiled at her. "And your pa and I could surely do with some help on the computer! You're good with the livestock too and sorting the seaweed and you can put your culinary skills to use anytime!"

Padraig looked at Mairead in earnest. "I think what your mother is saying, Mairy, is you've plenty to offer – look at y'self, gal! You don't need all that alcohol to get attention. Glossy locks like a true gypsy girl... My looks, eh?"

He gave her a cheeky smile and added more quietly,

"You are beautiful, chara, but drink takes that away – changes your lovely character, making you ill and... er... drugs, well, they can be lethal."

"Yeah, thanks, Pa. I know all that now."

"We would like to trust you out with your friends, Mairy, but can you see how it worries us, after the last time?"

"I do," said Mairead, and suddenly she brightened. "Mrs. Kelly had an idea!"

"Ah, what might that be?" Padraig asked.

"Catrina has a cousin, Eileen. She's nineteen, and is willing to chaperone me to the youth club if that's OK?"

Aoifa looked across at Padraig doubtfully. "Well, chara, can we meet Eileen before we agree to anything? And maybe Catrina can come over here sometimes, too?"

Her pa added encouragingly, "Give all this a go, eh? Put that fire and passion to good use, Mairy?"

Mairead nodded, giving her parents a small smile as she and the girls left for school.

"Well, Pad, she's been very accommodating this past month and has paid all the money back now. Let's see about this Eileen, then?"

"Ach, OK. We have to set her free sometime. Have faith that a guiding light will shine down on 'er an' she'll turn a corner."

Padraig left for work, but his body language told her that he was none too sure, and if Aoifa were honest, nor was she.

After lunch, Aoifa was taking Rafa on a surprise visit to see Rachel, with Flynn too. The sky was a clear blue flecked with pink fluffy clouds, the promise of a hot afternoon. Aoifa's head was full of her family's wandering and wayward ways as she and Rafa walked along. Her most vibrant daughter was leaving them, taking her music and colour with her. She would miss her with all her heart, and she didn't see it coming. "Damn it, Ma!" feeling immediately ashamed, yet it made her feel angry sometimes, this lack of knowing, creating confusion as if her head were full of cotton wool. And what about Mairead? Hmm. Mairead was on a different journey entirely, but at least their talk had gone well that morning; that to be grateful for. Siobhan was a bit of a closed book, but surely the door would open and gradually she would let them in. She would think about Lois later.

They turned off the beach, soon reaching the moorland, which was covered in bright yellow gorse, sea lavender and white and blue heather in striking abundance, and she breathed in the heady scents as they walked by. The sun was beating down through the canopy above, rays of sunshine illuminating the colours of nature. They soon reached the stream and there was no hurry as they all stopped for a rest.

"Rafa, your life is so straight-forward. You don't have decisions to make, just going with what life throws at you, yet I guess you too have to work out the answers, eh?"

Rafa just shook his head and gave a snort in response.

Aoifa clambered up onto a rock and took out her lunch from her rucksack. She glimpsed out through the trees, spotting a large cruiser in the distance, no doubt making its way toward New York. It brought her thoughts to Lois, where she too would be headed soon. Her two daughters with their exuberance of youth gone from Muir Farm to place their roots elsewhere. Aoifa sighed. When they all left, would she just be a void without the surrounding energy? Would her thoughts ever contain that vitality of old? A feeling of guilt suddenly came over her – had she been bossy with the girls when the messages came, smug even? Rubbish. She cared for her girls, always leading with her heart. She quickly pushed the thought away, knowing her overriding motive had always been to protect them.

Aoifa's thoughts drifted to Rachel, and she felt excitement about seeing her as she jumped back onto Rafa, who was waiting patiently. She would get some water for him and Flynn at the pub as the heat from the sun intensified.

They set off slowly in the bright sunshine, winding their way through the ferns and brackens as the ground bees buzzed around them, soon reaching the road as the pub came into view, and there was Rachel hanging out some washing.

"Hi, Rach!" she shouted.

"Aoifa! I didn't know you were coming…"

"Wanted to surprise you. Oh my goodness, you look blooming!"

"Four months gone and feeling on top o' the world!"

"It suits you, Rach. Pad and I are so delighted for you both." Aoifa dismounted and they both hugged. "The best Christmas present ever, the patter of tiny feet!"

"Yeah," said Rachel, grinning happily. "Come in, I'll make some tea."

Aoifa loosed Rafa into the paddock, filling a bucket with water for him and Flynn as the two girls linked arms and went into the pub.

"Bren – we have a guest!"

"Aoifa! Come to share our good news, no doubt!"

"The best. And you'll have the school ready for him or her too!"

"Him," said Rachel.

"Wow! To help with the heavy stuff, eh, Bren?"

"To cause havoc more like!" Brendan replied with a grin.

"Huh… gotta be easier than girls!"

They took their tea to sit on the patio, overlooking the moors.

"Phew. Hot for you, Rach?"

"Nah. Used to reach forty degrees in the tropics."

"Didn't get the Atlantic storms over there, though?"

"No, and I missed them, but I may eat my words one day with climate change. Anyway, how is everyone, Aoif?"

"OK, thanks, but with some changes ahead."

"Oh?"

"Niamh is leaving us. She captivated the circus folk! Maybe just for a while… who knows?"

"What about her schooling, then?"

"Well, she's got all her GCSEs and it's what she wants. You know, with her passion for music and dance… now acrobatics too. I will so miss her," she added, welling up.

"I know you will." Rachel squeezed her hand. "I expect she'll visit, though."

"Lois is waiting on her interview with the WWF. She's not saying much, talks to her da, not me. Who knows why."

"Can't you tell her what's comin' then, Aoif?" said Rachel, her eyes twinkling.

Aoifa was quiet as she gathered her thoughts. She helped herself to a piece of cake, averting her eyes as Rachel waited patiently.

"I must tell you, Rach. I no longer have the second sight. It went with Ma. It's still causing me anxiety with the kids asking things, too," she said bleakly.

Rachel looked puzzled. "But I thought you were born with the gift of it, Aoif. Where can it have gone?"

She shrugged. "I have to cope with life as it comes now like everyone else," she added with a forced smile. "Finding it quite a challenge if I'm honest. Mairead is the biggest problem. She's been out drinking and worse."

"She'll mend her ways, Aoif, once it's out of her system, you watch."

"I truly hope so. Anyway, enough of my woes!"

Aoifa wiped her eyes, composing herself. "You know summer every year, we have a bit of a do. We thought – a beach party?"

"Oohh… be fab! We can all help."

"Only if we do it before you get too big!"

"Oh you!" said Rachel, giving her friend a playful punch. "Bet you never got big!"

"Don't you believe it, bigger with each one!"

"Oh nooo," Rachel groaned.

They both laughed and walked slowly along the path out toward the wood, going over old times.

"Hey, Aoif, heard anything from Laurel?"

Aoifa looked away. "Not lately, no. She's been seeing a bit of Sean, though."

"Yeah. D'you think they're suited?"

"Not sure. Time will tell. Have you noticed a change in he…?"

"In what, Aoif?" But Aoifa shrugged and changed the subject.

"Hey, how's the school coming on?"

"Main building's finished next week! We're planning the landscape now, with a forest school in the wood nearby. It's all so exciting."

"I'll say. Unbelievable."

Aoifa looked out across the moorland. "Will you look over there – must be young grouse nesting in the summer heathers. I see young gannets and terns on the seashore too."

They both wandered on quietly, watching the moorland birds picking their way across the wetlands.

"Listen, Aoif, any time you want to talk… but you'll know what to do, for sure."

"Thanks, Rach, you're a good friend. I've so missed our chats."

Aoifa felt cheered as she returned to Rafa for their journey home when Rachel whispered some parting words,

"Two down, three to go. In the nicest possible way – time for you and Pad, eh?"

Aoifa smiled at her thoughtfully and waved as Rafa trotted off with Flynn running along behind. It was late afternoon when they reached the woodland, with shadows and the quiet of dusk approaching.

"Rachel is so wise, Raf. Must be all that travelling. Nothing phases her, even having a baby at forty. But then she always had to make her own mind up, not like me, having it done for me.

Spoilt I am, had nothing to worry about, till now. Time for me and your da, apparently." Rafa bobbed his head up and down in response. "It's OK for you. All you have to worry about is the weather!"

Aoifa pondered on that, looking out at the azure sky, a burnt orange sun and a mere wisp of wind, but she knew a storm could come across the Atlantic at any time. Rachel had mentioned climate change too, so it must be real, as she would know the science behind it. Aoifa told herself she needed to be more aware of it, catch up with the rest of her family. Especially now, as she no longer knew what was coming.

"Come on, Rafa, your ma's got stuff to do!" She let Rafa go, giving him free reign as they took off at speed. Aoifa gripped skilfully with her knees, allowing him to dictate the rhythm of his stride, kicking up clouds of sand as he went. She felt the exhilaration, and as she leaned forward, she could see the soft waves coming slowly toward them. Throwing back her head, Aoifa laughed loudly, her hair tangled and free, her arms and legs naked to the elements, Rafa's ears pricking up as the farm came into view. As they reached the end of the bay, he slowed to a gentle trot and Aoifa turned to smile at Flynn as he caught up.

"Well done, Raf. Good going in this heat."

She petted him affectionately and they soon reached Padraig, who was sorting his seaweed on the edge of the bay.

"Hi, Pad, what a gorgeous day!"

"Nice to see Rachel?"

"Definitely. Given me some new ideas, too!" She carried on past him, leaving Padraig with his mouth gaped open.

When the girls came in from school, they prepared a salad. Aoifa picked some summer fruits and Padraig cleaned the rotisserie ready to roast their home-bred pork. They all sat around way into the evening until the sun began to set, a wonderful midsummer sight, as it slowly disappeared behind the clouds on the edge of the sea.

As dawn broke the next morning, with swirling hot mists along the horizon and a bright pink sun peeking out above the hills behind the house, Clara and Mairead were up early baking cakes when Aoifa walked into the kitchen.

"Another glorious day, girls! Let's have a special tea in the sun later! First, I'll race you all down to the beach for a swim!"

At 5pm, tea was laid out on the patio and Aoifa called the family together. Clara had picked a posy of flowers, so the table looked a blaze of colour with scones, jam, pretty cakes and sandwiches.

"Oh, Ma, this looks a treat!" Niamh exclaimed.

"All the work of Clara and Mairead this time."

As everyone sat down, Mairead exclaimed, "I recommend the lemon drizzle!" whilst Clara cried, "No! Chocolate one's best."

Their pa settled the argument. "Well, I think we'll all be havin' a piece of each anyways!"

It was a happy family scene as they chatted and enjoyed their tea in the blistering afternoon sun. Aoifa helped herself to some more tea, then tapped a cup for silence.

"Now, as you all know, we usually have a summer party, but I'd found the prospect rather daunting, then your da and I had a talk…" And with that, all the girls shouted at once, with Mairead the loudest.

"Oh, please, Ma, down on the beach, like before, yes!"

Clara added, "And I'll make the cakes again!"

Aoifa told them definitively that alcohol would only be for the grown-ups and the disheartened look on Mairead's face didn't escape her as she carried on. "…with family and friends too, in August, for Mairead's and your pa's birthday. Also to say our farewells to Niamh."

Her voice broke, but she was beaming at everyone.

"Now, there's one more thing," said Aoifa as she looked around to catch their attention once more. "I need to tell you something very important."

She glanced across at Niamh, who shot her a knowing look. Padraig caught her eye too, raising an eyebrow as a hush came over the group.

"Have you all noticed I've not enlightened you with any messages, any foresight, these past months?"

Aoifa looked around at the girls, waiting for a response, and Mairead spoke first, "You didn't tell us about the snow or the storms, did you, Ma? Or," she whispered quietly, "even me."

"An' you didn't know about Rachel's baby," said Siobhan.

"Or great Aunt Beth, Ma," added Lois.

Aoifa shook her head.

"An' you didn't know about Grandma? Or Conor coming?" Clara said meekly.

"You see, girls, I know nothing of the future anymore."

Aoifa's voice was shaking. "My second sight passed with your grandma. So I cannot help nor warn you of what lies ahead. We'll all have to cope with life as it comes now."

She felt the blood draining from her face as she looked around with bated breath, waiting for the shock to subside and the storms of protest to begin. There would be an outcry surely – but nothing happened. Open, disbelieving faces looked at their mother, but no one spoke. Aoifa didn't know what to make of it.

"Well, aren't you going to gripe or groan or something? I can tell you no more of your future!"

Still nothing. Aoifa decided to ask them one at a time. "Girls, this has been a real worry for me and I need to know how you all feel. Lo?"

Lois looked awkward as she fiddled with her empty glass.

"Well, Ma, I don't mind. I quite like not knowing what lies ahead."

Aoifa nodded her acknowledgement, unsurprised.

"Niamh?"

"Actually, I'm not sure it will affect me, as I've decided on my future anyway!" she said with a wide smile and her mother smiled back.

"Mairead? I was hoping to be able to guide you, warn you perhaps, but it's not to be."

"So, it means you'll never know what I'll be doin' in future, Ma?" asked Mairead as a flicker of a smile crossed her face.

"I don't think I will ever know, no, Mairy," Aoifa told her gloomily. "Sheve?"

"Well, I have my imagination, Ma, so I'll be OK, I think."

Aoifa might have guessed Siobhan would be circumspect. "Clara?"

Clara had had time to think. "Well, maybe Grandma took it away because she wanted to give it to someone else, Ma?"

Her parents looked at her thoughtfully as it flitted through Aoifa's mind, *Mairead perhaps.*

That would help her, but she replied, "You may be right, chara."

Padraig had been listening to the conversation.

"Your ma has helped us all these years. Now we have to start figuring things out for ourselves. We'll all be OK if we go with our own truth, our own hearts." He smiled one of his enchanting smiles and they all smiled back.

Aoifa and Padraig continued to sit in the garden as the sun went down, a golden ball of purple in front of them. There were wisps of light cloud coming across the sky and a hazy mist was hanging above the inky blue of the sea, giving a sense of mystery to the surrounding landscape. Aoifa felt enormous relief that she'd come clean about her own truth and that the girls had taken it so well. Padraig put his arm around her as she looked out at the night closing in, the sky now full of stars like a million miniature pearls of wisdom. Aoifa had no foresight anymore, but she hoped with all her heart that some positive energy had passed between them that afternoon which would help to guide her family toward a promising future. In particular, she felt they had definitely made a breakthrough with Mairead, as she had left the table with a jovial grin on her face.

18. FAMILY VALUES

After her truth had come out, Aoifa was watchful to see if there were any repercussions, but everyone went about their lives much the same as before. Maybe the girls were better prepared for the world than she had previously thought. As she planted her vegetable seedlings, Aoifa's mind whirred around the subject. *But what of my fate? Well, I'm just not meant to know that anymore, but how can I reconcile with that?* Aoifa sighed and turned her thoughts to good times ahead.

She was really looking forward to their summer party, an opportunity for some proper family time with Padraig's and Mairead's birthdays too. Mairead. She certainly seemed to have turned a corner since they had Eileen on board, who was proving to have a positive influence on their wayward daughter.

As Aoifa stopped for a tea break in the searing heat, Padraig came over to join her and she welcomed him with a big hug.

"Greet me like that anytime!" He made to grab her, but Aoifa pushed him away good-naturedly and went to put the kettle on.

"Mairead came home on time again Friday, Pad. She's really trying hard. I've seen a change in her, too."

"Well, her time-keeping has improved. What changes do you see, then?"

"She's become thoughtful, quieter. She's probably taking her studies more seriously."

Padraig rubbed his chin. "But I've not seen her studying much, chara? She spends a bit of time reading and on the computer…"

"Well, we suggested that, Pad. There's one week to go before her exams. Let's trust her now."

Padraig nodded and carried their tea out to the patio where they sat in a shady spot.

"Didn't they take the loss of my messages well? I'm so relieved. M'bes they're all glad, Pad? M'be they thought I was always interfering!"

"Nah. They're growing up, is what it is."

"You're right. I just wish I felt grown up about it!"

"You've been OK so far, though, right? No more worries now. Gotta finish some repairs afore weather breaks." He made to go. "See you later."

Aoifa's thoughts were interrupted when the gate clattered and Niamh came rushing in, her eyes sparkling.

"The ringmaster called me today, Ma. He's such a cool guy! Wants me t' go Saturday mornings to get to know the ropes."

"Good idea, Nevey. Be nice to get to know everyone before you start," she said with forced enthusiasm.

Niamh nodded agreeably and took herself off to change. Aoifa sighed then Clara suddenly appeared behind her.

"Hi, Ma!"

"Hey, you!" Aoifa turned, punched her playfully and looked around. "Where are Siobhan and Mairy, then?"

Siobhan suddenly ran past her. "I'm here, Ma. The air is burning. Can you smell it? Hot. Sounds like a desert island?"

Aoifa laughed, shaking her head. "Where's Mairy, Sheve?"

"Not sure. She may have gone to Catrina's."

Hmm, Aoifa thought, *it's only Thursday*. "Didn't Lois bring you all in the car?"

"No, we walked. She had to see the school secretary."

Aoifa raised an eyebrow, but the girls knew no more. She carried on preparing the vegetables when Lois came rushing up the path, bright-eyed, her face flushed.

"Ma – you'll never guess what? I have to go to America… next week and I can't believe…"

"Lo, sit down. Clara, fetch your da."

Aoifa put her arm around her daughter's shoulders.

"Oh, Lois. I knew you could do it."

Padraig came to the door looking very agitated. "What's up in here?"

"Lois has some news!" said Aoifa.

"I have a trial period, Pa, with the World Wildlife Fund. I have to go to America for a week! What d'you think of that?"

Lois' hair was all over the place, her face red with excitement as she paced up and down the kitchen.

"I had an online interview – sorry I didn't tell you, but…"

"No matter, chara. Main thing – it went well!"

"I'm liking it! No… I'm loving it!" Lois took off upstairs, laughing, and Aoifa knew she would never look back. It was written all over her face. Yet, it was a joy to see Lois' happiness; this was her dream come true. Then it crossed her mind that she felt quite different from when Niamh announced her imminent departure from the fold.

"Maureen? I'm sorry to trouble you, but is Mairead with you?"

"Yes, she was, Aoifa. They have a Speaker's night at the club. Eileen will drop her back later. Didn't she tell you?"

"She must've forgot. Thank you, Maureen, and sorry to be a bother. Just being a mother hen, you know."

"Yes, I know," said Maureen in an understanding tone.

Early the next morning, the day was already warm, but Aoifa noticed some heavy clouds on the horizon as Padraig pulled on his waterproofs.

"Is there a storm due, my love?"

"Yeah, reckon so, Aoif. I'll be off to work with Roma before it catches us."

"We need rain. The air is so heavy."

She put her arms around his neck affectionately.

"Hey, what's that for?" A smile curled around his lips.

"No reason, my love. Just take care."

"Save it for later, though…"

He gave her a cheeky look and was gone just as Lois came skipping down the stairs.

"Wow!" she cried.

"A celebration breakfast for everyone, Lo! It's not often you get to go to America. You know, you've partly your uncle Liam to thank for it, too."

"Yes, it was really kind of him. I'll give him a call."

"Well, tell him about our summer party too, eh? Be after you get back and just before Niamh goes…"

Aoifa's words faltered, and she was aware of Lois watching her as she continued cooking.

"It's OK, Ma. Nevey and I will both be happy, and you've still got Pa, haven't you?"

Aoifa started, as she didn't understand the comment, but let it go and called the girls down for breakfast.

"You off down the beach this morning, Lo?"

"Sure. I've something to check on. You want to come along?"

"Can I? Be lovely, take a walk too."

Encouraged by the pleasant channel of communication between them, Aoifa smiled to herself and they soon set off as she looked out at the threatening clouds coming their way.

"Your da says the rains are comin'."

"We need some, Ma. Phew!" said Lois as they reached the cave. "I've been treating an otter with an injured foot, so m'be you need to hang back?"

"Sure. I'll sit an' watch out for the storm!"

"Hey, look – she's waddling toward me, escaped her pen! Ready to leave now, me thinks."

"Your calling has come, Lo – to work with these animals."

"Yes. I hope so, with all my heart."

"Will you look at those horses frolicking an' your da trying to catch them, too! You get on, Lo, I'll wait here a minute."

Aoifa sat on a nearby rock, amused by the horses' refusal to co-operate. It focussed her mind and helped her to stay calm. She and Lois may be about to have a significant conversation and she so wanted it to go well.

Lois soon returned and they both watched the otter making its way across the sand, back to its natural habitat. It was a moving scene because Aoifa knew it was one which heralded Lois' future.

"All good, Ma. She's fine now."

"Brilliant. Another life saved," said Aoifa and they both set off for their walk.

"Lo, I wanted to ask you something. Have you no concerns about my lack of messages?"

Aoifa observed her daughter carefully, noticing a wisp of a smile cross her face as Lois avoided eye contact and considered her reply.

"I actually think it will change our relationship forever, Ma."

At this, Aoifa started to tremble. She couldn't see Lois' face because her froth of red hair had fallen forwards and turned away to conceal her anguish.

"That's what I was afraid of, chara." She wrung her hands and watched the turbulent sea, congruent with the torment she felt inside and a pained expression on her face.

"No, Ma. You misunderstand. I mean for the better." Lois turned, giving her a big smile.

"What do you mean, Lo? I can't tell…"

"That's just it, Ma. I never really wanted to know my future anyways!"

As Lois rejoiced triumphantly, Aoifa didn't know whether to feel relieved or bewildered. Ah well, best not dwell on it, not now, at any rate. Lois was happy. That was the main thing. They hugged one another and slowly made their way back home. Aoifa felt an immediate shift in their relationship and with it a freedom from responsibility which she had never expected.

The family had finished clearing up after supper that evening when there were loud rumblings overhead. Padraig was right – a storm was coming – then the heavens opened. Luckily, the horses were safe in their stables and all the livestock were inside the barns, with Flynn indoors.

"Well, the garden needs it, Pad."

"Yes, everything needs a soaking, the crop field and water tanks too. Just don't want more than we bargained for." He looked gloomily out of the kitchen window.

"I'm going to help Lois upstairs now. Will you…"

"Yeah, I'll keep my eye on the storm, as they say."

The atmosphere between her and Lois had definitely improved as they enjoyed an easy exchange in her bedroom.

"What do you think they'll be like, Ma, in WWF? Young like me or old fuddy-duddies like you and Pa? But now you won't know – just have to guess like the rest of us!"

"Hey, that's enough, young lady! I think the team you work with are likely to be young – university students maybe?"

"But Ma, I'm not one of those, am I?" said Lois nervously.

"No, but they obviously think you've plenty to offer anyways… Now what will the weather be…"

Before she could finish her sentence, there was an almighty crash outside and Aoifa yelled over the bannister, "What was that, Pad?" but he had already left the house.

Aoifa looked out of Lois' bedroom window, craning her neck to look back at the sea. Late spring tides were coming, and colossal waves were crashing mercilessly onto the beach.

Suddenly, Padraig threw open the front door.

"Aoif, the tides are rising over the fence below, there's flooding and more to come… Can you help?"

Aoifa quickly threw on her waterproofs and ran out to face the storm. The winds had picked up and she struggled to stay upright as she and Padraig secured the barn doors and their equipment.

Making their way toward the bottom fields, the heavy rain burned Aoifa's face and sea mist obscured her vision as she pushed forward. The giant waves were encroaching onto their boundary now, huge walls of water ravaging the lower fields. A fence had already been taken and their sheep shed was at risk. It was an unimaginable sight. The rain came down in sheets, blossom was stripped from the summer plants and the ancient trees blew horizontal, when all of a sudden a shaft of silver lightning lit up the treacherous sea and Padraig yelled up to her, "Aoifa… stay there! It's violent…"

She stopped in her tracks and watched in horror as he tried to hold the shed on the lower edge of the field, but then it went. With one almighty deluge, it was taken over the wall. The waves continued to overwhelm the field, momentous in height and landing with tremendous force, taking their shed right out to sea. Aoifa stifled a sob, a feeling of terror coming over her as she watched Padraig take the full force of a wave, disappearing for a moment, but then he surfaced with difficulty and, before a second onslaught, managed to retreat back up the hill.

They both stood in the porch and watched in vain as the storm continued to rage, taking their old wall too as it collapsed into a pile of rubble.

Aoifa began to tremble, and Padraig put his arms around her.

"It's OK, chara. It'll come no higher. Can all be mended."

They both knew the threat would diminish as the tide slowly turned, and as the worst passed, they took themselves indoors to dry off.

"No more worries, girls. A bad'un this time, but it's all fixable."

A general quietness came over the family that evening as they listened to the storm gradually moving away, the prospect of summer returning, and Padraig reassured them,

"The tempest abates and safe for bed now."

When they were all alone, Aoifa burst into tears.

"I should have known, Pad, about the storm. We could have saved…"

"Ach, no, chara. We could have saved nothing. Now, stop."

He stroked her hair and Aoifa eventually rallied.

"Pad, I've had a thought…" she said, sniffing, but feeling brighter.

"Chara, don't worry about the storm. It's only taken an old shed an' a bit o' wall. Safe 'ere up on the hill…"

"Then why do you look so worried, Padraig O'Brien?"

"Ach… my livelihood threatened, I guess! Need to check all the kelp enclosures. Not to worry for now."

"Anyway, it's not that," she told him with a secretive smile.

"Oh?"

"Fetch us some wine and I'll tell you my plan!"

When Padraig returned and poured out a glass each, Aoifa continued.

"The kids are growing – and going – and we need to replace the void with a bit of fun! So every Thursday, we'll go to dinner, theatre, cinema, day trips, visit friends…"

"A date, you mean?"

"Exactly!"

"Why, Aoifa, do we need it?"

"No, I don't think so – but it'll be nice anyway!" Aoifa told him breezily.

"Does it include… you know…?"

"Oh you!"

"Because we could have a practice now if you like… take our minds off that storm, eh?" He took his wife into his arms and the night stretched out long ahead of them.

The day came to take Lois to the airport for her trip to America, and as she was due to leave, Lois turned to her mother.

"Thank you for everything, Ma, and for not telling me what lies ahead. Now it will be a real adventure!"

Aoifa couldn't speak, as tears poured down her face.

"It's only for a week, Ma, not a year!"

"I know, and you'll be fine. We all love you. *Slán!*"

Aoifa shouted goodbye in their local dialect and Lois reciprocated. She jumped in the car and Padraig drove off as Aoifa turned to Niamh.

"Be your turn next, chara." She shook her head in disbelief at the imminent fragmentation of her close-knit family.

The family sat around the patio table and Aoifa thought of something to cheer everyone up.

"Let's plan that party for when she comes home – we've less than three weeks!" Aoifa announced.

"My party?" Mairead's face lit up.

"No, Mairead, not yours. Everyone's. It just happens to be near your birthday!"

Great discussions ensued and no one could agree on who to invite, so Aoifa gave in and told the girls everyone could come.

"A lot of work – but then I have you all to help, don't I?!" She told them firmly but with a grin on her face.

When the girls went their separate ways and Aoifa sat alone, she could hear a soft melody on the piano, faltering, quiet, then it stopped. She waited, and it started again, a familiar tune, an Irish folksong. Clara was getting better. Aoifa was overcome once more. Oh, how much she loved these girls and now one was gone. Rubbish! Only for a week. *Now get on, Aoifa O'Brien!*

After a few days of Padraig being quieter than usual, she knew he was missing Lois, so decided a ride out together would be good for later that day when Aoifa spotted the postman coming up the drive.

"How do, Reg. Anything much today?"

"Yon got sommat official 'ere, lass."

Aoifa frowned and took the white envelope from him.

"Thanks, Reg. Be nothin', just some votin' stuff for the elections."

As she went inside, Aoifa felt more concern than she had shown to Reg. It was a letter from the school, which she opened quickly. As she read it, her legs felt weak, and she sat down. Apparently, Mairead had been missing school and had many pieces of homework outstanding. She breathed deeply to compose herself and decided she wouldn't jump to conclusions until they had both spoken with her. Aoifa mechanically went about her chores that day, and when Padraig came in for lunch, her stomach was churning as she artfully avoided eating much, telling him, "Come up and have some tea with us around 5pm, Pad?"

Padraig looked surprised but didn't question it.

"OK, sure. See you later."

Mairead walked in at the usual time.

"Hi, Ma, so hot today."

"For sure, Mairy. How's your day, busy?"

"So-so. Just got to ring Catrina." She took off to her bedroom.

A while later, Aoifa took out the strawberry muffins she had made earlier and, as Padraig came in, called Mairead down to join them.

"Phew, another hot one!" he announced. "Calm as a mill pond now. These weather systems!" shaking his head.

Aoifa looked at them soberly. "Sit down, both. Pad, we had a letter from the school."

Mairead took an intake of breath. "What about, Ma?" she asked, and Padraig looked from one to the other.

"So, you've been missing lessons and there are numerous pieces of homework outstanding, Mairead." She turned to Padraig. "Just when we thought things were all good – and exams coming up too."

"Ah, that's where they're wrong, Ma. They think I've been skiving off, but I haven't, see!"

"Tell us more, Mairead," said her father sharply.

"It's like this. I took on board your suggestions for improving my maths, and the computers in the library are brand new, so I've been in there…"

"So where's the homework, then?"

"Still there, Da!" Mairead explained with a bright smile. "They hadn't any paper, but I can print it all tomorrow."

As she and Padraig exchanged glances, Aoifa visibly relaxed.

"That's a relief, Mairy. Make sure you hand them in, then, and I'll call the office."

"Sure, Ma. Can I go now?"

Aoifa nodded, smiling gratefully at her daughter. Nearly fifteen, a worrisome age, to be sure!

After she had left, Padraig turned to Aoifa, "Did you look into her eyes, Aoif? D'you think she was tellin' the truth?"

"Yes, of course I do. It's not always written in the eyes, Pad!" said Aoifa with a little chuckle. "You and your gypsy ways! You're makin' too much of it."

Mairead came downstairs a few minutes later. Her parents were still in the kitchen, and as she passed them by, she called out, "Your gonna have to trust me, Ma and Pa, as I'm soon to be the oldest, you know!"

She gave them a saucy look and disappeared outside.

Aoifa's heart missed a beat as the reality of what Mairead had said hit her. But just maybe her ma was shining a light down on her errant daughter and their family values would be upheld.

Everything would turn out grand then and Mairy would be fine. Perhaps they should treat her more responsibly, though, and maybe she could do some babysitting for their date nights in the future.

Aoifa smiled indulgently to herself at the thought.

19. THE SEA MACHINE

When Laurel arrived, there was no one at Home Farm, so she went outside to look around. Shielding her eyes against the sun, she could just make them out. Aaron, Sean and Conor were bringing the cattle over with Casey and Brody to the fresh grass by the house. "I don't know why they go to this trouble every week, takin' them cattle back and fore. Beats me," Laurel said to herself as she made her way back then picked up the phone.

"Hi, Aoif. What's new? Lois – interview in America? Wow. Got meself a week's holiday, to help with the party. Be grand. See yuz Monday!"

As she made her way upstairs, Laurel pondered over Lois' departure. *Like her da that one*, she thought, *with the ole wanderlust, stuck up an' all.*

Laurel looked around the bedroom at her belongings scattered everywhere and chuckled. She'd more or less taken over the room! Then she heard the boys coming in, deep in conversation.

"Ach, Da. It's na ready, yet."

"I think get Liam's take on it, lad, afore it's finished?"

Laurel didn't catch the reply but crept down to the hallway and listened at the kitchen door.

Then Conor spoke. "I canna keep it a secret from Clara much longer, Sean. Canny that one!" Laurel walked into the kitchen.

"Ach, lass, didn't see your car!" Aaron exclaimed.

"Did'na expect you, Lors. How long you stayin' then?" added Sean.

"I left a message yesterday – should listen to 'em once in a while, Sean. Stayin' long enough to see what youse all bin up to!" she replied with a sly smile.

Sean and Aaron exchanged glances and Laurel knew she'd overheard too much.

"I've brought us some nice steak fo' t'night!"

The boys all smiled – she knew they loved her cooking.

It was another scorching day, so she kept a low profile that afternoon, focussing instead on preparing a delicious meal, and they all came in to eat as the sun went down.

"Aoifa's comin' over t' see us on Monday," Laurel told them.

"Don' see enough of that gal," Aaron said, "what with Lois gone to America, although heaven knows why, and Niamh off to the circus! That's a turn up, eh?"

Laurel soon lost interest in the conversation and took herself up for a bath, leaving the boys to clear up, but she couldn't help lingering to listen to their chatter, as there seemed to be some secret afoot.

"So, if Aoifa's comin' over, Sean, let's get Liam too? They can take a look together?"

"Ach, you know they're divided, them two?"

"Not this time, lad."

"Be a first, then! I'll call him."

Laurel frowned. She didn't like Liam.

Since she'd convinced Aaron to refurbish the bathroom in pinks and greys, she always felt herself relax as soon as she entered. She lit a candle and filled the sumptuous claw-foot bath with a sea of bubbles, lowered herself in with a glass of wine, lay back and closed her eyes.

Laurel had decided the coming week would be pivotal in her relationship with Sean. She needed to know where she stood. As she lay luxuriating in the soft, scented bubbles, she considered her situation. Did Sean want her – or did he want a housekeeper? Because that was not in her life plan! With his mop of red hair and easy manner, he was quite a catch in a rugged sort of way, but he rarely made a move on her. It always had to come from her. She would do her very best this week. *Look good, cook good*, she thought with a smile, and yes, she would ask him outright what he wanted. He may blow her out, but she had to take that chance. She'd been coming here for over six months now and her time was running out.

The next morning, Laurel put on her swimsuit, ran out into the glorious sunshine and straight into Aaron.

"Ach, lass, the lads are on some repairs this mornin'. Can you help?"

Laurel groaned. "It's too hot for heavy work, Aaron. I need a swim first anyways! Just gimme an hour and I be there!"

Aaron's face fell, but he said nothing.

She carried on down to the beach and fell into the azure blue sea. It was so warm! As she was swimming her lengths, she saw Conor out of the corner of her eye making his way toward her and moaned. "What does he want?" Laurel didn't much care for Conor. He seemed to have eyes all over the place, real flighty. He didn't miss a thing and they rarely spoke.

As he reached the sea, he called out, "Um, Sean's callin' for yer."

Laurel ignored him and kept swimming. He came closer to the shore, and she could see him taking his shoes off.

"OK, OK. I'm comin'," she shouted gruffly, so Conor turned and headed back.

Laurel put on her towelling robe and made her way up to the yard, then she spotted Sean locking up the larger barn.

"So, what d'you want, Sean – and what d'you keep in there anyways?" she asked cheekily.

"Oh, nothin' much, lass, just stores and supplies. Help us wi' mendin' this fence now. Got blown in the storm."

She looked at him sulkily. "I'll get dressed first."

As she went indoors, Laurel knew there was something else in that large shed. He was always in there and it was kept locked. She put on her old jeans and t-shirt and went back to help them.

As they worked, Laurel had an idea.

"It's Sunday tomorrow, Sean, a day off! Such gorgeous weather. Let's go out for the day, to some private coves o'yonder – take a picnic. How about it?"

Sean was measuring the planks and didn't reply for a minute as Laurel waited patiently.

"Ach, big day on Monday, Lors. We got Liam comin' to discuss a bit o' business. I have to stick around and work tomorrow."

Laurel stood up and dropped the wood she was carrying.

"What's he comin' for, Sean? It's somethin' in there, isn't it?"

She pointed toward the locked door on the other side of the yard.

"M'bes," he replied without looking up.

"Well, what is it? Tell me, then!" she yelled at him, although Laurel knew this approach never worked with Sean. He simply shut down and usually walked off, but she couldn't help herself.

"I'll tell you soon enough, gal. But tomorrow's out!"

He looked her in the eye as if the matter was closed.

Laurel glared back and stamped her foot.

"Well, if you canna tell me, then I canna help you!"

She marched out of the yard, pushing past Conor, who was sweeping up, then called back to him fiercely,

"Youse can help him now!" and she went back down to the beach.

As she lay down on the soft sand, raising herself up onto her elbows and looking out to sea, Laurel's face was taut as anger raged inside her. As she lay there, breathing steadily, it slowly dissipated, and she decided to try once more to tempt Sean away the next day. She would tidy the house, make them a special meal, win him over with her charm. She was good at that. But suddenly a guilt crept over her. She'd been short with Conor, and Sean was fond of Conor. She'd better make good there, too.

Supper was a silent affair around the table that evening, then Sean spoke up,

"Now, young Laurel, everything's ready for Monday. So, where d'you wanna go t'morrow?"

"Yippee!" she cried as she gave him a peck on the cheek, but he scolded her lightly, wiping it off with the back of his hand.

"Steady on, now!"

She jumped up and fetched a mouth-watering dessert for the table. "Conor's favourite chocolate pudding!" she announced.

He gave a small smile, nodding his gratitude, and Laurel knew she had absolved herself.

The next day, the sun shone brightly through Laurel's bedroom window as she leapt out of bed, smiling and muttering to herself, "Today's the day!" After a quick shower, she put on her denim shorts to show off her bronzed legs and a pink floral off-the-shoulder blouse. She prepared their picnic, putting in Sean's favourites, pork pie, cheese and onion crisps and ham sandwiches. She'd even made some flapjacks for the occasion. As she popped some lunch for Aaron and Conor into the scullery, she selected a bottle of wine, then turned and grabbed another.

Laurel checked the time. It was already 11 o'clock and she looked outside just as Sean was crossing the yard.

"You ready, then?" she asked him, running over to take his hand.

"Och, chara, wouldn't touch them, been clearing the cattle shed…"

"Oh, yuk!" Laurel said in disgust and ran to the kitchen to wash as Sean went upstairs, chuckling to himself.

The promise of a lovely day stretched out ahead of them as they set off around the headland, which would take them to a small, secluded bay.

"You got enough 'ere, gal?" Sean asked, looking at the bags.

"All the usual, Sean, spare clothes, towels, sunscreen, hairbrush, aftersun…!"

"Blimey!" Sean exclaimed. "Aftersun… I thought that was a bottle of plonk!"

"Ah… got that too!"

Laurel laughed as she picked her way across the rocks, avoiding the barnacles. She reached a small cove and called out to Sean,

"Swim?" and before he could reply, she'd removed all of her clothes and ran, laughing, into the tranquil sea.

"It's fab – come on in!" she yelled, frolicking in the waves and looking back at Sean's stunned expression, her body bare to the elements.

"Feels so much better like this, the water next to your skin, real cool. Come on, Sean, join me!"

"Hate swimmin'!" he retorted, avoiding her gaze.

"Ah… spoilsport! Find a nice spot for us, then," she shouted back, leaning back but taking care not to spoil her hair and make-up and glancing back at Sean to check if he was watching her, but he was absorbed with laying out the rug.

Before too long, Laurel walked up the beach boldly, flaunting her nakedness. As she reached the rug, she lay down facing him and smiled shamelessly.

"I better dry off before dressin'," she told him, amused at his coyness as Sean seemed unable to look at her.

"Well, we canna eat wi' you like that, Lors!" He threw a towel at her.

"Just thought you'd like to glimpse dessert!" she quipped, bringing herself closer to him.

"Not out 'ere, Laurel! It's public. Put some clothes on."

"Well, it don't look very public to me, Sean O'Connell. There ain't no one 'ere!"

Irritated and embarrassed, she grumpily threw her clothes back on.

Sean lay back, covering his face with his cap. "It's hot, alright, in this midday sun," he said.

"'Ere," Laurel told him sharply, "you can open the wine, then." She thrust the bottle at him, making him jump.

He poured out a glass each and they tucked into their picnic. After Sean's lack of interest in her playful advances, Laurel felt the euphoria of earlier slipping away. They ate in silence, but the wine gradually warmed her inside as the sun warmed her on the outside and Laurel felt herself relax once more.

"Another glass?" She held up the bottle.

"Gettin' me drunk now, eh?" Sean asked with a flicker of a smile.

As Laurel could see his mood mellowing, she seized the moment.

"Sean – where are we going?"

"Eh?"

"Us, you know, this?" She gestured to them both.

"Who knows, Lors? It's OK, isn't it? Like we're doin'?"

"You mean me comin' 'ere and takin' care of yers?"

She knew she was sounding rattled now and Sean was taken aback.

"Well, I wouldn't put it like that…"

"I would, Sean. This is the first time we've done anything together in six months, and even now, we're not exactly together, are we?"

He looked uncomfortable now as Laurel continued.

"I mean, are we in a relationship, Sean?"

Sean mumbled his reply, but Laurel didn't hear, so made a suggestion. "Come on, let's walk."

They packed up the remains of the picnic and wandered down onto the beach. The wine had quelled Laurel's agitation, but it also gave her Dutch courage to fill Sean in on a bit of her history. They ambled along the warm, soft sand, into the shallows, allowing the ripples to wash over their feet and Laurel began,

"You may as well know a few things about me, Sean."

He looked at her with a pained expression as if he was finding their heart-to-heart rather disconcerting.

"What?"

"Two years ago, I was in a relationship, then I lost his baby. He was a bad sort anyway, so I walked, but it devastated me, to be honest."

"Yeah, I see that, Lors. You over it now?"

"Well, as much as you get over that sort of thing," she said, not without contempt, "but I don't want to be hurt like that again." She gently took his hand. "So, we an item, Sean?" she said, smiling hopefully at him.

Sean stopped and turned to face her. "You sayin' you want us to get married, Lors, or what?"

Laurel looked at the shock on his face, but it was now or never, and she added,

"Well, I'd like to know if we have a future, Sean. You know, settle down, m'bes have a family?"

Sean sat down on the wet sand, but she couldn't make out his expression as she waited for a response. Then she stood in front of him, blocking the sun and looking into his eyes. "Is that what you want, too?"

He looked away into the distance, seemingly transported to some other place, and Laurel called him back to the present. "Sean?"

He took a deep breath before he spoke.

"Well, now, that's put me on the spot, like. Need to think on it, eh?"

With that, he got up and walked up the beach, leaving Laurel staring after him, open-mouthed.

A quiet mood hung over them all afternoon, and that evening, Laurel took herself off upstairs, concluding that although she was none the wiser about their relationship, tomorrow she would find out about his other secret – the one inside the locked barn.

The next morning, a vehicle was coming up the drive as Laurel came downstairs. *Liam's early*, she thought crossly.

She opened the front door. "Morning, Liam."

Laurel was wary of Liam. She knew he didn't like her, and he was always such a cold fish. He greeted her with a smile but didn't move.

"Hello, Laurel. Didn't know you were here. Stayin' long?"

Not that it's any of your business, Laurel thought, but answered politely enough, "Well, I've come for the party, actually. Helping Aoifa with the food an all that, so. Coffee?"

"Yeah, why not, thanks."

A while later, she watched Liam and Sean take their coffees over to the big barn. She was tempted to follow but decided not to push her luck. She would wait and go with

Aoifa, as she and Sean were not quite back on an even keel after their talk the day before.

"Right, Aoifa was bringing lunch and she was to bake some scones. Shouldn't be hard." She chuckled at the metaphor. 'Hard'. Yes, she would make scones and give one to Liam!

At midday, Aoifa pulled up in their old car and Laurel ran out to greet them as Mairead jumped out, thrusting a bottle of champagne at her.

"What's this, then, gal?"

"Well, I owe you that, remember?" said Mairead.

"Aw, you needn't 'ave bothered, kid. You was in enough trouble that night!"

Mairead looked away, clearly embarrassed.

"But made up for it since," said her mother approvingly. "Summer holidays now, so just a big party to look forward to – and Mairead to help since she be the oldest!"

"Ma!" Mairead snapped from behind her.

"Yeah, but we can all help, Aoif. And you can tell us what's gonna happen, too!"

Aoifa looked uncomfortable at this, which puzzled Laurel. They all went inside and started to lay out the lunch as Laurel whispered to Aoifa that she wanted a quiet word later and Aoifa nodded. The men trooped in for lunch, and as they sat around the table, Aaron spoke up,

"So, this is an unusual family gatherin'. Well, not all family." He glanced at Laurel, and she felt her face darken.

"I think if I could take this opportunity..." Aoifa began but was interrupted.

"For what, Aoif?" asked Liam curtly. "It was Sean's idea, wasn't it?"

Sean grinned mischievously. "Let's tuck into this lot first, then we'll see!"

Aoifa began again. "Look, there's something I must tell you all."

A silence fell around the table and Mairead was the only one smiling.

"This is not easy for me, and it may come as a shock," she began, visibly nervous now. "You may have noticed that I haven't given you any messages lately? Well, I've lost my second sight. It went with Ma, m'be she took it, m'be not, but nonetheless, it's gone. I have no more idea of what lies ahead than you do." Aoifa spoke curtly as if concealing her true feelings as she looked cautiously around the table.

Laurel's face was a picture of shock and disappointment. "So, would that be… never, Aoif?" She looked accusingly at her friend.

"Probably, Laurel. I'm sorry."

Aaron was next to speak. "Ach, chara, donna be sorry now. Not your fault and we're all grown-ups, ain't we, Mairead?" he quipped, ruffling his granddaughter's hair.

"Yeah, Grandpa, we has to find out for ourselves!" said Mairead, laughing out loud as if she found it all very amusing.

Laurel glanced around. Was it only she who felt anger? She looked across as Liam spoke up.

"So, Aoif, no more bossin' us about, then, eh?" he said with a wry smile.

Aoifa glared at him, and Aaron intervened,

"Laurel, some cake out in the scullery, I think?" but she continued to stare out of the window.

"Laurel?" Aaron asked again, startling her.

"What?!" she shouted angrily.

Aoifa stood up and took Laurel's arm as they both went out to the scullery to make tea.

Laurel stomped around, unable to think clearly after Aoifa's revelation. How would she know about her future now?

"What's the matter, Aoifa? You've gone pale. It surely isn't your future that's affected – it's everyone else's!"

Aoifa didn't reply but marched back to the table and replied to Liam,

"I know you've never cared for my messages. In fact, you always berated them, tellin' me I was a control freak, but others have appreciated them, Liam O'Connell!"

Liam gave a small triumphant smile, but no more was said until Aaron intervened.

"Come on now, all in the past. We need to move toward the future, eh, Sean?" said Aaron decisively. "That's why we're all here, after all!" The atmosphere slowly improved as he changed the subject and Laurel brought in some tea and scones.

"Eh, Liam, what a storm t'other night. Lost a fence or two, mind."

"We lost a shed and more, Pa." Aoifa's face paled at the memory.

"Ah, well, none of you believe us. These storms are gettin' worse," Liam declared as he looked around shaking his head as Sean stood up and told them,

"Aye, but that's where I come in. Come with me an' I'll show yer."

Everyone made their way outside, but Laurel had no enthusiasm, especially not with the limelight on Sean, but she wasn't going to miss out and caught up with him. What was it all about anyway? Sean took out his bunch of keys and selected the biggest one as Liam patted him on the shoulder.

"Intriguing, Sean. What's all this, then? To do with climate change, bringing yourselves into modern times – finally?"

Aaron touched his arm. "No judgement yet, son. Wait till youse sin it."

Sean opened the heavy door and they all trooped in. The barn was nearly the size of an aeroplane hangar and in front of them was what appeared to be just that – a small aircraft.

Everyone stood in stunned silence as they surveyed Sean's invention.

Liam walked forward first, touching the metal arms and looking inside, then he turned and grinned at his younger brother.

"Go on, lad, enlighten us. What's it for, then, for God's sake?!"

"What you said, Liam. Climate change. Mainly, it's for collectin' Padraig's seaweed then it'll adapt to pickin' up bits of metal, plastic and the like," he said proudly. "To help the planet. A design in the makin'. Be ready in a few months."

Liam had a look of pure astonishment on his face.

"Well, you always wuz a dark horse, Sean, but this! It's spectacular. But will it work?"

"I've tested the theory on a smaller version, so yes, for sure."

"You need investment, though, right?" asked Liam, his face lighting up at the prospect.

"No. Thank you. Got sponsored by the authorities but maybe going for'ard. We'll see."

"What d'you call it, son?"

"The sea machine – says it all, eh?"

Liam remained deep in thought. "Be ahead of the game wi' this, lad! Need to license it, though. I might be able to help…"

Laurel touched Aoifa's arm and whispered,

"The love of his life, Aoif. That's what this is."

Aoifa smiled at her. "Be room for more, Lors."

The girls made their way out of the barn, leaving the men to ponder over the details, and wandered back to the house.

Aoifa seemed distracted as she gazed around the garden.

"Garden's lost its colour since Ma left."

"Yeah, no flowers. I must put some in," Laurel replied dismissively. "You OK, Aoif? You seem away with the fairies!"

"Not anymore, apparently!" Aoifa snapped and Laurel was taken aback.

"Just joking!"

"Yes, but my brother wasn't, tellin' me I'd been bossy!"

Laurel ignored the remark and continued,

"I'm sorry you won't have the sight, Aoif, for any of us. Was hopin' you could tell me my future, like!"

"Well, I can't."

Aoifa's sharp tone was uncharacteristic and perturbed Laurel. Suddenly, she was contrite.

"Sorry, Lors. My brother always manages to provoke me, somehow or other."

"Which one?"

"Liam, of course. Not Sean; he's a kindly soul. Clever too, by all accounts."

"You know him better than most, Aoif. A closed book, though?" she smirked. "Not sure where we're goin, Aoif, if anywhere. Broached the subject yesterday an' he side-stepped it. Anyways, after seein' his latest development, I know where his love lies."

Laurel knew she sounded bitter, but that was how she felt.

"What do you want, Lors?"

"More than anything, Aoif, I want a child."

Aoifa muttered something, but Laurel didn't catch it.

"Does Sean? Have you asked him?"

"I've tried an' he didn't say, but if you hadn't lost your sight, you could have helped me, couldn't you? You've let me down, big time!"

Laurel was seething, but Aoifa held her ground.

"Calm y'self. There's only one thing for you now."

"What's that?" Laurel held on for some snippet of hope.

"I know nothing of my brother's desires, Lors. You need to ask him directly, otherwise someone will get hurt." Aoifa added kindlier, "And you've had enough hurt in your life."

Laurel nodded, as she knew Aoifa was right.

They walked up the garden to where Mairead was waiting.

"Come on, Ma! Cat's coming!"

The men were crossing the yard, as the group were to go their separate ways, and Aoifa called out as she jumped into the car,

"Good luck, Bro! I knew you'd come up with something clever! No message, just a hunch!" and she waved to them all dismissively then Liam called out,

"See you at the party on Saturday!"

Laurel was soon left alone with her thoughts as she cleared the dishes away. She and Sean would have an open exchange later once and for all. There were things about her past that Sean was unaware of, but she needn't tell him for now. She hadn't mentioned her depression nor how she'd been to anger management and had been careful to keep those violent outbursts from him. Anyway, if she had a baby, they would go away; she was sure of it. Sean could chase his desires, as long as she could have hers. Laurel clapped her hands with glee at the thought! If she had her child, he could spend all day making his silly machines if he wanted to, but her clock was ticking, and she needed to know. One thing she did know was Sean was kind-hearted and surely she'd be able to persuade him. Give him a boy to take on the farm!

Laurel noticed the door to the large barn was open, so she sauntered over and soon heard him humming an Irish folk song. It surprised her; Laurel had never heard Sean sing. She put her head around the door, and he was polishing the wings of his strange machine as she called out,

"Hey, Sean. I'm gonna open that bottle of champagne Mairead brought. It's bin on ice, nice an' cold for celebrating on a lovely evenin', eh?"

Sean stopped humming immediately as if he'd been stung and stared across at her.

"Sean, you gone dumb or what?" She let out a laugh.

"Ahh… gotta finish off here, lass. You put it ready an' I be across in an hour."

Laurel was satisfied with that, as it gave her time to spruce up. She went upstairs, put on a short skirt with a white gypsy blouse, curled her hair, dabbed on some expensive perfume then a touch of lipstick and checked herself in the mirror. How could he turn her down? She knew the way to go was to compliment Sean on his new invention; after all, it was pretty important to him, and she wouldn't deny him that.

She made her way downstairs, took the champagne out into the garden with two glasses and some peanuts too. It was going to be a while till supper. The sun was still warm in a cloudless sky, and it looked to be a warm summer's evening. She didn't have long to wait, as Sean soon came ambling towards her in relaxed mood, reassuring her, and she greeted him with a kiss.

"I knew this would come in handy!" she told him, holding up the champagne. He took the glass from her with a shy smile.

Laurel raised her glass.

"Congratulations, Sean. I am so impressed by your new invention. You always were a clever sort and now youse gonna save the planet!" she said, beaming at him. "Come and sit by me." She tapped the bench next to her.

"Ach, well maybe this stretch of the coast, Lors, not exactly the planet! An' I'm too dirty t' sit there," he laughed and put himself on the seat opposite.

Laurel shrugged and handed him some nuts. She needed to warm him up.

"So, when will your machine be sea-worthy, then?"

Sean frowned a little. She guessed he was surprised at her keen interest.

"Maybe by New Year's."

"Well, I'll raise a glass to New Year's, then." They may have two things to celebrate by then, she thought with a cryptic smile.

They chinked glasses as Laurel continued.

"How long you bin inventin' it, then?"

"Almost a year now and can see the way to finishin' it! Liam definitely showed his support."

He was really starting to open up now.

"Your efforts will pay off, Sean, and you'll get what you want. I'll support you too, help out an' that." Laurel looked at him encouragingly.

"Pleased to hear it!" he added with a smile.

She topped up their glasses. "There is just one small thing I would like in return," she added furtively.

Sean stiffened. "What might that be?" His face turned serious.

Laurel thought, *now or never.* "I want a baby, Sean."

It was as if Sean had stopped breathing. He was dumbstruck, with his glass still held out toward her. Time stretched out between them with neither speaking then Sean lowered his eyes and put his glass down. Laurel hadn't intended to blurt it out quite like that and tried to soften the blow.

"I thought maybe you'd had time to think after yesterday."

She moved slowly from her seat across to sit on his lap, but he shuffled away nervously, leaving her in limbo.

"Not time enough to think yet, Lors."

Laurel pressed him. She had to know.

"You must have considered it, though, Sean?"

Laurel moved ever closer and held her breath.

"No, I haven't, Lors. I have never wanted children," he said flatly, looking up into her eyes, which had gone icy cold. Laurel stared back at him. Although the sun was dazzling, she couldn't look away. She felt her temperature rising, and her mouth turned from a sexy pout to a hard red line as one hand formed a fist and the other clenched around her glass, which broke, sending shards of glass across the table. Still, neither of them moved. Laurel ignored the glass but maintained her fixed cold expression as she replied.

"That saddens me, Sean. It saddens me very much."

They continued to sit together and gradually she felt her heart rate slowing, the tension easing, as she looked out to sea. It would just take a bit more time then she knew he'd come round.

"Ah, look what I've done now, chara. I'll clear this then make us all some nice dinner."

Sean got up and left, muttering about stuff to do, whilst Laurel took the bottle indoors, popped it in the fridge and looked to see what she could make for their supper.

As she cleared the glass away, Laurel was sure of one thing. She just had to make sure Sean had a few drinks one night and he would soon forget he didn't want a baby! Also, she knew better than anyone how persuasive she could be when she put her mind to it. A devious smile curled around her red lips as she took the broken glass and popped it in the bin.

20. CHANGING TIDES

Lois jumped out of the car even before Padraig had put the handbrake on and ran into the melee that was her family. Flynn too was running around like the place was on fire and everyone was talking and hugging at once. Aoifa smiled warmly at her eldest daughter, then held her close.

"Lovely to see you home, Lo. The girls have prepared a welcome lunch – a practice for the weekend – the party, d'you remember?"

"I do, Ma. So, who's coming?"

"Now, that's a very good question!"

"Everyone!" added Mairead as they all went into the house.

The family sat around the kitchen table, tucking in with gusto and waiting to hear all about her trip.

"Not eaten since I left New York, Ma, too excited!"

"So, what were the boys like, Lo?" Mairead's eyes were gleaming.

"Trust you, Mairy!" said Lois but offered no reply.

"An' what animals did you see?" asked Clara shyly.

"I didn't actually see any, Lara, just learning about them for now."

"I can hear wild cats, Lo, and sirens, and I smell cat poo, too!" said Siobhan quietly.

"More like boat horns, Sheve, and no wild cats round here!" Niamh was bemused. "You going back for good, then, Lo?"

"For good? Who knows! I begin my training programme in September, but, hey, you be gone before me!" Niamh's face shone with pride at her own imminent adventure.

"So, it's yours, Lo? The job is yours?" asked her mother, wide-eyed.

"If I want it, Ma, it sure is!"

Clara couldn't contain herself as she whispered to her older sister,

"Do you want it, Lo? Are you going to live in America?"

"I am, Lara!" A look of ecstasy spread all over her face.

There was a loaded silence from the family then her ma told her,

"We are thrilled for you, Lo, truly thrilled," as the girls all whooped at once, but her father was more circumspect.

"Come for a ride, later?" he asked her softly.

"Love to, Pa. I'll miss the horses, but they'll be waitin' on my visits!"

"Clara will keep them warm for you and Ma, too," he told her with a small smile, but all Aoifa heard was the word 'visit'. So she really was going for good.

After lunch, as it was such a beautiful sunny day, Aoifa suggested she and Lois went for a swim together. They both quickly changed and made their way to the beach, diving into the silky warm water in unison.

"So, what was the best bit about your trip, Lo?"

Lois kept swimming without so much as a pause as Aoifa struggled to keep up with her.

"Seriously, Ma?"

Aoifa was puzzled, stopping to tread water and looking over at her. "Yes, why not?"

"Well, it just feels strange. You never used to ask me anything, cos you always knew!"

Aoifa resumed her swimming. "Those days have gone, chara. Just showing an interest like any normal mum now," she said brightly.

"Then I'll tell you. I met a boy!"

"Oh, Lo!" gasped Aoifa as she turned around with a splash. "What's he like?"

Her face lit up. "I'd rather not say much in case I jinx it! Put it like this," she added coyly, "he's a bit like Pa. Long dark hair, sparkly eyes, a lovely smile and very easy-goin' too!" She laughed and frolicked in the water.

Aoifa smiled happily at her daughter. "Couldn't do better, chara, if he turns out to be anything like your pa!"

Lois suddenly added, "Don't tell Da, will you?"

Although surprised, Aoifa nodded. They finished their swim, then wandered up to the house and bumped into Padraig, who was preparing the horses.

"Just change, Pa. Back in a min!" Lois called out, and as Aoifa looked at Padraig, she sensed some tension in him.

"Chara, you seem worried?"

"Ach, it's nothin'. Just pleased Lo's back safe an' sound."

"Then why are you not cheerful?" she asked tentatively. It wasn't very often Padraig was troubled by anything.

"I am, chara," he replied with a forced smile.

Aoifa took his hand. "You're not, Pad. Is it about Lois?"

"Nah, she's lookin' on a bright future for sure. Be a nice ride out in a minute."

"So, what is it, my love?"

"Ach, nothin'. You wouldn't understand anyways," he muttered.

"Try me."

"Well, it's about Siobhan, how she sees and smells things even when she's *not* tellin' a story. Keeps comin' back to haunt me, Aoif. You see…"

"See what? Och, don't make anythin' of that, Pad. She imagines it all. Her storytellin' is improving, have you noticed?" Aoifa laughed it away and Padraig nodded.

"Yeah. That be it, then."

Lois soon returned, ready for their ride, and Aoifa was still pondering their conversation when a car pulled up in the yard.

"Hi, all!"

"Hello, Lors," said Aoifa, smiling as Lois stifled a groan behind her.

"Come for me marchin' orders, Aoif. Told yer I'd help!"

Marchin' orders, considered Aoifa, *now there's a good idea*, then immediately chastised herself. Laurel wasn't that bad.

"Now then, good timing, because we've sorted the menus. Can you bring some bread rolls and make a potato salad?"

"Easy-peasy. And I wanna ask Lo what those GIs are like!"

Aoifa frowned at her friend. Lois wasn't joining the forces!

"Hiya, Lors." Lois was always wary of Laurel, usually giving her a wide berth.

"Youse in good spirits, then, Lo. Must've gone well o' the water? Are those American men all they're cracked up to be?" Laurel teased.

"Gimme a break, Lors," said Lois, throwing her mother a glance. "I ain't going for the men. Working with animals, you know."

"You talk like blokes dunna exist, Lo. You must've noticed them!"

The smile disappeared from Lois' face. "I do, but I have my career to think on now."

She turned on her heel and went over to take Rafa from her pa.

"Oops, upset 'er now, Aoif."

"She'll be OK. Takes her studies seriously that one."

Mairead came running out of the door. "Hi, Lors! You come wi' my present, then?"

"You cheeky hussy!" Laurel quipped. "Anyways, when is it and what d'yer want, eh?"

"Actually, it's tomorrow an' I'll be fifteen," Mairead said proudly. "Can I whisper to you what I want?"

"Yeah, as long as it's less than the price of a pint!"

Mairead looked guiltily at her and replied,

"Only a tiny bit more than that, please, Lors."

Laurel walked across and planted a few notes into her hand.

"There you go – and make it last this time!"

Mairead shouted her thanks and ran off upstairs. "We're all off to the youth club tomorrow, Ma, and dunna worry – Eileen'll be there!"

Aoifa passed Laurel a coffee and they sat out in the sunshine.

"Hope it's fine on Saturday, then, Aoif."

"Meant to be. How's things back at the farm?"

"Oh, much the same. Sean alwuz workin' on that machine. I'm waitin' till Saturday – take my chance after a few drinks!"

Aoifa was slightly alarmed. "Carefully does it, Lors. Sensitive one, is Sean."

Laurel stood up, hands on hips. "You tellin' me what…?" Then she stopped and sat down again. "No, is OK. I'll go easy, o' course."

"Must make a start on Mairy's cake now. Look, take these."

Aoifa handed her a basket of potatoes and they went their separate ways as she called out to Niamh to come and help.

"Why not make one big cake to share with Da? Mairy won't mind."

Aoifa agreed, and as they worked together in the kitchen, it occurred to her how much she would miss Niamh, in so many ways. *It's always those left behind who suffer the most*, she thought ruefully.

Later that evening, Aoifa and Padraig were sitting together.

"So, Aoif, what do you buy a mischievous and misguided fifteen-year-old for their birthday these days?"

"Aw, that's not fair, Pad. She's not misguided! She's bin really trying lately."

"Hmm. Well, I not sin it. In a better mood, is all I can say. Grateful for that wi' all you women!"

"Oh, you rascal, Paddy O'Brien! Be lucky you're surrounded by wenches. Could be a room full of rugby players."

"Aye, be less trouble an' all!"

Aoifa shook her head. "We'll see when Rachel's comes."

The next morning, the girls burst into Mairead's bedroom to a chorus of 'Happy Birthday', scattering her presents onto the bed. Mairead sat up, rubbing her eyes as Aoifa brought in the cake.

"Smells of liquorice, Ma," whispered Siobhan. "M'bes the black I did on Roma's mane."

"But that's just a drawing, Sheve…" said her mother.

Padraig popped his head around the door. "Liquorice cake?!"

"Na, just Siobhan's funny ideas!" shouted Mairead. "Hey – thanks, everyone!"

The family worked together that day, baking and making dishes from the menu. As they chatted, Aoifa did a head count of their guests and could feel her blood pressure rising. That was a lot of food! They worked tirelessly, stacking the finished dishes in the old cheese cabinet out in the scullery. By evening, it was nearly full and Aoifa was exhausted.

"All done, girls. Looking good!"

"The flowers look pretty, too, Ma," as Siobhan arranged them in a vase, "but d'you think they cry when you cut their stalks?"

"Not sure what you mean, Sheve," Aoifa replied. "But we give them water just in case, eh?" she told her with a smile.

Niamh stood back to admire the results. "Me thinks I'm gonna miss all this cookin', Ma!" she grinned. "Not as like!"

Aoifa gave her a withering look but chuckled all the same.

A while later, Padraig walked in carrying a box of barbecue meats. "Plenty here, Aoif, including our own sausages. Bren's bringing the veggie ones for Rachel."

"And me, Pa!" added Lois.

"Oh, donna tell me, chara…"

"Yep. Gone veggie!"

Aoifa sighed to herself. "No more surprises now cos I hope to just go with the flow tomorrow!"

The next morning, as Aoifa opened her eyes, dawn was just breaking. She peaked out of the window and breathed a sigh of relief. A sunny day with not a cloud to be seen and

Padraig was already in the yard tending to the animals. Quickly throwing on some old clothes, Aoifa ran downstairs and called out of the kitchen window,

"Guests arriving at 10am, Pad. No storms to spoil it today!" and he came in for breakfast.

"Mairead got back in one piece last night, then, Aoif?"

"Sure, not late at all, then I heard Eileen driving off. All good."

They heard little footsteps coming down the stairs.

"The early bird catches – the first lot of jobs!" Padraig called out.

"Oh, Da! Not had breakfast yet!"

"Just jokin'," he said kindly. "Go put your pretty togs on for the party instead!"

Clara giggled. "I want to look nice, y'know," she said timidly.

"Ahh… can't think whys, young lady! Young Conor be working today!"

"Working, Pa?" she said indignantly. "It's a party!"

"Only on the barbecue, the coals an' that."

Just then, Conor popped his head around the door.

"Early, son?" Padraig smiled broadly at him.

He had taken to calling him 'son' now and no one had objected. Aoifa had noticed how lately Clara had become quite shy around Conor. He was at least a head above her now, must be rising fourteen, although no one knew when his birthday was, least of all him!

A car was approaching and Aoifa strained her eyes to make it out.

"What's this?" she cried as Declan and Megan got out and Aoifa greeted them warmly but couldn't remember inviting them. She noticed Megan's earthly beauty, which brought back a few memories.

"Surprise, eh?" Declan shouted as they both gave her a hug.

"So, am I going mad?" Aoifa laughed to conceal her embarrassment.

"Not at all, chara," said a voice from behind. "This was my doin'!"

She turned around to face Padraig, a look of pleasure on his face, and Aoifa took a sharp intake of breath, feeling a twinge of something inside.

"Oh, you scoundrel!" she said, turning to them both. "Good to see you anyways. Look, take your stuff over to the bothy and settle y'selves."

Mairead came out of the house carrying a tray of food to take to the beach as her mother took in her pale face and dishevelled appearance.

"How much more carryin' we gotta do, Ma?"

"Well, all hands, Mairy! Nearly done now, then we can all go an' freshen up." She looked at her pointedly.

Conor and Padraig brought out the beers, wines and soft drinks.

"Hope the wind don't pick up, chara, or these paper cups be gone!"

"Weather looking OK still?"

"Some clouds over yonder, but I'll keep an eye."

"We're all off to change now. Don't you forget to do the same!" She shot him an accusing look, knowing how Padraig preferred his casuals to anything which had seen an iron.

Aoifa opened her wardrobe. Megan had raised the bar. Yet, she looked down at her own shapely bronzed legs, admitting they looked pretty good, and boldly selected some denim shorts, a fitting t-shirt and embroidered blouse loosely over the top. Her curly red hair was gleaming as it fell in folds around her shoulders. She added a touch of make-up, popped on some pretty sandals and hopped down the stairs. *Time to shine!* she thought to herself, but not entirely believing it. Time to do a spot of pretending again, more like, but she saw the humour in it this time.

As she went outside, Aoifa saw Liam's Range Rover coming into the yard and the family jumping out.

"Och, what a day for this, eh?" Liam exclaimed as Emma and Aoifa embraced.

"You know Declan and Meg?" Aoifa asked as Megan came across the yard, tall and svelte, in a stunning pair of white trousers and black top, her long layered blonde hair bouncing around her pretty face. Emma shook Meg's hand and Aoifa noted her usual warmth but saw that she smoothed her skirt and checked her own hair as she walked away. Her brother was not so subtle as he held Megan's hand just a little too long.

"Here's Grandpa!" yelled Niamh.

"Ah – our wanderer returns," said Aaron as he got out stiffly from their old car, "with them American airs and graces, no doubt!"

"Aw, Grandpa, they're grand over there. I loved it!" Lois told him.

"You be marryin' one of 'em afore too long, then!" he quipped, and she turned away to conceal a smile.

"Hi, Mairy!" Laurel called out as she ran toward them carrying several bottles. "Take these, quick, afore I drop 'em."

"With pleasure!" Mairead replied, but her mother rescued them then told everyone,

"Padraig's at the beach startin' the barbecue. Go down and get y'selves a drink."

Suddenly, it was mayhem, everyone shouting at once when Catrina and Eileen walked into the garden and Mairead took them by the hand. "C'mon, you two, down t' the beach!"

Mr. and Mrs. Kelly made their way slowly up the path toward Aoifa.

"Hello there. Nice day for it too, Aoifa."

"Maureen, Dennis, lovely to see you."

Aoifa smiled at her friends and took them down to the beach. The tide was going out and the aquamarine sea was as calm as a mill pond.

"We'll have several hours before the tide turns. Now, come and find some chairs," she told Maureen. "Ah... there's my friend from school, Rachel, bloomin' in her pregnancy, and Brendan – he runs the pub where they're building the new school. You must have heard of it, Dennis?"

The Kellys nodded and Dennis replied,

"A big undertakin', but brilliant, indeed. They need it o'there."

Aoifa spotted Rachel turning the spit.

"Hey, Rach, this is men's work!"

"You don't see what I have to do in the pub!" she said, smiling happily. "Anyways, this meat's nearly done – an' you're all welcome to it!"

"Better get everyone over, then."

Aoifa looked around and called out to the girls to help.

"Where's Mairead?" But no one knew, so she asked Siobhan to hand out the cutlery.

"Ma, I can hear the quarries workin' today."

"Really?"

"I can, Ma, but I smell something too, oranges and reds, hot flowers!"

"No, chara, that's the rotisserie," said Aoifa, wishing Siobhan would save her imagination for a more suitable time.

The guests began to tuck into the feast laid out before them. Aoifa took her plate and sat alongside Emma, with Liam and Aaron on the other side and the young ones all together some distance away.

"This is lovely, Aoif. Amazing salads – by your girls, no doubt!"

Aoifa nodded absent-mindedly at Emma as she'd spotted a sailing boat coming into shore and dropping anchor. Two people disembarked, then, to her surprise, walked up the beach towards them. Ah – it was Aunt Beth and Uncle David! This would surprise everyone, especially Liam.

"Hi, there." Aoifa stood to greet them. "Lovely to see you both." She led them to the refreshments. "You arrived in style, then!"

Aunt Beth smiled and nodded politely.

"I'll do some introductions later, but first, come and have some food. Look, Lois will serve you."

Aoifa was determined to make them feel welcome. She wanted above all to make friends with her ma's long-lost sister and positioned some chairs close to the family group.

"Would you like some white wine, Aunt? A beer, Uncle David?"

They both accepted and Aoifa noted their improved mood on the last meeting.

Padraig brought the drinks over and whispered,

"Youse a dark horse sometimes, chara! Why didn't you tell me…?" as he smiled good-naturedly at her.

Aoifa looked at him accusingly.

"You can talk, Pad. What about Dec and Meg, then?"

Padraig shot her an awkward look. "I thought you'd be pleased!"

"Thought *you'd* be pleased, more like!" she replied with a sardonic smile and turned away.

As Padraig sat down to eat, Mairead came over to ask if he would take them all out in his big fishing boat.

"Ach, chara, too many of yuz now. And look, some clouds comin' over." But Mairead protested rather too loudly, inviting a few scathing glances.

"Oh, Pa – it's for my birthday!"

"Now, Mairy, quiet down, lass. Gimme half an hour and we see," he replied firmly, closing the subject down for a while at least.

Aoifa turned to him. "Is the weather to change, then, Pad?"

"No, chara, be OK I think."

Aoifa returned to her seat and her heart missed a beat as she overheard Liam telling their aunt of her lost sight.

"That's right, isn't it, Aoif – no more messages, eh?"

Beth was looking at Aoifa rather intently and it unnerved her.

"Yes, it's true, Aunt."

Aoifa began to tremble as a feeling of guilt came over her and she had no idea why.

Beth seemed to be looking vaguely into the distance as she spoke, "It was the same for Cara when our mother passed," and added as an afterthought, "but hers came back."

Aoifa had so many unanswered questions but refrained from asking them. "Maybe mine will return too, then."

"Well, I hope not. Just causes trouble," Beth declared fiercely.

"I'll just refresh the drinks," Aoifa stammered, but Beth wasn't finished as she continued in a whisper,

"There are some things in life which are best kept hidden. Can't have everyone knowing your business. It's not right."

Aoifa did indeed go to fetch the wine to conceal her discomfort, glaring at Liam, yet she noticed even he was looking uncomfortable now. When she returned, Emma touched her arm supportively as they both went to replenish everyone's glasses. She was eager to disguise the dark mood which had come over their little group, but she had no idea what to do or say and Padraig saved the day as he stood up and shouted,

"Right. Who's comin' boatin'?!"

Mairead laughed triumphantly, punching the air and shouting, "Yes!" as she led everyone down to the fishing boat which was tethered near the rocks.

Aoifa watched them all running down the beach, grateful for the distraction, as she observed the choppy waves and the murky greyness beneath, but she trusted Padraig implicitly. He would take no chances.

She was suddenly jolted out of her reverie as her aunt spoke to her.

"I am so glad, my dear, that your mother removed your sense of the future. Hopefully, she has seen fit to remove evidence of the past, too. So we don't need to dwell on it any longer, do we?" As she spoke, her face lit up with a radiant smile which Aoifa had never seen before and she smiled back, lost for words once again.

She simply nodded, excusing herself to join Emma, Rachel and Meg as they carried the plates and dishes up to the house. Declan was dismantling the barbecue and called out to Aoifa as she passed,

"Hey, Aoif, you seen Sean? Did he go with the boat?"

"Nah, he hates boatin' and swimmin'!" shouted Laurel scornfully.

Aoifa glanced around and spotted someone in the distance, near the rocks. She screwed up her eyes against the dazzling sun, watching as they swaggered unsteadily up the beach. Then she saw the red hair. It was Sean! She sneaked away and went over to him.

"Sean! What's up? Why can't you walk?"

"I dunno, Aoif, like my feet won't work. Not feelin' too good…" And with that, he fell over.

"Sean, get up!" She shook him, but he didn't move.

Aoifa ran quickly up the back path to the house to fetch Laurel.

"Lors – what has Sean been drinking?" Alarm and suspicion were written all over her face. "He's crashed on the sand – out for count!"

"Well, hmm, I may have overdone it a bit…"

"Overdone what?"

Aoifa stared icily at her friend but didn't wait for an answer and told Laurel it was best she took him straight home and to fetch Declan to help. Pushing her anger and disgust away, Aoifa walked back along the beach toward Beth and David, who were deep in conversation with the Kellys, and Aaron had joined them.

"We canna ignore this climate change, as my grandchildren keep tellin' me."

"Shall we make our way back to the house for tea? Tide's comin' in now," Aoifa interjected and her aunt Beth stood up.

"No, thank you, my dear," she replied. "We need to sail back before dark. It has been lovely."

She smiled warmly and Aoifa felt encouraged.

"Come again, Aunt, please. You are always welcome. Have some supper next time."

"Thank you, my dear, but you must come to us, and…"

David interrupted her, "Come along, Beth. Weather's changin' now."

Aoifa watched as Liam accompanied them down to their boat. The sun slipped behind the clouds, a greyness shrouding them as they walked away.

"Take care now," Aoifa shouted, a sudden wind taking her hair as she gazed out to sea, frowning instinctively at the approaching clouds.

Rachel and Meg were preparing tea when Aoifa walked in.

"How long have they been out in the boat now, Rach?"

"Maybe a couple of hours. They surely won't be long, eh?"

"No, not with the clouds comin' in," she muttered.

"Shall I check on the numbers for tea, Aoif?" asked Meg.

"Please," replied Aoifa distractedly as the wind rattled the door, large raindrops splattered on the window, and she tried to ignore it. "I wanted to bring out Pad and Mairy's birthday cake and hoped they'd be back by now."

"Ah, wait a bit, then," suggested Rachel. "There be an onslaught of youngsters all wanting some any minute!"

Aoifa took cups of tea through to the sitting room for everyone, then excused herself and popped upstairs to look out of the window. She scoured the coastline for the boat, but visibility was poor, and the mists were closing in as the rain increased. As Aoifa left the bedroom, she stopped abruptly as she heard some muffled sounds, like someone crying. She checked the bedrooms, Lois' then Niamh's, then Mairead's, which she shared with Clara. As she pushed open the door, there was Mairead, soaked to the skin and sobbing into her pillow.

"Mairy! What's happened? Where are the others?"

Suddenly overcome with emotion herself, Aoifa took in great gulps of air. Mairead made no sense and surely there was a smell of alcohol too? She managed to undress her, put her pyjamas on and tuck her up in bed when Mairead spoke,

"Ma… was chasin' me…"

"Who, chara, who was chasin' you?" But Mairead had drifted off to sleep.

Aoifa composed herself then went downstairs and walked right into Declan.

"Dec, Mairead is upstairs. She's sopping wet and making no sense. But where are the others and the boat? Look at the storm!"

Aoifa burst into tears and found herself talking, not to Declan, but to her ma.

"Please, Ma, keep them safe. I don't know what's happening."

Declan was about to speak when the door flew open, and everyone rushed in.

"Oh, thank God!" Aoifa cried, running up to them.

They were a bedraggled group, all drenched through and talking at once when Niamh grabbed her mother.

"Ma… we… lost Mairy, but we saw her leave the water…"

Aoifa cut in, "It's OK. She's here, in bed. But what happen–"

Padraig shot her a cursory glance and she stopped mid-sentence.

"Go dry yourselves, Lois, find some towels… We have a birthday cake to eat!" The house was then filled with a rendition of 'Happy Birthday', once for Padraig and once for the absent Mairead.

It was almost midnight when Aoifa and Padraig sat down in the sitting room and Aoifa got to hear what had happened on the boat.

"Well, was all good to start with, Aoif. We moored up and they were messin' about catching crabs in the rock pools. Then we set off again, all havin' a bit of a sing-song, when Mairy started playing up, saying she wanted to do the rowing. I think she'd had a drink or two on the beach, to be honest."

Aoifa's face fell, and Padraig rubbed his eyes.

"Anyways, she dropped the oar into the water, and we all watched it float away." Padraig shook his head in disbelief. "Then the wind picked up and the rain started, so I tried the engine, but Mairy grabbed the pulley. It broke,

241

and she fell over the side. I couldn't believe it. All happened so quick."

Aoifa could see he was close to tears.

"Luckily, she was able to swim to the rocks, make it out of the water, then she carried on along the cliff. Conor jumped overboard, rescued the oar and we managed to steer the boat to shore. It was a terrifying few minutes. I felt so responsible. Several of the kids were crying and Catrina was sick overboard."

He put his head in his hands. "I hope she doesn't tell her parents. I played it down as best I could, Aoif, telling them Mairy was safe."

He sighed wearily. "Is she OK, then, Aoif?" he asked worriedly and Aoifa told him,

"She's upstairs asleep now. Ma helped her to safety, I'm sure of it. You did well to hold it all together, Pad. Although it must have been terrifying for Mairy. I found her sobbing in her bed, Pad, like she was terror-stricken. She told me…" But Aoifa let it go. "We can talk about it tomorrow."

As they made their way upstairs, Aoifa remembered something.

"When Beth and David went to their boat with Liam, I noticed him pass her a large envelope. What do you think it was, Pad?"

Padraig just looked at her blankly and shrugged, shaking his head.

"Another thing, Aunt Beth said some disturbing things today, that some folk should have secrets and what's in the past should stay there – and Liam agreed!" she added grimly.

"Strange goings on, Aoif," he replied wearily. "I think we both need a good night's sleep. It'll all look better in the morning."

21. RACHEL AND THE SCHOOL

The morning after the party, Padraig was making a cooked breakfast for everyone when Declan and Meg walked in through the front door.

"Hey, what's this, Pad? You spoiled us enough yesterday!" said Dec as he took the cutlery from Aoifa to lay the table.

"Energy for the drive home!" said Padraig amiably and Aoifa added,

"Our very own sausages, proven good for a hangover, Dec!" as she glanced across at Meg, who looked positively fresh-faced and clearly with no hangover at all as she helped Padraig with the cooking.

Did Pad just put his arm around her as they stood at the cooker? Pah, get a grip, Aoifa. He was just moving past.

"Sleep well over in the bothy, Meg?"

"Oh, it's fab over there, Aoif, just the sounds of the sea, breeze in the trees and summer fragrances from your garden. Heaven!" said Meg, smiling gratefully as she put the sausages in the range to keep warm. "Beats the calling of the cows at our place!"

Aoifa smiled back warmly and called for the girls as she whispered to Padraig,

"Not sure there be many takers for that this mornin', chara, and especially not Mairy!"

No sooner had she spoken than Mairead came running down the stairs.

"I'm starvin', Pa. Plenty for me, please!"

Padraig looked across at her, shaking his head in surprise.

"Great party yesterday," said Declan as everyone sat down and they all chatted about the day's events, then Clara spoke up,

"It was funny, Pa, when Mairy fell in."

Mairead scowled at her younger sister, but Clara was blithely unaware of the trouble she had caused and continued,

"She swam all the way to the rocks, Ma. I couldn't have done that!"

A proud smile crossed Mairead's face as Clara carried on. "We caught a lot of fish, you know, and crabs too!"

"Not crabs!" Aoifa muttered, but she was pleased this was Clara's residing memory of the outing and smiled appreciatively.

After breakfast, as Declan and Meg picked up their bags and walked out to the car, Meg took Aoifa's hand and placed it on her tummy.

"No hangover for me, Aoif, just a delicious breakfast for a new little one!"

Aoifa gasped, but Megan put her finger to her lips, adding,

"Early days!"

As they jumped in the car and left, Aoifa felt as if a load had been lifted from her shoulders, suddenly snapping out of her thoughts as Lois spoke to her.

"What's up, Ma?"

"Nothing at all, chara," she said with a strained smile.

"So, why are you frowning, then?" Lois persisted.

"Oh, just tired after yesterday."

Although, Aoifa knew the truth. It was time to face Mairead, who, by her buoyant mood and the way she had tucked into a hearty breakfast, had clearly put yesterday's incident behind her. The boat accident was all due to Mairead's drinking again and it seemed that whenever there was trouble, Mairead was at the helm. The outcome could have been far worse – and anyway, who had been chasing her?

Padraig had built a raised patio area at the bottom of the garden which looked out over the bay, and later that afternoon, she and Padraig were sitting at the old oak table on some hand-carved chairs which were dotted all around. Aoifa wished she could relax and enjoy the vista, but it was not to be, as, by their invitation, Mairead was on her way over to join them.

"So, Mairead," said Padraig. "Here we are again."

Aoifa noted an edge to his voice as she swallowed nervously, observing Mairead's defensive stance, with her taut body, crossed arms and sullen expression.

"I dunno know what you mean, Pa. Done nothing wrong."

Padraig sighed deeply, glancing over at Aoifa before continuing.

"You know that's not true, Mairy," he said in a calmer tone. "Had you been drinking at the barbecue?"

Mairead started flinging her arms about and stomping around the patio.

"You canna deny me a drink or two for my birthday!" she screamed, and Padraig gave a measured response,

"Mairy, please, come and sit. I don't think I'm an unreasonable father…"

"Well, I do!" she yelled, which Padraig ignored, and he waited a moment.

"We all need to remember you are only fifteen, Mairy, well below the legal drinking age. I have no problem with you having one drink or even two on your birthday, but you must have had more, as you couldn't keep your balance on the boat, your behaviour was erratic, and your speech was slurred. It was potentially very dangerous out there!"

Aoifa picked up the panic in his voice now.

"I dunno what erratic means. I just fell over, that's all. The boat was bobbin' about," she said sulkily.

Padraig, clearly irritated, frowned, his lips forming a thin line, and Aoifa cut in,

"Mairy, you lost the oar, broke the pulley and there were many lives at risk. The whole incident was because of your behaviour. Anyway, you mentioned about someone chasing you. Can you please explain that? We are your parents and still responsible for you," Aoifa spoke kindlier, "and we care deeply about you."

Mairead's face suddenly crumpled and she burst into tears.

"Yes, Ma, there was someone."

She was crying hysterically now as if the tears had been bottled up for some time. "He… he was waiting for me, I think. I'm not sure." Mairead took some deep breaths and sat down on a chair, rubbing her face. "When I reached Lois' cave, he came out and hit me with his bag!"

Aoifa and Padraig stood up, horrified, and went over to her. Aoifa put an arm around her, and Padraig paced the garden in a rage and, his face contorted, asked her directly,

"Mairead, did you know this man?"

She tried to catch her breath, pushing her thick tousled hair from her face.

"M'bes. I'm not sure." She sniffed. "I ran off as quickly as I could, but he was behind me, then he climbed up the rocks and headed off towards the road and I came home."

Padraig sat next to her. "We must find this person, Mairead! If you knew him…?"

"No, Pa!" then her crying subsided. "I mean, if we find him, he may come after me again! Anyways, I can't prove anything, can I?"

"We can't just let it go, Mairy. What was he doing there anyway?"

Mairead hissed at her mother. "How would I know? I just wanted to get home! I was soaking wet… and scared." She burst into tears once more.

Aoifa squeezed her arm comfortingly. "Of course you were." She made a face at Padraig, who was rubbing a frown from his face, clearly exasperated, as they seemed to be going round in circles.

"Mairy, let's talk on this another time, but please acknowledge your part and let's see no more of that behaviour, eh?" her pa told her.

Suddenly, to their amazement, Mairead muttered an apology.

"Accepted, Mairy," said Aoifa, but Padraig hadn't finished.

"We will revisit this, as I have had an idea which I'll talk over with your mother. For now, keep close to Eileen, eh? She's a sensible girl."

"Yes, Pa." Mairead nodded humbly, turned and left.

As her parents watched her go, Padraig moved to sit by Aoifa.

"She is indeed a worry, chara. What was all that about – that man?"

Aoifa's thoughts were a blur as she shook her head, pulled away gently and smiled weakly.

"It's your birthday tomorrow, Pad. You deserve a celebration, too."

"Sure. Look, gotta go, Conor's waiting. Ach, I'm sure it'll work out."

He made his way down to the seaweed farm with the horses walking steadily behind him and Aoifa picked up her spade to resume her gardening when Niamh came out to the garden.

"Hi, Ma," she said cheerfully and Aoifa looked up, *a ray of walking sunshine when I need one!*

"Hi, Nevey. So, you ready or what?"

"I am, and more!" Niamh replied. "Would you and Pa take me, please? Circus is on a site not too far and I have lots of stuff!"

"Of course – but your room'll be empty, chara?" Aoifa replied pensively, her angst of earlier returning.

"Not at all, Ma. My bed'll still be there!" she said with a cheeky grin.

Aoifa looked over at Niamh's vibrant, happy face.

"Your da and I are so proud of you, following your dreams…" But she couldn't finish.

"I will be happy, Ma, as long as I'm dancin' and playing music!"

"Aww, come on, grab that spade and give me a hand." Or she'd be blubbering all over again.

Later that afternoon, before Padraig finished work, the family were discussing his birthday.

"Pa and I are going over to Rachel's for lunch tomorrow, a day out on the horses, and we'll see youse all later on."

"Ma, I can hear bells ringing, and look – the number forty is in the clouds outside with a smell of poppies and horses' hooves on the wind!"

"That would all make a wild story, Sheve!" Aoifa exclaimed, but Siobhan frowned.

"That's not a story, Ma. It's for Pa's birthday tomorrow." Aoifa nodded, trying to conjure up the image.

The next morning, the sun shone brightly through the kitchen window and Aoifa turned to Niamh as she came downstairs.

"A perfect day for our ride out, Nevey!"

"And a perfect day for a birthday, too!" said Padraig as he came in through the door.

"HAPPY BIRTHDAY, PA!" the girls shouted, showering him with presents and giving him a bear hug.

"Ach, girls, you're embarrassing your old pa! You've not spent all your pennies, have you?"

"Of course," shouted Lois. "And you're worth every one!"

"Can I open them later on, then?"

Mairead made a face. "No, Pa! Now, please."

"I'll open one, then. I like to keep them!" He took one from the pile. "It's soft. Hmm. From Niamh. Ahhh… knitted gloves! Just what an old man needs, eh?" he quipped.

"No, Pa, they're for cold days…"

"I know, chara, just pulling those long legs of yours!"

"You all be OK today, girls? We're off in a minute." *Bliss* crossed Aoifa's mind as she popped upstairs to freshen up before they left. She caught a glimpse of herself in the mirror and smiled her approval, knowing Padraig loved her gypsy skirt and ribbons in her long hair giving her a wild look as she skipped back down the stairs.

"Right," she shouted, "we're off!"

"Wow, Ma, colourful or what!" cried Lois. "I think your hair's even longer than mine now."

"Like twins, more like," Padraig added, standing back and smiling as he looked around proudly. "You're all like angels to me. That's the truth," he muttered.

Aoifa noted the colour in his cheeks and a tear in his eye as he spoke.

"Come on!" she said. "Before you get even more maudlin!"

Roma and Rafa seemed to know it was a special day. Rafa was particularly frisky, bobbing his head and flashing his soft brown eyes to them as they went down to the beach.

"Brown Mane is following, Pad," Aoifa whispered.

"Ach, no matter. Pretend you've not sin 'er! Anyways, Clara and I are going to work on 'er one day!"

"Really? Be hers, then?"

Padraig was non-committal. "Maybes." But she noticed a furtive smile curling around his lips.

The sun was high in the cloudless sky when they reached the bay, and the tide was coming in as they walked the horses slowly through the ripples. Aoifa could feel Rafa loosen up as they reached the sea edge, his head falling down and his muscles relaxing, but his ears pricked as always, an awareness from living in the wilds along the Connemara coastline. The gulls were soaring above them and the terns pecked along the seashore in their wake.

"Look, Pad!"

In the distance on the rocks, there were half a dozen Atlantic seals lazing in the sunshine with some pups too.

"They's always here now, chara, when I come across to the farm."

Aoifa moved Rafa closer to Roma and whispered, "Behind!"

Padraig turned around and Brown Mane was frolicking in and out of the tiny white waves, chasing the gulls away, which were on her tail. They could hear her playful whinnying, an immature sound, as she was not yet two years old.

"Come on!" Padraig shouted. "Let's give her a run for her money!"

The two horses didn't need any encouragement. They took up the signal and started a fast trot which quickly turned into a canter right across the bay. Aoifa felt her colourful skirts billowing behind, her blouse falling off her shoulders and her hair gathering salt and sand as they went. This was where she felt alive, whole, and safe in the hands of her beloved horses and her husband, surrounded by the joy and beauty of her surroundings. She knew her ma was out there too, watching, listening and waiting.

Gradually slowing to a trot, they approached the path to the moorland and Aoifa gave him a provocative smile as she caught up.

"What a way to spend a birthday, eh?" They steadied to a gentle walk, pulling up to halt at a familiar watering hole. They released the horses to take their fill and found a soft patch of grass to sit in the sunshine as Aoifa took Padraig's hand.

"Now, have your lifelines got bigger yet. Let me see," she joked.

"Ach, get away!" he quipped, taking her into his arms. "Not enough to stop me kissin' yer!"

"Now, chara, be serious a moment," he told her as they sat up.

Aoifa let out a groan. "Not today, Pad!"

"Yes, today, chara. I have a plan."

Aoifa scowled. "I hope it's a happy one."

"Well, I hope so, too. It's about Mairead."

"Nooo… not now!"

"Aoif, I think Mairy knew the man who attacked her. I don't know more and I don't know why, but he must have been from the village. Maybe he has a resentment against her."

"How can that be, Pad? She's only fifteen!"

"Yes, but she has… a colourful history, you must admit. Anyways, I think she should leave that school."

"What are you saying – leave school, Pad?!" Aoifa turned to face him, incensed by the idea. "But she has a good brain, too!"

"Na, not leave school, exactly. Just leave the company she keeps."

"What then, go to college up in town?"

"No, closer to home." He looked across at her steadily. "To Rachel's school."

Aoifa held her breath, lost for words until she thought about it then a broad smile crossed her face.

"Well, they're having a sixth form too, probably fewer pupils…"

"So, what d'you say, then, eh?"

Padraig jumped up animatedly with his hands on his hips and stared hopefully at her.

Aoifa took a deep breath. "Well, she'll meet a new crowd. But more to the point, what will Mairead say?"

"A tiny stumbling block!" he said, chuckling out loud. "First, we need to ask Rachel."

They mounted the horses and set off through the bracken under the shade of the trees. It was as if a magic cloak had been placed around them, a protective cloak to help them solve a problem as an aura of excitement hung in the air.

As they arrived at the pub, Brendan came running out. "Ah… here he is, the birthday boy!"

Padraig jumped down and patted his friend on the back. "Good to see you on this nice day, too!"

"Come on in. They's all waitin'!"

"Who?" asked Aoifa curiously as she led the horses into the paddock.

Brendan opened the pub door and there was a huge uproar.

She and Padraig looked around, spotting a few familiar faces.

Rachel laughed, giving them a hug. "Let me get you a drink and they can raise you a toast!"

Padraig was hesitant, as he hated being the centre of attention, but Aoifa pushed him forward and he was smiling all the same. Rachel led the way to a sunny corner of the garden where they sat under a large striped umbrella with a view of the moors and mountains beyond.

"Thirty-five again, Pad?" asked Brendan, his eyes twinkling.

"Ah, close," Padraig quipped, "but the grey hairs are a'comin' anyways!"

Aoifa took in Rachel's pretty appearance in her floral smock showing an obvious bump now, with her lustrous black hair in a tidy ponytail, as she turned toward Aoifa.

"Roisin be bringing lunch out soon. A day off for us, too! Great barbecue last weekend, guys, thanks. Nice to see Dec and Megan again."

"Ah… some news afoot there. She won't mind me telling – they're expectin' too, Rach! I think they've been waiting a while."

As Aoifa spoke, she shot Padraig a glance, but he simply smiled distractedly, and she felt a touch of relief deep inside.

Roisin came out with their birthday lunch – veggie lasagne for Rachel and some local fish cooked in garden herbs with a huge bowl of salad and home-made bread on the side.

"Wow, Rach, you have been busy! This looks delish."

They all tucked in as Aoifa and Rachel caught up on some local news and the girls' plans.

"You'll miss them, Aoif."

"Niamh goes tomorrow. I'm no longer sad, though. She and Lo have made brave decisions and we're so happy for them."

"So, Rach," Padraig asked her directly, "is the opening of the school on target, then?"

Rachel's face lit up. "Just completed the interviews. We've a full staff quota startin' in three weeks' time!"

Aoifa opened her eyes wide, in awe of how it had all come together. She wondered how they would bring up the question of Mairead as she glanced over at Padraig, but Brendan opened up the subject for them.

"Pad, what was the matter with Mairead last weekend? I saw her comin' across the rocks crying as I was helping Dec with the barbecue."

Padraig suddenly became very serious.

"We've been having some problems with Mairead, Bren. Although," he corrected quickly, "she has improved of late. We don't like the company she keeps in the village and..." Brendan frowned as he waited. "She fell off the boat. Got home OK, but she was attacked by a local chap, and we got the impression that she may have known him."

Aoifa caught Rachel's anxious expression and added,

"We're worried about her group of friends, but she is a clever girl, Rach – good at maths and a whizz on the computer..."

"What do you think you'll do, then?" asked Rachel anxiously.

All of a sudden, there was huge applause from inside the pub and Roisin came out with a double-layer chocolate cake, followed by a few local friends, applauding and singing loudly.

"It was forty-one, wasn't it, eh, Pad?" whispered Brendan.

"Well, how d'you know that?!" He looked accusingly at Aoifa, who was beaming and clapping the loudest.

Padraig cut into the cake and shared it around with everyone.

After the crowd had dispersed, Aoifa answered Rachel's question.

"Well, Rach, we thought, maybe, that's where you'll come in."

Rachel had a stunned expression on her face as she spoke. "Our school," she said quietly.

"Exactly!" replied Aoifa.

Aoifa and Padraig waited patiently as Rachel took a deep breath.

"Well, we can give it a go, but no promises. Our first challenge, then, eh?"

Aoifa sighed and clapped her hands excitely. "And our biggest challenge is to convince Mairead!"

Padraig nodded gratefully to them both, smiling with relief. Brendan went to replenish their drinks and they all sat on some deckchairs in the afternoon sun.

"You must be so excited, Rach. You've a lot going on just now!" Aoifa said as Rachel leaned close to her.

"Talking of babies," she said quietly. "Laurel was telling me that she and Sean have plans, too. Did you know, Aoif?"

Aoifa almost choked on her drink. "Well, not sure about plans, exactly. Between you and I, m'be they're a bit one-sided at the moment."

"Oh, I was under the impression…" said Rachel, but Aoifa cut in,

"Don't think Sean knows much about it, if I'm honest, Rach."

The subject fizzled out and they sat together enjoying the sun, but the matter had disquieted Aoifa as she pushed thoughts of Laurel away.

"Come on, let's walk on the moor. Love it over here. More rugged this side of the headland, abundant with wildlife, eh."

"Welcome here anytime. See over there, high on top o' the mountain ranges, they's letting out lodges. Look, you can just see them, beautiful by all accounts. Anyways, hope to see more of you when your gals have gone, eh?"

"For sure. I'll miss them, but we can go walking, can't we, explore a bit." She looked dreamily across at the mountains. "Mairead will be the oldest at home, then, but you know, Rach, my belief is that Ma will look down on her, hopefully give her the gift instead of me. She left me a message sayin' as much when she passed, you know."

"Do you think she'll learn those spiritual ways like you, Aoif? We can hope, can't we?" Rachel replied solemnly as the boys caught up with them and they collected the horses from the paddock for the return journey.

"Dunna know if my stomach will take a ride quite yet, chara. Would hate to lose all that lovely food!"

"Ach, Pad, you're tougher than that!" Aoifa quipped back as they jumped on the horses. "Phew, still hot, but what a grand day. Thanks so much! *Slán!*"

They walked slowly down the path and out onto the moor, the horses sensing their relaxed and satiated state and in no hurry either.

As they walked in the amber sunshine, Aoifa spoke quietly.

"You heard the news about Megan, then, Pad?"

"I did, chara. A long-awaited event, I believe?"

Aoifa looked across at her husband, searching his face for his innermost thoughts and Padraig pulled Roma up to a halt.

"Why are you looking at me like that, Aoif?"

Aoifa kept Rafa walking slowly on as she replied. "I know I don't get messages anymore, but I get hunches, you know!"

Suddenly, Padraig caught up with her and jumped down, pulling her down too. He gently pulled her hair and she found herself enveloped in his arms.

"Well, this time your hunch is wrong, chara," he said reassuringly as they kissed, and she felt his love in the embrace.

All that crossed Aoifa's mind at that moment was that she would have to watch out. She didn't want paranoia taking over from where the messages left off. They carried on their way and Padraig turned to her.

"Lois told me about her new beau, too." He flashed her a happy smile, but Aoifa detected something else hidden behind.

"Ah, yes. Apparently, he's just like youse!"

"She canna do better, then."

"Modesty'll come on your next birthday, Paddy O'Brien. Anyways, that's exactly what I said!"

"So, everyone's happy, chara. Lois, Niamh, you, me and even, maybes, Mairy! A turn up, eh?"

"Yeah, a new start. She'll be OK. Ma will see to it, too."

That evening, it was bedlam at Muir Farm. The girls had made an interesting selection of dishes for supper, but Niamh could eat none of it.

"Ma, I will never eat again. My stomach is doing somersaults!"

"What, even before youse reach the circus, chara?!" joked Padraig. "Sure enough, tomorrow takes you on a journey, Nevey. You ready?"

"More than ready, Pa. Doin' what I love best in the world – an' getting paid for it an' all!"

Aoifa looked at her apprehensively. "Come back an' visit, won't you – and keep in touch?" she added, her voice trembling.

"You know I will, Ma. You are everything to me, all of yers."

As they made their way upstairs, Aoifa knew it was time to talk to her ma that night, to make sure a light was shining on Niamh. And Mairy too.

22. CONOR AND THE WOLVES

Conor thought wolves were the most spiritual animals on Earth. They were so true to themselves, and in a way, he felt that they were kindred spirits, and he had a natural affinity with them and their ways. Wolves had apparently been a big part of his family going back centuries; that's what his grandpa had told him anyway. When Conor put his mind to it, he believed he too had wolflike qualities, being a bit wild, fearless, independent, with an endless desire to roam. Deep down, he knew that person was still inside of him, and he often felt a yearning to go back to his roots from where it all started.

Conor was sitting in his favourite spot on the garden wall overlooking the moors with the bay in the distance. He was more than fourteen now, having been at Home Farm for two years, and he was in a quandary over whether to stay or not. Every day, he wondered where his brother was and so wished he knew. Although very grateful to Aaron and Padraig for taking care of him and giving him a home, Conor thought maybe the time had come to take back control of his life. He was nearly a man; there was no doubt about that. He could feel it and he often craved company of his own age.

Like any good wolf, Conor was an observer. It was his panacea, what he did to resolve any problem, to observe and examine before taking action. You could say he was cautious like the wolf in him, but he had been considering his circumstances for some time now and felt he was heading toward a decision.

As he sat pensively looking out to sea, Conor's mind wandered to the O'Brien girls and his thoughts troubled him. Two of them gone, but they'd be fine. Mairead was taking a dark road, to be sure. What would become of her? "You travels you're own road. No one can do it for yer," his pa used to say. Wolves do that. They keep their own counsel and show by example. Padraig and Aoifa were great parents in Conor's book, but sometimes kids don't follow kindness; they choose something else and have to meet their own destiny. Siobhan was a funny one; he worried about her too. He knew his way of describing things wasn't always right, but her ways were funnier than his. She was different, alright. All that storytelling, even when she wasn't telling a story!

Conor stood up, brushed the sand from his feet and put his trainers back on. It was late and he had a lot of jobs that afternoon. As he set off toward the moors, his mind continued to wander. The omega of the family, ah, yes, Clara. Conor was amazed that Lois had found the fish pendant then given it to Clara. That was not luck; it was fate, like too much of a coincidence. He had made it many years ago and now it had found its way to the right place. She was such a lovely gal, not brave, but the kindest heart anyone could have, and he had enough courage for the both of them. The wolves had seen to that.

He made his way over to the cattle as they stood together across the moor, watching him. Their long horns and dazzling black coats always impressed him and they took no persuading to move from one pasture to another. He just looked into their eyes, deep pools of inky black to match their gleaming coats, and they trusted him, all fifty strong of them, and just followed where he went. Every time Conor looked into the eyes of any animal, Casey and Brody especially, and they looked into his, he just got them and they him. He felt at one with them all like there was a wolf deep inside of him, guiding him, showing him how to make the connection. The dogs usually scampered on ahead as they did now, ready for a day's work, but they were company as much as anything, Conor's constant companions. As he approached the cattle, the leader of the herd, Nuala, recognisable by her crooked horns, always came up first. She then led the herd away across the moor and the sandy plains leading to the island some distance away, where they would stay for a full three days, then he would bring them back. Aaron always came with him too and he would be over on the shores now puffing on his pipe, waiting patiently for Conor to join him. He loved his cattle.

As he walked, Conor contemplated his lot. He loved working with wood; it was what he did best, and he spent all of his free time working alongside Sean. Whilst Sean put his magic machine together, Conor was building his own boat with wood he'd collected from the forest just like his da had done. He had completed the shell; next he would put in the seats and the roof then equip it, but for that he needed to save his money. He was sure Clara would like it, and when it was ready, he would take her to where he began his journey. He would also show her his casket full of wolf hair which had been passed down through his family for generations and which he used for making tools. These always brought him luck – they had brought him to the farm. She wouldn't believe him, but he knew it to be true.

Aaron didn't spend so long helping him and Sean these days, preferring to sit alongside his range whatever the weather, leaving the care of the animals and the land to him mostly. Sean was pre-occupied with his new machine, and much was left in Conor's hands. He didn't mind, though, not one bit, and enjoyed the responsibility if he was honest.

Conor had always been able to sense what was going on, to work things out long before they happened. Not a second sight as Aoifa had, so he'd understood, no, just a knowing. Aaron had been a real da to him and he'd been watching him lately as he spent more time resting and he wondered if Sean had noticed it.

There was Nuala waiting patiently, her big brown eyes staring at him dreamily. She knew what lay ahead. He patted her shoulder as she stood, stolid, calm whatever the weather. Conor looked around, but Aaron was nowhere to be seen. He patted Nuala once more and told her he would be back as he turned and headed towards the farm. Aaron would be in the barn talking to Sean about his machine; he did that a lot these days too.

Conor loved to work alongside Sean, and if he left, he would miss him for sure, he surmised, shaking his head to clear the indecision. Sean always had time for him except when that Laurel came, then he never saw him. *Alwuz in a bad mood, that gal, too. She was what his ma would call a scary one. Dunno what Sean sees in 'er. Not sure 'e does, really.* Conor didn't like her because she bossed him about. *A good leader doesn'a do that. Wolves don't do it; they're clever, so they don't need to. But, I must say, she makes a grand chocolate cake!* he admitted with a smile.

When he reached the barn, it was all locked up. Sean must have gone out, as he noticed his old truck was gone. The sun was beating down now and if they didn't get the cattle across soon, the heat would stop it and the tide would turn.

Conor stopped his pondering as he looked around for Aaron, but there was no sign of him anywhere. Aaron never missed a cattle drive. Casey and Brody were running ahead of him; they were confused too.

Suddenly, his heart beat faster, louder, and Conor picked up speed, breaking into a run, the wolf in him sensing the urgency. He needed to be there. On reaching the house, he clicked open the old front door and the heat of the fire hit him.

He looked across the room and there was Aaron, fast asleep next to the range. Despite his closeness to the fire, his face was pale, white even. Conor went over and gently shook him by the shoulder.

"Aaron?" He spoke quietly to him, but Aaron did not move.

The grandfather clock was ticking quietly in the corner as the dogs came over and stopped in front of their master. Casey licked Aaron's hand, but Brody, the older of the two, stayed at Conor's side.

Conor's heart slowed right down. He brought the footstool over and sat on it, looking into the fire, feeling the intensity of the heat. He glanced up into Aaron's face; he looked so tranquil with his eyes half-closed, and Conor knew he had gone. He'd seen it before and was in no doubt. Cascy and Brody lay down at their master's feet and Conor put his head in his hands and sobbed.

He sat there a long while until his tears passed. He knew he had to do something like he had done before, but this time, although Aaron had shown him love and given him a life beyond anything he thought possible, Conor was not family. It was with a heavy heart and a coldness in his soul that he picked up the phone. He loved Aoifa and wanted to save her pain, but he could not any more than he could save his own. He accepted the truth of the task ahead just like any wolf would do.

"Aoifa? Please can you come? It's your da…"

Aoifa had put down the phone before he had finished. She was already on her way. What would happen now? Conor was shaking, his mind in overload. His decision whether to stay had been taken from him. He would have to go. The farm would come to Sean, and he may want to make changes, even bring Laurel in or they would sell it. Conor sighed with a sad resignation that he would no doubt have to move on once more.

He soon heard Sean's old Land Rover coming up the drive. As he came through the door, Sean avoided eye contact and touched his shoulder as the tears rolled down Conor's cheeks, the loss of his own parents coming back to him. The door latch clattered again, disturbing the tranquil scene, as Aoifa ran over to him and took Conor into her arms, embracing him like he had never known before. He stood still, unable to move or respond, but the gesture brought enormous comfort to him, his tears gradually subsiding. One by one, the family all arrived, then Liam and Sean took their pa upstairs and laid him out on his own bed.

The family went up to be with their pa and Conor stayed downstairs. He sat on the stool and looked across at Aaron's empty chair. The dogs lay on the floor next to him, their heads bowed too, in the knowing way dogs have. Conor heard Aoifa reciting a poem, one he was not familiar with.

"Because I have loved life,
I shall have no sorrow to die
I have sent up my gladness on wings,
To be lost in the blue of the sky
It is with my loved ones I shall be.
I will think of you as you can think of me
and speak to you all from the deep of sea."

Later in the evening, after the padre had visited, the rest of the family departed. Only Aoifa and Sean remained. They invited Conor to sit with them in Aaron's study, which Conor had never entered previously, and he sat down nervously, overwhelmed with grief, his mind whirring.

"Conor, you did a wonderful thing, being here for Pa. He passed peacefully; it was a heart attack."

"Like my da," Conor whispered, looking down, wringing his hands.

"Broken heart, too," muttered Sean as he perched on the edge of the armchair, tense and taut with grief. Aaron's parting had been so sudden they were all reeling from the shock.

"The poem I read, Pa wrote himself," said Aoifa, looking into space. "The saddest part of all, we never said goodbye," she added as her voice broke and there was a moment's silence between them, then she continued, "We want you to know, Conor, that Sean will run the farm and we would love you to stay and continue as before? You've been an enormous support to Pa, and we know that's what he would want."

Conor glanced up at them both with a small smile, but words eluded him as he realised how important this family were to him and he felt overwhelmed with relief.

"This is your home too, if you want it," Sean told him.

A flood of gratitude washed over him, and Conor knew he must stay. Yet a part of him wanted to move on, make his own living and not depend on these lovely people. His thoughts were jumbled, but he couldn't let them down. They had been kindness itself to him and he had to be true to them. He would stay, for now at lcast, if not forever.

"Yeah, we make a good team," he nodded and smiled across at Sean then got up. "I'll get us a nice pot of tea." He left them alone and went to put the kettle on.

"Ony thing t' help for now, Casey," he told the Collie as he trotted over dejectedly, his tail low. Conor stroked him affectionately, but Brody didn't move at all.

Conor stayed down in the living room that night, trying to make sense of things. A strange power had brought him to the barn that night, and into the heart-warming ways of this dear family. Otherwise, where would he be? Although he had to admit his heart was not here, he would travel the road with them; they were, after all, family to him. Conor had a plan, but he would be patient. A good wolf is always patient. Then, after Aaron had been laid to rest, within a respectable time, he would follow his own heart and the rest of his life would begin.

23. EARTH, FIRE, AIR AND WATER

It was the end of a chapter of Aoifa's life. Her ma and now her pa, gone. She couldn't take it in. "Damn it!" she shouted as she drove home. Oh, what was the point of dwelling on regrets and recriminations? "I'm done with that!" she mumbled. Messages wouldn't bring her pa back anyway, she thought miserably.

Aoifa sighed, an intense sadness gripping her as the grief took hold. So, her ma had taken her gift of foresight and now she'd taken her pa, too. *I wish you'd take my bitterness, Ma, because it will finish me!* Aoifa growled and banged the steering wheel to release her growing tension. *I'm supposed to be of Water – trusting, forgiving, flowing freely through my life. Huh, not anymore. It's impossible to stop the world from turning. Well, Ma, you've turned mine upside down!* Aoifa screamed at the elements all around her, which were shaping her future but no longer in the way she had envisaged.

Home Farm had been in the family for centuries and thank God for Sean and Conor – at least the farm would stay. The thought helped to ease her gnawing pain deep inside.

Aaron had played such an important role in Aoifa's life. He'd been the mainstay of the family, stalwart, solid, entirely reliable – he was of Earth, like Padraig. A touch of a smile curled round Aoifa's mouth. Now she understood the attraction. An evening breeze came in through the car window and, pushing her hair back from her face, she found it wet with tears. Aaron had left his legacy, a truth, an honesty, his belief in core Christian values. He had been a benevolent man, a true example of rightful living, and for that she would always feel extremely lucky and grateful.

By the time Aoifa arrived home, she felt more composed and compassionate. The anger toward her mother passed as she managed to find the courage to explain to the girls what had happened. They couldn't believe it and had myriad questions, which Aoifa did her best to answer.

"Why couldn't we say goodbye, Ma?!" shouted Clara.

"Because, sweetheart, sometimes death happens like that. Taking the good folk quickly without letting them suffer."

Clara looked desolate, giving a slight nod, the idea consoling her.

That night, Aoifa lay enveloped in Padraig's arms, listening to the lapping of the waves and the nocturnal calls of the birds and animals out on the moors. The stars were shining brightly as Aoifa gazed out at them but with unseeing eyes.

"He didn't suffer, Pad, passed in his sleep. That's a comfort to me."

"Best way, Aoif. We will all miss him very much, a font of wisdom, to be sure. Your ma had the messages, but your pa always found a solution to any problem. We can learn from that."

"Yes, he left us all with so much," said Aoifa as she added wistfully, "Love never dies, does it, Pad?"

"No, chara, never." He held her tight until she fell fast asleep.

It was one month later. Lois was leaving in a few days' time. The school open evening was coming up, so Aoifa and Rachel were having a day out together.

As Rachel's Land Rover stopped in the yard, Aoifa looked out and noticed her friend had a bit of trouble getting out.

"Ach, I need a stepladder, Aoif!"

They both laughed as Aoifa called back,

"Don't get out – we'll n'er get yer in again!"

She grabbed her bag, ran to the car and they set off. "Cloudy today, mind. May get a shower later."

"Well, no matter. Retail therapy's good whatever the weather, eh!"

They travelled along the coastal road toward the town. The sun was nowhere to be seen and clouds were steadily creeping in across the Atlantic as the seagulls screeched their displeasure. Aoifa watched the scene, and a sadness came over her as if brought on by the change of weather.

"I can't believe Lois will be gone in a few days, Rach. Too many folk leaving us," she added quietly.

"I been thinkin' on that, Aoif. Why not get in touch with your spiritual past, fill a void, eh? You always found solace in the spirit world."

Aoifa contemplated her friend's wise words as they chugged along.

"I think maybes your right. I will revisit the special place I used to with Ma," she said, the thought comforting her. "I can talk to Pa, too. You know, Rach, with all the beauty of this place," Aoifa gestured toward the bay, "this is our little bit of wild utopia; that to be grateful for." She looked out at the scene ahead of them, a late summer vista of fading greenness travelling the contours of the bay as they passed forests, moorland, hills and marshlands interspersed with rugged rock formations. Immersed in thoughts of their homeland, they travelled along in companionable silence, eventually broken by Aoifa as she spoke excitedly,

"We spoke to Mairy – and guess what? She can't wait to join you! We explained the sixth form didn't open until January and she was actually disappointed!"

"That's grand news, Aoif. Our sixth form tutor is accomplished in all the sciences, so should focus her skills."

"That's settled, then!" Aoifa announced, clapping her hands and breathing a loud sigh of relief as Rachel broached another subject.

"Tell me about Mairead's element of Fire, Aoif?"

"Well, Mairy is very passionate by nature, Rach, and is a bit of a pleasure-seeker, alright. We're hopeful she'll be more open-minded when she makes new friends and channels her passions in other directions, especially when she sees your state-of-the-art equipment!"

"Yeah – hopefully inspire her. Can I ask, what makes you think your ma will send Mairy the gift, then?"

"Ma left a message for me just before she passed, saying to look out for my girls and especially... Sadly, she didn't finish her sentence, but surely, she'll get that Mairy is travelling down the wrong road?"

"So, she didn't mention anyone by name?"

"Well, no," said Aoifa, "but Mairead needs guidance the most, doesn't she?"

They soon pulled up in the car park in the centre of town and Rachel threw her jacket into the back.

"Ach, it's so humid, Aoif."

"We need a storm," said Aoifa as they made their way to the shops and Rachel soon stopped to look in a shop window.

"Hey, this is very on trend, as Lois would say. Let's go in."

They browsed inside and Aoifa selected one or two tops for Lois' trip and a pretty cardigan for herself.

"They's all too small for me in here! I could feed two babies with these at the moment!" laughed Rachel, looking down at her chest.

Aoifa laughed. "Sure it's only one in there?"

"Cheeky!" she replied, giving her a playful thump.

By the time they had walked around a while and several purchases later, it was time to stop for lunch.

"Look," said Aoifa. "I love this place, squishy leather sofas, very cosy. Now, Rach, after spoiling us on Pad's birthday, this is on me!"

"Ach, give over," replied Rachel, but Aoifa insisted.

"Sit yoursel' afore you fall down!"

They soon settled with a coffee and waited for their food to arrive.

"Did I tell you we had a lovely break a few weeks back? It was heaven, Aoif, to get Brendan away from the pub!"

"Sounds lovely," said Aoifa pensively.

"You two should go. Hey, I could look after the girls, get to know Mairy!" she said with a wink. "By the way, d'you ever find out who that bloke was, who went after her?"

"Yes, he's in her class and he was just hanging out in the cave when Mairead came by. He thought she was spying on him, so he pushed her out the way. We let it go, Rach. Mairy wanted it." Aoifa shook her head doubtfully. "Sooner she moves on the better," she added grimly then a big smile came across her face. "Pad and I could go away for my birthday!" she said excitedly. "It's a no-brainer! Chase away my sadness for Pa a little, eh?"

Aoifa felt a sharp pain and pushed it away as she smiled at her friend and Rachel looked at her carefully.

"Don't bury that, Aoif. You must miss him so much. Talk about it?"

Aoifa blinked back the tears. "I can't, Rach, too raw, but thanks."

Rachel smiled warmly then brightened.

"Why don't you take one of those lodges up in the mountains? Roisin and Donald said they're lovely."

Aoifa's face lit up. "You know, I think we will!"

They enjoyed a nice lunch together then resumed their shopping. Rachel had just managed to find some maternity tops when suddenly the heavens opened.

"Wow! Quick, Aoif."

Aoifa grabbed their bags, and they made a run for the car, the rain coming thick and fast with a promise of more as menacing clouds filled the sky. Rachel quickly opened the door and they jumped in.

"Thank goodness we brought the Land Rover – look – floods up ahead!"

Sure enough, as they drove along the coast road, Aoifa looked out at the voluminous waves crashing onto the beach.

"Will they come over the wall?" Rachel asked anxiously.

"Probably get through OK. We're well up off the road," Aoifa replied.

It was a hazardous journey, the rain horizontal, and sure enough, gigantic waves did come toward them, tumbling treacherously under their vehicle which luckily held firm, although up ahead the floods were covering the road.

"It's drivin' in off the sea with the tide coming in, but this is built for these conditions," Rachel reassured them as she drove slowly onward.

The road soon turned inland, and they both breathed a sigh of relief as they headed away from the swell of the waves and out of danger.

"Phew, that was a close one," Rachel gasped.

When they reached Muir Farm, Aoifa jumped out, grabbing her bags, and Rachel pulled away quickly, keen to get home.

"Bye, Rach. Take care now."

Later that evening, she and Padraig were sitting each side of the range and the girls were settled in the sitting room.

"These flash storms are becomin' more frequent, eh, Pad?"

"Didn'a get it here, Aoif. Very localised they are. Hard to predict, too."

"Right, Paddy O'Brien, never mind the storms. You and me are going away on a long weekend!"

Padraig dropped his newspaper and looked at her in surprise.

"Oh, we are, eh? Where and when, may I ask?"

"On my birthday. There are some deluxe lodges up the mountain past Clifden. I've reserved one already!"

Padraig took her hand and pulled her onto his lap.

"Just you an' me, then, eh?"

"Well, we could take the tribe if you like… but I dunna think the horses would fit! Rachel's gonna come an' stay here for us."

Padraig smiled. "Long overdue," he said, kissing her affectionately.

A few days later, they were all loading Lois' bags into the car and Aoifa watched her eldest daughter as she said goodbye to her sisters. *She looks so grown up*, she thought, *in her smart jeans, open neck blouse and her hair up in the clever way she does it.*

Clara was crying and Siobhan was expressing her emotions in her usual way as Lois gave them all an enchanting smile.

Mairead was standing tall and smiling confidently at her older sister.

"I'm the oldest now, so I'll look on them for yer!" she called out.

Aoifa nearly corrected her but stopped herself. "It'll do no harm to give her a bit of responsibility for that," she muttered to herself.

Padraig came outside to join them, and Lois turned to her parents. "This is it, then."

"Not IT!" said her pa. "Just a new direction, eh? But you'll come back down this road to see us, won't yer, gal?"

Lois had tears in her eyes as she replied, "Always, Pa."

The three of them jumped into the car and set off. On their journey to the airport, Aoifa knew Lois' departure would define their relationship – they would part as good friends and not just mother and daughter. At the airport, when Lois turned to board her flight, her expression a mixture of excitement and expectation, Aoifa was overcome with pride as she took Padraig's hand, wiping her tears as they watched Lois walk away.

Later that afternoon, back at the farm, the phone rang.

"Yes, Rach, we'll all be there. See you later – and good luck!"

Padraig pulled up in the new car park in front of a wide red ribbon which travelled across the front of the school. There was a throng of people and the local mayor, in full regalia, was welcoming everyone. He soon cut the ribbon, declaring the school open, which was followed by huge applause as Rachel invited everyone inside for a buffet. Aoifa had tears in her eyes. It was a proud moment for the town, and it was all credit to her friend, who had seen the project through from start to finish and her daughter was to be a part of it.

"I be coming here in a few months, Ma. It's so exciting!" whispered Mairead. "Can I maybes stay at the pub once in a while, to make it easier for you?" she asked.

Aoifa was unsure. "Well, settle in first, then we'll see. It's not far for me to drive you anyways."

After a tour of the school, the family made their way home in awed silence.

A few weeks later, there was a knock at the door and Rachel walked in carrying her overnight bag.

"Hello! All ready for the off?"

Aoifa hugged her warmly then started fussing around the girls, but Rachel put her hands up.

"Look, they're all good girls. Just go!"

Padraig took their bags out to the car as they waved goodbye and set off.

"Got you away at last, then, Pad?"

"Yep, just you and me and a birthday to look for'wd to! Think we'll survive?" he asked with a saucy smile.

"We'll do more than that, Padraig O'Brien!" said Aoifa suggestively.

Two hours later, they were on the mountain pass, winding their way upwards with glorious, panoramic views of the mountainous terrain stretching out as far as the eye could see.

"Oh God, Pad. It's stunning. We can almost see Lois in America! Apparently, we have to walk the last half a mile. Good we got our walking boots."

They pulled up in the car park, took their bags and provisions out and prepared to continue on foot.

"Gorgeous late summer weather too, chara." Padraig shielded his eyes from the bright sunshine then reached into one of the rucksacks. "Well, got the champagne!" He held up two bottles.

Aoifa shrieked with delight. "Better go easy on that stuff or we be fallin' off the edge of these mountains!"

Giggling as they went and struggling with their bags, the lodge soon came into view.

"That must be it, Pad. It's fabulous!"

Sitting in the middle of an acre of land with spectacular views out across the Atlantic Ocean, the lodge looked very welcoming as it gleamed at them in the bright sunshine. Aoifa opened the front door and looked inside at the modern decor, a carved oak coffee table in the centre displaying a pot of fresh lavender, pastel-coloured drapes to match the chintz sofas, with a huge wood-burner in the corner. The floor was of polished cedarwood, giving a warm hue throughout, and the galley kitchen was in a pretty cornflower blue.

"Oh, it's stunning!" Aoifa gasped.

Padraig chuckled as he walked around. There were two bedrooms and a luxurious bathroom with a claw-foot bath in pure white with shiny brass fittings.

They unpacked, ate a light lunch then set off for a walk to check out the area. There was an old brick bothy at the bottom of the garden, and as they passed it, Padraig noticed the door was ajar. He pushed it and inside there was a stack of chopped wood in the corner, but he was surprised to see some flattened old bales on the floor. They went through a small gate leading onto a well-trodden path which meandered around the side of the mountain. Sheep were grazing on the side of the hill, free-ranging as far as the eye could see and gazing up at them curiously.

As they followed the track, Padraig suddenly stopped, and his eye followed the route downwards.

"This must go to the bay, look. M'be couple o' miles?"

Aoifa pushed her hair back from her sun-drenched face and wiped her brow. "Phew, another day!" she said. "Let's go back now, follow that circular path around. I've put some wine on ice and I need it already!"

Back at the lodge, Padraig laid the fire for the evening.

"I bet it gets cold up here at night, Aoif."

"Not with a cosy fire and you to keep me warm! I've found some candles, too. So, which bag are all my presents in, then?"

"Now, the best presents are the smallest, isn't that right?" he said with a wink and Aoifa was mystified.

As darkness fell, they enjoyed a delicious meal by candlelight next to a roaring fire as they watched the flames flicker around the room, the reflections bouncing off the honey-coloured walls.

"So romantic. Takes us back, eh?" Aoifa gave him a sideways look.

"Promises, eh?" said Padraig. "Let's sit out on the verandah, Aoif. There's a full moon and the air is so clear up here. Look at all those stars!"

As they sat together enjoying the last of the wine, Padraig started. "What was that crack?" But there was nothing to see, only shadows of bracken and bushes in the moonlight.

"Ah… all manner of wildlife up here, Pad. Let's go in so as not to disturb."

They retired early after a long day, and as they lay together in the luxurious white bedlinen, Aoifa turned to Padraig.

"I've been thinking back to the times I was in close touch with the elements, Pad. You are my most compatible element, you know. Earth and Water – a symbiotic partnership. Perfect." But Padraig was already gently snoring. Aoifa lay in his arms, sighing contentedly as she felt herself drifting off into a deep dreamy sleep.

The next day, Aoifa awoke as the sun was peeking in through the curtains. *It's my birthday*, she thought, *without Ma or Pa, but with my best friend*. As she listened to the whistling breeze and the puffins calling outside, she suddenly sensed something, a veil, a shroud, touching, floating around her and a pull deep inside. It was her ma visiting her. She shivered and Padraig rolled towards her, taking her into his arms as he whispered,

"Happy Birthday, chara. The champagne's ready!" and they both laughed.

"For breakfast, you devil!"

"And why not? We're gonna need some after…" He didn't finish as he took her in a passionate embrace.

Later that morning, Aoifa was luxuriating in a bath full of bubbles when the room suddenly darkened as if the sun had gone in. She glanced up at the frosted window as a shadow passed over and it puzzled her. She got dressed and went out to the kitchen where Padraig was reading the paper.

"Pad, were you outside just then…?"

"No, chara, too relaxed to move! Why?"

"A shadow came across the window."

He went out to check but returned and told her, "Nah. Must have been a cloud."

"Hmm," was all Aoifa replied as she looked out at the sky, a clear sapphire blue with not a cloud in sight. She put on her new stripey summer cardigan over a white t-shirt and jeans, they prepared a picnic and walked out into the dazzling sunshine as two birds of prey came soaring high above them.

"Pad, look!"

"Ospreys, a rare sight. Must be near their nest, then, flying together."

They watched them a moment, mesmerised, then walked down a plethora of pathways, cutting between the purple and white heathers when Aoifa stopped and bent down.

"These tiny orchids, Pad, only grow at these altitudes on the rock face. So pretty."

They soon found a patch of grass to sit on overlooking the plains below with the sea and islands beyond.

"Such beauty, chara. No one to disturb, just sharing your birthday with nature this time, eh?"

"Just as I like it," she replied softly, "and you, of course."

Padraig poured out the drinks and raised a toast, "To you and another forty years or more!" he told her, but Aoifa's face darkened. "Hey, chara, what?"

"Glad we're away, not home to miss Pa." She gulped back a sob.

They sat in silence a moment then Padraig added, "Don't hide the pain, Aoif. Share it."

Aoifa quickly flashed her eyes at him, "Not you too! Rachel said that." Then she softened. "I know," she whispered. "Just not now, eh? Look – Clare Island way in the distance. Clara was born of Water too." Aoifa looked out for a moment, deep in thought. "She is such a sweet child, Pad, so home-loving, motherly even!"

"She's like you. Have you noticed she spends time at the end of the garden, doing goodness-knows-what these days?"

"She buried one of the green stones next to old Bessie. Maybe she talks to her."

After their picnic was finished, they lay back and dozed in the warm sunshine until it popped behind the mountain and Aoifa shuddered as a cool breeze came over the hill.

"Come on. I've a meal to prepare!" Padraig exclaimed.

"Is that right? Spoiling me, eh?"

"Aye. An' you've not had your present yet!"

Aoifa looked at him fondly. "I can wait. I've enough here a'ready."

She yawned indulgently as Padraig took her hand and pulled her up. They made their way back, winding around the stony path and up toward the lodge when suddenly Aoifa touched Padraig's arm and whispered, "Over there, look, by the bothy!"

There was a flash of someone closing the door.

"Who can it be, Pad?"

Aoifa went up to the lodge as Padraig tiptoed quietly back down the garden. She watched him open the bothy door when someone came out, shoulders bent with a guilty air about him as he and Padraig came toward her.

"How do!" she said, smiling at a young man very bedraggled-looking but with a friendly face.

He grunted something back which she didn't quite catch, and Padraig introduced him.

"Aoifa, this 'ere's Kane. He lives around and about and was just passing," he told her, with a glint in his eye. "I've asked him up for a drink."

"Of course, welcome," Aoifa said and stood back to allow him in, whispering to Padraig, "The shadow…"

Aoifa fetched a beer for everyone, and they all sat down.

"D'you live out there, then?" she asked him, pointing to the bothy.

"Well, ony sometimes when I's passin' by."

"That's OK," said Pad. "We won't say anything. So where do you live when youse not passin' by?" he asked with a glint in his eye.

"Way over yonder, boat down b'low," Kane answered vaguely.

"I see. Travellin' life, then?" said Padraig.

"Must be goin' now," he said, and within a second, he was gone, without touching his beer.

"I dunno, Aoif, but there was sommat familiar about that lad. Have you seen him afore?" he asked, scratching his head.

"I'm not sure I have, but I know what you mean."

Padraig made a start on dinner whilst Aoifa popped her cardigan on and enjoyed a glass of champagne, watching the sunset out on the verandah. Padraig soon came out to join her, carrying a small box.

"For you, chara." She smiled gratefully. It was a silver charm necklace. Padraig opened up one of the charms and inside was a tiny picture of her ma and pa then two other charms displaying Lois and Niamh. She studied them all carefully then stifled a sob.

"Thank you, my love. Now they will be close to me forever." She embraced him warmly.

"I felt Ma here this morning. Came to wish me Happy Birthday, too."

"I know. I felt you shiver. You always did that when the messages came."

They both stood up to go inside and Aoifa turned for one last look out across the sea.

"Out there, Pad, d'you see? An array of lights beyond Clare Island. What is it?"

Padraig scoured the dark ocean and stopped to focus.

"Ach, chara, the moon and sun playing tricks but pretty all the same." They both went inside, closing the door.

Their last evening was spent absorbed in a romantic comedy on the TV with their second bottle of champagne and both vowing to return for another break in the future.

The next morning as they made their way down the hill, Aoifa looked back at the lodge, glistening in the early morning sun. With her family in mind, she held her necklace tight as it occurred to her they hadn't heard from Niamh since she left. She knew how forgetful that girl was and would surely be enjoying herself too much!

Their arrival at Muir Farm caused an uproar as the girls ran out to greet them with Rachel walking slowly behind.

"So, how've you been?" Aoifa asked, beaming at everyone and turning to Rachel cautiously. "And you, Rach, more importantly?"

"All good, Aoif. Little angels. Looked after me a treat!"

"Come, I'll make some tea an' we can have a chat in the garden."

"I'm gonna leave you to it," Padraig announced. "Got some horses to exercise!"

Clara called after him, "Coming too, Pa!"

Aoifa waved them all away. "Well, we gonna have us a private chat, an' Rachel can tell me what little monkeys you bin!"

"Ach, no, Ma. I've been good, honest!"

"That'll be the day, Mairy!" But Aoifa was grinning in hope as the girls took themselves off.

"Before you ask, Aoif, Mairy has behaved impeccably. Even got me breakfast in bed! I don't see the problem, meself!" quipped Rachel.

"I dunna know who you're talkin' about, Rach! Well, must've brought the best out in 'er!"

"I been looking at these girls like you, through the elements, Aoif. I can see Clara is like you, of Water.

Sensitive, kind and hard-working too – she never stops! Spent her time up the garden mostly. But Siobhan – what's this imagination of hers? Unusual, I'd say."

"Hmm. I know it bothers Padraig," Aoifa told her and Rachel added,

"Her senses seem to blend together somehow. She's the Air element, sometimes there, sometimes not, in her own little world…"

They finished their tea and Aoifa handed Rachel a gift as a token of their gratitude then helped to carry her bags to the car, and she set off, waving happily as she went.

Later that evening, Aoifa told Padraig what Rachel had said about Siobhan.

"She talked about her senses, Pad, how they came together in a strange way. She didn't exactly say, but implied she was off with the fairies a bit."

Padraig looked away before he replied.

"Was she concerned, Aoif?"

"I don't know, but I think she was keeping something back."

A while later, it seemed that Padraig had nodded off, so Aoifa got up to go upstairs when suddenly he roused and spoke to her quietly,

"Sit, chara."

It startled Aoifa, but she did so.

"Many years ago, Aoif, my father used to express himself in exactly the same way. So, you see, it's happened in the family before."

Aoifa's eyes opened wide. "Really, Pad, I never knew."

"Because we never talked about it, not inside the family, nor out. Folk thought he was off with the fairies, too." He looked intently into the fire, then muttered as an afterthought, "And worse."

"She certainly lives up to her element of Air anyways!" said Aoifa lightly. "Well, we're not gonna worry about it now after such a lovely weekend." But she held her ma's charm tightly in her hand.

Suddenly, Aoifa's eyes opened wide, and she gasped, her face twisted as if in pain.

"Oh, Pad. Maybe it's Siobhan who will receive the gift instead of Mairead?"

Padraig looked across at her, a bewildered look in his eye.

"We'll just have to wait and see, then, won't we?" he said as he got up and they made their way upstairs to bed.

24. A TIME OF SURPRISES

It was late October and Aoifa and Padraig were having lunch together.

"It was magical on top of that mountain, Pad. Earth and Water amidst earth and water! The best bit – apart from the obvious," Aoifa fluttered her eyelashes at him, "was my present. I shall add to it when…" but she pushed away the thought of the other girls leaving home.

Padraig appeared thoughtful. "We could put a lodge up there, you know, on the edge of our land." He pointed to the small wood up behind their farmhouse.

Aoifa frowned, considering the idea. "Overlooking the Atlantic Ocean. Mmm. Beautiful," she replied dreamily.

"An escape for city-dwellers and a bit of bread an' butter for us! Keep you out of mischief, too!" he said, grinning.

"Like I do nothin' round 'ere. Hey, I could even run away to it, meself! Be expensive, though?"

"Not if I do it meself with young Conor. We've our own timber. Make it sustainable, you know, eco-friendly-like?"

"God, you are so wise, Paddy O'Brien. Maybe when I reach your age…!" She sniggered after him as he left to gather his seaweed haul.

That afternoon, following Rachel's suggestion, Aoifa was taking herself to a special place she used to visit with her mother, but as the girls arrived home from school, Mairead reminded her,

"Eileen's takin' Cat and me to the school disco later, Ma."

Aoifa's face clouded over, but she pushed her worries away, as Eileen had been an excellent chaperone.

"Ah, yes. Just serving soft drinks, are they?" she asked casually.

"I suppose so." Mairead mumbled something under her breath.

"What d'you say, chara?"

"Just one drink now and again would be nice!"

"Ah, well, that time will come. Have a nice evening, then."

Aoifa sighed. Now she needed her quiet time more than ever. There was a breeze in the air and the sun was hiding behind the clouds, so she threw on her jacket and set off.

Padraig was up ahead with his cart full of seaweed, and she waved as she moved away from the beach up onto the moorland. As she passed blue-flowering heathers and tiny mauve asters, the seagulls and terns hopping out of her way, she could soon see the small lake in the distance.

Aoifa had avoided this area since the loss of her mother and now her pa's passing still felt raw. Yet, as she approached, she felt a sense of peace, a serenity enveloping her and a visceral thrill rising up inside as she sat on their special rock. The lake looked magical, shimmering in the silvery-grey sunshine and Aoifa shivered, conscious of an ethereal presence, a warm sensation shrouding her. It was her ma. Fearing her presence may prove ephemeral, she spoke and immediately felt her senses ignite. Sounds and smells were sharper: the waves trickling loudly over the sand, noisy rustlings in the bushes and the fragrance of flora and fauna, more intense. The gulls were coming into roost, their callings loud and clear. Ubiquitous autumn colours of russets, amber and gold illuminated by the sun's rays seemed to come alive as they shone from above. As a mystical aura surrounded her, her thoughts floated in her subconscious.

Aoifa usually flowed through life as if on a wave, but lately she had a strong desire to protect everything she held dear, as images of her own element of Water crept in. The world would turn, the world would spin, yet Aoifa knew she was the only person she could control now. Conscious of her body and her soul within, keeping her mind still, she owned her thoughts, feeling the air around her until she felt the water, cool, flowing, calming, her body floating within.

Holding her charms tight in the palm of her hand, Aoifa watched the sun drop lower still, creating long shadows across the lake, and shafts of coppery sunlight filter through the trees. As she breathed deeply, she gave her worries back to nature, to the sea, then she stood up to reconnect with the physical, placing her hands on the rock, smooth, cool and so solid. She fondled the leaves on the trees, felt the soft sand between her toes and breathed in the heady fragrances to bring her back to the present.

Aoifa put her shoes on to make her way home. As she walked, images of her pa came before her eyes and she swallowed back the tears, leaving her sadness behind to float away with the elements.

Later that evening, the family all played board games and Aoifa enjoyed the playful banter which ensued, as it kept her focussed. Finally, the girls were exhausted, so they took themselves off to bed and she looked up at the time.

"Pad, it's 11 o'clock! Where's Mairy?" He sat up with a start, rubbing his eyes.

"I'd better see if she's comin'." He went outside to check.

A few minutes later, he returned followed by a rather stoic Mairead.

"She was standing in the porch. Goodness knows why."

"Mairy – bit late, eh?" Aoifa asked, but she got no response.

Mairead continued to stare at them, and Padraig was clearly piqued.

"I got nothin' from 'er either!"

"Has she been drinking, Pad?"

Mairead's eyes darkened as she declared sharply, "No, I have not," and promptly marched upstairs.

Aoifa made to follow her, but Padraig touched her arm.

"Leave her, Aoif. She's had a fall-out, I reckon."

When Mairead came down to breakfast the next day, she was back to her normal self. "So, what youse all up to today?" she asked cheerfully.

Siobhan held up her drawing pad, but Clara asked, "Pa, can we do a ride today, please?"

"I'll tidy up this morning then take yer!"

"How was the disco last night, Mairy?" asked her ma.

"Ach, bit boring. Not many there and the music was rubbish!"

"Thought you seemed a bit down when you got back. Ah well, be meeting new friends before too long!" Mairead ignored the remark.

"Ma, is Laurel coming over to Home Farm soon?"

Aoifa avoided her eyes. "I really don't know, chara."

"Can you call her for me? She offered to lend me sommat."

"Now, we don't need t' keep botherin' her, Mairy."

Aoifa glanced at her, but Mairead had already walked off.

One week later, Aoifa was in the garden contemplating the idea of a lodge when Mairead came rushing out.

"Ma – it's Laurel on the phone!"

"Hi, Lors. Today? I can drop her by later?"

When she rang off, Mairead was waiting expectantly.

"Ahh… you called her, then, Mairy?"

"Just wanna go see them, that's all!"

"OK, we'll take the girls."

"Oh, Ma, really?"

Aoifa glared at her. "Yes. Really."

When they arrived at Home Farm, Laurel was waiting in the yard.

"Not sin you here a while, Aoif. Not since the funer–"

Laurel stopped as Aoifa burst into tears.

"I know," Aoifa sniffed, trying to compose herself. "Feeling bad about it, to be honest."

Laurel linked arms with her friend. "Come on in. I put the kettle on a'ready. This girl 'ere wants sommat, me thinks!" She linked Mairead's arm too and they walked toward the farmhouse.

"Why do youse always think the worst?" Mairead laughed wickedly.

Aoifa looked at them uneasily as she got the mugs out and Siobhan and Clara said they were going to see Sean's machine.

"He'll love that," murmured Laurel sourly.

Aoifa sat down next to the range opposite her pa's chair for the first time since his passing, but surprisingly she felt OK, as if he were sitting there. Mairead and Laurel had gone out to the scullery to fetch a cake and, quite by chance, she overheard snippets of their conversation.

"…I got plans, Mairy! A baby, yeah. But… say nowt… our secret… look, have this… promise t' keep quiet?"

Laurel came back into the kitchen, beaming and carrying a huge fruit cake.

"Aoif, I'll just take some out to Sean and the girls."

When Laurel had left, Aoifa spoke up. "Sit with me, Mairy. What do you want from Laurel, then, chara?" But before Mairead could reply, Clara burst in through the door.

"Sheve is so funny sometimes, Ma!" she exclaimed and Aoifa eyed her warily.

"Why, Lara?"

"I could see sparks out there," said Siobhan, "and there were lots of smells in the barn."

"I've no doubt, Sheve. Sean's got so many engines in the making!"

"No, not engine smells, Ma, but smoke and somethin' sizzling. There was a rainbow of dark colours, and I could hear shrieks of laughter, too."

"Ah well, just part of the machine magic," said Aoifa dismissively. "Come on, girls, we must get back."

As they all got up to leave, Aoifa looked sideways at Mairead.

"You look like the cat who got the cream, Mairy."

"Do I, Ma?" She gave her mother a small smile.

On the journey home, Aoifa was troubled by what she had overheard. What did Mairy know about a baby and what had Laurel given her? She didn't have time to dwell on it because as they arrived home, Padraig was waiting with Brown Mane, and Clara jumped out of the car.

"Pa! You got him to wear his new bridle!"

Padraig smiled. "By the time your birthday comes, he be ready for a ride!"

Clara whooped with joy, stroking Brown Mane affectionately as he looked at her through his soft brown eyes, his ears pricked, and Clara walked him back to his new stable.

As nature prepared itself for the winter months ahead, Aoifa felt an inner peace and a quietening of her spirit. It was coming up to the anniversary of her mother's passing and she'd been making regular visits to their special place where she'd felt a tangible connection with her, a reprieve from her angst inside. She seemed to have so many worries at the moment and was pleased she had found the courage to ask her ma to help Mairead.

Clara's birthday arrived and a delicious tea awaited the girls' homecoming. As they arrived, Padraig put his head around the door with Brown Mane alongside.

"This one 'ere's waiting for his first ride!"

Clara jumped up and down excitedly. "My best present, Pa!"

"Come, everyone, tea first!" Aoifa told them.

"Where's the birthday gal, then?" Conor popped his head in, handing Clara some sprigs of lavender and a small present, which turned out to be a wooden trowel he had made especially. She got up to give him a hug then stopped as her parents exchanged looks and Aoifa told him,

"Come and join us, Conor!" but Clara wasted no time, swallowing her cake in one and shouting,

"I'm ready, Pa!" as she, Padraig and Conor went off for a ride.

Later that evening, the phone rang.

"Bren, Hi. How's things?" Aoifa paused, then shrieked, "That's wonderful news! So he shares a birthday with our Clara! Finn. A beautiful name. Please give our love to Rachel and we be over to wet his head soon!"

Padraig opened a bottle of wine to celebrate and this time even Mairead was allowed a small glass as they all raised a toast to wish Finn a long and happy life and Aoifa added happily, "Not forgetting Clara too!"

A few weeks later on Christmas Eve, Aoifa was in the bathroom when she heard the front door click.

"Pad, is that you?" she called down the stairs. Pulling on her sweater, she ran down to see and there was Niamh, standing in the hall giggling with her arms full of presents.

"Nevey!"

"I wanted to surprise you!"

"Come here."

They hugged excitedly. "Let me see you. Just look at that hair, gal, it's grown – you've grown! It's all that acrobattin' and jumpin' around!"

"Niamh!" cried Clara as she ran downstairs and flew across to her sister. "You staying for Christmas?"

"Well, that's the plan – if you'll have me?"

"I think we can fit you around the table, chara. You're skinnier than ever anyways!"

Mairead came down to see what the commotion was all about.

"Oh, Nevey! Youse got our presents, then?"

"Cheeky as ever, Mairy!" Then Siobhan appeared from nowhere.

"I could hear horses' hooves and smell loud music and there were fireworks in the air, and I knew it was you!"

Niamh turned to look at her. "Still tellin' stories, Sheve!" she chortled.

Padraig came in and stopped in surprise.

"Who have we here?" he grinned. "Brought the music back into this house, chara!" He drew her in for a warm hug.

At the mention of music, Aoifa glanced across at her youngest daughter, aware of her developing piano skills, but Clara appeared not to be listening.

"Come on, let's decorate the tree and Niamh can make her usual gingerbread men to hang up too," she told them.

The next morning, Aoifa looked out of the window. The sky was a deep pink tinged with purple above an aquamarine sea with just a wisp of breeze on the air. "Perfect," she said to herself, putting on her most colourful outfit and skipping downstairs where she and Niamh prepared the vegetables.

Lunch was well on the way when Sean, Conor and Laurel arrived, all rejoicing when Niamh went out to greet them. Aoifa gulped and looked away as they entered, as her pa had always been the first to walk through the door. Padraig opened several bottles of his bramble wine and they sat down to an enormous spread with the biggest turkey in the centre, bronzed to perfection.

As they all tucked in, Padraig raised a toast to Lois, adding, "She's probably sunbathin' right now!" and chuckled when Sean, quite out of character, raised a toast to their da too and they all lifted their glasses once more in silent respect.

Laurel soon turned her attention to Niamh.

"So, tell us about circus life, eh, Nevey?"

"Too much to tell, Lors. Would take all of lunch."

"We got time, gal!"

"What's the best bit?" asked Mairead.

"The circus folk! Oh an' the step dancin' and playing my fiddle to the pony dance and learning acrobatics and training all the animals!"

"That's all, then, chara?" asked her pa with a lop-sided grin.

"What else is there, Pa?"

"All those good-lookin' gypsy boys!" Mairead chirped.

Niamh replied coyly, "Well, maybe there is one…!"

"Ah, see, I knew it. She got a glint in her eye, Ma," said Mairead smugly.

Aoifa looked across at Niamh wistfully. It was a blessing to see her again, a vision of laughter, light and colour, a ray of sunshine breaking through the cloud which hung over her in the absence of her pa.

"So, how long you staying?" she asked.

"Until New Year's Eve, then there's a party in the Big Top!"

"Oh, can I come?!" asked Mairead boldly.

"Only circus folk, Mairy. Why, haven't you a party of yer own to go to?"

Mairead suddenly looked downcast. "Well, one of the girls from school is having one, but I'm not allowed to go."

"Now, Mairy, you've not asked, my girl!" said her pa, eyeing her directly. "Maybes. If Eileen is going."

"Ooh, can I, Pa? Eileen is going. Be my last time to see all my friends, too."

"Why, Mairy?" Niamh looked at her curiously. "Where you off to?"

Mairead smiled haughtily. "To Rachel's new school!" she said proudly, and Laurel chipped in,

"Mairy's goin' ta turn over a new leaf!"

Mairead's face darkened and her smile disappeared, but she had an answer.

"Actually, Lors, it's because they have a brilliant maths tutor and that is my best subject!"

Mairead had closed the matter once and for all in her bold, inimitable way and Aoifa secretly hoped she would never lose her sauciness as she looked at her fondly. After lunch was finished, there was much hilarity as Clara and Siobhan handed out the presents.

Padraig came in after feeding the animals, and as he opened the front door, the wind preceded him.

"Ach, wind's changed. Remember that snowstorm last year? Dunna want any more o' that!"

Sean looked out of the window. "We canna stay late. Got our animals t' see to an' all."

Then Laurel shouted, "Hey, we ain't goin' yet – open one of those bottles we brought!"

Aoifa caught Sean's eye, so he pretended not to hear. They left after supper and the girls went into the snug to watch a film. After clearing up, Aoifa and Padraig sat in the quiet of the sitting room in front of the fire with Flynn at their feet.

"A nice day, chara. You enjoy it?"

"I did, Pad. All went well. Peaceful too." She fingered her charm necklace. "And I still have Pa close, thanks to you."

New Year's Eve came around and Niamh had returned to the circus that afternoon, dropping Mairead to her party on the way. Aoifa closed the curtains and lit the fire as Padraig brought in the wine and they all sat down to a special meal.

"Got a vodka spritzer to go with the wine this evenin', Aoif!"

The girls tasted a sip, but Clara went to the kitchen to spit it out in disgust. "Oh, Ma, this is poison. Don't drink it!" she cried, making everyone laugh when Padraig added,

"One day you may change your mind on that, Lara!"

At 11pm, there was a knock at the door.

"That'll be the taxi with Mairy, Aoif. I'll go."

When he opened the door, Padraig swore to himself. The taxi driver was holding Mairead up and she couldn't keep her eyes open, her make-up was smudged, and her black hair tangled around her face. She just managed to slur a greeting of "Happy New Year – hic – Pa," waving a wine bottle at him.

He grabbed her sternly, thanked the driver and took her immediately upstairs to bed. When he returned, all he said was, "Thank God for Rachel."

Aoifa wondered what had happened to Eileen but figured she couldn't be expected to watch over Mairy forever.

There was one week to go before Mairead started her new school and they were sorting out her clothes upstairs when the telephone rang.

"I'll get it, Ma!" Mairead ran down the stairs two at a time.

"Just a minute. I'll get Ma."

Mairead called her mother down, but she was already there.

"Uncle David! You know just the other day, I was saying…" Then Aoifa stopped, and her face went white. "I don't understand, Uncle. What happened on the boat, then?"

Aoifa's face fell as she listened to his explanation. If only she hadn't invited them over; it would never have happened! She was only vaguely listening to him now… "So sorry, then, bye."

Aoifa put down the phone, tears flowing down her cheeks as Padraig came in through the door.

"It's Aunt Beth. She's passed, Pad. They had an accident on the night of our party, all that time ago…" She broke down and was unable to finish.

"Come, chara. Mairead, put the kettle on."

He led her to the sofa, telling her gently it must have been the storm.

"No, it was my fault!" she screeched. "Such was my desire to find out about the past. Now I shall never know anyway, and she's gone. She must have suffered so from her injuries, Pad!"

Aoifa put her head in her hands and the grief poured out of her.

"Chara, they could have had a boat accident any time. Calm now."

"But it was because of our party! Drat the loss of my sight, or I'd have…" Aoifa wiped her tears away harshly. "They even had the funeral, Pad. The memorial service is on Saturday."

Aoifa's lips were trembling as she tried to control herself, but she felt so weary and so very sad.

"Mairead, make some tea for your ma and put sugar in it. I must go out to finish, but I won't be long, chara."

Aoifa sat with her tea untouched and Clara alongside.

"Why, oh why, did it have to happen like that?" she shouted. "She was fit and well when we last saw her."

Clara looked worriedly at her mother and held her hand.

"At least you became her friend, Ma, didn't you?" she said meekly, making her mother smile.

"How right you are, Lara. We did become friends in the end, in spite of the past."

It was three days later, and the family were preparing to travel up to the memorial service. Aoifa remembered to put on her charm necklace and called out to the girls to hurry up just as Mairead replied,

"Must I go, Ma? I didn't really know Aunt Beth."

Aoifa turned on her angrily, "Yes, we must all go, Mairead. Life isn't all about having a good time, you know."

Padraig raised his eyebrow to her as he put on his coat and Aoifa knew she'd been overly harsh. In truth, she was cross with Mairead because she had done little to change her ways, yet she looked across at Padraig apologetically as they all walked out to the car.

When they arrived at the church, she approached Liam and Emma at the entrance, giving them both a hug.

"Li. What a shock this is."

Aoifa was dismayed at how distraught he looked, more so than at his mother's funeral, and she touched his arm gently.

"You OK, Li?" But he turned away and Emma told her,

"This has hit him badly, Aoif. Aunt Beth and Liam were very close."

This took Aoifa by surprise, but she said nothing, just put her hand on her brother's shoulder then returned to Padraig, who had found some seats. It was a solemn service, following their strong catholic faith, and Aoifa took Padraig's hand to contain her grief as tributes were made by David and some close friends. Afterwards, David told them to follow him back to the house, where a meal would be served.

As they drove through an elegant housing estate and turned into the drive of a rather imposing house, Mairead gasped.

"Cor, this house is huge!"

"Now, Mairy," warned her pa. "Not to gloat over." But he caught Aoifa's eye as they travelled around the turning circle to park the car in a paddock at the back. When Aoifa got out, she could see that the property stood in a couple of acres of formal garden. Liam was standing at the front door, clearly feeling better as he welcomed them warmly, offering drinks and directing everyone to the dining room.

"Liam seems at home, Pad," said Aoifa, smiling politely at everyone.

As they joined a short queue for food, she noticed Liam was in the kitchen talking animatedly to a tall young lady who was obviously the caterer. Then she saw a strange thing. He put his arm tightly around her shoulders, drawing her in and kissing her cheek, and Aoifa gasped.

"What is it, Aoif?" Padraig asked irritably, as people were looking at them.

"It's nothing, Pad." She looked down to deter any attention.

Liam came out to serve them with the same lady alongside and it was obvious that they were getting along famously with their heads close together. Aoifa was horrified. Her brother had gone too far and in their deceased Aunt's home, too. She looked around for Emma, who was nowhere to be seen.

The family took their plates to sit in the sumptuous drawing room as Danny and Scorcha came to join them.

"Poor Aunt Beth," said Scorcha, visibly upset.

"I know, chara," Aoifa retorted kindly. "We couldn't believe it and after our party too."

"Now, Aoif, don't start that again," Padraig said gently, putting his arm around her. "She enjoyed our party and we enjoyed having her; that to be grateful for."

After they had eaten, Dan suggested they all went for a walk around the garden and the girls were only too pleased to get some fresh air.

Aoifa got up and went to join her brother in the kitchen. It seemed he was still cavorting with the same young lady.

"Liam, can we talk, please?"

"Sure, Sis."

As he led her away, Aoifa turned on him.

"What are you doing flirting with that young lady, Li? Behaving badly, I would say, up to your old tricks and at your aunt's funeral too!"

Aoifa was candid with him, as his blatant behaviour had not only embarrassed her but had been wholly inappropriate. Liam didn't speak immediately and seemed thoroughly disconcerted by Aoifa's accusation.

"I wasn't… I mean, I didn't…"

He was clearly lost for words.

"All over her, you were, Li. I can tell by the guilty look of yer."

"No, Aoifa, you've got it wrong. She's… just Nell."

Aoifa wasn't prepared to listen to his lies any longer as she turned and walked out into the garden to join the others. Her heart was pounding, and her hands felt clammy at their exchange. She was appalled. Liam was undeniably prepared to tarnish the family's reputation, at a time when a modicum of decency was definitely required.

She spotted Padraig at the bottom of the garden and gestured for him to join her. She was red-faced by the time he caught up with her.

"What's goin' on, Aoif?"

"That young lady doin' the food, Liam was actually flirting with her, outrageous it was, in front of everyone!"

"Hmm. She was rather attractive…" Padraig added distractedly but with the suggestion of a smile.

Aoifa glared at him, then smiled to herself to conceal her true thoughts. She was fully aware that her occasional feelings of jealousy were often misplaced and just maybe she had misjudged her brother! The word 'paranoia' came to mind again. Maybe it was all the grief? Aoifa shook her head, sniffed, and reached out to touch the fronds of a bamboo plant close by to help keep her head.

They wandered around the beautiful gardens, soon reaching two converted barns behind the main house. The first one was in darkness, but there was a lamp on in the second. Aoifa became curious and they went to have a quick peek. There was a lady of indistinguishable age sitting in semi-darkness at a desk in a wheelchair, with a wood-burner glowing in the background. She was unaware of their prying eyes, as she had her back to them. They both turned away quickly, suddenly ashamed of their snooping, when Scorcha called them from the house to say there was a celebration cake and a small speech was about to be made.

Inside the hallway, Padraig and Aoifa stood at the back and Aoifa spoke quietly,

"Who was that person in the barn, Pad? They couldn't walk."

"It looked to me like self-contained accommodation, Aoif. She may be staying on vacation or be renting the barn. Anyways, nothin' to do wi' us. Let's spend some time with Uncle David before we leave."

They all went across to him and Aoifa addressed him warmly,

"Uncle – thank you for inviting us today. Please come and visit us – we'd love to see you and hope you'll not be too lonely here," nearly adding, 'in this huge house', but she stopped herself.

"Thank you for coming, Aoifa. I will miss Beth greatly, but I won't be lonely. I do hope we will meet up again," he smiled then turned to rejoin his guests and they all made their way out to the car.

25. NEMESIS AND THE DARK

First thing the next morning, Aoifa was in the hall reaching for their coats.

"So, Mairy, we're off to visit Rachel today, check everything's ready for school on Monday."

Mairead made a face. "Aw, Ma, do I have to come?"

"Rachel would love you to meet little Finn, chara."

Mairead knew she needed to keep Rachel on side, so she agreed, and they set off.

"How far is it anyways?"

"Just three miles – half as far along the beach, though, with the tide out. You could cycle to school, you know!"

"Ma! You canna be serious. The weather's too bad round 'ere!"

As they travelled along, Mairead pondered on what the other pupils would be like because Callum had told her they were a bit posh around there.

"How many in my class, Ma?"

"I think eight girls and four boys."

"Yuk. More girls, then!"

Mairead cringed and her mother gave her a disdainful look.

"New friends, Mairy, eh? Now, baby may be asleep, so quietly does it."

Mairead nodded and wondered how women coped with all that, the crying and dirty nappies too. They soon pulled up at the pub and Rachel came out to greet them with baby Finn in her arms as Aoifa jumped out and ran up to them.

"Ooh, Rach, he's awake! How are you both?" she cried, holding out her arms for a cuddle, and Rachel smiled proudly.

"Doin' OK, I think, but I know nothing and need to ask you!"

As they made their way into the cosy sitting room, Aoifa asked Mairead if she'd like a cuddle.

"Och, Ma, I dunna know how to hold him!" She looked down on the baby, who was glancing up at her with his big blue eyes, rosy cheeks and shock of dark hair.

"He's got your hair, Rach."

"Really, Mairy, poor Finn – mine's so unruly! Coffee and scones, both?"

"Be lovely," Aoifa replied gratefully as Mairead followed Rachel into the kitchen.

"You ready for Monday?" Rachel asked, handing her the mugs.

"Think so. Bit nervous, though."

"You'll get to know the other kids in no time. May take a few weeks to settle in properly."

Mairead was aghast, as she'd imagined going out with her classmates right away. Maybe Rachel knew they weren't her type? This made her more nervous still as they took the coffee through.

"Do the students come to the pub, Rach?"

"Not really, Mairy – too young! In the class above, they do."

That pleased Mairead, but she asked no more, deciding it best to wait and see.

As they all sat down, Mairead told them, "I'll probably miss my old friends," noticing her ma and Rachel exchange a look and wondering what it meant when Aoifa spoke brightly.

"You'll make new friends quickly enough, chara. Don't worry on it."

And Rachel added brightly, "They're lovely families around 'ere, Mairy. You'll probably get invites to their houses pretty soon," but Mairead felt a flicker of disappointment at that idea. Weren't there any youth clubs or discos around there? And what were the other pubs like?

"Can I get some more scones, please, Rach?"

"Sure. Help yourself."

Mairead popped to the kitchen and rummaged in the tins but could hear her ma and Rachel speaking in low voices and she crept to the door to listen.

"I've had some quiet times with my Ma, Rach."

"Has it helped?"

"Definitely. I asked if Mairead can have the gift to stop her going down that dark road, too."

"Ah. Be a good day when Mairy changes her ways, to be sure."

Mairead was fascinated by the idea of having her ma's gift, but she'd had no messages. Well, she thought huffily, she'd just have to plan her own future and didn't know what the problem was anyway. What dark road? One thing was certain – she definitely knew how to have a good time!

As she returned, Finn was having a breastfeed and Mairead couldn't take her eyes away.

"Cor, Rach, he's pullin' your boobs, a'right! Won't they stay like that?"

Rachel and Aoifa laughed. "Well, they may not be quite the same, Mairy!" said her ma with a chuckle. "But it's best for baby."

Mairead wasn't so sure and didn't think she wanted her nice boobs to be pulled around like that. Pah! It seemed to her they all wanted babies round there at the moment, but she was sure Lors was too old anyway as she turned to listen to her ma.

"So, Rach, do we need to get anything more for Mairead? What about sport and outdoors?" asked Aoifa.

"Oh, Ma," Mairead groaned. "You know I hate sports!" But Rachel added,

"Well, Mairy, there's a climbing wall, forest school, tennis courts, up-to-the-minute sports hall and a new thirty-metre swimming pool!"

"An' I hate swimmin'!" she exclaimed, but her mother told her,

"Mairy, wait an' see. I think you'll be impressed by it all."

Mairead shook her head, knowing all of that was a waste of time. After her maths lessons, all she wanted was to hang out with her friends. If she had any, she thought grimly, and with that, she jumped up.

"Ma – I have to get back to call Cat 'bout t'night."

Her mother nodded unsurprisingly, and Rachel smiled. "A last fling, eh?"

Aoifa added, "You can still see Catrina at weekends, Mairy."

Mairead was doubtful. They may not be her friends once she left, but she must keep in with them, especially the boys. They were the best! Mairead rallied as she thought of the partying that evening – with the money Laurel had given her.

On the way home, her ma told her,

"Your da and I have to go into town later, t' see someone about putting a lodge up on the hill. Girls both at tennis club till later."

"Eileen's collectin' me soon, then, Ma."

"Don't be late back tonight, chara."

"Aww, Ma, gimme a break!"

Aoifa shrugged and smiled, telling her to make sure she got the taxi by 11pm.

After her parents left, Mairead dashed upstairs and threw on her jeans, t-shirt and new shiny bomber jacket. She put silver and pink braids in her jet-black hair to show it off and some of Catrina's pink lipstick would look a treat. She needed some high heels, so borrowed some of Niamh's that she'd left behind. Fab!

There was a knock at the door, and she called out of the window. "Coming, Eily!"

Mairead retrieved the money from its hiding place and tottered downstairs.

"Be a good night, Eil, afore I move schools!"

"Be nice for yer over there, too," said Eileen, but Mairead felt that she seemed a bit too pleased about it.

"Yeah, but I'll miss all of yer!"

They carried on in silence, and as they pulled up at Catrina's house, Mairead remembered to swap her high heels for trainers from her bag then made her way up to Catrina's bedroom.

"Can I borra this pink lipstick, Cat?" she asked and, without waiting for a reply, dropped it in her bag.

Mrs. Kelly gave them all some tea then they were ready to go. As they reached the youth club, everyone was standing outside and Mairead called out of the window,

"What's up, Cal?"

"Tom's not turned up an' no one else's got a key."

Mairead groaned, then Aidan invited them all over to his.

"Let's do it, girls!" Mairead exclaimed, but Eileen's expression said otherwise.

"We canna go, Mairy. Your da wouldn'a like it."

"Ach, Eil! I gotta let me hair down s'times!"

"Please, Mairy. Come back with us t' Cat's?"

"No, I'm going," she announced defiantly, and with that, she flounced out of the car and jumped into Aidan's.

When they arrived at his house, Mairead went to the cloakroom and looked in the mirror. "Lookin' good, gal!" as she applied the pink lipstick, then went to find Callum.

"Hiya, Cal, you got some dosh t'night?"

He looked back at her warily. "Yer never paid up last time, Mairy."

"Ah, but I've loadsa cash now!" she said, waving her purse around.

She paid him then helped herself to a drink. Callum soon returned, carrying a bottle of vodka and handing Mairead a small packet.

"Thanks," Mairead purred at him then took the vodka and drank from the bottle.

"Mairy, don't have all that with the candy too. You wanna stand up!" he told her nervously, but Mairead took another long swig, laughing as she handed it back to him. Someone put some music on, so she and Callum danced to the beat as he put his arms around her waist, and they moved together. She glanced at him provocatively.

"I'm likin' this! Gotta a smoke, Cal?"

"Nah. Too much for yer with the dope!" he laughed.

"Nothin's too much for me. Look, plenty o' cash left!"

Before too long, Mairy had difficulty standing in her high heels and her head began to spin.

"Need some air," she told him, giggling. "This vodka's a bit strong, ain' it?" They both went outside and sat on a wooden bench. "Aww, look… Here comes Fred," as the dog ambled up to them.

Mairead leaned over to give him a hug when she fell, landing on top of him, and Fred turned on her, catching her hand.

"Ouch!" Mairead shouted. It hurt and her hand was pouring with blood, but she couldn't stand up. "Cal, get me up, will yer!"

"Hey, you better wash that, Mairy."

Mairead giggled. "Nah, get me a towel."

He fetched one then wiped away the blood as she staggered into the kitchen for a refill.

"Get me another hit, Cal, t' forget 'bout that little cut," she said, and he got up.

"I'll go see Rory, then. Back in a minute."

Rory, thought Mairead, *that ole thief!*

She sat in the kitchen and was feeling more relaxed now, but she definitely needed more to get a proper high. Callum soon returned and popped something in her drink, which she downed in one, grinning at him.

"See – sure can take it – this is how I roll!" she said suggestively as she leaned on him. "Whey-hey, Cal, dig this music. The room's movin' now, ain' it?" she slurred.

"Mairy, your arm's still bleedin', look. We better do sommat about that – what d'you do to the dog, eh?" Callum laughed.

"Fell on 'im and he didn'a like it!"

Mairead lost all track of time and space as she swayed to the music, but then she could hear someone calling her from a long way off.

"Mairy, we gotta get you some stitches, gal."

She tried to stand up, but her body was rigid, and she couldn't open her eyes. She heard a siren, getting louder, closer, then all of a sudden, everything went black.

When Mairead woke up, she looked at her bandaged hand. What on earth…? She couldn't remember a thing. All she knew was it hurt like hell. She called her ma, who came running upstairs.

"Oh, Mairy, you had an awful time, chara. Callum dropped you home and told us you'd reacted to the drugs the hospital gave you for the dog bite."

"Ah…" Mairead tried to recollect.

"Yes, that was a nasty dog at the youth club and Callum kindly took you to hospital. Rest, now. Should be fine by Monday, though, no stitches. You were lucky."

Mairead lay back in bed and enjoyed the hot chocolate her mother had brought her. She quite liked having a bad hand if this was the treatment! Phew, her head throbbed. She had a feeling it wasn't the hospital drugs that made her funny last night, though, and she thought with a devious grin that she must've had a great time at Aidan's. Just a pity she couldn't remember any of it.

Monday came around and Mairead was up early, ready for school.

"Ma, I'm real scared now," she said as they went along in the car.

"It's OK to be scared, Mairy, the others will feel the same. I'm sure it'll be a lot of fun, too," said her ma comfortingly.

They pulled up in the car park and Aoifa found her form teacher, introduced them to one another then waved goodbye.

The first day seemed to whizz by with Mairead finding her way around and meeting the other students. She had to admit it all looked grand and lunch was really cool. She quite liked two classmates, a girl called Shannon and a nice-looking boy called Dara, older than her with lovely long brown hair and a friendly smile. She hung out with them most of the day, and when school finished, she hopped into her ma's car with a broad smile.

"All good, Ma! Loved it!"

Her mother breathed a sigh of relief as they set off home.

Mairead was grinning from ear to ear as the family sat down to dinner that evening.

"What did it smell like, Mairy?" asked Siobhan.

"Well, Sheve, not that awful musty smell. It's brand new, yer see!"

"And what was the playground like?" asked Clara excitedly.

"Well, I don't do playgrounds anymore, chara," she replied kindly, "but it did have real fancy equipment."

She turned to her mother. "Made a couple o' friends already, Ma."

Aoifa looked optimistic. "Well, an excellent first day, then, Mairy."

Her pa was watching with interest. "You liked the teacher, Mairy?"

"Yeah, but we didn't do much work. The computers are grand, though, Pa, real state o' the art."

Padraig's face lit up and he was clearly impressed.

After a couple of weeks, Mairead came home with some news.

"Ma – they're starting a youth group on Friday night an' Rachel said I can stay over."

"OK, that's good of her, Mairy. Fine by us, then."

"Yes!" She punched the air with excitement.

"Maybe you can give a hand with Finn?"

Mairead's face dropped; she didn't know that was part of the deal.

Padraig added, "Sounds like things are working out for you, chara?"

Her face brightened as she thought of something. "Yeah, Pa, I like it. Maybe get to meet some locals in the pub too!"

"Now, chara, don't start that – Brendan will kick you out!" But he was grinning, probably because Bren wouldn't really do that.

Friday came and Aoifa dropped Mairead off at school with a rucksack for her sleepover.

"Have a great time and be no trouble, now!" she called after her.

After school, Mairead made her way to the new community centre, where the youth leader was waiting with two other students.

"How many are comin', then?" she asked him.

"I dunno. Maybe this is it!" he laughed and Mairead wondered where Shannon and Dara had got to.

They waited a while then the leader announced that they best advertise it for another time. Mairead had a long face, but she didn't care for the two that had turned up anyway.

"See youse all on Monday," she told them then walked the mile along the road to the pub.

"Hi, Rach," Mairead said dejectedly as she walked into the kitchen, tickling Finn as she passed him by. "Not many turned up at the new club. Mores next time, I hope." She sat down heavily in the kitchen.

"That's a shame, Mairy. What will you do now?" Rachel asked gently.

"I'll not be a bother, just go up to the bedroom an' listen to music."

"OK, then. See you later for some supper?"

"Nah, thanks. Had some at school. See yer tomorrow."

Mairead trooped heavily up the stairs, threw her bag on the bed and groaned to herself. "That was a sham. Where was everyone?"

Mairead looked out of the window and hung her head disappointedly. The moors looked spooky in the twilight, but the tide was out, and a full moon lit up the sandy bay in the distance.

Deep inside, Mairead felt anger rising. She wished she were at her youth club; the boys always gave her a drink there and a smoke if she was nice to them. Well, she'd spent all her money and had none left anyway. It just wasn't fair. If she were at home, Cat would've lent her some and she could've had herself a good time.

She looked out across the bay toward the lighthouse and gazed over to the rocky peninsular. Then she remembered something – Lois' booty! It was still there in the cave – that boy hadn'a taken much, he'd told her so – and she knew Lois hadn't taken it. It was worth a fortune, Laurel had said. She could fetch it now then go on to the pub before closing! It wasn't even properly dark yet. She quickly put on her boots, anorak and threw her rucksack onto her back. With the tide out, she could cut across the bay; her ma had said it was quicker.

She put a pillow in her bed, like she'd seen on TV, and opened her door quietly. Rachel was seeing to Finn, and Brendan was busy in the pub, so she crept downstairs and out of the back door. As she made her way across the moor, the moon lit up the path leading to the bay and, realising how much she missed her friends, she quickened her pace. She missed getting high too. That was brill and it took all her worries away, except when that dog appeared. She'd stay away from him this time.

Mairead was halfway across the bay when dark clouds obscured the moon, throwing her into darkness, then the heavens opened. Pulling up her hood, she sheltered under a rock. The wind picked up as Mairead watched the sea turn from calm to raging in a matter of minutes, but she set off into the storm resolutely. Her ma's comment about her going toward the dark came to mind, but it wasn't the dark she wanted – it was fire, passion, that she craved! Pah! She hadn't heard anything from her grandma, so she would have to get her own kicks.

The rain was horizontal now and her feet were already sopping wet, yet Mairead felt driven. Nothing would stop her from getting the booty. It could buy her a lot of good times! She felt compelled to keep going; something was willing her forward and she was powerless to stop it, but she didn't care a jot.

She must be nearly there, but it was so dark and misty it was hard to see properly. Soaked through to the skin, Mairead started to shiver and pulled her coat tighter around herself. Suddenly, the moon disappeared completely, and everything went black. Blinded by the darkness, she froze but then remembered – her phone had a torch! She took it out of her bag, put the light on and set off once more, looking into the murky distance to get her bearings. She could hear the crash of the waves and looked out to sea. It was lucky the tide was going out. Suddenly, there was a huge clap of thunder followed by lightning, and Mairead caught a glimpse of the caves up ahead, which spurred her on. The thought of an exciting evening kept her spirits up – one last trip! Then her grandma would help her to walk into the light. She just knew it.

She turned the torch light up and could see the rocks now. Moving steadily over the wet sand, squelching as her boots were full of water, Mairead pushed on through the driving rain, eventually reaching the familiar craggy rock. She clambered over it toward the cave entrance. At least she would soon be out of the rain.

Once inside the cave, Mairead searched with the dim light and saw something sparkling high up on a ledge. As she moved further in, she felt colder even than outside and shivered – but there it was! A pile of what appeared to be rubble, but it was gleaming at her now, calling her... She just had to figure out how to reach it. As she ventured deeper into the cave, her torch seemed to be dimming and a flutter of panic passed through her. She began to climb up the rock face, which was very slippery, but she managed to get a foothold as she neared the top when she stopped a moment to listen. It sounded like the tide was coming in. It couldn't be. It had been going out, hadn't it? Anyhow, she would be high up in the cave, so no matter. She didn't think waves came that far up the beach – may be that climate thing Lois had talked about. Anyway, it couldn't be the tide turning yet, must be water trickling from above, and she kept moving upward towards the ledge.

Eventually, she secured her foot in a cleft of rock and managed to reach it. Propping up her phone to see, she selected all the precious items plus anything undamaged.

Her bag was soon full to bursting, so she threw it onto her back, but it caught her phone. She tried to catch it but missed and it fell to the floor, disappearing into a rock pool with a splash. "Oh, no way!" she cried as she was plunged into inky blackness.

Mairead felt herself panicking as she quickly began to make her way down the rock face – but her foot was stuck! She pulled it with all her might, turned it, wiggled it, but it was trapped in the cleft, and it felt numb with cold and so did her hands. "Damn it!" she shouted, her voice echoing eerily around the cave. Mairead banged her fist onto the rocks as tears of fear and frustration rolled down her face. She so wanted to get out of there! Water was definitely coming into the cave now. As she remembered the colossal waves down the bay earlier, she began to shake, stifling a sob as she thought with increasing dread, what if she were stuck there all night? Then there was a sudden rush of water, and an enormous wave flooded the cave. She had to move her foot and get out! She twisted it one more time and yelled with pain, but eventually it freed. "Thank God!" she cried but felt a jolt as she lost her footing and found herself waist-high in freezing cold water. Mairead had no idea how far it was to the cave entrance and her chest hurt as she pushed forward through the deep icy water. She was finding it hard to breathe as it seemed to be getting ever higher up her body. The waves were deafening now, rolling in at regular intervals, and one almost engulfed her, but she held her breath and scrambled up again, only to be overcome by a second. For the first time in her life, terror filled every fibre of her body.

She caught sight of the inky ocean outside, the moon illuminating the choppy waves as they continued to come rhythmically toward her. Her shoulders were now submerged as one wave after another came over her and she felt something pulling, pulling her under. She struggled to stay upright, pushing against the tide, but it was so very hard. Her bag was so heavy, but she mustn't give it up and she battled on yet seemed to be getting nowhere. The water was freezing, and she couldn't feel her hands nor her arms, and her heavy boots were weighing her down. She had little strength left as her whole body was soon submerged and her head felt so heavy. She just couldn't think anymore. If only she were a better swimmer, Mairead knew she would beat it, but there was only one thing waiting for her now and it closed in on her: total darkness.

26. IN THE EYE OF THE STORM

The next morning, Clara had an idea.

"Pa, can we take Brown Mane out on the beach today?"

"You want Conor to come on Rafa, too?"

"Yes, the three of us!" Clara shouted excitedly.

"Sounds a good plan – he needs t' practise his canterin' anyhow. Hey, Aoif, what time is Mairead getting home?"

"Why, Pa?" asked Clara. "Does nobody know where she is?"

"Yes, of course, she's with Rachel at the pub," her ma told her. "She be here for Sunday lunch, would never miss that!"

"Funny noises out on the moors today, Ma," said Siobhan. "I can taste the colours rising up from the moor, greens and blues like water, and smell heavy purple clouds, a strong smell. It hurts my nose."

Aoifa looked at Padraig wondrously as he sighed and got up to begin his repairs after the storm but avoiding Aoifa's beady eye.

"I thought the thunder passed last night, meself," he muttered. "See youse all later." He left Aoifa to unravel Siobhan's ramblings.

Aoifa was wondering how Mairead had enjoyed the new youth club and decided to give Rachel a call, but there was no answer at the pub, so she tried her mobile.

"Hi, Rach. Ah… both out walking young Finn on this bright morning… No youth club? What a shame. She was excited on it too. Still, she does like her bed that one!" Aoifa chuckled to herself. "Tell her to call me when you see her, then," and she turned to Clara as she came off the phone.

"Such a storm last night. Come and check the animals with me, Lara?"

The geese and chickens were running around causing mayhem, as the wind had blown out the door to their coop, which Padraig was fixing. Clara went over to help and Aoifa propped up a temporary measure to help contain them all, out of harm's way.

"At least them pesky piglets are safe, Pad." She grimaced. "Good news yesterday about the lodge, then?"

"Yeah, Brian's going to draw up some plans for us. No charge as long as he gets his wood for the winter!"

"All's fair, then!" Aoifa smiled at him in excitement. "We surely can start the groundwork soon?"

"When weather turns, I reckon."

Just then, Siobhan came running out.

"Ma, it's Rachel again – sounds hot!"

Aoifa shook her head as she took the phone.

"Hi, Rach… Mairy's not there? She did what? Don't worry now, she'll have gone for a walk, may even be on 'er way home. I'll check her mobile again. Just wait a bit."

When Aoifa came off the phone, her heart missed a beat. Siobhan had been right; Rachel did sound hot. She was in a proper panic, and with a new babe and all, she didn't need this. Aoifa's mind was whirring as she ran out to tell Padraig.

"Pad!" she called. "Mairead's done a runner! You wait till I get my hands on that daughter of ours." Her face was contorted with anger.

Padraig dropped his tools. "So, where is she now?" he called back.

"I dunno. At the moment, I don' much care either! Put a pillow in 'er bed, she did!"

Aoifa turned, marched into the house and tried Mairead's mobile, but it went dead; the battery must have run out. She frowned and tried to think where she may have gone and decided to try the Kellys. With no youth club, she may have got Eileen to pick her up.

"Good mornin', Maureen. Did you hear from Mairead at all? So… she never arrived?" Aoifa's tone softened, her voice breaking. "Thanks anyways. She be on her way here, then." She tried to keep control.

Padraig came into the house and looked at Aoifa's white face.

"So, Aoif, if she put a pillow in 'er bed, when did she go out?"

"Rachel had no idea. Mairy didn't tell them she was going." Aoifa was wringing her hands now. "They were expecting her at the Kellys, Pad, but she never turned up. Didn't pick up her phone either."

Siobhan and Clara were sitting at the table, drawing. "I can see a black noise, Ma, and that smell has come back."

"Oh, Sheve, not now!"

Aoifa's patience was at breaking point and Padraig came over to her, gently touching her arm as Clara whispered,

"Is Mairy somewhere, Ma? Do we know, does anyone know?"

"Not yet, Lara, no," her pa replied more calmly. "She be somewhere between Clifden and Galway…" he said, trying to lighten the mood, but Clara burst into tears.

"That means she may be anywhere, Pa! I think she is somewhere closer than that!"

Aoifa began to shake and took Padraig to one side.

"What if she's run away, Pad, or worse, run off with one of those lads from school or what if that boy's come after her again?"

"Now, chara, no jumping to conclusions. There be a simple explanation. Let's ring all her friends."

Padraig looked up some of their names and Aoifa dialled the numbers, but the response was the same from each: no one had heard from Mairead.

The phone rang again and Aoifa grabbed it, but it was Rachel, so she put it on loudspeaker.

"Oh, Aoif, I don't know what to say. We feel so responsible. I didn't see her leave, didn't hear anything either…"

"Rach, please don't feel that. Mairy has a mind of her own and a strong will pulling her… and she just follows it…"

"Bren and I've been thinking, Aoif. It's possible Mairy slept here and went off early this morning, taking her things. She could even have gone for a long walk; her phone must be out of juice."

The idea pacified Aoifa and she nodded to Padraig, a fleeting smile crossing his face. "Why don't we all sit tight and wait a while. If anyone hears anything, we can call."

Rachel agreed, as there was nothing more to be done.

When Aoifa put the phone down, she felt drained. There was a tension in the room, and as the clock ticked by, an apprehension, a fate was forming before their very eyes. Padraig and Aoifa sat together with the girls on either side as the radio played wantonly in the background.

Aoifa looked out at the warm sunshine, the storm of the night before long forgotten. "She's out there, Pad, somewhere in that sunshine."

Yet Aoifa's spirit, her soul, her very being were not flowing like water anymore as she felt the panic rising up inside, forming a knot, a familiar feeling of late, only this time the worry was much closer to home. Aoifa's residing thought was, *please, Ma, keep the paranoia away.*

She walked slowly to the open door, Flynn sidling up to her as she looked into his sad eyes and stroked his soft fur, then whispered with her back to the others, "Please, Ma, show us the light. Take us to the light. I feel the dark pulling, but I can turn. Please show us we can all turn and help Mairead to turn too."

Siobhan and Clara sat quietly talking amongst themselves and Padraig got up to put the kettle on. The room was quiet, the silence palpable. Aoifa told them she was going upstairs to be alone a while. She wanted to communicate with the elements and her ma too.

As she sat at the window in her bedroom and looked out to sea, Aoifa sent her thoughts out into the ether, to connect with the ebb and flow of the water. The cerulean sea was a sheet of pure tranquillity after the storm, but Aoifa couldn't feel the gentle flow. Her emotions, her thoughts, her soul, her body, all felt trapped.

"Oh, Ma, I wish I knew she were OK, my little Mairead. Where is she?" she stuttered. "What if she has met with some calamity, something of her own making. What is her fate, Ma? I have a dark feeling deep inside, but I pray it is otherwise. Tell me – is she footsteps in the sand now, which will be washed away as the tide comes in? Has her element been at work – pulling her toward the darkness? Is it her time? No! She can still turn, see the light. I can see her now, walking along the beach…"

Then Aoifa came to: the beach! *Of course! We didn't search the beach! She will be lying in the sun, sitting on the rocks, turning to the light. She will surprise all of us.*

Aoifa ran downstairs. "Pad… we didn't search the beach. She would have walked that way to see her friends… Quick!"

Padraig was stoking the fire but turned to her. "I'll go with Conor, take the horses," he said, jumping up quickly.

"I'm coming. We'll take Brown Mane too."

It was a statement and Padraig didn't argue as they went to prepare the horses.

"Stay here, girls, in case Mairead comes home," Padraig told them gently.

They soon arrived at the beach, where Conor caught up with them, jumping onto Brown Mane, and they searched from one side of the headland across to the other, as far as the eye could see. The tide was out, and when they had covered the expanse of sand, they looked up and saw Laurel and Sean waving from the rocks. Maybe they had found her! Aoifa could see Laurel was beckoning and calling to them and they all set off at top speed toward them and Aoifa galloped on ahead.

"Lors – have you found her?" she called out breathlessly.

"Lois' cave, look in there, maybe…" but her voice was lost in the breeze, although Aoifa had heard her clearly, as she had thought the same but hadn't wanted to venture there. Now, she led the way.

Lois' booty, she thought. Mairead needed money. She always needed money.

As she pushed Rafa forward, stoically and with a steely determination, Padraig and Conor followed behind.

The sun was shining brightly. It felt much milder as if spring was upon them, just a flicker of wind but not a sound on the air. Even the birds were quiet. Aoifa reached the entrance to the cave and she and Padraig dismounted. Conor took the horses away and they entered on foot.

Aoifa suddenly took on a different life form. She felt weightless as if she were being carried, floating above the sand, and her heart had stopped. Padraig took her hand. It felt cold like lead, but her feet kept moving. She felt as if her body were there, but she was not, as if she were an apparition walking ahead of herself. Aoifa lifted up her eyes, terror gripping her. She knew they were in the right place. Then they saw her.

Aoifa's hands fell to her side. Her legs fell from beneath her as she crumpled onto the sand alongside her beloved daughter and looked straight into her beautiful, dark, lifeless eyes. Padraig rushed over, but her body was cold, wet.

It was bright inside the cave. There was no darkness, just a pure white light. Mairead's face was lit up by the radiance of the sun and her hair was shining like ravens' wings framing her pale face. Her body was folded over with her heavy bag thrown some distance away.

"The booty was what she wanted," Padraig stammered as he too fell to the ground. There was a stunned silence. The only distant sounds were of ghostly echoes above them as the sea played its usual tricks high up in the voids of the cave.

They both wept horrendously, convulsively, and Aoifa wailed piteously as Padraig took Mairead into his arms, rocking her, and Aoifa held her hand as if it had more life than her own.

Aoifa suddenly emitted a gut-wrenching scream.

"I should have known, have stopped it, have saved our daughter from the darkness, Pad!"

Aoifa was suddenly frantic, chaotic. "Pad – if we lift her and run, take her quickly to the hospital, maybe, maybe they can…"

She was hysterical now, irrational even, she knew that, and she no longer cared about the paranoia because she knew it would come. This was all her fault! The dark had taken her daughter and she had been powerless to help her *because she didn't have any messages*.

"No, chara." Padraig's voice was taut, raspy. "This was Mairead's own doing. We did our best, but the darkness took her." He broke down, sobbing silently, his hands over his face and his body limp.

He had told Aoifa the truth, but she didn't believe him. The paranoia had set in. Carefully dropping Mairead's hand, she stood up. She had let Mairead down. She had let her whole family down. Aoifa turned around and walked slowly out of the cave and over toward the moor, to the rock. She would tell her ma that she had made a big mistake.

Her ma hadn't been listening, Aoifa just knew. It was all too late.

She made her way to Muir Farm, but she didn't know how to walk into her own home anymore. How do you continue with the privilege of your own life when you have allowed your daughter to die? How do you put one foot in front of the other, go to sleep, get up in the morning? What happens to the torment, the eternal damnation, the guilt? Would they ever go away or get worse day by day?

Aoifa made herself walk up to the house where her daughters were waiting. They knew. Their faces were red raw from crying. Padraig took her into his arms as she entered. He had told them what had happened, that Mairead needed the money to spend that evening, but the tides had taken her, and it had been a terrible, unavoidable, tragic accident.

Siobhan cried out to her. "That was the black, Ma, and now I smell red!" she wailed as Clara clung onto her ma's hand and buried her face in her skirt. Mairead was no longer with her, but these girls were, and she would love them more than ever. She would prevent anything from happening to them if it meant losing her own life.

As she walked in through the door, it felt to Aoifa like she was walking through glue, purposefully, mechanically, her mind a blank, but she kept pushing, wading onwards. She'd bury the pain and carry on.

During supper that evening, they all held hands, and each sent a personal message to Mairead on the wind, out to sea where she was at peace now. After their meal, which no one had touched, Padraig led Aoifa outside. He took her into his arms as they stood connected by their love and grief, looking out across the bay where the tide was now high and across to the cave which was once again filled with water and where Mairead had drawn her last breath. He then spoke to her with an intensity she had never heard before.

"Everyone had loved Mairead very very much, but she hadn't loved herself, chara. She always wanted to be something, somewhere or someone else, always searching. Her end belied her means because she had walked on the dark side. One drug or drink was too many for her and one hundred not enough. We tried with all our hearts to reach her, to do all we could, but it had not been possible. The bad energies got to her first. She was mistaken, Aoif, because she was fine as she was, but she didn't believe us. Remember her in her earlier happiness, not in her final hours of desperation, and always remember her for her lovely, funny ways."

"But, why, oh why, Pad, didn't Ma send her the gift?"

Padraig said no more, only tightened his hold on her in an attempt to ease her terrible pain he knew was deep inside and would be there for a long, long time. They stood together for an eternity, united in their grief, then Padraig spoke once more,

"Connect with your ma and she will confirm to you the truth, chara."

Aoifa did hear the truth from her ma. She heard that she had to be responsible now there were no more messages. She had to keep her water flowing, keep her thoughts and her actions moving, start to trust again to keep the rest of her family safe. So, she hadn't been responsible? Aoifa decided her first task would be to help ease her family's pain and forget her own. '

Although Mairead has gone, we always have to remember those who are still with us. That will be my spiritual objective now, she told herself, *to be responsible for their happiness and wellbeing.*

27. AOIFA'S CHANGING WORLD

Niamh and Lois came home the minute they heard the devastating news. Niamh was totally distraught, very emotional and bursting into tears at the drop of a hat. Lois, although upset, was less surprised and far more pragmatic, telling her parents they had done all they could to help Mairead.

The funeral had been a small, private affair and so painful that Aoifa had difficulty recalling the details. Both girls stayed on for a further two weeks, for which Aoifa was hugely relieved. Niamh gave her constant practical support and Lois stayed around the younger girls, answering their questions as best she could. Yet the burden of grief felt the greater to Aoifa because she didn't entirely understand much of it herself – there would always be unanswered questions about that fateful day.

Four months had now passed and, true to her word, Aoifa had strived to put her family first. Although everyone told her the accident was no one's fault, she still believed otherwise. After the gift had left her, there was no doubt that Aoifa had found parenting difficult. It should be common sense, shouldn't it, if your errant teenage daughter was out drinking and worse, you would actually deal with it? But she simply didn't know how, so had allowed Padraig to take the reins, which now added to her guilt.

After her older daughters had returned to their new lives, Aoifa knew she had to take responsibility and she had tried, she really had. It was just sometimes the answers didn't come. When Siobhan gave out about her senses exploding and Clara became emotional, asking probing questions, and Niamh cried down the phone and Lois told her what to do and Padraig just showed love and compassion, Aoifa usually came adrift. She would always end up talking to her ma, but deep down she knew she was on her own now.

When she admitted her failings to Padraig and her friends, they all said the same: *It was the sadness, Aoif; It would pass, Aoif; Don't be too hard on yerself, Aoif*; except Laurel, who simply told her to snap out of it and get on! Maybe she was spot on. Much of her angst, after all, seemed to be fuelled by self-pity for all her losses, pure and simple. What could anyone do about it? Nothing. She was such a failure and would just have to accept it. Trouble was, Aoifa hadn't been able to feel anything for a month now, no emotion whatever. It was as if someone had poured cold water all over her.

It was a sunny day at the end of June and Aoifa had gone down to the beach for a swim. The sea was a deep cornflower blue and as calm as can be. She glided through the warm water with rhythmic, easy strokes and looked out at the beautiful vista around her but with unseeing eyes. Platitudes, she thought, banal pleasures. Aoifa saw little beauty in anything anymore. As the soft silky water slid over her body, she concentrated on every breath, filling her lungs with clean oxygen-filled air.

Turning on a wave, the flow of the water and her motion perfectly synchronised, Aoifa emitted a scornful laugh – would she ever know happiness again? Her, a pretty useless parent if ever there was one, that her own daughter goes and kills herself. Oh, not deliberately of course, but there was no doubt that Mairead had been on a self-destruct path. A glimmer of hope permeated Aoifa's negative thoughts – was it purely because Mairy had been born of Fire that she took the dark road? Stopping to tread water, she spoke aloud,

"Nah. It was because I never taught her how to avoid the dark in the first place or she would still be here."

She turned vigorously and plunged deep into the water when she heard a splash and looked around as Padraig jumped up in front her.

"Penny for them!"

"Oh, Pad. You scared me."

Aoifa swam away, rebuffing his friendly approach, but he caught up with her, his strength and ability overtaking her slim, svelte shape.

"Lovely day for this, Aoif. Sea's warm, too."

Aoifa didn't reply. She was aware of being aloof, but it was easier than pretending. These days she was unable to deal with life on life's terms and definitely unable to connect with her family. It had come to that.

"You been here a while, chara. Let's get home afore the girls?"

Aoifa sighed as she left the water, throwing her towel around herself as they walked slowly up the path.

"I'll make us some tea," Padraig told her, and she shrugged.

As they reached the front garden, Aoifa fell languidly into a deckchair, and she'd just closed her eyes when Padraig reappeared with a tray of refreshments.

"Piece of Clara's nice sponge?"

Aoifa took it from him, avoiding his eyes as she muttered her thanks.

"Make the most of this sun, eh? Midsummer's passed already!" he told her. "I bin thinking. How about we follow through our plans for the lodge now, Aoif? It's been on paper a while, but seaweed harvest is slow, so Conor and I have some free time."

Aoifa made no response and just stared into space. Despite her best efforts, she was perpetually consumed with grief and guilt since Mairead's passing and knew it would take a miracle for her to feel a part of anything again. "Chara, would you at least consider the plans with me?"

Aoifa glanced across at him. Why was he being so kind when she felt as if she had fallen into an abyss and was trapped on all four sides?

"I don't know why you bother, Pad. If I cannot keep our daughter alive, what good am I? Best carry on without me now."

Aoifa watched the blood drain from her husband's face, noticing the grey hairs around his temples for the first time, his features drawn and pinched, but she remained unmoved. Padraig said nothing and they sat together but as separate as the day was long when Padraig broke the silence.

"We are falling apart, Aoif. Our family is breaking up into warring fragments."

She looked at him vacuously as a stream of tears fell down his cheeks, but she remained silent. Harshly wiping his eyes with the back of his hand, he spoke more vehemently.

"Tell me one thing, Aoifa – are you the only person who matters here? We lost Mairead four months ago and never once have you asked how I feel nor shown concern for our daughters for weeks now."

Padraig's sharp words jarred Aoifa, and she looked at him directly as if seeing him for the first time, but still she felt no empathy, her own tears dried up long since.

The garden gate flew open, and Clara ran down the path exuberantly then stopped before them.

"Why is everyone upset?" she asked, her joyful expression vanishing, but Padraig was quick to reassure her.

"It's nothing, chara, just old stuff. Is OK now."

He looked at Aoifa piercingly. "Isn't it, Aoif?" But Aoifa just watched as Padraig took the girls inside and left her staring, unblinking, after them.

Later, Aoifa prepared tea silently and mechanically, her thoughts more scrambled than ever. After the girls had gone to bed, Padraig didn't finish off outside as usual. Instead, they cleared the supper dishes together when suddenly he stood facing her with his hands on her shoulders.

"Aoifa, we cannot go on like this. I want you to know we all love you, but we miss you, your love, your kindly ways. We want you back. It's like you don't live here anymore." Padraig spoke soothingly as if to a child, but Aoifa didn't respond, and it frustrated him. "Is that what you want – to no longer be a part of this family? Can you answer me that? Sit, please, and answer me."

Aoifa curled into an embryonic position in the armchair, gathering her cardigan around herself and gazing out of the window.

"Of course not. I live here too."

"Well, you wouldn't know it. You don't speak to me anymore nor take any interest in our girls. We all lived together in such harmony once, do you remember?"

Aoifa drew her eyebrows together, her eyes downcast, her sickly pallor giving her a haunted look. What could she say when she felt nothing?

Padraig spoke more quietly. "Aoif, do you think we don't miss Mairy too? I also have feelings of overwhelming sadness and guilt, you know. Wish I'd done more." But Aoifa had shut down, her face set.

Padraig paced the room concealing a sob, then continued angrily. "The girls are suffering, Aoif. They have no mother anymore. You seem to care for no one except yourself! What about the older girls and do you even know about Scorcha's depression? You never even called Liam back. If you continue in this way, we will all be better off without you!" Aoifa felt something shift within. He was giving her an ultimatum. "…you are being very selfish!" she heard him say.

Suddenly, she raised her eyes as if to speak and he looked at her hopefully.

"I have to go to bed now," she told him.

Padraig sighed heavily and walked out of the front door, slamming it behind him as Aoifa took herself upstairs.

When she awoke the next day, Padraig's burning words from the night before still in her head, she knew they had reached a turning point. She had to turn, but could she? Could she ever be there for her family again? She would go to her special rock to try to gain momentum and perspective and ask her ma to give her strength or Aoifa knew she may lose them, and she didn't want that – did she?

For the next seven days, Aoifa asked her ma for guidance, not expecting any messages, just a sign, a feeling, even a thought to help her function again. However, at the end of a week of heartache and soul-searching, Aoifa still felt nothing.

Day seven was a Saturday and Aoifa decided to take a picnic and spend the day surrounded by all things visceral, connected to earth and water, her element and of nature itself.

It was a warm, overcast day, but the birds were high in the sky and the curlews were gathering food along the shoreline. Although the puffins were nesting in the rock face and coming to gaze at her curiously, Aoifa didn't see them. As she finished her lunch with Flynn alongside waiting for the crusts, the sun peeked through the clouds, so she threw off her cardigan and Aoifa's hand was drawn to her necklace. She held the charms in her palm as she pushed her feet into the warm silky sand and considered the five family members they represented. At that moment, she heard rustlings as Siobhan and Clara came into view, smiling and walking tentatively toward her.

"Hi, Ma," said Clara, nervously fingering her ponytail. "We wondered where you were," she muttered shyly.

For the first time in what seemed like forever, Aoifa's heart melted at the sight of her daughters as a horrific thought entered her head, the charms still in her hand – *What if one of these two lovely girls ended up on my necklace next?* A shiver ran down her spine as she realised Padraig had been right, *they did need her.* Instantaneously, she felt a bright light shining down on her, awakening her, to show her the way. Could it be from her ma? Emotions welled up inside as her juices began to flow, her element coming alive once more. She held out her arms and the girls ran into them, Clara sobbing and Siobhan muttering in her usual way. They all hugged one another for a long moment, hot, happy tears rolling down Aoifa's face as an immense relief washed over her and she thought, *the truth has prevailed. I am their mother.*

Eventually, she let go of them, picked up her bag and they all ran shrieking with laughter, barefoot, through the rippling waves with Flynn frolicking behind. She looked up at the sky, an array of pinks and mauves, the sea a glimmering expanse of turquoise with the emerald hills in the background, and Aoifa felt herself connecting with her homeland once more, the water and colours of nature bringing her back to life. She looked wondrously at her daughters, their hair shining wet from the spray, the joy on their faces at having their ma back, and her heart lurched. They made their way home, arms linked, talking animatedly, and as they reached the garden, Padraig was waiting for them. Aoifa looked at him with warmth in her eyes and love in her heart and he smiled back.

Aoifa had encountered a spiritual awakening that day. Whether from her ma, or through working her element or from trying to do the right thing, it mattered not. Her sadness was still there, but she would rise above it and trust that one day maybe it wouldn't hurt so much.

The next day, Aoifa turned to Padraig, smiling coyly.

"I'm going to call Lois, Pad. She needs to hear from her ma," she announced, wringing her hands. "I'm nervous to have left it so long."

Padraig grinned back at her, his happiness unmistakable.

"You'll make her day, chara."

"Lo – it's Ma – how are you? Your first big project, eh, with dolphins? Oh, that clicker thing you mentioned. Ah… we have to download one of those apps – course we can do that, don't be cheeky!"

Padraig was sitting alongside, chuckling to himself.

When Aoifa came off the phone, her face was radiant as she exclaimed, "Niamh next!"

"Do it!" said Padraig. "You're on a roll, gal!"

"Hi, Nevey, how's things? …Yes, much better now, thanks." Aoifa felt her voice breaking and took a deep breath. "Coming our way? Wow, the girls would love to see you in action! Let us know when, eh?"

Aoifa rang off and told him, "Now, Liam," then mumbled, "Well, maybe not yet," as her courage escaped her and added brightly, "We are lucky, Pad, to have such beautiful girls, eh?"

"An' to think you almost forgot about that!" he said with a smile.

The following week, they all went to the circus. Niamh held a pivotal role, leading a display of acrobatics on horseback, step dancing and playing her fiddle – with her family in the front row. It brought light back into Aoifa's life just to see the smiles on their faces as they watched the performance with rapturous delight.

A week later, Aoifa came running downstairs as Padraig was enjoying a cup of tea with his newspaper in front of him.

"Hey, you didn't tell me we were off on the razz, Aoif?"

"Ah – we're not. Rachel, Laurel and I are off into Clifden to a swanky restaurant."

"Make a nice change for yer!" he said, smiling. "Now, don't go runnin' off with any of them fancy men o'there, lookin' as pretty as a picture!"

Aoifa went to sit on his lap. "Now, why would I do that?" she said demurely, her red hair falling in curls around her shoulders. "And dunna do that, you'll ruin my lace skirt and lipstick too!" She pushed him away, stood up and grabbed her handbag. "See youse all later, then. Don't wait up!"

Aoifa set off for the train station, collecting Rachel on the way. The journey only took thirty minutes and Laurel was waiting on the platform.

"So, Lors, where we goin'?" asked Rachel.

"Booked us a smart hotel for once!" Laurel told them.

As they walked through the town centre, Aoifa looked in the shop windows at all the pretty summer clothes and wondered why she didn't visit more often. Soon arriving in the central square, they followed Laurel to a large, elegant boutique hotel, making their way up the wide marble steps flanked by high steel pillars, through the revolving doors and into the poshest foyer Aoifa had ever seen.

"Phew, we'll need a mortgage to eat here, Lors!" she whispered then saw Laurel and Rachel exchange glances.

"Our treat anyways, Aoif," Rachel said.

"Ah, you two, now…" Aoifa objected, but they ignored her, stepping into the lift up to the first-floor restaurant with panoramic views over the town, and a smart waiter showed them to their table.

"Wow," Aoifa whispered. "Stunning or what?"

After they had ordered their drinks, Aoifa said what was on her mind.

"Girls, it's been a while…"

Her friends nodded, looking at her sadly, then Laurel spoke too,

"Aoif… I want to say…" and Rachel piled in,

"Oh, Aoif, Bren and I are…"

Then all three girls shed a tear, oblivious to curious glances from the other guests, and Aoifa held up her hand.

"I'm so sorry to have been out of contact for so long. I… we've… been heartbroken."

Her friends took her hands and Rachel spoke up.

"Nothing to explain, Aoif. I… I shouldn't have let Mairy out of…"

Then Laurel interjected, "If I hadn't told her the booty was valuable…"

Aoifa looked at her two friends intently.

"We couldn't save her, girls. It was Mairy's own journey. I was mostly at fault. I was her ma and mostly wasn't her ma, too."

Aoifa's face was downcast, her voice thick with emotion as she squeezed their hands and her face drained of colour. There was a moment's silence then she added more lightly,

"Got the others t' think on now," as she took out a tissue, cleared her throat and continued, smiling. "So, let's look at this delicious menu…"

Their exchange had cleared the air and they soon fell into their usual banter when Laurel told them some news. "Sean and I are going to start a family – he's agreed!"

Aoifa let out a cry louder than intended. "Wow, Lors, you kept that quiet!"

"Yeah, but don' say nothin' to him. Meant to be a secret, see!"

Aoifa and Rachel smiled, and they all enjoyed a luxurious meal in sumptuous surroundings overlooking the aurora of city lights and with waiters appearing at a click of their fingers.

On their way home, Rachel broached the subject of Laurel's news.

"Aoif, what do you think – about Sean?"

Aoifa shook her head. "Hmm, not sure. Surprised me, I'll say."

The next morning, Aoifa told Padraig about her evening, her relief at making amends for her absence. She also told him about Laurel's secret plans.

"Well, now, that's a turn up." Padraig's face was expressionless as he brought up another subject. "Now, we can look at those plans…"

"Ah, yes, but I've one more amends to make first. Uncle David doesn't know about Mairy. We owe it to him, Pad. Take a drive over with the girls on Sunday?" Padraig agreed.

When Sunday morning came, Aoifa awoke feeling unexpectedly nervous. "Must we go, Pad?" she groaned. "He may ask all sorts of awkward questions."

"You said yerself, chara, we owe it to him." He threw back the covers, pulling her out of bed.

The girls got themselves ready. Clara chose some pretty leggings and matching top and Siobhan put on some jeans with a simple t-shirt. Aoifa wanted to wear bright colours and chose an orange sleeveless dress with a cream cardigan and matching sandals, as an expression of her new-found joie de vivre.

As they were driving along, Padraig pointed out a new log cabin which was being built along the coast.

"Look at the finish on that, Aoif. Beautiful wood cladding, much like our lodge will be."

"Getting excited about it now, Pad."

He squeezed her hand as she detected a look of pure love in his eyes.

An hour later, they pulled up in front of David's stylish home and Aoifa saw someone at the kitchen window. Soon the front door opened. She got out of the car and held out her hand with a smile, recognising the elegant young lady who had been the focus of Liam's attention at the funeral.

"Hello – er…"

"Nell," she replied with a warm smile.

"Yes, Nell." Aoifa turned to the others. "You know Padraig, and Siobhan and Clara."

"Don't you have other daughters too?" Nell asked.

Aoifa stumbled over her words.

"Erm… yes… but Lois now works in America and Niamh is working away too."

She quickly asked if David was home to change the subject.

"Yes, he is. Please come in." Nell led the way into their luxury kitchen, also used as an attractive living space.

Aoifa looked at this calm and composed young lady, wondering what she was doing in Uncle David's house as David soon came striding down the hallway, his arms out to welcome them.

"Hello, all! Long time no see. Nell, pop the kettle on, would you?"

They all settled around the large marble-topped central island whilst Nell brought out a sponge cake and David asked unexpectedly,

"Don't you have another daughter at home, Aoifa? What was she… Maureen?"

A silence fell upon the group and Aoifa looked at him sadly.

"Mairead." She gasped. "It – it's why we've come. Oh, Uncle, she… she died. It was a tragic accident, you see." Aoifa's face crumpled and she burst into tears as her uncle came across and put his arm around her shoulders. "She… drowned. It's been unbearable…"

Aoifa became completely overwrought as Nell handed her a tissue and Clara climbed up onto her lap when Padraig stepped in,

"It's been hard for all of us. Some months have passed now, so we're each finding our own ways of coping…"

David expressed his condolences and Padraig thanked him as Aoifa collected herself and moved the subject on.

"David, may I ask – we're thinking of building a holiday lodge. You have some barns you let out? Any tips for us?" She sniffed, taking some deep breaths as Nell poured them all some more tea.

"Ah, you mean the barns at the back. They're in long-term use, not for holidays. Nell and Aisling live there – she be coming in now, Nell's called her."

"Ah, a sort of long-term rental, then?" asked Padraig.

"Well, I guess. Been here a while now."

The front door opened, and Nell pushed Aisling's wheelchair toward them. Aoifa was struck by the warmth in her smile as Aisling held out her delicate hand. "So pleased to meet you," Aoifa told her, and Aisling moved to greet the others. Clara giggled and did a curtsey as Aisling responded with a cheeky grin,

"Well, I'll not be seconding that!"

"I can see hoops in the air and smell bells on the wind," Siobhan told Aisling excitedly, who looked at her curiously, adding,

"That's very poetic, now. English is my subject. Always very taken with novel turns of phrase, to be sure!"

They all opened their eyes in amazement as they listened to Aisling's mellifluous words and Siobhan moved closer to her.

"I smell candy floss now, my favourite!" she exclaimed.

"I'm afraid we've none of that!" added Nell.

Padraig told her to shush, but everyone laughed good-humouredly. It was soon time for them to leave and the girls offered to push Aisling out to the front drive to say goodbye.

Later that evening, Padraig and Aoifa were sitting in front of the TV when Padraig took her into his arms. Aoifa smiled one of her old smiles, happy and engaging as she kissed him then suddenly sat up.

"Pad, I been thinking on those girls."

"Aww – don't talk on our girls just now…"

"Not our girls, those girls!" Aoifa exclaimed, letting out a chortle. "Nell and Aisling. I suppose being lodgers, they be good company for Uncle David?"

"Aye, I guess so, chara." He went to embrace her again, but she pushed him away playfully. "That one, Aisling, seemed rather taken with our Sheve, didn't she?"

"Hmm." Padraig sat back. "Not sure what it was, Aoif. Taken with 'er or bothered by 'er!" he said with an enigmatic smile.

"Come on now, Pad. She's a proper character is our Sheve!"

Aoifa took a sip of her wine. "You know, on another subject, Aunt Beth, Liam, Lois, none of them liked the second sight and we'll probably never know why. You know the gift always comes down the female line, so it'll be to Clara or Siobhan next. As soon as they pass puberty, it'll become apparent." Aoifa nodded emphatically.

"Well, my money's on Clara, with her gentleness, Aoif."

"Mmm, she does have an ethereal glow about her, but perhaps Siobhan, Pad? She's got some funny ideas, you must admit! I'm sure Aisling sensed something special about her. Anyways," Aoifa mused, "are we sure it's bypassed Niamh, with her passionate ways?"

"But what about Mairead… wouldn't she have told…?" Padraig didn't finish and Aoifa just shrugged.

"I must say, never seen her so upset before," she said vaguely.

Padraig poured them out another glass of wine and the subject was soon forgotten as their passion was re-ignited after a long period of absence from their lives.

28. PADRAIG, CLARA AND THE HORSES

Conor came rushing through the farm gate one Saturday morning.

"Mornin', son." Padraig smiled at him. "So, all measured up for the lodge in the middle o' that copse of mighty pines and birch above the house. Aoifa chose the spot, overlooks the ocean, see. We've plenty o' mature pine seasoned an' stored behind the barn. Soon get the straights sorted with the chainsaw but may need t' take some more trees from up top."

"Ground bit dry just now, Pad?"

"Yeah, need to wait for the rains t' come, first, lad. Problem then is how we get the timber down from over yonder."

Conor was suddenly attentive. "Yeah. That'd be a problem, for sure." But Padraig thought he spotted a smile cross his face.

"So, we gonna get holiday-makers 'ere, then?" he asked.

"Aye, but don't worry – they won't bite yer!" Padraig told him, ruffling his mop of unruly hair. "So, this mornin' give the tools a clean an' sharpen? Clara and I are poppin' out on Brown Mane and Roma."

"OK," said Conor and headed for the tool shed.

Soon the horses were ready to go as he and Clara led them out into the yard.

It was during these trips that Clara frequently confided in Padraig, often mentioning her friendship with Conor, and he had an inkling that maybe she had hopes of more. What if something became of it? Conor was almost a man and Clara just a young teenager, yet Padraig knew in his heart that Conor was as sound as could be. Although just lately he had detected a faraway look in his eyes which rather unnerved him. What if he left them? Clara would be devastated.

He gave her a leg-up, jumped onto Roma and the two of them set off up the rocky path.

"So, Brown Mane coming on well, Lara?"

"He's grand, Pa, the best! Got tricks to teach 'im an all!"

"Oh, what might that be?" he asked, cocking his head on one side.

"You have to wait an' see!" Clara chuckled as she trotted on ahead.

"Right, then, lass. I'll wait on yer!"

"Pa?" Clara was waiting for him at the top. "Did you know Ma's going to write her memoirs in the new lodge?"

"Did she tell you that, Lara?"

"No. I know cos she hasn't done it yet an' she likes her quiet times."

Padraig considered this. "But why does she need t' come 'ere on 'er own?" he muttered to himself but immediately dismissed the thought.

"A lovely idea, Lara," he told her cheerfully, "but we have her back, is the main thing."

During the period of Aoifa's emotional and physical absence from their lives, Padraig had spent precious time with the girls, riding with Clara, storytelling with Siobhan, which had brought them closer. It had been a blessing but in disguise, as he had lost his beloved wife in the process and his heart missed a beat as he recalled that distressing time. In truth, Aoifa had no idea how much the loss of Mairead had impacted on him. He just knew it was best not to burden her with his grief, as she still suffered from periods of self-doubt and recrimination herself, but it was the paranoia which bothered him the most. Since that miraculous day when their lives had returned to relative normality, Aoifa had refused to discuss it and that worried him too.

Padraig knew in his heart all the agonising in the world wouldn't bring Mairead back. He had to focus on his other girls now, be more of a hands-on father, as somehow

Mairead had slipped through that net. The sun popped out from behind a cloud and brought him back into the moment as they made their way along the track above the house. Padraig glanced at the clouds gathering overhead and crossed his fingers. "We'll head across the moors and then back down to the bay. Tide be out then."

"Pa, can I tell you a secret? I've been practising a song for Ma's birthday."

"On the piano, Lara? She'll love that."

"An' I love playing, but I'll never be as good as her," she said quietly.

"Yes, you will, chara. Just enjoy it along the way." He contemplated what a kindly soul Clara was, and it warmed his heart.

They meandered through the small birch wood leading to the moors as a spec of blue sky appeared.

"Maybes a fine day, Pa."

"Mmm." Padraig nodded doubtfully.

On the edge of the moors, they snaked their way down toward the bay, the horses enjoying the slow amble in the rising heat. They were approaching a small copse when Roma pricked up her ears and Padraig pulled her up.

"There's a rider approachin', Clara." But they couldn't make them out in the dark of the wood, so they waited patiently.

"Pa, it's Conor!" Clara shouted.

"On horseback?" Padraig exclaimed.

Conor came into view with a huge grin on his face.

"How do! Meet Keefe – means clever and handsome like his owner!"

He halted a few feet in front, the horses eyeing each other warily.

Padraig jumped down and went to pat the Connemara pony of huge proportions, taking the horse by its bridle and looking deep into his soft brown eyes as he shot a glance at Conor.

"So, who's this, then, lad?" he asked.

"He's mine, he is," Conor told them in serious voice. "Aaron… left him, for me," he choked, and as if to qualify, "He's for workin' too, though."

Padraig held out his hand and Conor took it.

"You deserve this, son. You've shown hard work and loyalty itself to our family. We are all proud of yer."

"I've given my horse a new name!" Clara cried. "He's called Quinn. That means clever, too!" she told them, beaming with delight.

"Well, now we're a team, eh!" said Padraig.

"Pa, can we take Keefe and Quinn to see Clare Island?"

"Let's do it, Lara."

They walked down onto the beach, three abreast. Keefe stood a head above the others, a fine white steed with brown patches across his back, a long white mane almost reaching the ground, matching his fine luscious tail which he was swishing around excitedly, and the largest eyes Padraig had ever seen.

"Easy to handle, lad? You up for a fast'un?"

With that, Conor lurched forward, taking off across the bay, and the other two followed in hot pursuit. When they arrived, the horses snorting and sweating in the heat, they were all in need of a drink.

"Let's lead 'em up to the lake then check out the treehouse," Clara suggested as they all dismounted, and Padraig led them in single file along the track which zigzagged around the shores of the island. When they arrived at the lake, the horses took a long drink then Roma took them away to find the lush grass. Keefe followed readily, having developed an instant bond with his companions.

"So, did you know 'bout Keefe, then, son?"

"I never knew, Pad, then yesterday, he arrived. Al at the pub bin lookin' after 'im, brought 'im on, like. He's about three and can help us with the timbers on the lodge!"

Padraig grinned. "Ah, that's what you was smilin' 'bout earlier!"

As they headed up the rock face to the top, the heat was oppressive, and Padraig took off his rucksack to find some drinks. They sat down at the base of the treehouse when a gust of wind took them by surprise and heavy clouds began to close in.

"I think we're gonna have a shower," said Conor.

"Hmm," said Padraig. "Is humid, for sure. Come on, let's inspect the treehouse afore it comes."

Clara went ahead, pushing through the bracken and ferns when she stopped.

"Pa, look, it's a little tree like by old Bessie in our garden! Same shiny stem too!"

Sure enough, there was a tiny sapling at the base of the tree, but Padraig was bemused because he couldn't see anything gleaming, just an ordinary young tree.

They made their way up the rope ladder when another gust of wind almost buffeted Clara off the worn-out slats. They quickly climbed into the little house as Padraig shouted,

"Sit, Lara, afore you get blown down! Son, we should go tie up the horses, winds'll spook 'em," so he and Conor quickly made their way back.

"Let's put 'em inside the thick pine copse t' shelter," said Padraig.

When the horses were tethered and they turned to leave, the sky darkened and the heavens opened, heavy rain falling around them in torrents. Retracing their steps through the undergrowth, they were soon soaked through, and the terrain had become very muddy and slippery. The tall pines on top of the cliff were blowing horizontally and there was a sudden flash of lightning giving the landscape an ephemeral eerie glow. The rain was unrelenting as the storm gathered momentum, the path becoming obscured by fallen branches. Padraig tried to climb back up the rock face but failed to find his footing when there was an almighty crash from behind. Conor had slipped down the side of the cliff.

"Con!" he called out. "You OK?" His words were lost in the melee of the storm, so he inched his way downwards to take Conor's hand, but he kept slipping. Eventually managing to grab a fallen branch, Conor pulled himself up to safety. He was bruised but otherwise unhurt and they climbed up the rock together, both exhausted as they reached the top.

"Phew, Con, this is really treacherous – we must get to Clara."

They struggled on through the deluge and debris, but there was no let up, the winds stronger than ever and the clouds overhead ever more forbidding as Padraig mumbled to himself, "Didn't see this comin'."

He surveyed the damage occurring before their eyes as branches cracked above their heads and fell, blocking their path.

The treehouse came into view as Padraig stumbled the last few metres, falling into the mud-splatted bushes. He grabbed the ladder which was thrashing around perilously then hauled himself upwards into the driving rain, followed quickly by Conor.

As they climbed inside, Clara, sitting on the little stool he had made, turned to smile at them and Padraig smiled back, attempting to conceal his relief. She was weaving some dry twine using a small pick. Padraig hesitated and looked at her in surprise.

"You OK up 'ere, then, Lara?" he asked curiously.

"Grand, Pa. Why? You two bin swimmin' or what?" She looked at their wet, dishevelled state. "Or having a mud bath!" she giggled.

Padraig glanced at Conor then across at Clara's serene, happy face, the sun suddenly appearing as if from nowhere and shining her rays all around them.

"No, chara, it was the storm…"

He didn't finish his sentence because he realised that Clara was either unaware or unaffected by any storm as he and Conor watched in awe of her concentration on the job in hand.

"Didn'a see any rain up 'ere, Pa. Been hot. I found this little tool an' twine, so makin' a purse for Ma."

Padraig reached out for the rucksack and handed out drinks and snacks all round when Clara suddenly jumped up.

"Look, Pa, across the sea!"

He looked to where she was pointing, to an island out in the middle of the ocean.

"Colours of the rainbow way above that island," she exclaimed.

Sure enough, Padraig could see a display of assorted colours shrouding the island.

"I told you 'bout a storm, chara. It'd be the end of a rainbow over there."

Clara stood still, riveted by the spectacle. "But, Pa, it doesn't have an end, just shooting colours up to the sky!"

Padraig chortled. "Course it is, Lara. Now come on, the horses be worried."

They made their way down the ladder and along the path. Clara followed behind, singing quietly to herself and making no mention of the wreckage around them as Conor whispered to Padraig,

"So, Pad, no rain at the treehouse, then?"

"So it seems," Padraig replied quietly. "Just one happy girl in her little bit of heaven."

When they reached the horses, Padraig put his finger up to halt them and they all stood motionless to watch a family of otters which had stopped by and were cavorting on the muddy shoreline. Kittiwakes were weaving in and out of the rocks as guillemots and terns too were all coming out to fish in the wake of the storm. Padraig gazed in awe at nature doing its work along his favourite coastline and smiled indulgently to himself.

The horses were certainly pleased to see them, Quinn whinnying at Clara's approach. They all left the island, setting off at a canter across the bay as the tide followed them in and the sun came out once more, leaving the storm behind.

"Bring Keefe to meet Aoifa and have some tea with us, lad?"

"Be grand, thanks."

Aoifa was waiting for them in the yard at Muir Farm.

"So, who do we have here, young Conor?" She walked up to Keefe, her hand out gently for him to sniff.

"Aaron's gift left to me, for workin' on the farm," Conor replied shyly.

"You deserve every bit of him, too," she replied, her voicing breaking too.

"That's what I said, chara," Padraig told her.

They loosened the horses into the paddock and made their way to the house.

"Did you all miss that storm, then?" asked Aoifa as she beckoned them to come and sit around the table.

"No, we caught the storm on Clare Island," Padraig told her, "but apparently it missed Clara," he added with a wry smile.

Clara took her mother's hand. "I've made you something, Ma." She handed her the small purse, intricately and neatly bound together.

"It's beautiful, Lara, thank you, but how did you make it without any tools?"

"Oh, I found some tools in the cubby, Ma, but I don't know where they came from."

There was a moment's silence, then Conor whispered,

"I made them, Clara."

Clara took a sharp intake of breath. "But when?"

"I lived there a while afore I found Home Farm."

Clara looked at her parents in disbelief and back to Conor.

"Didn't you have any family?"

Conor's face fell. "I do have a brother, but I don't know where he is now."

Clara looked at him sadly.

"Do we know him? What was he called, Con?"

"I don't think so, Lara. His name was Kane."

Padraig looked across at Aoifa as their mouths gaped open.

"But surely we can find him. Can't we, Pa?"

Padraig smiled knowingly at Aoifa as he replied, "Maybe one day, chara," and she smiled back.

Clara went and sat next to Conor whilst Siobhan brought in the apple pie and cream.

"I smell excitement and hear the sound of bright colours on the wind! I can taste happiness too."

No one replied as they all tucked into their pudding and Padraig told them how Keefe was going to help them build the new lodge.

29. FATE AND FORTUNE

Every day for a week, the rain did come, and after it had passed, Padraig and Conor proceeded with the foundations for the lodge. They worked tirelessly for many weeks, preparing the timbers, following their plan, and the building slowly grew into a stunning masterpiece. It was an eco-friendly venture using sustainable materials, water from a borehole, heating from a wood-burning stove, electricity from solar panels and a wind turbine, also with its own composting system. In all, it would create an exceptionally small carbon footprint, which Padraig was especially proud of, making it more attractive to holiday-makers – and impressing certain family members too.

"What d'you think, son?" Padraig stood back to survey the results. "Lay the patio, some landscaping and we're done!"

Conor nodded happily. "'Tis a fine building – you can even see 'merica from 'ere!"

"An' we couldn'a done it without young Keefe, a treasure that one."

Conor smiled and gave a sideways nod to Padraig. Aoifa was standing behind them, and as they turned around, she gasped,

"Oh, Pad, this is fantastic and just look at that view!"

Padraig's face was glowing with pride.

"We need to celebrate!" she said, looking in through the windows. "Invite all our family and friends!" Then she felt her eyes filling up.

"What, chara?" Padraig went to her.

Aoifa sniffed and a lone tear fell down her cheek as she felt the old torment rising up inside.

"Mairy loved a party and we've not had one since…"

Padraig took her to sit on the grass and wiped her tears with his hand.

"She loved a party, alright. That we canna deny," he declared breezily, then became solemn. "She would be with us, chara, especially if we hang her commemorative plaque on the same day. How about your birthday?" he murmured, stroking her thick red hair.

Aoifa brightened. "That would be wonderful," she said, taking some deep breaths and pushing her sadness away.

"Look who's come to see you!" Flynn walked up to Aoifa and dropped his ball in her lap. She picked it up and gave him a hug.

"Come on, Flynn, the beach is calling."

Aoifa set off down the path and the men returned to work.

Aoifa and the girls spent the next couple of weeks decorating and furnishing the lodge, then one Saturday morning, the family sat down to discuss the party.

Siobhan shouted excitedly, "I can smell fresh pine and strawberries, Pa, and hear sunshine and taste the wind and hot wheels too!"

Padraig chuckled. "Can you now? Well, that'd be our first guests arriving!"

"And I'll make the birthday cake…" Clara whispered.

As Padraig explained about the plaque for Mairead, a hush fell over them all but no melancholy, simply a moment of respectful silence.

"I'm hoping the girls will come back for it," said Aoifa. "I hear from Lois but not Niamh – she must be busy with that boyfriend o' hers."

"Also David with his two nice houseguests," said Padraig, "and Liam's lot too, not seen them for ages."

Aoifa's heart missed a beat. She'd not spoken to Liam since Mairead's passing, living in fear of his judgement, or was that her paranoia again? She wished she knew.

Over the following weeks, Aoifa and the girls filled the freezer with party food. Rachel was bringing canapés, Emma would make desserts, Siobhan and Clara were making Aoifa's surprise birthday cake, so the plans were well underway.

The day arrived and Aoifa threw back the curtains at the crack of dawn. It was a glorious late October day with not a cloud in the sky. Aoifa knew she would have to be strong for the placing of Mairead's plaque, but she didn't feel it. In truth, she felt fragile, but she could always pretend like she usually did. No one would see deep inside her feelings of grief and loss which were still agonisingly painful, twisting her stomach as if it would break in two. She usually managed to replace it with gratitude for her other girls, but it never went entirely.

Aoifa showered and selected her new flowery skirt, neat white blouse with a warm cardigan and glitzy trainers. She had just twisted her hair into a shiny side plait with loose curls around her face in case she needed to conceal her sadness when little feet could be heard on the landing. She opened the door quietly.

"Lara! What are you doing so early?"

"Oh, nothing much, Ma."

Aoifa smiled at her, such a pretty sight, other-worldly like a dainty little fairy, the golden lights in her hair gleaming in the sunlight which filtered through the curtains. "Let's go down and get some breakfast."

"I've got a surprise for you later," Clara told her as they sat at the kitchen table.

Aoifa started in mock surprise. "Can't I have it now? Afore anyone else sees it!"

"No, Ma! Is not ready yet! Anyways, there's nothin' to see."

Aoifa frowned with an amused expression as she opened the kitchen door, allowing the sun and Flynn to enter. She could see Padraig letting the animals out of their pens, all squawking and squealing at the start of a new day.

Around mid-morning, a car came up the drive and Aoifa went out to greet their first guests.

"It's Meg – their new baby – girls, come!" she called out.

Everyone gathered around the little baby girl.

"This is Angharad," said Meg with a broad smile.

Siobhan exclaimed, "I can hear bubbles! How do you say…?"

"Annie for short!" Meg intercepted.

Annie was the image of her mother, a sweet little thing with a froth of blonde hair and pretty blue eyes. *A chip off the old block*, thought Aoifa, not without a touch of bitterness but immediately chastised herself. She didn't want that old chestnut back, yet she still felt the envy bubbling up inside as she looked at Meg, as stunning as ever in early motherhood. She had a deep suntan and her figure back already, her thick blonde hair gleaming, a picture of loveliness in her slim-fitting pale blue summer dress.

Padraig came over as Declan walked up to them both.

"We were so sorry about Mairy, but today we can all send our love."

He held Aoifa for a long moment and she was too choked to reply, instead turning her focus to Annie.

"Have a cuddle, Aoif!"

As Meg handed her over, Annie gave Aoifa a huge gummy grin, shaking her blonde curls and glowing with four-month-old chubbiness in her lacy pink outfit.

"She's gorgeous, Meg. She looks like you," Aoifa told her coyly, tickling Annie and making her chuckle.

Everyone helped with taking the drinks up the hill to the lodge, then at midday, a taxi came up the drive. Aoifa stopped and looked on in amazement as Lois got out. Shrieking with delight, she rushed over and wrapped her arms tight around her.

"Oh my, Lo, I never expected… I would say you've grown but don't you look swell!"

"Dunna say I've grown, Ma, bin trying to lose weight!"

"Perfect as you are!" Aoifa shouted. "Padraig – here!"

He came quickly, a tear escaping as he cast his eyes on his eldest daughter.

"Now, you didn't tell us…"

"I wanted to surprise you!"

"Well, that you did." A sob caught in his throat as he pulled Lois into a warm embrace.

Uncle David came next with the two girls then Liam and his family pulled up in their Range Rover. Aoifa stepped forward, giving her brother a welcome hug to deflect any hard feelings, but she didn't sense anything as they all hugged her back.

Sean and Laurel chugged up the hill in their old truck and Conor arrived on Keefe. Lastly, Rachel and Brendan with baby Finn turned into the drive and handed over plates of delicious canapés.

Padraig soon directed everyone up to the lodge, Rachel and Aoifa linking arms as they went up the path.

"Niamh not coming?" Rachel asked.

"Funny thing." Aoifa's face fell. "She was, then yesterday said she couldn't make it. She didn't sound her usual self either, Rach."

"Ah, boyfriend troubles, so!" Rachel said assuredly.

Aoifa nodded then turned her attention to the lodge up ahead and thought how stunning it all looked with the honey-coloured timbers under a canopy of lime green, rust and golden leaves casting reflections over the whole area. The drinks were at the ready on the table with Clara's huge flower display in the centre, and as the party gathered together, Aoifa cleared her throat.

"Well, thanks for coming one an' all. This is our new holiday lodge! All credit to my clever husband here and young Conor with the help of his assistant, Keefe – and not forgetting the pretty flowers by Clara!"

There was much whooping and cries of 'well done' as everyone chinked glasses, then Liam spoke,

"You've surpassed my expectations with this project, Pad, environmentally-friendly too, very impressive. Top class, lad!"

Padraig coloured under his scrutiny, but Conor was nowhere to be seen.

"Uncle Liam, eco-friendly is a thing now, you know!"

"Oh, is that so, young Lois. Be takin' over my business soon!"

"Hey," cried Emma. "I'd stay here any day! A real get-away from it all!"

"What, get away from us?" Liam exclaimed in mock horror with his hand on his heart and everyone laughed.

After the canapés, Padraig beckoned for them to walk down to the beach as he took Aoifa's hand and led the procession silently down the track. When they reached the cave, the sun was beating down with just a wisp of autumn breeze and it was hard to imagine the storms which frequently ravaged their coastline as Aoifa's thoughts drifted back to that harrowing day.

Padraig addressed the group with a few words about their beautiful daughter as he hung the plaque high up on the rocks. There were a few tears then everyone turned and made their way back up to the house, a close group of family and friends all mindful of that tragic time, when a young member of their family had been prematurely taken from them.

As they walked up the path, an appetising aroma wafted down from the barbecue, raising everyone's spirits. Very soon they were all tucking into the vegetable dishes, fresh rolls and barbecued meats and settling in small groups around the garden, the sun soon becoming hazy as it dipped behind a pink cloud. Finn and Annie were playing happily with some toys, overseen by Clara, and as Aoifa looked out on the jolly scene, her emotions were raw, as Mairead was never far from her thoughts. She turned around and noticed that Laurel was sitting alone, looking out to sea and nursing her glass of wine, so Aoifa wandered over and sat next to her, noting her pale complexion despite the hot summer and her long fine hair pulled back harshly off her troubled face.

"You OK, Lors?"

"Been better," was the sour reply and Aoifa waited patiently, but Laurel gave no more away, then suddenly a gentle melody could be heard coming from inside the house. Aoifa knew it was Clara playing the piano and her eyes glistened with unspent tears as Padraig came and sat alongside her, and when it had finished, Clara tiptoed out and whispered,

"Happy Birthday, Ma!"

"That was beautiful, Lara, similar to an old Irish folk song I once knew." She drew her daughter close. "Very special, thank you," her voice breaking with emotion and everyone clapping their appreciation whilst Clara sat beside her mother, her pretty hair falling forward to cover her modesty.

Liam leaned across to her. "You're very good, Clara, a natural, like your ma and grandma before you." Clara blushed.

After lunch, the party dispersed to go for a walk, but Aoifa hung back and stole her moment as she crept surreptitiously up to the lodge. She had taken to spending time there in quiet reflection, enjoying the solitude. As she opened the door, she stopped and sighed, allowing the tranquillity to wash over her. She entered the bedroom and opened a drawer to the bureau. Taking out her manuscript, she smiled reassuringly to herself. It felt comforting to hold it in her hands, her memoirs, written by hand in her very own journal. The hanging of the memorial that day had brought back some haunting memories. Would she ever be free from this guilt? It should have been her that went, not Mairead. She was the one who made the mistakes, not her daughter. She did the bad parenting. She was holding the journal close to her, her eyes closed, when the click of the front door interrupted her thoughts and she turned to see Liam walk in.

"Hello, Aoif. Thought I'd find you here."

Liam's arrival irritated Aoifa. She had needed some space, and this was her happy, safe place now. She mechanically put the journal back in the bureau as if it held no importance.

"Hello, Li. Just looking for something…"

"'Tis lovely to see everyone again with some sad memories, for sure," he said absent-mindedly as he wandered around and Aoifa nodded, avoiding his eyes as she breathed deeply to keep her emotions in check as he turned to her.

"Can we have a talk?"

Aoifa's heart sank.

"Must we, Li – today?"

"Yes," he replied definitively. "I'll make some tea."

He went over to the galley kitchen to put the kettle on and gestured to the two wicker armchairs positioned in the window overlooking the deep blue sea.

Aoifa sat down as Liam brought two cups and sat opposite her. She watched him take a deep breath, his face serious.

"You know how I never approved of the gift, Aoif?"

She nodded slightly.

"The time has come for me to tell you why. Something happened when I was twenty-one and you were sixteen, your sight not yet developed."

Aoifa sat up straight, preparing herself, when the door crashed open, and Siobhan burst in.

"I taste lavender, Ma, and the sound of cool air, but what is that burning?"

Aoifa smiled at her daughter as she brought her peculiar blending of the senses through the door.

"I think this is not the time, Li."

Aoifa stood up, washed the cups and left with Siobhan, taking her hand as they walked carefully down the steep track back to the house.

"So, Sheve, where is everyone?"

As Aoifa opened the front door, she was greeted by a loud rendition of 'Happy Birthday'. Her hands shot to her face in surprise as Clara brought out the prettiest cake in the shape of the lodge and adorned with candles. Smiling through her tears, she took a deep breath to blow them all out.

"Right," Padraig announced, "to the beach! This is a special one, you know, so all hands on deck!" but Aoifa shouted,

"No, it is not!"

Padraig laughed, grabbing her quickly and throwing her slight body over his shoulders. On the beach, there was much hilarity, and the girls couldn't stop giggling as the men hoisted Aoifa up, despite her struggling, to give her forty-one bumps and afterwards threatened to throw her into the sea, but that she did oppose vehemently.

"Absolutely no way, Padraig O'Brien, not in this new skirt!"

Brendan opened more champagne and eventually they all settled to enjoy their drinks in the afternoon sun, even managing to bring Aisling's wheelchair onto the sand as Aoifa went to sit and chat with her.

"It was really nice of you to come, Aisling." She looked at this waif of a girl with intelligent eyes and an easy smile.

Aisling smiled. "Call me Ash. Lovely to join in the celebrations and to say a final goodbye to your Mairead, too," she said softly. "You have two girls at home now and two away?"

"Yes. Clara is very practical and helpful, makes life easier for me! Siobhan pretty much spends her time writing and drawing. They're the best of friends, though – mostly! Do you work, Ash?"

"I do. I teach at Belfast University."

Aoifa's eyes opened wide. "Well, that's grand. What's your subject?"

"The mechanics of the English language," Aisling told her, catching Aoifa's attention. "I wanted to mention to you. Your Siobhan – she has a unique way of expressing herself, no?"

Aoifa laughed as she looked across at her daughter, always understated with her long shiny black hair in a ponytail, a pair of old jeans and t-shirt, her flawless complexion pale but vibrant and expressive.

"You could say that, Ash, baffles us sometimes! Isn't that right, Pad?"

"What?" He came over to join them.

"Siobhan's funny ways!" laughed Aoifa and Padraig's face grew serious.

"Why, who says?"

"Ash is an English professor."

His face clouded over. "So, is there something…?"

"I've not said a thing!" Aisling told him airily. "But it is certainly a rare and unusual gift… that interpretation of the senses."

Padraig sat down between them and scratched his head, but the conversation stopped abruptly as Laurel staggered over, her face red and her eyes bleary.

"Oh no, Pad," Aoifa whispered.

"Hey, Rach," Laurel yelled. "Let me take baby Finn for a walk, hand him over!"

Aoifa intervened, "Lors, come with me, somethin' to show you!" but Laurel resisted and tried to make a grab for Finn, who was playing happily on the sand.

Aoifa quickly stepped in and led her away by the elbow.

"Help me hand out more cake, Lors. See Finn later."

Laurel pulled a face as they walked off. "What is it with me an' babies, Aoif – never any chance t' get near one!"

Aoifa took her into the kitchen and made her a strong coffee.

"Tell me how you've been, Lors? You taken time away this summer?"

"Nah. Sean says they're too busy on the farm," Laurel told her crossly. "More like on that damn machine of 'is."

They sat on some deckchairs on the patio and Laurel soon fell fast asleep. Aoifa got up and no sooner had she arrived back at the beach than Liam waved her over to join him on the rocks. They sat together idly watching the youngsters cavorting around. The older ones were playing catch and the others were building sandcastles with the babies.

Aoifa observed Liam closely, took a sip of wine and waited. He seemed nervous, his eyes averted as he looked out to sea.

"I won't beat about the bush any longer, Aoif. Nell and Aisling are my daughters. They're twins."

Aoifa coughed and spluttered, her wine in her hand as the blood drained from her face, and she managed in a shaky voice,

"H… how… when…?"

Aoifa began to tremble as she gazed across the beach at the two girls, several years older than Danny and Scorcha and quite unlike Liam. Nell was a willowy blonde blue-eyed beauty, a quiet girl. Aoifa watched her long arms reaching for the ball. Aisling was petite in stature with a brown curly bob, smaller features with a permanent twinkle in her eye.

Aoifa looked across distractedly at the calm azure sea, the waves gently lapping onto the sand, the warm sunshine beating down, all discrediting her stormy emotions deep inside.

"You remember Nora?" Liam didn't wait for a reply. "I told Ma that she'd had an abortion, but she didn't. Then Ma's second sight told her otherwise and Aisling was paralysed from the waist down. It was all devastating. Then something worse happened."

Liam's eyes were downcast, his shoulders drooping.

"What?" Aoifa whispered, barely audible.

"Nora died shortly after childbirth then Ma knew the truth and it was all very traumatic, so Aunt Beth brought them up."

Liam looked away and Aoifa felt as if she were burning up inside, her emotions raw and intense as she shook her head in disbelief. She took his shaking hand, the truth overwhelming her as she thought of Aunt Beth and how she had misjudged her. Yet, Liam had kept this secret for so long, his pain must have been unbearable, but now it was written all over his face and it all fell into place – Nell and Liam together! How she had misjudged them all.

"So – do your family know, Li?" Aoifa asked gently.

"Emma does and has been very supportive. Dan and Scorcha know nothing, but I'm about to remedy that."

Aoifa blew her nose and gathered herself as she got up.

"Did Pa know?" she asked with bated breath, her energy waning as she suddenly wished everyone would go home.

"He did, Aoif, but I think he buried it."

"Liam – I am so sorry we had our differences, that I doubted you and you doubted me, but now I understand. Thank you."

Liam put his arm around her shoulders as they rejoined the group, ignoring a few questioning glances as they approached.

Aoifa went and sat next to Sean, who was just waking from a slumber in the deckchair. She sat, shell-shocked and vacantly rubbing her eyes when Sean spoke.

"Great afternoon, Sis, but must take Laurel back for safety now."

"Sure," said Aoifa, not trusting herself to say any more. She managed to say goodbye to her family with a fixed smile on her face even though her stomach was doing somersaults.

When everyone had left that evening, Aoifa and Padraig were sitting with their feet up before bed when Padraig raised his glass.

"To you, chara, for a lovely day and many more birthdays to come." He took Aoifa into his arms. "I didn't see much of you today, though. Where did you get to?"

When Aoifa lifted her head, her eyes were full of tears.

"Ah," Padraig nodded, "was an emotional day, to be sure. I'm glad we laid the plaque with that special verse for little Mairy, chara. She can see it for herself now out at sea."

Suddenly, tears were running down Aoifa's face like torrents. She pushed her hair back and Padraig sat up.

"Aoif – what is it?"

She told him everything about Liam, the twins, Aunt Beth and her ma, too. When she had finished, he stroked her wet cheek and she added bitterly,

"I didn't know any of it. Why didn't Ma tell me?" sobbing convulsively, her pent-up emotions pouring out of her.

"Hey, look on the bright side."

"Is there one?" she asked bleakly.

"Of course. We have two more lovely nieces and Aisling thinks Siobhan has a gift!"

"Yes, she said as much, didn't she?"

"More's likely she'll make a fortune from that imagination of 'ers," he chuckled.

No more was said as they made their way wearily upstairs after a thoroughly exhausting day. They were just getting into bed when the sound of horses' hooves could be heard approaching, followed by a loud banging on the front door.

"What the…?"

Padraig groaned as he took the stairs two at a time and opened the door as Aoifa watched from the landing.

It was Conor, very red-faced and totally distraught.

"Pad, come quick… There are problems… Laurel… and Sean…"

He stopped to catch his breath and steady Keefe, who was snorting loudly. Padraig called out to Aoifa not to worry as he threw on a coat and left to fetch Roma.

Aoifa watched incredulously from the bedroom window as they set off, shadows in the moonlight. No sooner had they gone from sight than the telephone rang, waking Siobhan as she ran into her ma's room.

"I hear navy blue and shooting stars and the phone is ringing!"

Lois appeared, steering Siobhan back to bed as Aoifa picked up the phone. It was Rachel.

"Oh, Rach, what's happening?" cried Aoifa. Rachel was sobbing. "Calm, breathe, Rach. Is it Finn?"

She heard Rachel's distressed breathing as she spoke.

"Laurel? Came to you? Ah, must have had a fall-out with Sean, then." But as Aoifa listened to her friend, her hands began to feel clammy, and her legs gave way as she staggered across to the bed.

Minutes later, Lois brought some tea and handed it to her.

"What's happening, Ma?" Aoifa was listening intently to her friend.

"Laurel… took Finn? But where? No, surely…"

Aoifa felt herself stiffen, her heart rate increasing. Rachel assured her that Brendan had caught up with them and Finn was safe, but she was shouting now,

"…not in a good place at best – and losing her mind at worst, Aoif. It was horrendous. We couldn't believe it was happening."

"Oh my God." Aoifa was completely overwrought. "Padraig has just left for Home Farm, and I don't know why." But Rachel did and explained it all to her.

After she rang off, Aoifa sat on the bed with her arms around her knees for a long time, trying to make sense of it all. Lois sat with her as her mother told her what had happened.

"Laurel tried to set fire to the barn and Sean's new sea machine, Lo, and there's only rubble left is what I understand…" Then Padraig could be heard coming in through the front door.

He came straight up to the bedroom, his clothes and face black with soot and muck from the fire. He had a quick shower then explained the situation to them both.

"The machine was saved, thanks to Keefe. The barn was locked, and Laurel had taken the keys, but he managed to pull the doors off, enabling Sean to bring his machine out – but the barn has gone, burnt to the ground, Aoif. Both the boys are OK, though."

"Well, someone was looking after them, then. Poor, poor Sean and Rachel too. Laurel tried to take Finn, Pad. Unbelievable."

Aoifa wrung her hands, her head throbbing as she thought about the catalogue of the day's events.

"Was Laurel drunk, Pa?"

"Not sure, Lo," said Padraig, but Aoifa told her sourly,

"Laurel's very sick, is what she is," the past creeping into her mind and her voice trembling. "An ambulance took her to hospital. She'll be safe now, or more like everyone else'll be," she said miserably. "Ironically, Sean said that he needed to take her home to keep her safe."

"'Tis a sad state of affairs," said Padraig, shaking his head.

Lois gave them each a kiss as she left the bedroom and Aoifa wasted no time. She stood up and began pacing the room tormentedly.

"I don't think I can take much more, Pad. It's one crisis after another. Damn the loss of my gift, damn Laurel – and damn Ma too!"

Aoifa looked at the distress and fatigue on her husband's face and turned away, throwing herself on the bed and burying her anger in the pillow as she emitted a bloodcurdling scream.

30. CLARA

When Clara awoke the next morning, she looked out at the murky aquamarine sea and the glistening trees outside her bedroom window. There had been a storm. She could feel it, smell it, sense it. She watched as the clouds moved slowly away, revealing a pink sky on a violet-blue horizon. White-gold mist shimmered above the water in the early morning light as the sun appeared amidst the cocktail of pretty colours. Yet, in all its beauty, the sea was still choppy, the wind whipping it up into a frenzy of white horses as Clara thought to herself, there was still menace afoot. Her ma had told her the autumn weather could be very unpredictable as it came across the Atlantic.

As her thoughts returned to the present, Clara wondered what all that commotion had been during the night. She dressed and, as she went downstairs, heard her parents mention Laurel's name.

"What's happened to Laurel, Ma?" she asked, entering the kitchen.

Padraig and Aoifa exchanged a look and her mother told her,

"She's not well, chara, and has been taken to hospital."

"Was it during the storm last night?"

"It was indeed. There was definitely a storm last night."

Her mother had that faraway look in her eyes again and Clara wondered what it had all been about, but the thought was soon replaced with her plans for the morning. She and Conor had planted their little green gemstones in different locations, and it seemed there were now three small saplings alongside and Clara wondered, could it just be coincidence? What made the tiny trees special were the gold specks on their leaves and trunk and she needed to check them out.

After breakfast, Clara made her way up to Bessie's memorial at the top of the garden. She knelt down and looked more closely at the tiny tree, the sun catching the gold highlights in her hair, which fell around her face. She reached out to take a leaf and touched one of the gold specks. It felt softer, smoother than the leaf itself, which was changing colour now as autumn approached, but the gold was still evident. Her hair fell onto a branch and the golden hues in both touched one another, glinting in the sunshine, as if as one. She stood back and examined its branches which seemed to be reaching for the autumn sun, perhaps aware that winter was approaching.

Clara snapped out of her daydreaming and turned to make her way up to the lodge, weaving through the brambles and gorse bushes which ran alongside the path. When she reached the back of the lodge where the small tree stood, Clara could hear her parents talking inside and she reached up to peek through the window.

"When I sit here at the desk," her ma was saying, "a black-headed gull sits in that beech tree watching me, Pad," as she pointed through the window and Clara quickly crouched down.

"They're making a come-back in these parts, chara," said her pa. "What do you do here anyway, Aoif, if it's not a rude question?" he asked lightly.

Clara suppressed a giggle.

"I'm writing my life story, Pad."

Clara raised her eyebrows at this, although it wasn't a complete surprise. Her ma had mentioned her memoirs, maybe that was the same thing.

"But you're only halfway through it, Aoif, unless you know somethin' I don't!"

Clara could hear the smile in her pa's voice and suddenly knew it was wrong to be there. She stood up, waved through the window and looked across at her mother but was unable to read her expression as the window opened.

"Lara, come on in. What are you doing out there?" her mother asked, sounding irritated and Clara felt guilty.

"Looking at this tree, Ma, and how it's grown," she called back.

Aoifa nodded and smiled at her thoughtfully as she put her head out to look.

"See the specks of gold, Ma?"

"Yes, Lara, just like the specks in your hair."

Her parents turned to leave, and Clara watched her pa lock the door as she went around to join them. Her mother was deep in thought, so she turned to her father.

"Can we take the horses across to Clare Island, Pa, before the weather gets bad again?"

Clara wanted to check out the third tree, see how they all compared.

"Aye, tomorrow, then," her pa told her, ruffling her hair. "We need to put the treehouse to bed for winter anyways. I'll tell Conor too."

"Be grand. Sun's out again today and storm's passed for now," she told him as they made their way back home, but she noticed her mother held back, looking out to sea with a wistful expression.

"Come on, Ma!" Clara shouted and Aoifa caught up with her, taking her hand as they walked slowly down the steep path together.

They were all preparing lunch when Siobhan came downstairs to join them.

"Hi, Sheve. What you been up to this mornin'?" asked Clara.

"Drawing the storm with all its colours, Lara, and telling the story of last night with all the dark lights, too," Siobhan replied.

"Pah! How can the lights be dark, Sheve?" asked Clara solemnly.

"When they're not bright and when they smell of oak leaves. You are silly sometimes, Lara. My story was about Rachel, too. She had a thick cloak around her and a strong smell of shaking and shivering. Was Rachel OK, Ma?"

Clara looked at her mother in surprise. "I thought it was Laurel who was ill?"

"It was, Clara."

Her ma gave Siobhan a warning look.

"Rachel called the ambulance, as Laurel was with her at the time."

The topic fizzled out as the lunch of cold meats, salad and a selection of breads left after the party were laid out on the table. They all tucked in heartily as Aoifa broached a subject which Clara always preferred to avoid.

"Girls, as you're both teenagers now, you need to be aware of the gift forthcoming from your grandma. We know it hasn't gone to Lois or Niamh, so it will come to one of you."

Clara really wasn't sure about the gift. Her ma's second sight hadn't helped Mairy, had it?

"Maybes Niamh will get it still! Do we need to worry about it, Ma?" she asked warily.

Her mother didn't look at her but replied carefully.

"I think it has probably bypassed Niamh. You are the element of Water, Lara. Your energies flow freely, but you need to contain and channel your passions and you'll feel it if it comes. Siobhan, you are Air, which means your ideas cannot be seen nor touched, only you feel them, yet you may see them. This will all mean nothing to you both until the gift touches you, then it will all make sense."

Aoifa said no more and immediately stood up to leave the table when Siobhan added,

"Ma, I can hear a mixture of cold air and warm sun today and taste a rainbow of colours too. Sometimes I see bells on the air like an old fire engine and it feels like fire has been and snow is coming," and with that, she left the room as Padraig started to clear away the dishes.

"Sean needs me and Conor to help with clearin' up over there this afternoon, Aoif. It's a mess, a'right," Padraig said sternly.

"I'll join you later, Pad," Aoifa told him.

Clara was puzzled. She didn't know about any mess at Home Farm. She shrugged; it was all a mystery to her as she took herself into the snug with her favourite book, but her thoughts kept drifting to the mysterious gift. She'd seen how the loss of it had affected her ma and she didn't want it.

How could it be a good thing? But maybe it would be grand to know what lay ahead? Maybe she could make plans for her own future, but would she have to take care of everyone else's too, like her ma did? Or could she plan a better future for the whole world, not just her family? That thought made Clara tingle all over as she thought of all the problems in the world Lois had talked about. She sighed, dismissing it all, and tried to concentrate on her reading, but her parents' voices filtered through.

"Clara is a very serene, spiritual young lady, Pad. She needs no help. Her spirit guides her already. Siobhan is the troubling one. She's an enigma, as she travels down her own rather strange path. I think I'll call Aisling. She never finished talking to us about her funny ways, did she?"

"Yeah, why not? Be good to understand her better, with or without the gift. Our girls all have their passions, you know, Aoif." He left the kitchen and put his head around the snug door. "Never apologise for your passion, Lara. Find it, walk in it, be proud of it!" he told her, grinning from ear to ear. "And just be happy, eh?" he added in a whisper and Clara smiled back at him contentedly.

The next day, they were getting the horses ready when Clara suddenly bursts into tears.

"I rang Niamh yesterday, Ma, and she was horrid to me. Said to leave her alone," she told them, snivelling, her face a picture of misery as she fastened Quinn's bridle.

"Niamh's not been herself, sweetheart. Says she can't make it home for a while. It's not you, chara."

Her ma suddenly became serious. "Maybe we should all go visit her?"

"Well, I'm not coming!" Clara told them and broke down once more, then after a moment, added, "I miss her, Ma."

Aoifa took her hand and gave her a leg-up. "We all do, sweetheart. You know – she missed out on your amazing piano-playing – that'll bring her back! It'll be OK."

Clara wasn't so sure, but the idea cheered her nonetheless.

The sound of horses' hooves drowned out her thoughts as Conor and Keefe came hurtling into the yard and she walked Quinn over to greet them.

Conor clicked his teeth. "Feel the air a'changin', Lara," he told her, giving her one of his brightest smiles, which melted all her worries away.

"Autumn's coming, Ma's favourite season. Mine too, when everything goes t' sleep. Always makes me think more!" she told him.

"As long as it makes yer talk less, eh?"

"Hey, mind yer tongue!" she yelled, then took off at a canter and yanked at Conor's mop of wild hair as she passed him by.

"You wanna race, gal, I'll show yer…!"

He lifted his reins, rousing Keefe, and overtook her, laughing loudly as they both made a fast trot down to the beach. When they reached the wet sand, both horses galloped full pelt across to the rocks on the other side, Clara taking the lead, as Quinn was younger, lighter, and Keefe struggled to keep up.

"'Ere – wait for me!" Conor shouted, but the wind had picked up and his voice was lost in the dust of the chase. The horses' tails swished in the cool morning air, their long manes blowing wildly behind them and their ears flicking back and forth with excitement. Gradually slowing, they came to a halt as they reached the rocks.

Clara felt exhilarated and smiled to herself, her passion ignited, as her da had told her, for two of her favourite things: being with Conor and riding Quinn. As they stopped, the horses were snorting at the rapid burst of energy, Keefe stamping his foot in agitation, and Conor cried out,

"He's not used to these sudden spurts, Lars, more of a steady worker, is Keefe!"

"Yeah. He's lazy like his da!" Clara replied, hooting with laughter.

Padraig was some way behind, so they waited for him to catch up.

"Look up there, Con. All the colours changin' in the trees already and the terns and gulls nestin' on the rocks with winter comin'.."

"Can be cold anytime now, chara. Seasons changing, y'know. Cold in summer and warmer winters. All back t' front if you ask me."

"When we're grown up, Con, maybe they'll change places!"

Padraig came trotting toward them rather more sedately and grinned at them both.

"Come on, you two, we'll head over to the Island, give them the last of the grass o'there."

They walked the extra mile down the beach, the sand no longer pale cream and golden caramel like in summertime but solid and wet in ochre, bronze and deep red tones, echoing the autumn colours of the ferns in between the rocks.

When they reached the island, they released the horses and Roma led them up to the lake.

As the sun disappeared behind the clouds and the sky grew darker, the trio followed the familiar pathway up through the craggy rocks, the bracken dark and damp underfoot.

"Hope we dunna get an 'urricane like last time, Pad."

"Nah, not today, lad, just dull after the storm last night."

When they reached the big old oak, Conor pulled down the ladder. "Look, Pad, some rungs have finally fallen off!"

Clara followed his gaze up the ladder when something caught her eye, a movement up above.

"Pa," she whispered, "I think there's someone up there."

Her pa looked at her. "Well, I better get up an' see, eh?" He hoisted himself up quickly, avoiding the broken slats, and Clara's hand went to her mouth nervously. "I saw someone, Con, in the treehouse. Pa's gone to check."

"Nah. Be the wind, gal," he told her.

Padraig soon shouted down to them,

"All clear. Come up, then, but mind how you go!"

Conor held the ladder for Clara, waiting until she reached the top. As she jumped into the little wooden house, she squealed and her pa quickly put his finger to his lips, yet why was he beaming at her?

There was a man sitting on the little wooden seat, several years older than her, with an open, impish grin. When Conor jumped into the treehouse, he froze immediately, rope ladder still in hand. Then, to Clara's surprise, he ran across and took this stranger into his arms. Suddenly, they were both in floods of tears.

Her pa spoke first. "Clara, this is Kane, Conor's brother!"

The two young men were unable to speak, hugging and crying as Kane patted Conor on the back.

"A'right, then, Bro?" Kane asked, laughing loudly.

Clara thought he looked a friendly chap, with long brown curly hair, small angular features and big blue sparkly eyes, just like Conor's.

"Oh!" Clara exclaimed. "This is the best! How did we find you here?" she asked, and Padraig put his hand up.

"That was my doin'," he chuckled. "Your ma and I knew he had been here because we saw him someplace, so one day I sat in wait and said I would bring his brother to him."

Conor was finally able to speak but still overcome with shock and emotion.

"Aw, Kane, I thought you was lost forever. Now you're back and…" He broke down once more and Padraig finished his sentence.

"You'll make your brother a happier man, lad!"

They all laughed together as Padraig took out some beers from his rucksack and a strawberry milkshake for Clara.

Padraig filled Kane in on how Conor had found them. Clara's eyes shone with pride when her pa said how invaluable Conor had become and how he was now part of their family. When they'd finished their refreshments, Padraig stood up.

"Come, Lara, let's check on those horses…"

He winked at her, and they both climbed down the ladder, leaving the boys together.

A single tear fell down Clara's cheek as they reached the ground. "Pa, you were so clever! I'm really happy for Conor."

"Family is important, chara," said Padraig, taking her hand as they made their way down the path, then the clouds suddenly parted, and the sun came out once more. The horses were grazing contentedly, their patchwork coats gleaming as they swotted the flies with their luscious tails, then lifted their heads, sensing their approach.

"Pa – can Kane come and work for us too?"

Her eyes were shining at the idea.

"Well, Lara, that's up to him. Maybes he has plans a'ready! We'll have to see. Whatever happens, the sun will shine on us all, chara," he told her, grinning and nodding his head.

Quinn gave a small whinny then immediately lay down and rolled in the grass, which tickled Clara. "Look, he's happy too, Pa!"

"Yes," Padraig smiled, "and are you happy, Lara?"

"I am so happy, Pa. Can I tell you something?"

"Go on," he told her.

"I love Conor." Her face went pink with embarrassment.

"Yes, Lara, I know."

He stroked her hair, looking at her fondly. "He's a good lad."

"Yes, Pa. He is."

Suddenly, there were rustlings in the bushes and excitable voices as the two boys joined them.

"Look, Kane, meet Keefe!"

"'Tis a fine creature, Bro. Where d'you get him, then?"

"I worked for 'im, see," Conor told him.

"He has worked very hard for him."

Padraig patted Conor on the back. "You must come and meet the family, Kane."

"Maybes," Kane replied warily, then a moment later, he spoke boldly. "Be grand!"

Padraig told him, "That's the spirit, lad. Look, come, walk with me."

Padraig led Kane away, leaving Clara and Conor with the horses. Quinn was nuzzling her cheek as she patted him affectionately.

"Hey, come back to the treehouse, Con. I wanna show you something."

As they climbed back up the rock face, Clara wanted to take Conor's hand, but held back. She watched him moving in front of her, his strong body and long legs taking one stride to her two. She observed how similar the brothers were. Conor's hair was thicker than Kane's and he was shorter, but they both had sunny characters. Clara suddenly felt sad at how they had no place to call home when she smiled to herself. Of course they had. They were home! As they reached the oak, Clara walked around to the back.

"Ah. It's still here. Look, Con, you remember we put the last green stone here for safe keeping and a little tree with gold specks has grown. There are three and it's the biggest."

Conor became thoughtful and knelt down, looking at it closely, the specks of gold on the branches and leaves sparkling in the sun. Clara took a leaf and stroked the speck of gold, some of it rubbing off on her skin.

"It's so soft, like gold. Feel it."

As Conor took the leaf from her, the gold seemed to vanish, leaving a sheen on his fingers.

"It's gone, Lara!"

"No, I still have it." Clara showed him a tiny pool of liquid gold in her palm.

She opened out her hand and it dropped onto the ground.

"Must be some sort of tree akin to the island, Lara."

They both sat down next to it in the misty sunshine.

"Your brother is so nice, Con. Happy to see him again?"

Conor looked down at the ground and examined the glint of gold. "Y'know, I'm so glad he's safe. He's bin livin' on 'is own too, with no one to talk to, not like you an' me, Lara. He's had no friends." Conor seemed so sad all of a sudden and Clara took his hand gently.

"He's got all of us now, though!" she told him brightly and he squeezed her hand back.

They both sat in silence a while, watching the horses in the distance enjoying the last of the sun.

"But you an' me's the best of friends, too, eh. That'll never change, will it, Lara?"

Clara looked up into Conor's bright blue eyes, a thick flock of hair falling across his forehead and a shy grin on his face.

"You're the best!" she said coyly, giggling up at him, thinking his eyes were the colour of cornflowers on a hot summer's day.

"One day," Conor became serious, "I'd like to take you to a place I call Nirvana. Will you come with me, Lara? It's very special, bit magical too. You never know what you're gonna find there."

"I thought Nirvana was a rock band?" Clara asked, her hazel eyes twinkling.

"Oh, it is too but means the same thing."

"Can we go there now? It sounds grand!" Clara became excited.

"No, we have to wait until you are gone sixteen, Lara."

Conor spoke in earnest, and instinctively, Clara's hand flew to the little goldfish on a chain around her neck.

"I made that fish, Lara. I'm glad you have it," he told her as Clara beamed up at him, her face shining with happiness.

"Come on!" she cried as they ran back down to the horses, jumped on their backs and made their way along the path to the beach in silence as something went through Clara's mind,

Now, no matter what happens, I'll always have a little piece of Conor close to me. She held the fish tight in her hand, her heart beating a little faster.

As they reached the beach, they took off together at speed across the vast expanse of sand, Conor's hair blowing wildly around his face and Clara's gold streaks glinting in the late afternoon sun. Dusk was approaching with long shadows ahead of them and clouds were collecting behind on the horizon. There was a sleepy stillness in the air.

The soft sand swirled about the horses' hooves as they reached the top of the bay, creating a cloud of dust around them, and the sun came out to greet them one last time. They both turned and watched the tide coming in and her pa making his way slowly up the beach with Kane on one side and Roma on the other.

As they watched, the sunset formed before their very eyes. The sun was a dazzling ball of amber-rose, casting silver-violet rays out over the indigo sea and catching the edge of the waves as they crawled up the beach. Then, as if from nowhere, a magnificent array of colours appeared above the horizon, high up in the sky and far far away.

They were both mesmerised by the spectacle before them.

"What is it?" asked Conor as Clara murmured,

"It's magic, Con. That's what it is." Conor turned to look at her.

"No, Lara. You are magic. '*Not everyone can handle magic. Some people are so accustomed to mediocre, they run from magic. Let them run. Let them have their blah, their boring, their basic, their beige. You keep standing tall in your magic and let the ones who can't handle it pass on by.*' I read this somewhere, Lara, and I thought of you."

Lightning Source UK Ltd.
Milton Keynes UK
UKHW010618240322
400544UK00002B/62